LaVyrle Spencer

That Camden Summer

BERKLEY BOOKS, NEW YORK

THE BERKLEY PUBLISHING GROUP
Published by the Penguin Group
Penguin Group (USA) Inc.
375 Hudson Street, New York, New York 10014, USA
Penguin Group (Canada), 90 Eglinton Avenue East, Suite 700, Toronto, Ontario M4P 2Y3, Canada
(a division of Pearson Penguin Canada Inc.)
Penguin Books Ltd., 80 Strand, London WC2R 0RL, England
Penguin Group Ireland, 25 St. Stephen's Green, Dublin 2, Ireland (a division of Penguin Books Ltd.)
Penguin Group (Australia), 250 Camberwell Road, Camberwell, Victoria 3124, Australia
(a division of Pearson Australia Group Pty. Ltd.)
Penguin Books India Pvt. Ltd., 11 Community Centre, Panchsheel Park, New Delhi—110 017, India
Penguin Group (NZ), 67 Apollo Drive, Rosedale, North Shore 0632, New Zealand
(a division of Pearson New Zealand Ltd.)
Penguin Books (South Africa) (Pty.) Ltd., 24 Sturdee Avenue, Rosebank, Johannesburg 2196,
South Africa

Penguin Books Ltd., Registered Offices: 80 Strand, London WC2R 0RL, England

This is a work of fiction. Names, characters, places, and incidents either are the product of the author's imagination or are used fictitiously, and any resemblance to actual persons, living or dead, business establishments, events, or locales is entirely coincidental. The publisher does not have any control over and does not assume any responsibility for author or third-party websites or their content.

PRINTING HISTORY
G. P. Putnam's Sons hardcover edition / January 1996
Jove mass-market edition / March 1997
Berkley trade paperback edition / January 2010

Berkley trade paperback ISBN: 978-0-425-23321-4

The Library of Congress has cataloged the G. P. Putnam's Sons hardcover edition as follows:

Spencer, LaVyrle.
That Camden summer / LaVyrle Spencer.
p.   cm.
ISBN 0-399-14120-0
1. Women—Maine—History—20th century—Fiction.
2. Divorced mothers—Maine—Fiction.—I. Title.
PS3569.P4534T48   1996   95-20055 CIP
813'.54—dc20

PRINTED IN THE UNITED STATES OF AMERICA

10   9   8   7   6   5   4   3   2   1

Many people rolled out red carpets for my husband and me when we visited Camden, Maine, in September 1993 to research this book. Rarely has a welcome been as total and spontaneous as the one we received in this charming seaside village. We fell in love not only with the town but also with its people. These are a few of the folks who bent over backwards to help:

John Fullerton of the Camden Chamber of Commerce
Elizabeth Moran of the Camden Public Library
Pat Cokinis, realtor
Captain Arthur Andrews of the lobster boat *Whistler*
Cap'n Andy's daughter, Cheryl
Dave Machiek and John Kincaid of the Owls Head
Transportation Museum
John Evrard of Merryspring Preserve

Also, thank you to *Victoria* magazine, whose July 1993 article on Edna St. Vincent Millay inspired this story; and to author Elisabeth Ogilvie, whose books, with their sublime Maine settings, were a constant reference during the writing of my own.

Those readers who are well versed in the history of Camden will find that I've taken many liberties with the actual dates on which some notable local events occurred. I hope my readers will overlook these liberties and enjoy the story for what it is: a work of fiction.

LAVYRLE SPENCER
Stillwater, Minnesota

To our darlings,
Amy & Shannon,
as you start your years of parenting . . .
may they be the best years of your lives.
And to our grandchildren,
Spencer McCoy Kimball and Logan Harrison Kimball . . .
may you grow up like the children in this story,
knowing love and limitless possibilities
and the freedom to be yourself.

That Camden Summer

One

Roberta Jewett had hoped for fair weather the day she moved her children back to Camden, Maine. Instead, a brew of needly rain and thready fog had followed the Boston boat all the way up the coastline. The water, tumbled to a smart chop by a persistent southwest wind, made for a hellish voyage. Poor Lydia had been sick all night.

The ten-year-old lay on the hard wooden bench with her head in Roberta's lap, eyes closed, complexion greenish. Her French braid was shredded at the edges like an old piece of rigging. Her eyes rolled open and she asked in a puling voice, "How much longer, Mother?"

Roberta looked down at her youngest and pushed the disheveled hair back from her face. Lydia had never been a sailor like the other two.

"Not long now."

"What time is it?"

Roberta checked her lapel watch. "Going on seven."

"Will we get there on time, do you think?"

"Let me check and see if I can tell where we are." She eased Lydia's head from her lap and pillowed it on a wadded-up coat. "Be right back."

1

She glanced at her other two girls, Susan and Rebecca, asleep nearby with their cheeks and arms flattened on a varnished tabletop. Around them other passengers dozed on the uncomfortable seating provided for those with the cheapest tickets. Some snored. Some had spittle gleaming at the corners of their mouths. Some roused now as dawn approached and the end of the run neared. Had this been a transatlantic voyage bearing immigrants to America, this cabin would have been designated *steerage*. Since it was the highly estimable Eastern Steamship Line running daily up the coast from Boston to Bangor, the brochure avoided such harsh terms in favor of the overblown moniker *third-class lounge*. But any mother who had herded her three children aboard and watched them spend thirteen miserable hours in this spartan setting without so much as a cushion for comfort knew *steerage* when relegated to it.

No panoramic views here, only minuscule portholes. Roberta made her way to one and found it beaten by plashes of rain that streamed astern as if thrown. The glass was fogged. She cleared it with her coat sleeve and peered through.

Going on seven A.M. and the sky was becoming murkily light. They should have already rounded Beauchamp Point off Rockport Bay. Putting her forehead to the chilly glass, she peered sharply astern but saw only a dark, hulking shoreline so blurred by weather it might have been there, might not. A bell buoy clanged and she peered in the other direction. Yes, there was Negro Island light. Almost home.

As they passed between the light and Sherman's Point

the sound of the buoy changed from a distant question to a nearby statement, and she watched it rock in the waves. Beyond it, the village at the head of the harbor was smudged by the downpour but visible. She studied it pragmatically, stirred less by nostalgia than by defensiveness.

Inside the protected harbor the water was calmer and the steamer leveled off. The featureless huddle on the shore took on identity: Mount Battie, which rose behind Camden like a great, black, breaching whale; the wharf where the *Belfast* would land; the skeins of streets climbing the eastern skirt of the mountain; the spires of familiar churches—Episcopal, Baptist and the Congregational where she had gone until she moved away; the omnipresent smokestack of the Knox Woolen Mill that supported most of the town and where she'd probably still be working today if Mother had had her way.

Somewhere out there the morning shift was heading toward the mill, probably to turn out wool for the uniforms of the boys *over there*. Other workers were heading to the lime kilns in Rockport. Grace had written that Camden had a trolley line now, and that the men traveled to Rockport on it.

Some of those men Roberta knew, she supposed, or had known when they were classmates in school. Some of their wives, too. What would they think of her now, returning as a divorced woman? Probably the same thing Mother did. What a disappointment Mother had been, her letters outspoken and bold: *No decent woman sunders a marriage, Roberta, surely you realize that.*

To hell with them all, she thought, let them think

what they will. If women could go to the battlefront as nurses, they could divorce as well.

Mother would not have come down to the wharf this early—her lumbago or some other convenient complaint would be keeping her in bed—but Roberta's sister, Grace, would be waiting when the steamer landed, along with Grace's husband, Elfred, whom Roberta remembered only vaguely.

The lights of the little seaside village poked through the blur, and she returned to her children.

"Rebecca, Susan, wake up." She shook each of them, then went to the bench to tip Lydia upright. "We're almost there." She sat down and tucked her youngest beneath an arm. "We're just entering Camden Harbor. How're you feeling?"

"Terrible."

At the table, sixteen-year-old Rebecca dragged herself vertical. A yawn and a stretch distorted her voice. "Is Lydia still sick?"

"No dog has ever been sicker," Lydia herself replied.

Roberta slicked a hand down Lydia's ragged braid. "Not for long. She'll feel better once we're on dry land."

"I never want to ride on this barnacle breeder again." Lydia's head fell to the hollow of her mother's shoulder.

"You shouldn't have to. This time we're staying. The house is bought and the job is mine and nothing short of a hurricane will force us to move again, agreed?"

Nobody answered. Roberta appealed to the pair at the table but they were slump-shouldered yet from sleep, their enthusiasm sapped by the long night at sea.

"Girls, come here." She gestured the two older ones

over. They rose with limp resignation and sat down at her right, her fourteen-year-old, Susan, resting against her mother's arm while Roberta spoke to all three.

"Listen, all of you . . . I'm sorry I couldn't rent a stateroom. I know it's been an awful ride, but we need every penny for the house and to get started here. You understand, don't you?"

"It's all right, Mother," Rebecca reassured. Becky never complained about anything. Instead, when the younger ones did, she chastised them. Lydia tried it now, with a slight whine in her voice.

"But I wanted to see the staterooms. The brochure said they have private bunks and real brass wash-bowls."

"Mother's doing the best she can," Rebecca chided. "And besides, what difference does it make if you puke in a brass sink or that galvanized bucket? Puke is puke."

"Mother, make her stop." That was Susan, becoming lucid.

"Enough, Becky. Now listen," Roberta said to all three, "straighten your skirts, fix your hair and gather up your things because we'll be at the landing soon. Feel that, Lydie? It's getting smoother. That means we're getting close."

They stood, shook their skirts down and buttoned their coats, but little repair was done on hair, and their mother neither badgered nor reminded them again. When the first blast of the steam whistle shuddered the floorboards, they looked as unkempt as if they had never touched combs or irons.

The knock of the engines slowed and they braced their feet wide.

"Make sure you've got everything," Roberta said, "especially your umbrellas, and let's go forward." They gathered up their belongings and moved to the part of the lounge giving onto a companionway that emptied onto the first-floor deck. Here the windows were more generous and other passengers already crowded, peering out, waiting to disembark. The girls stretched their necks to see above the heads in front of them.

"That's the Baptist church tower, see? And the smokestack from the mill. Remember I told you how my mother wanted me to work there? Do you see it?"

"Yes, Mother, we see." Becky replied for all three of them.

"I wonder if the children will be with Grace and El-fred."

"How old are they again?" Lydia asked.

"Very nearly the same as the three of you. Marcelyn is sixteen, Trudy's thirteen and Corinda, I believe, is ten."

"I hope they're not as weird as their names, and I hope they're not all stuck-up and holier-than-thou just because they've lived here all their lives and we've never been here before." In general, Lydia was always the negative one.

Rebecca played peacemaker, as usual. "For all we know, they think our names are weird. Besides, *I* think their names are dramatic."

"You think everything is dramatic."

"Everything but you. You're just a little naysayer."

"Girls," Roberta said, and they quieted down and waited among the other bedraggled passengers, whose eyes showed signs of little sleep and whose teeth were in need of brushing. A man behind them proved it by yawning hugely, tainting the air with garlic.

Susan pinched her nose and caught Rebecca's eye. "I think the buttons just rotted off the back of my dress," she murmured.

Rebecca giggled and received a strong nudge in the back.

"Ow! Motherrr!"

"Mind your manners, both of you," Roberta warned in an undertone, though the corners of her mouth were twitching.

"He should mind his," Rebecca whispered over her shoulder.

"Yes, he should," Roberta agreed. "Either that or we should all turn around and yawn on him . . . and there are *four* of us."

Roberta, Rebecca, and Susan began to snicker, and the amusement from one fed the others, drawing the attention of nearby passengers until Lydia looked up and tugged her mother's hand. "What are you three laughing at?"

Roberta leaned down and whispered, "I'll tell you later, honey-bun. Be on your best behavior now for Aunt Grace and Uncle Elfred."

"Mother, if you tell me that one more time I'm going to stow away and go back to Boston. And must you call me honey-bun, like I'm some mere infant in pinafores? I'm ten years old, you know."

Roberta smiled and affectionately rested the folded side of a fist on the part in Lydia's messy hair, then turned her attention to the cluster of people on the wharf that was just sliding into view.

She had ambivalent feelings about returning here, but the girls needed stability, and a little shot of family wouldn't hurt either. They had never known their grandmother, aunt, uncle or cousins, and it was high time they did. Let my family be tolerant, she thought. If they'll just be tolerant, that's all I ask. I'll provide for my girls and see that they make it to adulthood with a home and love and encouragement, but when I can't be there for them, I'll need my family to be.

The boat whistle blasted again and the *Belfast* hove against the wharf. The vibrations ascended from the floorboards through the soles of Roberta's shoes to the region around her heart, warning that for better or worse, after eighteen years, she was home again.

The four Jewetts descended the corrugated gangway huddled beneath two black umbrellas, and the sides of their skirts got wet before they were halfway down. A well-dressed man, hunched beneath his own black umbrella, separated from the crowd on the wharf and hurried forward, anchoring a bowler on his head with one hand while his coattails flapped.

"Birdy?" he called above the wind.

"Elfred?" she called back. "Is that you?"

"It's me all right. And these must be your girls." He came close enough that their umbrellas bumped and she could see he was the man she remembered, though he now sported a moustache.

"Yes, these three. Girls, this is your uncle Elfred."

"Come inside. Grace is waiting where it's drier."

He herded them along to the steamship office, a low-slung weather-beaten structure with sodden benches lining its outside walls and new electric lighting sending a glow through the windows. Inside, a heavyset woman wearing a high, fruit-trimmed hat opened her arms and rushed forward.

"Birdy, oh, Birdy, you're really here."

"Oh, Gracie, it's so good to see you!"

They hugged hard, blocking the doorway and the other passengers streaming around them.

"Our little Birdy has flown home at last."

"Heavens, I haven't been called that for a while." During the first few years of her marriage Roberta had returned home occasionally, always without her husband. But in the last ten years, as his philandering had escalated, she had stayed away, unwilling to face questions.

The embrace ended and the two women stood back to take stock of each other. Grace was only a shade over five feet tall, a firmly packed matron shaped like a cracker barrel, with a pudgy face bearing a large, unsightly mole on the right side of her upper lip. Her hair was tidily dressed and her clothing expensive. Behind wire-rimmed spectacles, there were tears in her blue eyes.

By contrast, Roberta's gray-blue eyes were dry and held, perhaps, a touch of reserve. She was a head taller than her older sister. Her clothes were cheap and wrinkled. She flouted convention by not wearing a hat, and her thick mahogany hair—coiled up inexpertly the previous afternoon, well before they had boarded the steamboat—had not been touched since. It drifted from its rat, which showed in places, and straggled along her neck without apologies from her. There were age lines sprouting at the corners of her eyes and a bit of girth developing at her midsection. Everything about her said, *I'm heading for forty and not ashamed to show it, and here are my three reasons why.*

"Come on, Gracie, meet my girls." The pride in her voice was unmistakable. "Girls, introduce yourselves."

They did so with impressive elocution and bearing, as if they had no idea they looked like a trio of ragamuffins. During the introductions, Grace hugged them all and Elfred removed his hat, bending over each of their hands in turn. He spoke their names and verified their ages, then finally turned to their mother to make up for the abrupt greeting outside in the rain.

"Well, Birdy, hello . . . gracious, how you've changed."

"Haven't we all, Elfred."

He was nattily dressed, his clothing brushed and his cheeks cleanly shaven above a gorgeous silvering moustache that tilted up at the corners like a smile. The rain released the scent of bay rum from his skin; it wreathed the air above his beautifully barbered head like perfume above a purple petunia patch. He had grown stocky and developed some silver at the temples, too, but at middle age—forty or so—it became him. He seemed to know it though, which spoiled the whole effect. His smile released the power of a surprising pair of dimples and long-lashed brown eyes that were true heartbreakers. Some sixth sense warned Roberta that he used them for that purpose whenever it suited him, and she suffered his gloved hand on her shoulder for a moment longer than it needed to be there.

"Welcome back to Camden," he said.

"Thank you. Is the house ready?" Elfred sold real estate and had arranged the purchase of her house.

"Now, Roberta, 'ready' is a relative word. I warned you, it needs work."

"Work I'm used to, plus I have three willing helpers. When can we see it?"

"As soon as you'd like, but Grace was hoping you'd stop by our house first for breakfast. Unless, of course, you ate on the boat."

"What we ate on the boat was cheese sandwiches last night about six o'clock. We're all ravenous."

Grace grew radiant. "Then you'll come! Wonderful! We've given the children permission to be late for school so they could meet your girls. By now they're dressed and waiting. Elfred, what about Roberta's trunks? Will you speak to the station agent about them? I imagine she'll want—"

"I'll speak to the station agent myself," Roberta interrupted.

"Oh . . . well . . . yes, of course," Grace said haltingly, her eyes flitting to her husband as if expecting to be told whose side to take. "Of course, yes, I imagine you will. Then shall we—"

"Mornin', Elfred, Mrs. Spear," a man said as he brushed around them on his way inside. He was dressed in dripping brown oilskins, Wellington boots and a plaid wool newsboy's cap canted low over his left ear. His face was windburned, his brown hair shaggy beneath the cap. He looked to be about Elfred's age.

"Hey, Gabriel, not so fast there," Elfred called. "Come and meet Grace's sister, Roberta, just in from

Boston with her three daughters. You might even remember her. She went to school here, but her name is Jewett now. Birdy, maybe you remember Gabriel Farley?"

"No, I'm afraid I don't. How do you do, Mr. Farley."

He touched his cap. "Mrs. Jewett," he said. "You're moving back to stay, I hear."

"Yes, I am," she replied, surprised that he knew.

"Into the Breckenridge house," Elfred put in.

"The Breckenridge house!" Farley cocked an eyebrow the color of old rope. It was very untamed, and made him look grumpy when he scowled. "Does she know what she's getting into?"

"Don't scare her, Gabe. She hasn't seen it yet."

Farley leaned an inch closer to Roberta and murmured as if in greatest confidence, "You've got to watch this fellow." Without elaborating, he tossed a teasing grin at Elfred and bade them farewell. "Well, good luck and nice to meet you. Got some supplies to get off the boat, so I'd better see the agent. Ladies," he said, touching his cap one last time.

When he had moved on, Roberta accosted her brother-in-law. "All right, Elfred, just exactly what are you getting me into?"

"The best house I could manage with property as scarce as hens' teeth these days. Since the trolley line came in and with wool production up because of the war, the town is booming. Now, are you sure you don't want me to speak to the station agent about your trunks?"

"Quite sure. I spent eighteen years with a negligent husband who was rarely around and I have no intention of starting to rely on a man at this late date. All I need is the street address."

"Just tell him it's the old Breckenridge place. He knows it's on Alden Street."

When she turned away to make the arrangements, Grace's eyes swung to Elfred with an expression that said quite clearly, *You see? I told you what she was like!*

When the trunk claims were stamped and a cartage dray hired to deliver her freight to the house on Alden Street, the entire troop repaired to Elfred and Grace's to have breakfast.

Much to the amazement of the Jewetts, Elfred boarded them into a shiny black touring car.

"This is really yours?" Becky exclaimed, awestruck.

Elfred laughed. "That it is."

"Gosh! I've never been in one before."

Neither had Roberta, but she immediately preferred it to a jolting, smelly horse and carriage.

Elfred drove them to a lovely three-story Queen Anne on Elm Street. It was apparent that Elfred did well selling real estate. Elm was obviously the thoroughfare to live on in Camden, with grand houses set far back behind broad green yards. Elfred and Grace's house was stately and large, painted a deep wine color with four different colors of trim on its fish scales and gingerbread. Inside, it was decked out with a plethora of polished wood, leaded glass and elaborate wallpaper. The furnishings were rich and formally arranged, the carpets imported, the light fixtures already converted to electricity. *But so painfully neat*, Roberta thought, glancing into the parlor from the foyer. *I wonder where they do their living.*

"It's beautiful, Grace," she said as Elfred stepped behind her to take her coat.

Mercy! she thought, thrusting her midsection forward. *Was that his body bumping me from behind while Grace wasn't looking?* Roberta turned, but so did Elfred, away from her to hang her coat on a brass tree in an entry alcove, and to see to the girls' coats, too.

Perhaps it was accidental, she thought, and said to her sister, "I insist on a full tour."

Elfred returned to face her at a respectful distance with Grace looking on. "Forgive me, Birdy—I may call you Birdy, may I not?" Rubbing his palms together, he flashed her a charming smile. "But since I'm the purveyor of real estate, might I suggest that *I* give you the tour while Grace sees to breakfast? That way I can point out some of the features of the house that make it most attractive."

Roberta was setting her tongue to inquire if he wanted to point out the fine points of her sister's decorating while he was at it. It took a great effort to bite back the words.

Grace advised, "Do it after breakfast, Elfred. Sophie will have it all laid, I'm sure." She tilted over the ornate banister and bugled up the stairs, "Girls, are you there?"

Three prim young darlings came down, all dressed in starched layers with oversized grosgrain bows in their hair. Their shoes were as polished as their demeanor when they were introduced to their three cousins.

The oldest, Marcelyn, acted as spokesperson for all

of them. "How do you do. Mother has set a special breakfast table for us in the solarium. Would you like to see it?"

The Jewett trio followed, mesmerized, their eyes lifting as they passed beneath the novel electric lights that burned away the April gloom even in the interior halls. In the solarium, a hexagonal room situated at a rear corner of the home, fine china was laid on a filigreed white iron table. Ferns, palms and orchids flourished on tiered metal racks while rain pecked at the windows and occasional thunder rumbled outside.

"Holy Moses!" Rebecca exclaimed. "You guys must be filthy rich!"

A couple of dubious glances flashed among the Spear girls, followed by a hint of giggling.

"What's so funny?" Rebecca asked.

"Do you always say exactly what you think?"

Rebecca shrugged. "Pretty much."

"Mother would have dyspepsia if we talked like that."

"Then do it where she can't hear."

Shocked surprise sent more quick glances among the hostess-cousins before Marcelyn politely invited her guests to sit.

"Is that what you do?" she inquired, fascinated in spite of her upbringing.

Rebecca was still gazing around. "What?"

"Say anything you want to behind your mother's back?"

"Heavens no. We can say anything we want to in front of her. If she doesn't like it, we discuss it and she gives us a little rhetoric about the pros and cons of good manners versus the impact of imperfect manners on one's independence. Mother, you see, believes in living your life the way you see fit."

"Oh, dear," Marcelyn breathed.

"Why do you say that?"

"Well . . . our mother would . . . I mean . . . well, goodness."

"Oh, I get it. Your mother wouldn't like such free-spirited talk from her chil—"

"Shh." Marcelyn placed a conspiratorial finger over her lips. "Sophie will be bringing breakfast in any minute, and she reports everything to Mother."

As if on cue, a buxom, gray-haired woman waddled in bearing a tray that dented her ample stomach. The girls sat primly while she placed steaming plates before them.

"There you are, some nice, piping kedgeree."

Lydia peered at the glob on her plate. "What is it?"

"What is it? Why, it's fish and rice in egg sauce. Every Mainer knows what kedgeree is."

"Well, we're not Mainers."

"But your mother was."

"Yes, but our mother doesn't cook much."

"Doesn't cook much!" Sophie stopped in her tracks. "Why, that can't be so."

Under the table, Rebecca nudged Lydia's leg, shutting her up. Sophie placed hot biscuits, butter and blueberry jam on the table, and Marcelyn asked, "May I have some coffee, Sophie?"

"Why, Marcelyn Melrose Spear, you know perfectly well your mother would give me the boot if I let you drink coffee."

"No harm in trying, is there?"

Sophie scowled until her single chin became three, and said as she left the room, "Now make sure you clean your plates."

The moment she disappeared Susan and Lydia set out to do just that, with manners leaving much to be desired. They slurped and chewed with their mouths open and wiped their mouths with the back of their hands.

While they ate, Rebecca observed, "Melrose is an odd middle name."

"It comes from my great-great-grandmother on Father's side," Marcelyn explained. "It is said that when she was thirteen she gave birth to her first child in the snow beside the Megunticook River, wrapped it in a fur robe and carried it down to the trading post, where her husband was stone drunk in bed with an Indian woman. She laid the baby between them, sliced off her husband's left ear and said, 'There, now maybe the ladies won't find you so pretty and you'll stay home where you belong.' They had eight more children, and the way the Indians told it, half of them were born with no left ear. Have you ever heard of anything so sad and pathetic and romantic in your life?"

"Hell's bells, what a drama it would make! We should write and perform it sometime."

Marcelyn was again shocked by a sixteen-year-old using the word *hell*, but nobody else said anything about it, so she replied, "Write it?"

"As a play."

"You write plays?"

"We write them all the time."

"And perform them, too?"

"Oh yes, we're always giving some kind of performance."

"For whom?"

"Why, for Mother, of course, and for our friends and our teachers—anyone who'll sit still long enough to watch, actually."

"Your mother sits and watches you put on plays?"

"Oh, most fervently. She'd stop any work to watch us do anything—act, sing, play the piano, recite poetry. Susan's already up to grade three on the piano, and Mother has begun teaching Lydia to play the E-flat recorder. I can play quite a few instruments, and we do trios together and sometimes quartets if we can convince Mother to join us. Actually, when we give plays we perform our own opening overtures on the instruments, then quickly skip backstage and assume our roles, then come back out front to play the closing piece again. Do you *never* put on plays? *Ever?*" She seemed as amazed by this cultural deficit as her cousin had been at the word *hell*. "I guess you don't."

"We, ah . . . um, no. I mean, we never thought about it."

"Do you play instruments? Any of you?" Becky looked from one blank face to another and thought she had never seen such an insipid group of girls in her life.

"No."

"Surely you recite, then."

"No, not that either."

"Well, then, what do you do for fun?"

"Well . . ." Marcelyn, still acting as spokesperson for her sisters, glanced at each of them, then back at her inquisitive cousin. "We stitch."

"Stitch! I said *fun*!"

"And attend chautauquas."

"Oh, how boring. I'd much rather *give* a chautauqua than watch one. What else?"

"Well, sometimes we go rowing."

"Not sailing?"

"Gracious, no. Mother would never allow us to sail. It's too dangerous."

"So I imagine you don't fish either."

"Pew, no. I wouldn't put my hand on a stinky old slimy fish. But we had a clambake once out on the beach at Sherman's Cove."

"Once?"

"Well, Mother didn't like us removing our shoes and getting our hems dirty."

Rebecca thought that over, chewing some kedgeree, discovering it was very tasty. "My mother doesn't care much about hems, clean or dirty. And there have been summers when we practically lived on clams and lobsters, anything we could get from the ocean free. She cares more about our minds and says that we must never squander one moment's time at inconsequentialities that will eventually cease to matter. But the imagination, she says, is a priceless gift, and we must cultivate it and any of our natural-born abilities at every opportunity. The next time we put on a play, would you like to come and try it with us?"

Marcelyn Melrose Spear beamed at her newfound cousin. She had inherited her mother's plain brown hair and—from some other unfortunate progenitor—a slightly bulbous nose. But she had landed her daddy's pretty brown eyes, complete with dark lashes and up-tilted corners, and they positively gleamed as she said, "Oh, Rebecca, do you really mean it?"

"Of course I mean it, and call me Becky. For our first play we'll do your grandmother's story, and if you want to, you can be the one whose ear we cut off, then you can do all the screaming and writhing and cursing, and it'll be a great opportunity to emote. Of course, we'll have to figure out what to use for blood, and we shall have to make a wig of black rags for whoever plays the Indian woman. Maybe one of our little sisters can be the baby, do you think?" She quickly assessed the ten-year-olds, Lydia and Corinda. "No, no, of course not, they're too big, aren't they? Well, we'll work on that problem when we get to it. We could always use dolls, couldn't we, and you younger girls can cry offstage. We must start working on the script right away!"

Marcelyn leaned forward and whispered, "Listen, everybody. We must form a pact. Anything that's been said this morning is not to be reported to Mother—agreed?" She aimed a warning gaze at Trudy and Corinda.

"But she'll ask," Corinda said.

"Then tell her we had a lovely chat and nothing more."

"But Marcy . . ."

"You want to put on plays, don't you?"

And so, within an hour of being introduced, the two oldest cousins set the temperament of their next meeting.

Meanwhile, in the more formal dining room, the adults had finished their breakfast and were enjoying hot coffee. Elfred sat back, playing with a toothpick and sending some unsettling grins to Roberta whenever Grace wasn't looking. Since Grace was getting down to brass tacks—which she, as the older sister, considered her beholden duty—she wasn't looking at Elfred much.

"Well, Birdy," she said officiously, "I've been waiting for you to mention . . . *it*."

"It?"

"The . . . well, you know . . ." Grace stirred the air as if she were folding cake batter. "The divorce," she whispered.

"Why are you whispering, Grace?"

Grace's demeanor stiffened a degree but she spoke aloud once again. "Don't be obtuse, Roberta. Did you really do it?"

"Yes, I did it."

"Oh, Roberta, how could you?"

Unruffled, Roberta echoed, "Oh, Grace, how could I not? Would you care to know how many women he philandered with over the years?"

Grace colored and whispered again. "Birdy, for heaven's sake!"

"Just a minute—do I understand you correctly? It's all right for him to philander, but it's not all right for me to speak about it in polite company? Is that it?"

"I didn't say that."

"No, but you implied it. Obviously you disapprove of my getting a divorce. So what should I have done? Stayed with him for another seventeen years and let him chase women for weeks at a time, and gamble away what little money he made and come back to me when his funds ran dry or when his other woman got sick and tired of him and threw him out? Because that's what he did, Grace, time and time again, until I just couldn't tolerate it anymore. *He* didn't keep my family alive, *I* did, and certainly he wasn't going to make my life or my children's lives any better, so I took the initiative. *I* divorced *him*."

"But George was so charming."

Roberta scarcely stopped herself from rolling her eyes. *Like your own charmer, Elfred here, who's sending flirtatious messages to me at this very moment, right across this very table?* He had that sneaky, insidious way about him, adopting poses suggesting private intimacy, then stealthily straightening up just before Grace swung her glance his way. He was sitting that way now, slightly off plumb with an elbow beside his coffee cup and an index finger faintly stroking his moustache. But above and below that finger his eyes and lips were telegraphing an unmistakable invitation.

Roberta disregarded him and replied to her sister, "You barely met the man, but you're right about that. He charmed one woman after another—thirteen of them, to the best of my knowledge."

"Nevertheless, Mother and I are both dead set against this divorce. What will people say, Birdy?"

"I don't give a dingleberry what they say, Grace. I had to do what was right for me and the girls, and I did it."

"Totally disregarding conventions!"

"Yes, just like George totally disregarded conventions."

"And you really plan to take this job as the county nurse and go flitting off across the countryside?"

"I've already taken it. I start as soon as we're settled."

"And who'll take care of your girls while you're gone?"

"I haven't figured that out yet, but I will."

"Roberta, don't be outrageous."

"What's so outrageous about supporting one's children?"

"You know what I'm saying. A divorced woman going from town to town—it just isn't done."

"Ahh . . . I see." Roberta studied her poor, deluded sister, who couldn't—or wouldn't—recognize that she had a husband who apparently thought all women were fair game. Most certainly he was giving that impression to Roberta, all the while he was silently mocking his wife.

Abruptly Roberta diverted the conversation to him.

"Tell me, Elfred, do you share Grace's low opinion of the state of divorce?"

Elfred cleared his throat, straightened in his chair and busied himself refilling his coffee cup. "You must admit, Birdy, not many women do it. And it *will* look rather fishy, your taking a job that'll carry you all over the countryside."

Grace leaned forward earnestly. "Listen to me, Birdy. Put your girls to work in the mill and you take a job there, too. That way you can be with them and with the townspeople, who won't have as much reason to question your motives."

"Question my motives!" Roberta leaped to her feet. "Good God in heaven, listen to yourself, Grace! You're telling me *I'm* the one who has to vindicate myself just because I'm the *female*! You'll wait till hell freezes over before you get any apologies from me! And as for putting my girls to work in the mill, not so long as I breathe air! They're going to have every cultural advantage I can give them—music lessons, and trips to Boston to the galleries, and the time to explore nature and create anything they want to create, and to use their hands and minds. To complete their education, first of all. None of that would be possible if I put them in the mill."

"All right . . . I'm sorry." Grace pressed the air with both palms. "It was just an idea, that's all. I merely thought that three extra wages would help, since you don't have a husband to support you anymore. Sit down, Birdy."

"I'm done sitting. Actually, I'm anxious to see my house, so Elfred, if you'd be so kind . . ."

Elfred wiped his moustache on a linen napkin and rose. "Anytime you say, sister. Would you allow me to give you that tour of our house first?"

"Another time, I think. It's been a long night and I'm anxious to get settled."

"Very well." Elfred pushed his chair beneath the table, fished for a pocket watch and flipped it open. "By now I should think the drays have arrived at your house with your things. Let's collect your children and go."

At the door, when coats were donned, Grace gripped Roberta's hands and pressed their two cheeks together. "Don't be angry at me. I'll come over soon and we can talk some more."

"Yes, do that," Roberta replied coolly.

"And you will go see Mother right away, won't you?"

"As soon as I have a free minute." Roberta pulled free of Grace's grip and closed her last coat button. "I imagine it's fruitless to hope that Mother might come to see me."

"Now, Birdy, don't be that way. It's a daughter's duty, and after all, you *have* been away all these years. She'll be anxious."

To give me another lecture about the evils of divorce, I'm sure.

"Girls, say good-bye to your cousins."

The girls exchanged friendly good-byes.

"And come over anytime," Grace told the children.

In the commotion of departure, Elfred made sure his hand was hidden from view when he touched Roberta's waist the way only a husband should touch his wife's, with a suggestive squeeze.

Two

"Elfred, stop it!"

She had let the girls run ahead through the rain while she and Elfred readied their umbrellas on the stoop.

"I beg your pardon?"

As innocent as if dew wouldn't sizzle on his you-know-what!

"You touch me one more time and I'll blacken your eye."

"Touch you? Why, sister Birdy, whatever do you mean?"

"You know perfectly well what I mean! And *don't* call me sister Birdy! I'm not your sister!"

"Very well. Is Birdy all right?"

"I suppose it'll have to be. Are we clear about where your hands belong from now on?"

"Oooh, you are a spunky one, aren't you?"

"Just keep your hands to yourself and we'll get along fine, Elfred."

Rendering a grin that would have charmed the scowl off a Quaker matron, he doffed his bowler and motioned her ahead of him down the walk. "As you wish. Shall we join the children?"

He drove them through the rain in his shiny black touring car. In the backseat the girls were agog, testing

26

the seat springs, exploring the vase on its bracket between the doors and asking Elfred if it had a Klaxon,
and would he toot it. He did so once while Roberta
kept to her corner of the front seat and looked out her
window.

"So, what do you think of our electrics?" he inquired.

"Electrics?"

"The streetcars."

"Oh. Well, they've certainly changed the town,
haven't they?"

"Pretty progressive for a town this size, wouldn't you
say?"

She watched a passing streetcar as it clicked by.
"Have you ridden one yet?"

"Certainly. Everybody rides the electrics. Quickest
way to get over to Rockland and Warren."

"Quicker than in your motorcar?"

"Well, I wouldn't say that, no."

"So many motorcars." After watching one pass, she
turned sharply to question her brother-in-law. "Do you
like yours, Elfred?"

"I do, but some of my customers refuse to get into it.
People still think the horse is more reliable."

"Do you?"

"No."

She may not have approved of Elfred on a personal
level, but everything Grace had ever written about the
man assured Roberta he had more than a pretty head
on his shoulders. "So," she asked, "if you were a
woman, you'd get a motorcar instead of a horse?"

"Oh, now wait a minute, Birdy, don't tell me *you're*
thinking of buying a motorcar!"

"Why not?"

"But you're a woman!"

She released a snort that told Elfred this wasn't his subservient wife to whom he was talking.

"With plans of my own."

"Be careful, Roberta. People will talk."

"About what? My getting a motorcar?"

"Well, you're divorced, Birdy." He had lowered his voice to an undertone. "You have to be more careful than most."

"There's no need to whisper, Elfred. My girls know I'm divorced, and they know the world takes a dim view of divorced women, don't you, girls?"

"Our father was never home anyway," Lydia piped up.

"And when he was, all he did was take money from Mother and disappear again," added Rebecca. "But the last time she refused to give him any."

"We think it's a good thing that she divorced him," put in Susan.

Roberta might have acted the slightest bit smug as she remarked, "It's been my experience, Elfred, that people will talk on general principles, usually because they haven't enough in their own lives to keep them occupied. That's the chief reason people put their noses into other people's business. Do me a favor, would you, Elfred? Take me down Main Street."

"What for?"

"I want to see what it looks like."

"It looks the same as always."

"It does not. Grace has written about all kinds of changes. I want to ride its full length and see them all . . .

unless, of course, you feel your reputation would be sullied by being seen with a divorced woman."

Her sarcasm, on the heels of Elfred's attempted hanky-panky, was taken as a challenge.

"Very well. One quick trip, then it's back up the hill to Alden Street."

"Very well, Elfred," she said with mock servitude, and sat back to enjoy the ride through the town where she'd grown up.

Even in the rain, Camden appealed. The mountains rose behind it in gentle curves, the little village looped at their throat like a necklace. Camden's shape was dictated by the horseshoe curve of rocky coastline that formed a calm, natural harbor made all the more calm by dozens of outlying islands that dotted Penobscot Bay and broke the backs of even the greatest storm-blown breakers threatening the Atlantic coastline.

In the years since Roberta had left, many yachting enthusiasts from the larger New England cities had discovered safe little Camden Harbor and had made it their home port. The masts of their pleasure crafts now shared moorings with Camden's own fishing fleet, though at this time of day—midmorning—the working boats were gone, along with their owners, poles and nets, out onto the rainy water to earn a living.

"In Boston," Roberta said, "we lived inland. It's good to be close to the water again. The sounds and smells are different by the water."

They sat for a moment beside the town docks, rocked by the engine of Elfred's touring car. Through the windows came the toccata of hammers from the shipyards, the polyphony of gulls, the contralto note of a lonely boat engine as the craft headed out. "Listen," said Roberta to her girls. "It's playing a composition."

"What is?" Elfred asked, but Roberta flapped a hand to shut him up while she and her girls—who understood without question—listened to the serenade of the seaside town. The salt air pressed heavily, like a cold, damp cloth against their faces. It smelled of rocks draped with seaweed that soured at low tide, the wood of docks swelled by years of dampness and the faint stench of the lime-burning kilns that drifted up from Rockport whenever the wind was out of the southwest.

When they'd heard enough, Roberta said, "Let's go, Elfred. Show me Main Street."

Main curved like an eel and climbed at the north end. The white wooden structures of the business section that Roberta remembered from childhood were gone, destroyed by fire in 1892. In their place were two- and three-storied buildings of red Maine brick. Though the buildings were different, the character of the town remained the same. Its roots had been put down by Calvinists, who valued hard work, Sunday worship and a sheltered seaport. If that port were of exceptional beauty, so much the better. If it faced the homeland where the town founders had left their loved ones, better still.

Roberta, like any traveler returning home, searched for familiar landmarks. On the white spire of the Baptist church the town clock still set the pace of daily life. Beside it the Village Green remained unchanged. Down at the Bean shipyard a four-master stood on the stocks, half completed, just like when she was a child. The little Megunticook River still plummeted over the falls at the head of the harbor, still passed the woolen mills, still turned its machinery. And the mill still reigned over the entire town, presumably with children on its payroll.

But progress had come to Camden in more than just its electric trolleys. A motor bus from the Elms Hotel came toward them, headed for the wharf with its load of outbound tourists. Telephone poles trimmed the length of Main Street. Concrete sidewalks followed the poles. There were water hydrants and streetlights and a new, expensive YMCA building. But the sign that snapped Roberta's head around swung from a building at the north end of Main where it curved upward to become Belfast Road.

"Elfred, did that sign say 'Garage'?"

"Now, Roberta, don't even think it."

"But it did! Turn around and go back there, Elfred, I insist!"

"Roberta, don't be silly."

"Damn and blast you, Elfred, when I say turn this car around, I mean it!"

In the backseat the girls started giggling. Rebecca said, "I think she means it, Uncle Elfred."

With a long-suffering sigh, Elfred braked, shifted gears and swung into a U-turn. While he waited for a carriage to pass, he said, "Roberta, I understand that you haven't had to answer to a man for a long time, but this time you must listen. Women simply cannot own cars because they cannot operate them."

"And just why not?"

They began rolling again, back into downtown. "Because you can break your arm cranking them. And because gasoline is heavy and clumsy to put in, and the motors break down quite regularly, and the carburetors need constant adjusting, and the darn things are cold in the winter and have been known to catch fire and burn right to the ground! And tires need patching, sometimes right out on the road, and what if that happens when you're all by yourself somewhere with no man to assist you? Roberta, please, be sensible."

"How much does a motorcar cost, Elfred?"

"You aren't listening to me."

"I'm listening. I simply am not agreeing until I explore the possibility further because, you see, I've thought about this for a long time. It's been a part of my plan. How much does one cost?"

He refused to answer.

"I can find out quite easily."

"All right," he said, exasperated. "This one cost eight hundred and fifty dollars. A roadster would be about six hundred, or thereabouts."

"I don't have that much, but nevertheless, I intend to buy one. I'll get the money somehow."

"Don't be ridiculous, Birdy. You cannot."

"Why not? You have."

"Yes, but I'm a man. Men can handle them."

"Oh, Elfred," she replied indignantly, "how you insult me without half trying."

"Birdy, you are the most ex*a*sperating woman!"

"Pull over." And after a beat, "Pull over, Elfred, I said!"

He did so, grumbling. "How you and Grace can be sisters is beyond me."

Elfred pulled over and stopped in front of the Boynton Pharmacy. The sidewalk was brand-new, and the car tilted slightly toward it while the engine continued to chortle and rock the car rhythmically. On the leather roof the rain sounded like grease spattering. It scrolled down the isinglass windows and turned the view of the buildings across the street into wavery images, like a washed-out watercolor.

Roberta squinted and put her face closer to the window. "Boynton's Motor Car Company," she read aloud. "Glory be, Elfred, you bought it right here?" Elfred refused to answer. The answer was obvious anyhow. Beneath that sign hung another: CAMDEN GARAGE. The smaller print on both signs was made illegible by the downpour.

"Girls, can you read that?"

Rebecca tried. "Not very well." She squinted. ". . . agency . . . storage . . . that's all I can make out."

"Storage? Do they store motorcars here, Elfred?"

"In the winter, yes, when it gets too cold to drive them and the roads become impassable."

"Where does one buy gasoline?"

"Birdy, please . . . your sister is going to be very upset with me if she thinks I assisted you with this crazy idea."

"Don't worry, Elfred, I shall absolve you of all wrongdoing. I'll make sure Grace knows that anything disgraceful was clearly my idea."

Elfred was beginning to realize this woman had a tongue like a double-bit axe and very much enjoyed nicking him with it in the hope that he'd squirm. But Elfred was no squirmer. He liked women, and this one in particular whetted his interest, with her single state, her sassiness, occasional cursing and footloose ways.

No man in his right mind would want her on a permanent basis—no wonder George Jewett had bolted—but as a distraction from a boring, overweight wife, Mrs. Birdy Jewett would do very well. Elfred began to anticipate the days ahead.

"One buys gasoline at the hardware store. Now may I take you home?"

Roberta grinned smugly and settled back against the seat as if a decision had been made. "Please do."

Alden Street was a mere stone's throw above downtown. The Breckenridge house was as old as Camden itself and during the last two decades had been owned by the final survivor of the clan, one Sebastian Dougal Breckenridge. Sebastian had spent his productive years at sea, and the sea had been his only bride. He had been content to live out his last rheumatic days within view of the ocean, where he could look down and see the steamers enter the harbor, watch the fishermen go out each morning and return each evening, listen to the gulls scold as they banked past his windows and remember his salty youth plying the trade routes across the bounding main.

People around town remembered the days when Sebastian had kept his place shipshape, when petunias had flowered in the beds beneath the front windows, when the anchor that lay scuttled in the soil of the front yard had been kept a glistening white. But many years had passed since Sebastian's creaky old joints could endure the torture of kneeling to weed a garden, or his arthritic arms support a paintbrush, or his feeble mind remind

him that the house needed care if it was not to tumble
down the hill into Camden Harbor.

Roberta gaped at the place and felt her stomach drop.
"This is it?"

"Holy smut," one of the girls whispered, followed by
only silent disbelief from the backseat.

"Elfred, you can't be serious. You spent my money
on *that!*"

"Two hundred dollars isn't much, Birdy. I could have
gotten you a much nicer place on Limerock Street for
four hundred, but you said two was your limit."

Two hundred for the house, two hundred for the motorcar, that was what she had planned. Now she owned
a hovel and could afford exactly one-third of a car, and
had no way of getting the rest quickly.

"Oh, Elfred, how could you? Why, it's nothing more
than a . . . a derelict!"

"It's got a good sturdy foundation, and wood stoves
that work, and windows that close."

"Without glass," she said, looking up. On the second
floor one pane had been covered with a sheet of wood.
Surely the place had not been painted in a decade. Not
by anything except gull shit. There was plenty of that
on the shingles, and below the window ledges, and
across the front of a shallow front porch where a line
of birds trimmed the railing whose spokes were as irregular as an old sea dog's teeth. Through the lower-
level windows Roberta glimpsed the effects of Sebastian
Dougal Breckenridge—predominantly what looked to
be stacks of newspapers and glass floats from Portuguese fishing nets lining the sills.

"Glass can be replaced," Elfred said of the upstairs window.

"Not by me, it can't. I'm no glazier, Elfred!" Roberta's disillusionment was fast growing into blazing anger.

"You said you had three good helpers, so I took you at your word, that you wanted to save money on a structure that could be fixed up. I assumed that you had set aside some money for that purpose."

"Well, I didn't! Not this much! I said fix up, Elfred, not rebuild!"

Roberta sat glaring at her new domicile.

"Do you want to go in and look?"

"No. I want to suspend you from the tallest tree in Camden . . . by your heel tendons, Elfred Spear!"

"Roberta . . ."

". . . then sell chances on when you'll finally rot and drop off."

Elfred covered his mouth with one hand and smiled behind it while she stewed in tight-lipped anger.

"Oh, come on, Roberta, at least go in and have a look."

She was so distraught she got out of the automobile without an umbrella and marched up the weedy yard without waiting for anyone.

"Shoo!" she yelled at the gulls. "Get your streaky asses off my front porch!" Elfred quickly turned off the engine and rushed to catch up with her with an umbrella. He did so at the bottom of the porch steps where she had come up short and set her teeth to keep from cursing at him. Upon closer scrutiny it appeared the porch itself would rot off before Elfred did! The floor had holes in it where feet had gone right through. She stood with her hands on her hips.

"This is deplorable. Just deplorable."

Elfred urged her up the steps, picked his way across the good boards and opened the front door. She preceded him into what she supposed was a parlor. Wonder of wonders—it had electricity! But the wires were strung outside the walls and the bulbs hung bare. There were newspapers everywhere. The walls had been papered with them. The old man had collected them and they stood in sagging stacks around the edges of the room along with empty glass jars and more of the Portuguese floats. Soot stained the ceiling above a heater stove, and trash littered the floors. The place stank of urine and decay.

Roberta announced, "I want my money back."

"I can't get it back," Elfred told her. "The sale is conclusive."

Roberta marched up to him, grabbed his folded umbrella and jabbed it smartly into his belly. Elfred doubled forward and grunted.

"Oof! . . . Ro-Roberta . . . what in the . . ."

"How are we supposed to live in this? How, Elfred! Would you tell me that!" she yelled.

Elfred hugged his belly and stared at her, aghast. The girls had come onto the front porch and stood looking in dubiously. Rebecca stepped over the threshold and the others followed, picking their way carefully. Susan peered up a creaky-looking stairway that divided the two downstairs rooms. Rebecca walked over to a wall and peeled a strip of newspaper off, revealing ancient water-stained wallpaper behind it. "It won't be so bad,

Mother. Once we burn the newspapers and paint the walls."

Rebecca, however, was always the optimistic one.

"It's unfit for a polecat!"

A kitchen adjoined the living room. Lydia ventured into it and the others followed. She opened a door beneath a dry sink, releasing a fetid odor. What appeared to be a slop pail—empty, by some benevolent freak of fate—had left a permanent stain in the wood of the floor.

"Close that door, Lydia!" Roberta snapped. "And don't touch that filthy thing again. He probably pissed in it, for all we know!" To Elfred she snapped, "I suppose there's no bathroom."

"No. Just an outhouse."

She turned away, too angry to face him.

"Listen, Birdy, you said two hundred dollars. This is what you get for two hundred dollars."

"Two hundred dollars I could have spent on something livable while financing the rest with a mortgage."

"You told me you didn't want a mortgage, so I figured it could be repaired with a little help."

She spun on him, pointing at a wall. "You repair it then, Elfred, because I don't have time! I've got to go out and earn a living for my girls! And while I do it, am I supposed to leave them in this?" She was shouting by this time, gesturing rabidly. "*You* stuck us with this skunk's nest! *You* make it livable! And while you're at it, you *pay* to make it livable! Lord help me, I trusted you, Elfred!"

Elfred was backing away because Roberta was brandishing the umbrella again. He spread both hands as if to ward her off. "All right, Birdy, all right . . . I will. I'll take care of it."

"And do it quickly, because this is no fit lodging for my girls!"

"Very well, I'll see Gabriel Farley right away."

"Yessir, you will," said a deep voice from the front room, and Gabriel Farley himself materialized. He stepped through the doorway into the kitchen and said, "Hello again."

"Well, where did you come from?" Elfred asked.

"Figured you could use me. If these ladies were going to live in old Sebastian's wake, it'd have to be fixed up some." He crossed his arms, cinched his hands beneath his armpits and scanned the tops of the walls. "Wouldn't mind giving you an estimate."

Roberta brushed off her palms and shot him an acid glance. "Well, that was fast," she remarked dryly.

"Lucky thing we met at the wharf or I wouldn't have known this place was going to be lived in again."

Roberta wondered just how lucky.

"So you're a carpenter, Mr. Farley?"

"Carpenter, painter, general tradesman all rolled into one. I can fix most things."

Her glance shifted from one man to the other. "Couldn't be you two are in cahoots now, could it? Like maybe Elfred just *happened* to purchase this wreck for me, and maybe Mr. Farley just *happened* to be conveniently coming into the steamship office as we were standing there, and now he just *happens* to have the time on his hands to repair this piece of junk. At what kind of inflated prices, might I ask?"

Farley said nothing, only stood as before with his

hands clamped under his armpits, studying her from beneath his wiry eyebrows. He was big, and the oilskins made him look bigger. He was calm, and his spraddle-legged stance made him look calmer. He had feet the size of dories that made him look as if nothing could tip him over. But no overgrown lummox was going to intimidate Roberta Jewett.

"Well, am I right, Mr. Farley?"

Gabe Farley, unruffled, turned to study Roberta Jewett more closely. First divorced woman he'd ever seen, and he wasn't sure what to make of her. There she stood, confronting him and Elfred with her suspicions, just like a man would do. No fear, no compunctions, just out with it! Didn't care much about her appearance either—that was evident right from the get-go. Stood there with her hair looking like a patch of swamp grass after a hurricane and her coat all crinkled and hanging unbuttoned. No hat, no gloves, no prissy posturing. She stood with her feet just about as widespread as Gabe's own, and he thought, Whew! Are the women going to be talking about this one behind her back!

The men, too.

"Well, now, Mrs. Jewett, you could be right," he said, one-handedly removing his cap and scratching his skull. He angled the cap across his temple again and tugged the brim down till it hid his right eyebrow. "Could be wrong though, too, so I guess it's up to you to decide if you want my help or not."

"Well, answer me straight, Mr. Farley. Are you in cahoots with my brother-in-law?"

"Nope."

She had expected a lengthier denial. Surprised by his

monosyllabic reply, she turned away and wandered the room. "Well, even if you are, I guess there's no problem because Elfred just agreed to finance the repairs on this house, didn't you, Elfred? You see, Mr. Farley, I don't have any money. Well, that's not exactly true. I had four hundred, but Elfred took two to buy this junk heap, leaving me with two hundred, which I intend to use to buy a motorcar."

"A motorcar," Farley repeated, the way an uncle would say to a five-year-old, "To Africa . . ."

"Don't you laugh at me, Mr. Farley!"

"I'm not laughing at you."

"Yes, you are. I'm not an idiot, nor am I incapable of making decisions for me and my girls, and I've decided I shall own a motorcar, come hell or high water."

"Bully for you, but we're not settling the question of whether or not you want me to repair this house."

"Ask Elfred. He got me into this mess. He can get me out."

Elfred cleared his throat and came forward. "Go ahead, Gabe, work up an estimate and bring it to me. We'll work it out somehow between Roberta and me. She's got to live somewhere, and this—I'm afraid—is it."

"All right, I'll look around. Excuse me," he said to Roberta, touching his cap and leaving the room.

The girls had gone exploring, and two of them called from the front porch. "Mother, come out here!"

She went to join Rebecca and Susan, who were standing at the porch rail, looking out through the rain. "Look, Mother," Becky said enthusiastically, "we'll be able to see the harbor from here, and all the boats, and

the islands. I'm sure we'll be able to see them once the
rain clears. And the sunrises! Oh, they'll be stunning,
Mother! Just imagine, this railing and floor fixed, and
our old wicker out here, and something with a delicious
smell blossoming there beside the steps"—she jumped
over two broken boards and turned at the far end of
the porch—"and maybe a hammock here in the shade,
for hot summer afternoons, and I'll write a poem about
the harbor and stand right here at the top of these steps
as if this were the stage at the Opera House and deliver
it for you while you recline on the cool grass with your
toes bare and your throat lifted to the sky." She turned
to her mother in appeal. "I know it looks bad now, but
we don't care. We love it. We want to stay."

"We've already picked out our room," Susan put in.

Roberta studied her daughters a moment. If there was
one force that could stop Roberta on a dime, it was her
girls. She was here. She had bought this rattletrap.
They—bless their ignorance—thought it could be a
home for them. Suddenly she bent back from the waist
and laughed. "Who says I'm poor when I have riches
like you? Come here, girls." She opened her arms. They
came and nestled up against her and linked their arms
around her waist. There they stood, like three fishermen's knots in the same rope, watching a lacework of
rain skim off the porch roof and peck into the sodden
earth below. The scent of fecund soil was primal, and
the touch of the air rich and damp with the promise of
summer's green. The mountain at their backs protected
them from the prevailing southwest winds. The earth
dropped before them, and with it the houses and trees
and commerce between them and Penobscot Bay. Below

and to the right a section of roof on the Knox Woolen Mill presented a sheeny sheet of slate, and beside it the brick smokestack knifed up into the drear heavens where rain-mist shifted like smoke.

A mackerel gull banked past, bleating a series of raucous yells, then flapped wings while settling onto the weather vane of a shed roof in a yard below. Roberta watched it all the way, till it perched and stopped shifting its tail. In Boston they had lived too far from the water. Gulls spoke differently inland than they did within sight of the ocean. The Atlantic's presence gave these gulls a brashness she loved. Nobody could tell a Camden gull it must be quiet, or obedient, or proper, or that it must conform, or that it could not fly singly.

Maybe she'd taken her cue from the gulls.

"I'll need some help from you if we stay," Roberta told her two older girls.

"Sure, Mother."

"Of course, Mother."

"And we won't have much, I can tell you that right now. But neither will you be working in that mill." She looked down on the dark gray slate roof.

"We don't need much," Rebecca assured her.

"You'll be alone a lot. Do you mind?"

"Who's the one who taught us 'When you have imagination, you're never alone'?"

"That's my girl." She jostled Rebecca, then both girls at once.

The mackerel gull came back, still alone, still scolding. She watched its black eye gleam and its head twist in curiosity as it balanced above them, looking them over.

"Houses have never been very important to me," she commented. "Long as they're warm and dry and have a modicum of laughter in them, and maybe some books and music, that's enough, right?"

"Right," the girls replied in unison.

"So we'll stay."

Rebecca's and Susan's grips tightened on her waist, and Roberta fixed in her mind that she'd made the right decision. All it took was deciding it was so, and from that moment on she'd be content with her decision.

"Where's Lydia?"

"Upstairs exploring."

"Shall we go find her?"

Smiling, the three went to do just that.

Lydia was indeed exploring the house. She had read some of the newspaper headlines on the wall from as long ago as thirty years. She had culled some colorful glass floats from the flotsam left behind by Sebastian Dougal. They were scarlet and aqua blue and saffron yellow and would look just dandy hanging on the porch rail in the summer. She set her favorite one at the bottom of the stairs, then looked up, daydreaming, humming. "Sorry her lot who loves too well . . ." Earlier that year, at her school in Boston, she had played the part of Josephine in *H.M.S Pinafore* and was transported now to a ship on the briny sea. Dreaming of it, she doubled over with her forehead on her elbow and ran her entire arm up the gouged handrail, humming all the way to the top. "Heavy the sorrow that bows the head . . ." she sang as she idled her way into the rear bedroom, the one that looked out at Mount Battie. Its ceiling followed the steep roofline, and on one end it had a pair of long, skinny windows that reached to within inches of the floor. Before them, Mr. Farley was on one knee, examining the wall around the window and whistling very softly between his teeth. His whistling sounded like ducks' wings when they flew low over your head.

"Hello," she said.

He stopped whistling and looked back over his shoulder. "Oh, hello."

"I'm Lydia."

He pivoted on the balls of his feet and let his weight settle onto one heel, resting his forearms on his knees, letting his hands dangle between them.

"It's nice to meet you, Lydia. I'm Mr. Farley."

"I know. Are you going to fix this house for us?"

"I think so."

"It's quite a mess, isn't it?"

He let his gaze rove as if following the shape of a rainbow. "Oh, I don't know. It's not so bad." He pointed with a knuckle while keeping the wrist over the knee. "That window in the other bedroom needs replacing, and it looks like it'll need almost a whole new front porch, but the roof is shingled with slate, and she's good for another hundred years."

"This is going to be my room," Lydia told him.

"Oh?"

"Mine and Becky's and Susan's. Mother will take that one." She pointed behind her.

"Have you talked it over already?"

"No, but Mother pretty much always lets us have our way."

"She does, does she?"

"Pretty much. Unless it would hurt somebody, or be bad for our minds. We want to stay, so I know she'll say yes."

"Why do you want to stay?"

"Because we have a grandmother here, and cousins and Aunt Grace and Uncle Elfred, whom it's time we got to know, and because there's an opera house here which Mother says we'll frequent, and exceptionally fine schools, and if you attend high school here you don't even have to be tested to go into college, they just let you in. Did you know that?"

Amazed by her spiel, Gabriel cleared his throat. "No, I didn't."

"Mother says education is paramount."

Mother does, does she? Gabriel studied the precocious child. She was no higher than his armpit and rather the ragamuffin in scuffed brown high-top shoes with knots in their strings and a sacky brown pinafore-shaped dress whose patch pockets sagged. Her sandy braid was in disrepair; a fringe of hair had worked loose from it and she frequently shoved it back from her temples. Her nails were dirty. But her cheeks were rosy and her eyes as bright as a tern's. Moreover, her vocabulary and elocution put Gabe's own to shame. He peered at her more closely.

"How old are you?"

"Ten."

"You speak awfully well for a ten-year-old."

"Mother reads to us a lot, and encourages us to be inquisitive about words, and to create."

"Create what?"

"Anything. Music, poetry, plays, essays, paintings, even botanical exhibits. Once we wrote an opera."

"An opera," he repeated in undisguised surprise.

"In Latin."

"My goodness."

"Well, we tried it in Latin, but we made so many mistakes that Mother got tired of correcting them, so we changed it to English instead. Do you have children?"

"Yes, I do. I have one daughter, Isobel. She's fourteen."

"Susan is fourteen. Maybe we'll all be friends."

"I'm sure Isobel would like that."

"And Rebecca is sixteen. Susan and Rebecca do everything together, but I'm the baby and sometimes they won't let me. But at least they let me put on plays. Well, I'd better go now."

She swung around and collided with her uncle Elfred, who had just reached the top of the stairs.

"Oopsy-daisy!" he said, sidestepping.

She looked up. "I'm sorry, Uncle Elfred. I was just going to find Mother."

"She's downstairs on the front porch with your sisters."

Lydia clattered off down the steps and Elfred joined his friend in the rear bedroom. "Well, what do you think?" he asked, stopping beneath the unlit lightbulb and reaching into his vest pockets for a cigar.

Farley rose. "About the house or about her?"

Elfred trimmed the cigar with his teeth. His burst of laughter sent the brown nubbin flying toward a mopboard.

"Take your pick," he said, striking a match with a thumbnail and puffing to light the stogie.

At that moment Roberta had climbed halfway up the stairs and was being followed by her girls. She swung around and shushed them with a finger to her lips and motioned them to stay where they were. Keeping to the edge of the steps where they wouldn't creak, she tiptoed to the top and flattened herself against the wall, straining to hear what she could.

Farley said in a lowered voice, "She doesn't care much what she says, does she?"

"Or how she looks," Elfred added.

"Or how her children look."

"She's got plenty of what a man likes to get his hands on though, and that's all that matters, eh, Gabe?"

Farley chuckled. "Well, I did get over here pretty fast, didn't I? But, hell, I never met a divorced woman before. I was curious."

"So was I. So I . . ." Elfred harrumphed. The smell of his cigar smoke drifted out past Roberta.

"So you what, Elfred?"

"Well, you know . . ." This slyly. "I tested her a little bit."

"Tested her? Why, Elfred . . ." This with teasing approval. "And you a married man."

"It was just in fun."

"What'd she do?" Farley was nearly whispering.

Though she heard no answer from Elfred, she imagined an off-kilter grin implying whatever a randy mind wanted to imagine, before Farley replied in elongated tones, "Elfred, you devil you."

And both men laughed.

"Yessir . . ." She could tell from his speech that Elfred had the cigar clamped in his teeth. "She's a fiery one, Gabe. Regular little spitfire." He must have removed the cigar from his mouth as he went on in the confidential tone of one worldly stud helping out another. "A word of advice, though. Warm her up a little first. She's got a belligerent side."

"Thought you said you only tested her."

"This was over the house."

"The house?"

"She blew a cork when she saw the condition it was in and jabbed me in the gut with my own umbrella. Damnable temper on her. Damnable."

Farley laughed. "My guess is you deserved it. And I'm not talking about the condition of any house."

Roberta had heard enough. With her face afire she stomped squarely into the room and confronted the two men. During that moment of arrested motion when everyone present knew exactly what the whispering and snickering had been about, she fixed her glacial eyes on Farley.

"When can you begin work?"

Farley hadn't even the grace to blush. "Tomorrow."

"And, Elfred . . . *you shall pay.*" Her manner gave second meaning to the statement that nobody could mistake. "And you shall make sure Grace knows about it, so there's no trouble later between her and me."

"I'll make sure."

"And *you*"—she skewered Farley with contempt in

her eyes, putting a distasteful subtone in the word—
"shall make sure you complete the job and get out of
here in the shortest time possible, is that clear?"

"Yes, ma'am," he said. "Anything you say."

She executed an about-face as regally as if dressed in
hooped taffeta, and headed for the door. "The drays
are here with my belongings. Would you please help the
teamsters unload."

It was far from a request: It was an order issued in
the tone of one whose disgust is so complete she can
cope with it no other way than to turn her back on the
subjects of that disgust.

When she was gone, Gabe and Elfred exchanged silent messages with their eyebrows, then snickered once
again.

Three

Her furniture was as ill kempt as she, a lackluster collection of pieces that would serve the purpose of holding people or possessions, but would do nothing, aesthetically, to enhance their lives.

"Oh, don't worry about the rain," she told the draymen, "just bring it right in here!"

"Perhaps you should stay with us tonight, Birdy," Elfred said.

"Not on your life. What would you do with four of us?"

Elfred didn't know what they'd do with four of them. He had suggested the polite thing but was, in fact, relieved she didn't take him up on his offer.

"This is our house. These are our things. We'll get along. Well, don't just stand there, Farley, make yourself useful! You too, Elfred."

Elfred got soaked. It gave Roberta a vindictive lift to see him gazing down at his wet wool suit, worrying about it shrinking two sizes. Farley, still in his brown-colored oilskins, fared much better, so she made sure he helped the draymen carry the heaviest pieces, including the upright piano that she hoped would leave him with a hernia the size of a turnip.

Whisper, would they?

Damned foul species. Let them haul like beasts of burden: That much men could do. But in Roberta Jewett's book, they were good for little else.

Elfred quite disliked being put upon to do such physical labor and decided he needed to get to his office the moment he could conveniently scramble off.

Farley went, too.

Roberta sent the girls upstairs with instructions to unpack some cartons of clothing and bedding. She went into the living room and perused the collection of crates and trunks stacked in one corner like a Chinese jigsaw, wondering where she might find kitchen equipment in all those boxes. It was nearly midday and the girls would be getting hungry. She should go find a grocery store and put in some supplies, light a fire to take off the chill, attempt to unearth her teakettle and the washbasin and some buckets, rags and towels. Suddenly it seemed too overwhelming to face. Besides, the air coming in the open front door—though damp—brought the smell of the ocean and of the earth greening and lilacs budding, and the sound of gulls and distant bell buoys, which she'd always loved. So she located the legs of the marble-and-claw-foot piano stool sticking out of the mountain of crates, removed a bunch of cartons from in front of the piano, opened the key cover, sat down and played "Art Is Calling for Me" from *Naughty Marietta*. She lit into it with robust energy, and ten bars in heard the girls begin to sing upstairs.

"Mama is a queen . . . and Papa is a king . . . so I am a princess and I know it."

Suddenly Roberta Jewett felt incredibly happy.

She had her girls, and a place to keep them, and a

job waiting. There was no husband to take what was hers or to make a fool of her anymore. Beyond the front porch the view of the harbor waited for her to enjoy anytime she wanted to lean against the doorjamb and bask. She had made a new start, and she and her girls were going to be very, very happy from now on.

With a nimble arpeggio she finished the song, spun around on the piano stool . . .

And found herself face-to-face with Gabriel Farley.

He was relaxed against the doorjamb with his hands tucked under his armpits as if he'd been there awhile.

Her face soured. "I thought you were gone."

"I was. I came back."

"Well, you might have knocked." She spun back to the piano, slammed the key cover and spiked to her feet.

"I did, but you didn't hear me above the racket."

"Racket?" Over her shoulder she quirked an eyebrow at him. "Why, thank you, Mr. Farley. How gracious of you."

Farley had been standing in the doorway for a full minute, watching and listening and wondering what kind of woman kept her front door open in the rain while she sat at the piano and ignored a mountain of moving crates that needed unpacking, and the fact that she was stuck with a wreck of a house that needed mucking out and scrubbing down before it was fit for human habitation.

"Actually, I rather enjoyed it. Your girls sing very well."

From upstairs Rebecca called, "Mother, who's here?"

"It's Mr. Farley!" she called back.

"What does he want?"

"I don't know." Then to him, "What *do* you want, Mr. Farley?"

He boosted off the door frame and came in. "Thought you could use a little help with the heavier boxes, maybe take a look at your stovepipes, make sure they don't have any squirrels' nests in 'em."

"No, thank you." She marched over to the mountain, selected a box and hefted it down. "We'll manage."

He came and lifted it out of her hands while they were still in midair, his height advantage making it effortless for him to pluck it from her.

She turned and gave him a dirty look. "Haven't you got some work to do somewhere?"

"Ayup."

"Then why aren't you there?"

"Got my own business, me and my brother. He's working at a job out by the Lily Pond and he'll get along fine till I get there. Where do you want this?"

The carton held her cast-iron frying pans. He handled it as if it contained nothing more than a thimble keep.

"In the kitchen."

He took it there and she followed, watching as he set it on the floor beside the iron cookstove.

"Look, Mr. Farley." She lowered her voice. "I heard you whispering and tittering with my brother-in-law upstairs. I think I have a pretty good idea of what that was all about, so why don't you just leave the unpacking to me and my girls and take your leave? I'm not the kind of woman you think I am, and you're not going to gain any advantage by hanging around here acting indispensable. I've got my piano inside. That's all I needed you for, and I thanked you for that."

He straightened his spine by degrees, angling her an amused expression.

"Why, Mrs. Jewett, you do me an injustice," he said, brushing his palms together.

"No, Mr. Farley, *you* do *me* an injustice. I told you before, I'm not a stupid woman. I know men and their ways, and I know perfectly well what preconceived notion the word *divorced* brings to their minds. Shall we at least agree that I'm bright enough to have figured out what you and Elfred were whispering about upstairs?"

Farley considered her for some time. By Jove, he'd never met a woman like her before, and if truth were told, he wasn't sure why he was hanging around here. Nevertheless, he decided an admission of his first mistake would put them on friendlier terms.

"Very well. Please accept my apology."

"No, I will not."

Farley couldn't decide whether to chuckle or gape. Never having had an apology flung back in his face before, he gaped. And thrust his chin forward as if he'd just swallowed a horsefly. "You won't?"

"No, I won't. Because it was rude and embarrassing what you did, and since I have no wish to further our acquaintance, I choose not to accept your apology."

A few beats passed before he muttered, "Well, I'll be damned."

"Good," she said, turning away with her nose in the air. "That would please me very much."

She disappeared into the living room, leaving him to gape further. He whipped off his cap, scratched his head (which didn't need it), looked around the kitchen, felt his curiosity about her gather steam, hooked the cap back over his temple (lower than ever) and followed her.

From the doorway between the two rooms he watched her clamber onto a packing crate and reach for a bandbox from high on a stack. The back of her skirt was a wrinkled mess, and the back of her hair was just plain awful. When she leaned forward the heels of her black high-top shoes lifted off the carton, and they, too, were scuffed and worn down so there was no sole left on them. He assessed her and made no more offers of help.

"I'll be going then."

"Yes, please do."

"So do you not want me to do the work on the house then?"

"Suit yourself. That's between you and Elfred. But if you do it, I'll want it understood, you're to knock before you enter and stop staring at my hindside the way you're doing right now. I'm not interested, Mr. Farley. Not in you or any man, is that understood?" She stepped down with the bandbox and faced him.

Off came his cap again and he scratched his head in a frenzy of astonishment. "Good God afrighty, woman, you carry a big stick, don't you?"

"Yes, I do. But you haven't lived in my shoes, so don't judge me, Mr. Farley."

"You'd better get one thing straight." He reset his stance and pointed at the bridge of her nose. "Women around here don't talk like that. And if you want to have any friends, you better not either!"

"Talk like what?"

"You know what I mean! Like . . . like *that*! Like you were!"

"Oh, you mean women around here pretend that men aren't whispering about them in salacious undertones behind their backs?"

"Look, I apologized for that!" He pointed again, but was beginning to get rosy in the face.

"And then added insult to injury by standing in the doorway staring at me as if I were Lady Godiva. Shame on you, Mr. Farley. What would your wife think?" She turned away, put the bandbox on the piano stool, lifted off the lid and let it dangle from its silk cord. From inside she lifted a black straw hat with a pink rose, and from beneath that a stack of folded scarves.

All the while he stood behind her, ill-tempered and embarrassed, prodded by her chastising into actually wondering what his wife would have thought. He shifted his weight from one foot to the other, then back again before defending himself with the most paltry excuse.

"I don't have a wife."

"I'm not surprised," she returned, standing with her back to him while tying a scarf on her head backward.

When it was in place Roberta turned to find him right where he'd been for too long, looking as though he'd like to clunk her a good one and send her reeling against the wall.

"What are you still doing here, Mr. Farley?"

"Damned if I know!" he spouted, and clumped through her parlor, across the porch and down the rickety steps into the rain. The last she saw of him was a flap of his brown oilskins as he veered left and stomped away.

"Good riddance," she mumbled, and went to work.

Gabriel Farley was a Mainer, born and bred, accustomed to the whims of the weather, but the damp and rain aggravated him that day. Well, maybe it wasn't *all* the damp and rain doing the dirty work. It was pretty hard to get a sassy woman like that out of your mind, especially when she had you pegged dead to rights about your motives in nosing around her to begin with. Especially when you'd excused your actions with a misguided remark like *I haven't got a wife.*

Damn it anyway, why had he said that?

He'd been ramming around most of the afternoon with his jaw set, glowering, before his brother Seth finally said, "What's eating you today?"

"Nothing."

"Something with Isobel?"

"Nope."

"Ma?"

"Nope."

"Well, what is it, then?"

"Mind your own business, Seth."

Seth continued measuring a piece of cross-bucking for the wide double doors he was making. He and Gabe were building a shed/garage for one of the rich summer families who had homes in Boston and cottages here. A workbench of plywood and sawhorses stretched down the center of the newly erected structure. Seth bent over it, slashed a mark, stuck the thick gold carpenter's pencil behind his ear and whistled softly between his teeth.

He knew Gabriel. Best way to get it out of him was to quit asking.

He whistled some more while Gabe worked on setting a small window, going outside into the rain and using his hammer, then coming back inside to do more of the same.

Pretty soon Gabe said, "I'm going to be starting a job for Elfred Spear tomorrow, so I'll leave you to finish this one."

"What's Elfred got going?"

"Well, it's not exactly Elfred's job, he's just the one who's paying me to do it."

"Oh?"

"It's the old Breckenridge house."

"You're kidding! That old wreck?"

"I went over and looked at it this morning. Structurally, it's pretty sturdy. And it's got a slate roof."

"Old Sebastian was crazier than a coot by the time he died. I can about imagine what the place looks like inside."

"Ayup, it's a mess all right, but nothing that can't be fixed with some soap and water and plenty of paint. Needs a couple of new windowpanes, and plenty of puttying around the old ones. Foundation needs some mortar between the stones here and there, but I can handle all that pretty easily. I'll be tearing off the whole front porch and putting a new one on. Might need you when I get to that."

"Just let me know when."

"Yup."

They worked awhile before Seth asked, "So who's Elfred carrying on with these days?"

Gabriel kept on sawing. "He didn't say."

"I feel sorry for that wife of his."

"What she doesn't know won't hurt her."

"Listen to yourself, Gabe. The man makes a fool of her, and him with three daughters to boot."

"You saying you never stepped out on Aurelia?"

"Y' damned right that's what I'm saying. We might have our little tiffs now and again, but I wouldn't do that to her." Seth worked a minute or so before asking, "You aren't saying you stepped out on Caroline, are you?"

"Good God, no. Not as long as she drew breath."

"Then how can you excuse it in a rounder like Spear?"

Gabriel dropped his tools, rubbed his eyes hard and sighed. He'd been unhappy with himself all day long, and damned uncomfortable about what had happened up at the old Breckenridge house. "Hell, I don't know, Seth. I guess I'm in a state right now. I'm just so sick and tired of this living alone."

"You're not living alone. You've got Isobel."

Gabe stared at his brother in silence, then walked to the unfinished doorway and stared out at the rain. Caroline had never minded the rain like most people do. She had often worked right out in it.

"Yes, I know. I've got Isobel. And the older she gets, the more she reminds me of her mother."

Seth abandoned his work and crossed the shed to stand near his brother. He crooked a hand over Gabriel's shoulder and gave it a squeeze. "Comin' close to the time she died, is that it?"

"Ayup. Every year at this time it gets bad."

The rain had drilled a trough below the edges of the new eaves. It made tiny explosions as it fell into the puddles there. Things smelled musky with renewal—the earth at Gabe's feet, the new-milled lumber above him. Out on the little lake known as the Lily Pond, frogs were singing as if they absolutely loved this weather. They were probably out there laying eggs. Robins were back and had nests built already. The other day, right outside their shop downtown, he'd watched a pair of mating loons doing a splendid, fluttering ballet on the surface of the water, like toe dancers. Spring—heartless spring—it was always difficult to get through spring without Caroline.

"You want to know how bad it got today?"

Seth dropped his hand from Gabe's shoulder and waited. Gabriel slipped his palms beneath his armpits and propped his weight against the unfinished door opening, continuing to stare out at the rain. "I ran into Elfred at the wharf, and this woman was with him— his sister-in-law, actually. Turns out she's divorced."

"Divorced! Aw, now, Gabe, you can do better than that!"

"Just let me finish. Turns out she's divorced and she's got three kids and she's moving into that mess that Sebastian Breckenridge left behind when he died. I heard that and I went hotfootin' it up there to see if she could use a carpenter." Gabe shook his head, a little abashed, now that he thought about it. "I mean, I was up there faster than a goose on a June bug. But she caught on to me, and let me tell you, Seth, she put me in my place. It was embarrassing."

Seth whapped Gabriel on the shoulder and started to laugh.

"So that's why you're in this puckered-up mood."

With the toe of his boot Gabriel pushed a couple of wood chips off the new pine floor into the puddle outside. "Yeah . . . I guess. Truth is, she made me feel like a jackass."

Seth went back to work. He hammered a diagonal onto the cross-buck door, then started searching out a length of cedar for another. He found a long one-by-six, picked up one end and eyed its length. "So what's she like?" he inquired offhandedly.

Gabriel boosted off the door. "Hell, she's a mess." He came back inside and resumed work, too. "Clothes, hair, house—you name it, everything a mess. Even her kids. They look like a bunch of orphans."

"So what are you standing here fussing about her for?"

"I don't know. Because I've got to go back there tomorrow and face her again, I suppose."

"Well, hell . . . maybe she won't be there if the house is that bad. Maybe she'll decide to live someplace else."

"Oh, she'll be there all right. Probably be sitting there playing her piano and singing her head off in the middle of all that filth. I tell you, Seth, it was the damndest thing you ever saw. I went back there after we helped unload all the drays, and there she sat, playing the piano as if there weren't a thing out of place. And her kids were singing upstairs! You'd have thought they were living in the Taj Mahal. But you know what? They're a happy bunch. And one of those little girls, the youngest one? Well, I want to tell you, that one's got a head on her shoulders. Nearly talked my head off. And language! Whew, I've read newspaper publishers that didn't use language that fancy. You know what she said? She said that she and her sisters wrote an opera. In Latin, mind you!"

Seth stopped working and gazed over in wonder. "How old you say this girl was?"

"Ten."

"Ten. Feature that."

"Ayup, ten."

They thought for a while, imagining themselves at ten.

Seth said, "Hell, I could barely wipe my ass by the time I was ten."

Gabriel laughed.

"I seem to remember that. Sometimes I had to wipe it for you." It was nearly true. Gabe was four years older than Seth, and his mother had often relied on him to be her helping hand.

Gabe's thoughts returned to the precocious Lydia. "How do you suppose a girl gets that smart by the time she's ten?"

"I don't know."

"The way she talked, her mother teaches them a lot."

"That'd be the . . . ah . . . the woman with the tacky hair and clothes."

Gabriel bent a wry glance at his brother. "What're you gettin' at, Farley?"

"This's the most you've talked about any woman since Caroline died, you know that?"

Gabe gave out a throaty sound, neither grunt nor chuckle. "You're demented, man. I told you, she's got a tongue that could fillet a flounder at six paces, and she's not any too ladylike."

"Let me get a look at her first, then I'll tell you whether I'm demented. You're the one who said you went sniffing after her 'cause you heard she was divorced."

"Well, maybe I did, but she's about as lovable as a water moccasin, so don't go spreading any rumors, you got me?"

"Yessir!" Seth squelched a grin. "Gotcha!"

The rain let up toward evening. Gabriel stowed his wooden tool caddy in the back of his Ford C-Cab, got in, set the spark on retard and went through four more steps before getting out to crank the truck. It coughed to life, and he lifted a hand in farewell as he got back in.

Going through all that rigmarole to start the truck brought the woman back to mind. She'd said she intended to buy a motorcar. Now that was just plain silly. First thing she'd do was break her arm trying to start it. And how could she remember everything she needed to know before she even gripped the crank?

Besides, what would people say? Ladies just didn't do things like that.

But then, in spite of how she protested, he guessed she was no lady.

Why in tarnation was he even wasting time thinking about her?

He'd think of something else.

It was a gol-darned pretty evening. Off behind Ragged Mountain the sky was clearing: You could tell by the peachy glow that lit its rim, though above it the clouds were still streaky gray-green like an old lobster's back. But they were in motion, lifting, dissolving in advance of a clear day tomorrow.

He took Chestnut down into town, then swung over to Bayview where his shop was sandwiched between the street and the rocky shore. He left the truck running on the street while he went inside. The doors were locked but Terrence, their clerk, had left some notes tacked to the wall beside the wooden telephone box: Mrs. Harvey had come in and was wondering how much they'd charge to replace a broken chair rung; the minister from the Congregational Church would like to speak to him about heading up a committee for cemetery cleaning; his daughter had stopped by after school and said she was just wondering what time he'd be home for supper; the Opera House was interested in having some stage props framed up for an upcoming production.

He dropped the notes on a dusty rolltop desk, picked out some price lists and catalogs and locked up again before climbing back in the truck to head home.

He lived on Belmont Street in a tall, narrow white house with a small shed out back to which he'd added a lean-to for his truck. From the shed a stepping-stone walk led to the house and was hooded by a white pergola just outside the kitchen door. He passed beneath it on his way through the yard, glancing at the canes of the climbing roses to see if any sprouts showed. They were all he'd kept of Caroline's flowers, and he carefully protected them with straw each fall, kept them pruned and fertilized all summer. The rest of the garden he'd long ago allowed to fall victim of the grass, and by now, after seven years, he couldn't even tell where the garden had been. Sometimes this saddened him, for when he thought of Caroline, he thought of her in a sunbonnet, wearing gloves, doubled over a hand cultivator, caring for the flowers she'd loved so much.

He stepped into the kitchen and was met by a reedy girl who had inherited his height and big feet, but little more of him. She was all Caroline's—from the buggy-whip thinness to the paprika hair. Though not a classically pretty girl, she had her pretty points. Her skin was as fair and unflawed as a sliced potato, but unlike that of most redheads, hadn't a single freckle. Her green eyes tilted up slightly at the corners and were framed by brows and lashes so pale they might have been illusions. Unfortunately, her ears even stuck out like Caroline's; she kept them covered at all times, out of self-consciousness.

"Hi, Daddy. I thought you'd never get here. I'm starving."

"You're always starving. What's for supper?"

"Fish cakes and boiled potatoes."

Fish cakes again. Mercy, he got so tired of fish cakes. But she did the best she could after school, more than a father should expect. Often he felt guilty that she had to spend so much of her precious free time on duties that a wife and mother should have handled.

"How was school?" he inquired, hanging up his oil-skins on wall pegs beside the door.

"Boring. Same old thing—Miss Tripton lectures, Mrs. Lohmer scolds, and Miss Bisbee treats us like children who can't be trusted for a minute while she's out of the room. Honestly, she still appoints a room monitor when she leaves!"

"Well, not long now till the end of the term."

He poured water from a teakettle and washed up while she put the fish cakes on two plates, dumped potatoes into a bowl, poured milk for herself and coffee for him. Drying his hands with a towel, he shuffled over and stood beside the table while she filled his cup.

"I met some new girls today."

"Girls? You mean my age?"

"One of them." He tossed the towel aside, and the two sat down and started smashing potatoes and spreading them with butter. "The other two were sixteen and ten."

"Well, who were they? How come they aren't going to school?"

"They will be pretty soon. They just moved into town and they're cousins of the Spear girls."

"What were they like?"

"The youngest one was smart as a whip. I talked to her the most. I think they're all pretty musical. Other than that, I don't know much about them, except they looked rather like ragamuffins."

"Where'd you meet them?"

"At the steamship office, actually, then I found out they were moving into the old Breckenridge house, so I decided I'd go up there and see if I could scare up a little business."

"Oh, yuck, nobody'd catch me living in that boar's nest. They must be awfully poor if they have to have a house like that."

"I think they are."

"Is their dad going to work at the mill?"

Gabriel took a swig of coffee, giving himself time to think.

"Ah, no, actually . . . there is no dad. Just a mother."

"Oh." Isobel grew thoughtfully somber. Because she had been reared primarily by Gabriel and recalled so little of her mother, it was difficult for her to imagine growing up without a dad. "Poor kids."

"I think they do all right. They certainly don't lack for imagination, and they seem to be a rather happy troop—singing, playing the piano, writing operas."

"Writing operas!"

"That's what she said—the little one, that is. Her name is Lydia. She said she and her sisters wrote an opera in Latin."

"My gosh! They must be brains!"

"I thought the same thing. Well, in any case, you'll probably be meeting them soon." He pushed back his plate. "Thanks for making the fish cakes, honey. Have you got studies tonight?"

She made a face. "Orthography and civil government. We're having examinations in both of them tomorrow."

He stood, picking up his stacked plates and cup. "Then leave the dishes for me. I'll do them later on, but first I have to work on an estimate for the Jewetts."

"The Jewetts?"

"That's their name, the new girls. Rebecca, Susan and Lydia Jewett."

Isobel shrugged and turned away. "I'll probably meet them at school as soon as they get there. I'll see if I like them or not."

"Ayup. Well, I've got that estimate to work on, so

you get your books and I'll leave half of the table for you."

They spent the next two hours sitting beneath the new electric light in their white-painted kitchen while the teakettle breathed a thin whisper of song. It was a comfortable room with a pressed-tin ceiling, bead-board wainscot and a curious combination of outdated and modernized equipment, evidence of the owner's ability to upgrade and remodel the house by himself. The lights were electric, the range wood-burning. The sink had a drainpipe but no faucet, only a pump. The oak table and chairs, fashioned by Gabriel's own hand, dated back to the year of his marriage, but the glass-doored cabinets were a recent addition and were tricked out with clear glass knobs, at Isobel's request.

A fluffy caramel-colored cat came and shaped herself into a loaf on a third chairseat underneath the table, tucked her paws and squinted into a doze. The rattle of her purring joined the music from the teakettle while night pressed its dark face to the windows. Three times Gabriel got up and refilled his coffee cup, then resumed working. Once Isobel got up and found herself two mo-lasses cookies. When she had finished munching and studying, she closed her book and looked up to find her father staring into space, his pencil idle.

"Daddy?"

"Hm?" Gabriel started from his reverie. For some odd reason he'd been thinking about that Jewett woman. "What?"

"Maybe you should give up and go to bed. You're staring."

"Am I? Well, I'm not tired. Just wool-gathering. Listen, I've got this estimate pretty much finished and I have to give it to Elfred Spear. You don't mind if I take it over there now, do you?"

"Tonight?" she said in surprise. "It's kind of late, isn't it?"

Gabriel checked his pocket watch. "Nine. That's not too late." He tucked the watch away, pushed back his chair, tamped his estimate together and reached for a light jacket. "Rain's stopped. Guess I don't need my oilskins. I won't be gone long."

She stretched, bending backward on her chair, both arms raised. "Okay, good night, Daddy."

"See you in the morning."

He went out without touching or kissing her, thinking how grateful he was to have her and worrying about two, or four, or six years up the road when she'd probably get married and leave his house.

Disturbed by the prospect of loneliness, he put it from his mind.

Outside, the grass was squishy between the stepping-stones, and the sky had cleared. Pinpricks of stars put bright holes in the deep blue velvet overhead, and somewhere spring peepers were fluting. Passing beneath the rose pergola he thought as he often did, *Miss you, Caroline.*

Under the lean-to it smelled of petroleum and the packed earth floor. Blackness surrounded him as he felt his way along the left running board to the front of the truck where he started the water drip into the carbide crystals of the headlamps. He swung open the lenses and lit the lamps, then did the same for the sidelights. Inside the truck he went through the regimen of adjustments—spark lever, throttle, emergency brake, choke wire and key—before finally getting out to crank the engine. Back in the driver's seat, he pulled down the spark lever to the running position, put the throttle back up, pulled the emergency brake halfway up and maneuvered the three foot pedals until finally he was rolling forward out of the open-ended shed.

Ridiculous of that Jewett woman to think she could do all that!

What was it that kept putting her back in his mind? He'd been thinking of her when Isobel roused him, and now again, though he could not for the life of him understand why. Probably just the motorcar, he thought—the sheer brashness of a woman thinking she could own one when she'd have to go through all this just to get the thing started. To say nothing of running it and keeping it in repair!

No . . . no, he thought. She'd be crazy to buy one.

But if he'd ever met a woman in his life who'd do a crazy thing like that, she was probably the one.

He pulled up in Elfred's yard and left the engine running as he crossed the beams of the carbide lights and approached the front door.

Elfred answered the bell himself, dressed in trousers and a smoking jacket. "Well, for heaven's sake, Gabe, what are you doing here at this hour?"

"Brought that estimate."

Elfred removed the cigar from his mouth and looked down at the papers in some surprise.

"At nine o'clock at night?" A sly glint formed in his eye as he accepted the sheets. "You *are* in a hurry, aren't you, Gabe?" He chuckled conspiratorially.

Gabriel lowered his chin and scratched his left sideburn. "Well . . . thought I'd get it taken care of right away, that's all. I can use the work."

"Sure, Gabe. I know how it is." Elfred cursorily glanced at the estimate and said, "I don't know why I even bothered to have you write it up. She's not the kind of woman a man says no to, is she?"

Gabriel put his hand on the doorknob, eager to be away. It was useless to protest that he had no ulterior motives in hurrying with the estimate after the wisecracking he and Elfred had done at the woman's expense.

With a wicked grin Elfred lightly slapped Gabe on the jaw, as if patting bay rum there. "Go ahead, Gabe. Give 'er hell."

Gabe stalked back out to his truck thinking, *Damn it but I hate that Elfred. He is one very repugnant man.*

He drove along through the spring night. Trees were budding and the runoff from the day's rain burbled along the edges of the street to the harbor below. Once again he heard the frogs and smelled the thawing earth.

Spring without Caroline—how bittersweet.

At home, he pulled under the lean-to and secured the car for the night, then walked slowly along the stepping-stones, under the pergola and into the kitchen, where Isobel had left the new electric light burning.

Wearily he pulled off his jacket, hung it and turned to face the room where he had taken care of so many domestic duties since Caroline had died. Isobel did her share, but so did he, often late at night like this when he was tired and would rather have gone to bed.

There was water in the reservoir and the teakettle.

He filled the dishpan and washed dishes, dried them, wiped off the table and put a nice neat little doily in the middle, just as Caroline had always done. It was one she'd crocheted herself. On it he put her philodendron plant, the way she always used to. With his damp dishtowel he wiped some fingerprints off a glass pane of a cabinet door, then folded the towel neatly and hung it on a towel rack he had made himself. His last duty was to pump water to fill both the reservoir and the teakettle for morning.

Pretty soon he'd put in a bathroom and some radiators, he promised himself. A modern stove, too. It was silly to have electricity and not make use of all the conveniences it could bring.

He'd have to make time to do the work, that was all.

Before he turned the thumb crank for the electric light, he looked the room over and found it satisfactory. Rugs neatly aligned at the sink and the back door, cupboard neat, chairs pushed in.

Just as Caroline would have liked it.

Near eleven o'clock, with plodding footsteps, he shuffled upstairs to his lonely bed.

Four

The Jewetts got to bed well after eleven P.M., awakened late and ate boiled macaroni in hot buttered milk for breakfast—the fastest thing Roberta could devise to slam on the table. Things were in such chaos that the girls couldn't find hair combs, so they took turns using their mother's. Neither could they find clean underwear or stockings so they wore the ones from yesterday. Their dresses were wrinkled from traveling, but nobody seemed to care.

Late heading off for school their first day, neither Roberta nor the girls made an issue of it as they set out together.

"Would you look at that," Roberta remarked, catching sight of the harbor below. "Like one of Lydia's glass floats." It had cleared overnight and the water took on so intense a blue it appeared as if the sun were lighting it from below rather than above. From three blocks up, the view was splendid. There were boats at rest beside the village docks and others heading out toward the silver-misted horizon. Some had white sails, some moved under steam power, their tracks spreading behind them like lifting wings. The many islands dotting Penobscot Bay looked like nuggets of ice with the sunlight melting their tops.

It was a noisy morning. The gulls were at it, and so were the workers at the Bean shipyard below. The tattoo of their hammers joined the more musical ring from a stonecutter's shed on Tannery Lane. "Listen!" Roberta hearkened. "In my oldest memories I awakened to the sound of those hammers." Other noises of commerce drifted up the hill as well—the clatter of the electrics, the burr of boat engines and the *chug-putt* of motorcars. All of these notes were filtered by the April morning into a fine harmony while the earth, washed by the previous day's rains, smelled brash and black.

Late or not, the Jewetts were enraptured by their new surroundings.

They walked beneath an eddy of gulls who scolded continuously. Susan eyed them and scolded back. "*Cree cree* yourselves!"

"Are they ring-billed?" Lydia asked.

"No, they're herring gulls," Susan replied.

Rebecca began reciting Swinburne.

> "The lark knows no such rapture,
> Such joy no nightingale,
> As sways the songless measure
> Wherein thy wings take pleasure . . ."

" 'To a Seamew.' " Roberta cocked her head and watched the birds. "A lovely choice, though these can't be mews, not on this coast. I agree with Susan. I think they're herrings."

Rebecca said, "I hope I like my English teacher."

"And my music teacher," added Susan.

"I like this town," Lydia, the pessimist, put in, surprising them all. "It's pretty."

It was a disjointed conversation but typical among the Jewetts. Their interests were so diverse that a stranger overhearing would have been addled by the quick shifts in topic.

At the school on Knowlton Street they met the principal, Miss Abernathy, an overfed woman around forty with glasses and wavy gray-streaked hair, which she wore in a chignon. She welcomed them but at one point checked her cameo watch and noted that it was nearly nine-thirty in the morning.

"School begins at eight, Mrs. Jewett."

"Yes, I know," Roberta replied, unruffled, "but we were reciting Swinburne on our way."

"Swinburne?" repeated Miss Abernathy.

"As in Algernon . . . the English poet?"

Miss Abernathy put her marbled pen in its holder and smiled indulgently. "Yes, of course. I know who Swinburne is. It's not common for our students to be familiar with his works, however."

"Oh, my girls are familiar with as many poets as I can get them to experience. And composers and authors as well."

"Indeed? So we have a trio of true scholars here."

"Scholars?" Roberta considered. "Maybe not. But they're inquisitive and they have imagination."

"Then they should do very well."

Roberta left them at school without the slightest doubt that's exactly what they'd do.

When she got back home, Gabriel Farley's strange-looking truck was parked on the street and he was sitting on her front step.

"What do you want?" she asked ungraciously.

He lumbered to his feet, reaching full height just as she reached the porch steps. "I'm repairing your house."

"Hmph." Right on by she went, into the house without even slowing.

He stood in the trampled weeds of her front yard, his gaze following her through the open doorway. From the porch straight back to her kitchen and out a doorway on the opposite end it was one clear shot. He watched until she spun right and disappeared behind a kitchen wall. His gaze swung to the rusty anchor half-buried in the dirt, then he curled his tongue around an eyetooth, sucked once and shook his head at his boots. He'd cooked his goose with her yesterday, that was for sure. Not that it mattered, because he really didn't like her much.

Resigned to the fact, he went to his truck to get his tool caddy.

After examining the outside of the house, he decided he'd better get the porch torn off and rebuilt first thing, because it was dangerous with the floor half rotted, and he'd have to cross it a hundred times himself in the next couple of weeks. The wrecking he could do alone, then he'd get Seth over here to help him rebuild it.

He climbed the porch steps, peered inside and heard Roberta dragging boxes around in the kitchen, unpacking things.

"Mrs. Jewett?" he called.

She came to the doorway between the two rooms

holding some blue kettles, wearing a dishtowel tied backward around her skirt. "What?"

"I thought I'd start with the front porch, if that's okay with you."

"I don't care where you start."

Abruptly she hied herself out of sight again.

"It's got to be torn off completely and rebuilt!" he shouted.

Her head returned for three seconds. "I said I don't care. Do whatever you have to, just don't bother me!"

He got a ladder, climbed up to the roof and started ripping off the porous wooden shakes, speculating about why the roof on the main body of the house had been done in slate. These houses were old, this one probably a hundred years or more. Sometimes porches and lean-tos had been added as afterthoughts. Dry rot had eaten this one.

He worked on into the morning and the sun grew warmer, the yard became littered with bent nails and broken pieces of silver wood. By noon he had the rafters exposed and was beating on one with a hammer when he thought he heard shouting.

"Mr. Farley?"

He looked down and saw Mrs. Jewett standing below, shading her eyes with one hand, squinting up. She still wore the dishtowel around the skirt of her mushroom-brown dress. Her hair was a fright and the armpit of her blouse was damp.

"Ayup?" he said.

"May I ask you a few questions about your motorcar?"

"Ayup. Watch out there." She stepped back and he

dropped a length of discolored wood. "It's not a car, it's a truck."

"Oh."

"A Ford C-Cab."

She glanced at it, then back up at him. "How long have you had it?"

" 'Bout two years."

"Do you like it?"

"Ayup, I do."

"Better than a horse?"

"How long's this going to take? You mind if I come down there and talk?" He'd been balancing his hips against the ladder and twisting at the waist to look down at her.

"No, of course not. Come ahead."

He slipped his hammer into a loop on a leather tool belt, backed down the ladder, and they stood their distance, separated by layers of shingles that gave off a smell like an old, unused shed. A sprawling ash tree, still bare, threw thin veins of shadow across them while they stood talking.

"Truck's much easier than a horse. You don't have to feed it or clean up after it. 'Course, in winter, around here, it can't take you the places a horse can take you, but then you've got the electrics to do that."

"Is a truck different from a motorcar?"

"Just the body. Chassis's the same."

"So it starts and runs the same?"

"Ayup."

"Elfred says a woman couldn't own one because she couldn't start it. Do you agree?"

Gabriel scratched a sideburn and glanced at the truck.

It was an odd-looking thing, doorless, with a black leather top shaped like an ocean wave that curved over the seat to create a roof. "That's hard to say. I've never seen a woman start one."

"Well, what's your guess?"

Gabriel's gaze wandered back to her. "Want to find out for sure?"

Her eyebrows twitched while she decided.

"Yes, I suppose so."

"All right then, come on. Let's see what you can do. Be careful there. Nails all over the place."

They traipsed across the clattery shingles onto the thick mattress of dead winter grass and he let her pass before him through the break in some scraggly, weed-choked irises and bridal wreath that edged the yard. He noticed she wore the same scuffed, run-over shoes as the day before. The street was paved in gravel and pocked with mud puddles after yesterday's rain. They skirted several and made their way to the far side of his truck where the side curtains were rolled up and tied out of the way.

"Get in." He motioned her up. "You might as well do it all, right from the start."

She stepped onto the running board, wrestled her skirt around the brake lever and sat down on the patent-leather seat.

"I'll take you through it step by step." He propped one foot on the running board and pointed inside as he spoke. "Now that lever right there on the steering column is your spark. It's got to be on *retard,* which is where it is right now. If you accidentally leave it on *advance* she'll kick back when you try to crank 'er, and chances are you'll get hurt. These things have been known to split skulls wide open. So this is important: Always set the spark on retard."

"Spark on retard," she repeated, and gingerly touched the lever.

Again he pointed to the steering column. "This right here is the throttle, and it should be halfway up when you start 'er. That gives 'er the gas."

"Throttle halfway up."

"And this right here"—he dropped a hand over the brake handle—"is the emergency brake, but it's got a lot to do with shifting, so make sure it's pulled all the way back toward the seat. You have to pinch the handles together while you pull . . . see?"

He moved his hand and let her give it a try.

"Good," he said. "Now, get out. We've got to go up front."

While she backed out of the truck, he stood back and watched the white knot of the dishtowel riding her spine, thinking if she were any other woman he would have offered her a hand down. But the tongue-lashing she'd given him yesterday had made him wary.

He led her to the front of the vehicle and pointed to a loop of wire protruding from the left side of the radiator. "That's the choke wire. Pull it out." She did, making no comment. "We could go inside the car and turn the switch on right now, but there's a little trick you can try that'll make 'er start quicker. You do like this—see? Pull up the crank three or four times with the switch off, and that draws more gas into the cylinder. Do it or not, it's up to you. Now back inside again. Come on." She followed him to the driver's side. "Just reach inside and turn on the key to the battery position. . . . Now, let's see if you can crank 'er yourself."

The crank had an unpainted wooden handle. When she reached for it, he pulled her arm back sharply. "Wait a minute. This is the most dangerous part. Always remember, you have to pull up. Never push down, because you want to get it on a compression stroke."

"Compression stroke?"

"That has to do with the engine, but you don't have to understand it. Just remember—always up, never down. And one more thing. Don't wrap your thumb around the crank. Fold it along the top, that way if she ever decides to kick back, your hand will fly free a little easier. Like this, see?"

He demonstrated, then moved aside and let her take over.

Gripping the crank handle, Roberta felt her heart dancing with apprehension. She glanced up and met Farley's eyes.

"It'll be okay," he said. "Everything is set right, so give 'er a try. If you can crank it, you can run it. Go ahead."

She set her jaw and pulled up so powerfully a muscle wrenched in her shoulder. The engine fired and Roberta leaped back with a hand over her heart.

"I did it!"

"Go on!" he yelled above the noise. "Get back in! You're not done yet!"

They both got in and the racket was awful, the engine rocking the machine till the two of them looked palsied.

"Okay, I showed you this before—it's your spark. It goes back down to advance while the engine is running, which gives the engine more power so it'll run smoother."

She put the spark where he said.

"Remember which one was the throttle?" he asked.

"This one."

"That's right. Put it back up."

She did, and the rocking leveled out somewhat.

"You want to drive 'er?"

"You mean you'd let me?" she replied, amazed.

"How else are you going to know if you want one of your own?"

She had to consider a moment before answering, "Thank you, Mr. Farley. Yes, I'd appreciate it."

"Hands on the wheel, then."

She gripped the wooden steering wheel and sat tensely on the edge of the seat.

"Relax some."

"Relax? Doing this? You cannot be serious!"

He smiled to himself and pointed down at her ankles. "Just sit back a little. Your skirt is hiding the floor pedals."

She slid back a few inches, still gripping the steering wheel as if it were a divining rod that was going to suck her down into the earth.

"Okay, those three pedals plus the emergency brake are what make it run." The three diamond-shaped pedals were arranged in a triangle on the floor. "The left one puts it in neutral, the middle one is reverse and the right one is the brake. First put your emergency brake halfway up and push the neutral pedal all the way down. Don't be scared—halfway up."

She followed orders with far less assurance than she'd

shown when she'd told Elfred she wanted to own one of these things. When the moves were made she let out a partial breath, but her knuckles had turned white on the steering wheel.

"Now push the emergency brake full forward and your foot all the way down, and that puts 'er in first gear."

She shifted cautiously and the car lurched forward, then began rolling down the boulevard, half on people's grass, half on the street.

"All right. Here we go. Use the throttle."

"Where's the throttle!" she shouted.

He took her right hand and guided it to the throttle lever. "Right there. Give 'er some gas now, slowly."

They accelerated and bumped along the Alden Street boulevards.

"Dear God, I hope I don't kill us both!"

"Turn the wheel." He turned it for her, steering them out onto the street. "Now take your foot off the left pedal and that'll put 'er in high gear."

They proceeded toward an intersection, bouncing when the wheels hit potholes and splattered muddy water up on the running boards. "Now try the brake . . . no the other foot!"

"It's confusing with three pedals."

"You'll get used to it. Look both ways at the corner, then just put your clutch in and that'll slow us down for a turn. Turn left and go up the hill."

She stomped on the clutch, and just as promised, they slowed. He helped her steer around a corner, then talked her through a ride that took them climbing up the foothills of Mount Battie.

"Relax," he told her again.

"I can't. I'm terrified."

"You're doing very well. Do you think you'll want one of your own?"

"Please, Mr. Farley, I can't talk and drive at the same time."

"All right, I'll shut up."

He sat back and watched her. She had gumption like he'd never seen in a woman before, and he couldn't deny a hint of admiration. He didn't know any other female who'd have gotten behind that steering wheel.

"Are you ready to try reversing now?"

"Oh God," she said.

"You'll do fine." He guided her through the process of slowing, turning around in a driveway and heading back down the mountain.

Halfway down, they encountered a car coming up.

"Mr. Farley!" she shouted. "What should I do!"

He resisted reaching for the steering wheel. "Just steer to the right."

She did, chanting, "Oh-my-soul, oh-my-soul," while he smiled to himself and waved back at Seba Poole, who gaped as the two cars passed.

"You're lucky I didn't kill us both, Farley! I never knew roads were so narrow!"

"You did just fine. Seba's still on the road and so are you."

She relaxed a little and asked, "Who was that?"

"Seba Poole, runs the fish hatchery at the outlet of Lake Megunticook. He likes to gossip, so word'll get around you've been driving my truck."

She flashed him a fast glance. "Too bad for you," she

remarked, garnering a study from him. It might have held a smirk; she couldn't tell.

After that they rumbled the remainder of the way down the mountain without conversing, but a grudging respect had been set into motion during the drive. She found him patient and good at explaining; he found her plucky and admired her grit in spite of her occasional shriek for help.

In front of her house she stopped and he showed her how to shut off the key and make sure she left the spark lever and throttle in the up position.

"So I won't break my arm the next time I crank it," he explained.

When the engine quieted, she heaved a sigh of relief and let her fingers slide from the wheel. No sooner had her shoulders wilted than they squared again resolutely.

"May I run through it one more time to make sure I remember correctly?"

"Of course."

"Spark on retard . . . ," She repeated what she'd learned without a slip—in the car, out of the car, touching each of the pertinent parts without actually starting the engine.

". . . throttle in the up position," she finished, meeting his eyes directly. "How did I do?"

"Perfectly."

They stood in the street beside the vehicle. She studied it as if evaluating. Finally, she said, "Elfred gave me a long list of reasons why a woman shouldn't even think of owning a motorcar. He says they break down quite regularly and the tires need patching and something up there needs adjusting all the time."

"The carburetor."

"Yes, that's it."

"Carburetors are touchy, all right, but I can show you how to adjust them. It's not very complicated."

"Elfred says gasoline is heavy and clumsy to put in."

"Not so heavy and clumsy you couldn't do it."

"Where does it go?"

"Gas tank's underneath the seat. Here, I'll show you."

He leaned into the truck and tipped up the seat bottom revealing a wooden floor with a hole through which the mouth of the gas tank projected. "You put the gas in here." He stepped back to let her see.

She bent over and peered at the spout. Beside it a wooden stick was tethered to a string.

"What's this?"

"A dipstick to find out how much gas is left."

She studied the increments carved into it. "Gallons?" she inquired.

"Ayup."

"Mm, simple." She dropped the stick and stepped back while he replaced the seat and brushed off his palms.

"So tell me, Mr. Farley. You can be honest. Do you think I'm crazy to want to own my own motorcar?"

"Well, you certainly can drive one. You've proven that today."

"There's a garage downtown where I could have it repaired when necessary, right?"

"Mmm . . . well, yes, if the trouble conveniently develops when you're in town. Elfred's got a point about these things acting up constantly. Do you mind telling me, Mrs. Jewett, what you want the car for?"

"I've got a job as a public nurse."

"Traveling, you mean?"

"Yes, all up and down the county."

"All by yourself?" He acted surprised.

"Yes."

"In that case . . ." He clamped his hands beneath his armpits. She was beginning to see the pose covered a range of tacit responses.

"In that case, forget about the motorcar?"

"Well, let me put it this way. I wouldn't want any woman of mine driving all over these mountains in one of these things."

"Yes . . . well, you see, Mr. Farley, it's my good fortune that I no longer have to answer to any man for what I do."

"You asked my opinion and I gave it."

"Thank you, Mr. Farley," she said. "Now I'd best get back to work."

She marched inside and left him standing in the thin veins of shadow from the naked ash tree. He went back to work wondering why she'd asked his opinion if she didn't want it.

Sometimes, from up on the ladder, he'd see junk come flying out the front door. Once she flung out some scrub water. Right afterward he heard the piano start up and stopped working to listen.

Strange woman, playing the piano between bouts of scrubbing.

A while later he smelled coffee but she didn't offer him any. Shortly before noon her mother arrived on foot.

"Mr. Farley," she hailed, "is that you up there?"

"Hello, Mrs. Halburton." She was tilted back stiffly, eyeing him with a grouchy expression on her face, a jowly overweight woman dressed in a pail-shaped hat, pressing a black purse against her diaphragm.

"I can't believe she hired you to fix up this old wreck. Why, it's hardly worth the match it would take to send the place up."

To the best of his recollection he'd never heard Myra Halburton greet anyone with anything but complaints. It gave him a twinge of pleasure to disagree with her. "Oh, I don't know. You might be surprised when I get all done."

She flapped a hand in disgust. "That girl's never listened to me a day in her life, and if you ask me, she's plumb crazy to put her money into such a shack. I can't imagine what Elfred was thinking. Plus a person has to walk up that blame hill to get here, and my legs are ready to give out on me. 'Course, she wouldn't stop to consider that!" Myra stumped on toward the house. "How's a person supposed to get in here anyway?"

"Stick close to the wall on that porch, Mrs. Halburton," he advised.

She picked her way to the door, complaining nonstop about the construction mess. "Roberta," she called, "you in there?"

Gabe heard Roberta answer, "Mother? Is that you?" Momentarily she appeared at the door while he looked down on her head through the shorn rafters. Her voice lost all color as she said, "Hello, Mother, come in."

"It's a fine how-do-you-do when a daughter doesn't even come to visit her own mother. I thought you'd come up to my house yesterday."

"I thought you'd be at Elfred and Grace's."

"That Sophie cooks too rich for me. Bothers my gall-bladder." Gabe lost sight of them as they moved into the house. "Merciful heavens, girl, have you lost your mind buying a place like this?"

"It's all I could afford."

"It smells like Sebastian Breckenridge's slop pail. That old man was crazier than a coot. Why, you can't keep three girls in conditions like this! What's it got— three bedrooms?"

"Two."

"Two bedrooms. Roberta, whatever were you thinking?"

"I was thinking that it might be nice for my children to get to know their grandmother."

"Well, of course it will be, which is why I waited for you all day yesterday."

"I had a busy day. After we arrived and had breakfast I had to meet the draymen here and see that our things were unloaded and get beds set up. It was nearly midnight when we got to bed."

Myra gave the place another once-over, grievance written all over her face. "This is all so unnecessary, Roberta. This is what comes of getting divorced. You had a decent home and a husband and now you've got this."

"How do you know I had a decent home, Mother? You never came to see it."

"Oh yes, blame me. You're the one who . . . who moved off the minute you got old enough, as if your family meant nothing to you."

"I moved off because I had to, to go to college. And I stayed with George because I had to. What else can a wife do? But I'm all done with that now. I can do exactly as I please."

"But the disgrace, Roberta. It's all over town that you've divorced him."

"He kept mistresses, Mother."

"Oh, please!" Myra slammed her eyes shut and held up both hands. "Please, don't be vulgar."

"He kept mistresses, one right after the other, women he could live off of, which he did until they finally realized he was nothing but a gigolo. Then they'd throw him out and he'd come crawling back to me, inveigling his way back into my good graces, asking for a new stake. Time and again I took him back, until I simply couldn't anymore. The last time he came back I locked the door on him and consulted the girls about getting a divorce. They encouraged me to get it, and I refuse to hang my head about doing what I had to to make a better life for me and my girls."

"But it just isn't done, Roberta! Not by respectable women. You don't understand. People whisper the very word."

"Of course I understand. I've already heard it whispered behind my back since I've been here."

"And it's obvious it doesn't bother you or you would have kept it quiet to begin with instead of trumpeting the fact."

"I didn't trumpet the fact. You and Elfred and Grace seemed to have done that for me, otherwise how would people have known even before I got here?"

"Who knew?"

"Farley, for one. I met him in the steamship office and he already knew. I certainly wasn't the one who told him."

"It just goes to show, people will talk, and how's a mother supposed to hold her head up?"

"You might try telling people that I've got three lovely children I intend to support on my own, and that I've got a job as a public nurse."

"Traveling all around the countryside unescorted? Oh, that'll really impress my friends. And speaking of that, how do you intend to get around?"

"I'm buying a motorcar."

"A motorcar! Who's going to drive it?"

"I am."

"Oh, heavenly days, there's just no getting through to you, is there? You were always headstrong and you still are. But mark my words, Roberta, you won't have any friends in this town, not when you flaunt your independence the way you do! Why can't you just take a job in the mill like the other women do? The girls could get on there, too, and help you out some."

"The mill again! Mother, we were arguing about the mill when I left here eighteen years ago!"

"You were always too good for the mill, weren't you?"

"It isn't a question of being too good for the mill, it's a question of what I wanted out of life, and it wasn't working in some closed room splicing felt ten hours a day for the rest of my life. And that's certainly not a sentence I'd impose on my daughters, either! They're bright girls, with imaginations and spirit. Taking them out of high school to work in the mill would crush that spirit and dry up that imagination, don't you see?"

"All I see is that you defied me years ago and went off to spend money your grandparents had left you to study nursing, of all things. And look what it got you. This house. This . . . pathetic house."

"Mother, why can't you be proud of me, for once in your life?"

"Oh, please . . ."

"Everything Grace does is perfect, but nothing I've ever done in my whole life has met with your approval."

"Grace follows the rules."

"Whose rules? Yours?"

"I didn't come over here to be insulted, Roberta."

"Neither did I. I came here thinking that maybe, after all these years, I might be able to get along with my family, but I can see I was wrong. All I get is criticism and admonitions to put my girls to work in the mill. Well, I'm sorry, Mother. I can't."

Myra touched her forehead. "You've given me a monstrous headache, Roberta."

"I'd offer you some stone root, but I haven't had time to unpack my medicines."

"I don't need stone root. I need to go home and lie down with a cold compress on my head."

"Very well, Mother. I'll tell the girls their grandmother stopped by and would like to meet them soon."

Her tone was acid enough to send Myra toward the door without a good-bye. Watching her go, Roberta thought sadly, why should there be a good-bye when there was no hello? No hug, certainly no kiss, only Myra sailing in on a billow of complaints, just the way it had always been.

Five

When Myra stormed out of the house Gabe was sitting under the ash tree with his ankles crossed, finishing up a cheese sandwich.

"That girl has always had the power to exasperate me. I should have known better than to come up here! Now I have to walk all the way back down, and what do I get for my trouble but her disrespect!"

Gabe sprang to his feet holding his sandwich tin.

"I can give you a ride back down, Mrs. Halburton."

"I'd be obliged, Mr. Farley. At least *some* young people know how to treat their elders!"

She tramped straight to the truck and he leaped forward to give her a hand up. While he was cranking the engine, Roberta drifted to her living room doorway and stood back, watching. Though her face was hidden in shadow he caught a glimpse of her hands, pressed fast against the dishtowel over her skirts. He'd heard enough to get the gist of their argument and to realize she and her mother got along like a pair of hens tied over a clothesline. He thought of his own mother, a kind woman with loving ways, and felt a twinge of compassion for Roberta, being attacked instead of welcomed after so many years away.

Myra complained all the way.

"Moves back here bold as brass with her divorce papers in her hand. Says she's going to get a motorcar. Says she's going to run all over the mountains in it and leave her children home alone. Says they *wanted* her to get a divorce. Hmph! Anything I've got to say on the subject rolls off her like water off a duck's back. She always thinks she's right. Always! Accuses me of playing favorites with Gracie. Well, Gracie never gave me a moment's worry, Mr. Farley, not one! But *that one*—from the time she could speak she was defying me. Gracie married a good man and had his children and made a good marriage, which is a woman's job. She didn't go running off to become a nurse! Why, it's no wonder Roberta's husband wasn't home much. What man would want to be when his wife came and went whenever she pleased?"

There was more, so much more that by the time Gabe dropped off Myra at her front gate he was ready to kick her out at ten miles an hour and watch her roll.

Watching Myra climb into Farley's truck, Roberta indulged in a rare moment of heavyheartedness. Her mother hadn't changed. She was still the autocratic oppressor of Roberta's youth. Part of the reason Roberta had left Camden was to escape her. How misguided she'd been to believe the intervening years might have tempered her mother.

Grace, Grace, the favorite had always been Grace. Grace, who used to play the songs on the piano that Mama liked; who wore her hair the way Mama said she should; who walked, talked, postured the way Mama told her to; who loved to hide around doorways and listen to Mama gossip; who garnered Mama's approval by becoming a gossip herself; who brought home a handsome, flirtatious swain able to turn his charms on Myra and blind her to his faults.

Grace, who stayed in Camden, married Elfred, gave him her inheritance to start his business, bore his children and had turned a blind eye to his extramarital forays ever since.

Obviously, Elfred still had the wool pulled over Myra's eyes as well.

Ten minutes after Farley's truck rolled away, Roberta was standing on a chair pulling some rotting curtains off a kitchen window when Elfred gripped her waist with both hands and said, "My, my, my, this is too tempting to resist."

She let out a screech as he doubled his arms around her belly.

"Elfred, let me go!"

"What if I don't? What'll you do?"

"Elfred, damn you!"

"What if I do? What'll you do?"

She shoved at his arms, but he was surprisingly strong.

"Elfred Spear, I'm warning you! I'll tell Grace what a philandering goat you are!"

Elfred only laughed. "I don't think so. You wouldn't do that to your only sister."

"I will! So help me, I will! Elfred, stop that!"

"Ooo, Birdy, you *are* packed nicely. How long's it been since you tussled with a man? I'm volunteering."

"Get your hands off me, Elfred!" She kicked backward. He grunted but hung on.

"I'll tell you something, Birdy. That's more fire than your sister's put out in nineteen years. A man spends all those years with a fencepost like Grace, he deserves a few diversions. Now come on, Birdy, why don't you and me just slide up those stairs and make a few bedsprings twang?"

"Elfred, you're the most despicable heathen God ever put on this earth. Now, let me go!"

Elfred laughed once more and slid his hand up her calf.

From behind him, Gabe Farley said quietly, "Hello, Elfred."

Elfred craned around, startled. "Oh, Gabe, it's just you! Whoo, you scared me."

"Did I?"

"Didn't know who it was." Elfred let his hands trail off Roberta. Gabe stood foursquare in the kitchen doorway feigning nonchalance when, in truth, he was feeling a faint twinge of revulsion.

"What brings you over here, Elfred?"

"Just came to see how the work was progressing and tell Birdy I'm footing the bill the way she asked."

"Work's progressing just fine. Got the whole porch roof torn off already this morning. Probably start rebuilding it tomorrow." Gabe sauntered into the kitchen.

"So I see." Elfred tugged at the waist of his trousers.

"Thought I should start with it so people could get to the front door safely. Mrs. Jewett, you need help with that curtain rod?"

Roberta scrambled down off the chair. "No thank you." Her face was burning scarlet.

"Something I'd like to show you out here, Elfred. You

mind coming outside with me?" He turned and Elfred followed.

There was nothing he wanted to show Elfred, but they stood in the yard pointing at the house and talking about what color to paint it. Eventually Elfred explained, "I was just having a little fun with her, Gabe. You know how it is."

"Ayup, I know how it is. You probably ought to watch your step though, Elfred. She's your wife's sister, and that's not going to look so good."

"But that's half the fun!"

"You know, Elfred, I don't think she was having quite as much fun as you were."

Elfred's eyebrows arched. "Oh, what's this? A different song than you were singing yesterday, isn't it, Gabe?"

"Well, maybe it is, but I happen to know she just had a row with her mother no more than half an hour ago, and the old woman was pretty hard on her."

"Why, Gabriel Farley, what's going on here? You wouldn't be wanting her for yourself now, would you?"

"Oh, come on, Elfred, use your head. You can't manhandle a woman that way. Why, I could hear her objecting clear across the yard. Supposing it had been Grace coming toward the house instead of me."

"You staking your claim on her, Gabe?"

Gabe dropped his chin and wobbled his head while Elfred continued with a wily grin, leaning close. "Here you are up here at her house, working every day. It'd be pretty easy, wouldn't it, Gabe?"

"That's *not* why I got you out of her kitchen."

"Oh no? Then explain it to me again."

Gabe raised his palms and let them drop. "What's there to explain? When a woman puts up a fight, you back off, Elfred. I shouldn't have to explain that to you."

"I told you, Gabe, I was just having a little fun with her."

"Fine, Elfred! Fine." Gabe presented his palms and let them drop. "Whatever you say. It just struck me that maybe we were both a little hasty to be making salty remarks behind her back when we didn't even know the woman. But if you want to make advances toward her, I won't interfere again. Now I've got work to do."

He turned his back on Elfred and bent to pick up his tool belt. When it was strapped on he attacked the porch floor, leaving Elfred to puzzle on his own. Finally Elfred swaggered up behind Gabe and stood like a sea captain watching his decks being swabbed.

"Well, Gabe, I tell you what. I won't horn in on your territory, but I'm going to keep an eye on you. After all, she's my sister-in-law, and I have to look out for her welfare." Giving a wicked chuckle, Elfred finally departed without bothering Roberta again.

Gabe eyed his touring car as it pulled away and thought what a real horse's ass Elfred was. Was it only yesterday he himself had been abetting the man?

In the kitchen, Roberta found herself grinding a stiff-bristled brush into Sebastian Dougal's filthy kitchen floor as if it were her brother-in-law's liver.

Though Roberta and Gabe kept out of each other's way as the day wore on, the scene in the kitchen remained in their minds. They might have put it aside, but sounds filtered into and out of the house reminding

each of them that the other was working nearby, pretending the incident with Elfred had never happened.

Finally, at three-thirty, Roberta wiped her brow with
the back of a wrist and listened. Nothing but silence.
She glanced down at her dirty dishtowel, untied it and
whacked at her skirt a time or two—wet at the belly
and dirty at the hem. She was too tired to care. What
a day. Lord, she hated housework. She hated Elfred. She
came close to hating her mother. She wasn't sure about
Gabriel Farley anymore, but it was damned uncomfortable having him working around here thinking who-
knew-what about her run-in with Elfred.

What was he doing out there anyway?

She stood in the kitchen archway looking across the
living room. The entire porch was gone, leaving the
room bright and the front doorway hanging four feet
above the ground. She tossed the dishtowel onto a
kitchen chair and went to the living room door. Farley
was standing in the littered yard with his back to her,
drinking water from a fruit jar. He had removed one
leather glove and held it against his hip while tipping
back his head. She watched him for some time, trying
to figure him out. He drank again, backhanded his
mouth and capped the jar. After tossing it onto the grass
he took his time pulling the soiled glove back on before
bending to start collecting the discarded shingles. He
loaded a bunch of them on his arm, turned and saw her
standing in the doorway.

And stalled as if encountering a bear in the woods.

She did the same.

For several seconds they faced off, distrustful and
staring. Finally, she spoke.

"I suppose you think I encouraged him."

"No, I don't." He carried the shingles a few paces and dropped them.

"But isn't that what *divorced women* do?"

"Elfred is notorious around this town for chasing women. Everybody knows it but his wife."

"He is pathetic."

Still stinging from Elfred's taunts, Gabe felt obliged to put up some argument. "That may be, but when a man runs around, there's usually some pretty good reason at home."

"Oh, that's a typical reaction . . . from a man!" she said disdainfully. "Naturally, you'd blame my sister for Elfred's peccadilloes."

"I'm not blaming your sister. I don't even know her well enough. I was just making a generalization."

"Well, make your generalizations somewhere else because I don't care to hear them! He's a family man with three daughters to consider. How do you think they'll feel if they find out their father is indiscriminately bedding any woman he takes a fancy to?"

He flashed the palms of two dirty gloves. "Look, I'm sorry I said what I did, all right?"

"Well, you should be because you men live by a double standard without considering what wives and children suffer when you have your *innocent affairs*. I know, because I had a husband exactly like Elfred!"

She spun and disappeared into the house, leaving Gabe to stare at the vacant doorway. Like many men in town, he'd often laughed about Elfred's adulteries and disparaged his wife for her ignorance. *That fat, bossy Grace Spear*, everybody called her. *No wonder*

Elfred stepped out on her. Elfred liked to flirt with women while Grace was in the room, and Gabe, like many others, had found it amusing. But watching him use his wiles on Birdy Jewett left Gabe questioning how funny it actually was.

Stacking shingles for a bonfire, he wondered about Roberta's husband. How many other women? Did her children know? Obviously, they did. Seemed a pitiful situation for youngsters to know their father was stepping out with a whole bunch of women besides their mother.

Intent on his thoughts, he was unaware of the children's return from school until one of them spoke—the little one he'd enjoyed so much yesterday.

"Hi, Mr. Farley! Look who's here!"

"Hi, Daddy!"

"Isobel! Well, for heaven's sake!"

"Susan and I met at recess," Isobel explained, "and I told her you were working for her mother so she asked me if I wanted to come home and see where they're going to live."

Rebecca exclaimed, "Our porch is gone!"

"I'm just about to burn it up."

"Oh, can we help you?"

"Oh, yes, can we, please?"

Susan took Isobel's hand. "Come on, let's climb in the front door and I'll show you our room! We can see the mountain from our window! Mother! We're home!"

The four girls went clattering over the shingles and started to boost each other over the doorjamb while Roberta came to stand above them.

"How was school? And who is this?"

"This is Isobel!" they chorused, while Lydia balanced on her belly at her mother's feet.

Gabe picked up a plank and strode across the yard. "Girls, wait!" He angled it like a gangway and they climbed it like sailors, bounced on it, babbling about school, Isobel, their teachers, the bonfire. He, with only one child, was accustomed to quiet and calm. This was mayhem as the girls bombarded the house, teetered on the plank and gabbled about four things at once. Somehow amidst the chatter Isobel's full name got through to Birdy.

"Isobel Farley?" she repeated.

"He's my dad," Isobel confirmed.

She met Gabe's glance from her high vantage point. In the midst of the frenetic scene the two of them exchanged a moment out of context, prompted by four exuberant adolescents who had no idea of the undercurrents between their parents. "Oh . . . yes, of course. Well, hello, Isobel."

Lydia said, "He's going to build a bonfire to burn the shingles. Can we help him, Mother?"

"Yes, please! Can we?"

"We're hungry! Is there any cake or anything?"

"Ah . . . oh, cake?" She prized her attention from Gabe to answer the girls. "No, I haven't had time."

"But we're starving!"

"I've got crackers."

They all trooped upstairs to see the girls' room, then back down to collect soda crackers before descending the plank and finding Gabe had ignited the stack of shingles. They headed straight for the fire, though none of them had changed out of their school dresses, which

Gabe had carefully trained Isobel to do. Instead, they collected shingles and fed the fire while Gabe stood back and tended it with a rake.

Without preamble, Rebecca began reciting, "By the shore of Gitche Gumee, By the shining Big-Sea-Water . . ."

"What's that?" Isobel said.

"That's *Hiawatha* . . . don't you know *Hiawatha*?" She paused and struck a dramatic pose. "I am Hiawatha, courageous Indian brave, fasting in the forest in the blithe and pleasant springtime. . . ." Without the slightest compunction she began to chant and dance as if she were wearing buckskin and eagle feathers. Her sisters picked up the cue and danced, too . . . around and around the fire, arms extended and bodies undulating while Isobel, as inhibited as her father, stared.

He watched her struggle to balance her fascination with a natural reluctance to join in. Once she glanced at him, wide-eyed, and he saw even clearer her wish to be like these girls. But she had been born an only child, had spent too many years alone to feel free amidst these irrepressible thespians of Mrs. Jewett's. He knew immediately they were not showing off for him: They were merely spontaneous.

Abruptly Rebecca broke off her chant. "I know!" she exclaimed. "Lobsters!" Her sisters stopped as well. "We could collect some if the tide is right and cook them in our bonfire!" She bounded toward the gangplank. "I'll ask Mother! *Mother!* What time does the tide turn?"

Roberta returned to the door above her. "About an hour ago."

"Then we've got to hurry! Can we go get some lobsters and cook them on the bonfire?"

"The bushel basket's in my bedroom full of towels." She turned away and her three girls scampered after her. Up the gangplank! Inside, with skirts bouncing! Momentarily they returned with Lydia in the lead, carrying the basket.

"Come on, Isobel!" she cried. "You have to show us where Sherman's Cove is! That's where Mother says the lobsters are!"

Isobel stood rooted and dazed. "May I?" She looked up at Gabe.

"Lobsters?" Nobody ate lobsters. They washed up on the rocks at high tide and made nuisances of themselves. Those who bothered to pick them up buried them for fertilizer.

Isobel shrugged.

He murmured at her ear, "Are you sure you want to eat lobsters?"

"I want to go along, please, Daddy."

He had his doubts about this wild trio, but Isobel had an eagerness in her eye that had been absent for a long time. Certainly she'd have more fun running off to Sherman's Cove than going home with him to share their lonely supper for two.

"Go ahead," he said, "but you should change your dress first."

"But, Daddy, if I do that it'll be too late!" Their house was the opposite direction from Sherman's Cove, and lobsters didn't stay in the rocks long once the air hit their backs.

"Oh, all right, go ahead. But tomorrow you change immediately after school, as usual."

The other three shouted a chorus of "Thanks, Mr. Farley!" and Isobel scurried after them. The last he saw of his daughter she was running to catch up with Lydia, who was skipping down the boulevard with the bushel basket over her head.

In their wake the yard grew silent except for the snapping fire. Roberta remained in the doorway. Gabe remained by the blaze. They recognized that their children were stirring up a friendship the two of them might not want to foster, but their reasons were selfish and had them feeling even more uncomfortable with each other. She said, "Well, I'd better go find some butter," and disappeared from the doorway.

He continued cleaning up the yard, picking up nails, feeding the fire, keeping some shingles for the girls to burn when they returned. Minutes later Roberta came down the gangplank carrying a bag of the sort used to haul groceries. Her hair had been neatened and her skirt changed. He turned his back to make it easier on both of them, and leaned over to pick up some shingles as she crossed the yard behind him. He knew perfectly well, however, that she was heading downhill to buy groceries and would have to carry them back up in her little mesh bag with the handles. She had only two feet while he had a Ford truck, and his mother had not been lax about drilling manners.

He turned from the fire and called, "Mrs. Jewett?" She stopped in the break of the bridal wreath. "I could run you down the hill in the truck."

"No, thank you, Mr. Farley," she replied crisply. "I

don't think it would do for the two of us to be seen together again in your truck. I'll walk."

He breathed a sigh of relief as he watched her move off in the direction the girls had gone.

His inclination was to be gone when she got back, but a responsible man didn't leave coals glowing to send up sparks and set a woman's house afire. So he finished raking the yard, scooped up the trash into a gunnysack and burned up most of the remaining shingles. His tools were in the truck and he was squatting beside a brilliant bed of coals by the time Roberta returned carrying *two* mesh sacks! The girls were with her and came lugging the bushel basket with their cache covered with seaweed. Their dresses were filthy and their shoes wet. Isobel's hair was hanging like sea grass. Everybody was talking at once.

"Look! They're positively huge!"

"Oh, the fire is just right!"

"Mother, where's the lobster pot?"

"Come and see them, Daddy! Rebecca knew how to put sticks in their claws so we didn't get pinched!"

There followed an admiring of lobsters with four disheveled girls trotting all over the yard, into the house, back out. Roberta passed behind Gabe with her two weighty sacks.

"You're still here, Mr. Farley. I thought you'd be gone."

"I didn't think I should leave the fire untended."

Walking the plank, she called, "You may stay if you'd like, and eat with us."

Lobsters? He shuddered. Moreover, he remembered

Elfred's innuendo. "No thanks. I'll be going home now."

At the top of the plank Roberta set down her heavy burden and turned around, rubbing her arms.

"You should have let me drive you," he said, feeling oafish for having let her carry tins and milk bottles up the hill.

She studied him as if deciding whether he was right. "I told you, I'm used to doing for myself. I can see you don't like lobster anyway."

He went home and ate alone. Sardines and soda crackers. Some tinned peaches, straight from the can. Two cups of hot coffee. Three cinnamon jumble cookies his mother had made. The kitchen was orderly and white in the glow of the new electric light. Caramel, the cat, came and nestled in his lap. He kept watching the wall clock, noting the purpling of light at the window, imagining the yard at the Jewetts' with lobsters boiling in a pot. He washed his fork and cup, watered Caroline's houseplant, swept the kitchen floor, shook the rugs and Isobel hadn't shown up yet. He bathed and shaved and still she hadn't come home. He kept imagining those coals and that unpredictable bunch she was with. Hell, for all he knew they'd have her walking barefoot across them pretending she was some Hawaiian volcano goddess.

He had put on clean clothes and decided to get in the truck and go back there to fetch her when she showed up, breathless and flushed.

"Daddy?" she called from downstairs. "Daddy, where are you?"

"Isobel?"

She came bounding up the stairs, taking them two at a time and tearing around the corner into his bedroom.

"Where in the world have you been this late?"

"Oh, I've been with the Jewetts, and Daddy, they're so much fun!"

"Don't you realize what time it is?"

"But you knew where I was."

"Yes, but I didn't think you'd stay this late."

"It's not even eight o'clock yet, and we were sitting around the fire. Mrs. Jewett got out a copy of Longfellow and she read us the first verse of *The Song of Hiawatha*, then everybody took turns reading a verse. They know some of them by heart! And they can pronounce all the Indian words. Kabibonokka and Mudjekeewis. An owl came and sat on that big tree in their yard and stared at us as if he were listening, too. And Mrs. Jewett called to it and it cocked its head and turned it clean around till it was looking backwards! She knew what kind of owl it was, too. A great horned, but it flew away without calling back to her, and its wings didn't make a sound. We're going to read the next five verses tomorrow!"

From a girl who was easily bored by everything from school to family visits, such exuberance impressed her father.

"Tomorrow."

"Yes, right after school, and Rebecca wants to make costumes and act it out, but I told her I don't want to do that. I'm no good at acting."

"How do you know? You've never tried."

"I just know. Besides, I don't like people staring at me. But I love the reading."

She always thought people stared at her ears, but he didn't know how to console her about them, so he asked, "How was the lobster?"

"Messy, but pretty tasty. Mrs. Jewett melted butter and fried rice cakes and we ate them with our fingers, sitting around the fire."

"You look it. Your dress is filthy. Now, why don't you wash up and leave your dirty clothes in the kitchen on the floor? I'm going to be taking the laundry to Grandma's tomorrow."

An hour later, when her room got quiet, he knocked on the door and found her sitting cross-legged on her bed, dressed in a pale blue nightgown, writing. He went in and sat at the foot of the bed, leaning back on one hand.

"What's that?" he asked.

"A poem."

"You're writing it?" She turned it facedown on her lap and looked self-conscious. "I thought you didn't like poetry."

"That was in school."

"Is it different at home?"

"It's different at *their* house. Everything's different at their house."

"Isobel," he said gently, "I know you had a good time with the Jewetts today, but they're a lot different than you. Their mother lets them run pretty wild, and I don't want you to get into that habit. You can't be staying out after dark, and traipsing off after school without changing your dress and eating around a fire like some savage Indian."

"Why, the Indians aren't savage! Have you read *Hiawatha*?"

"No, I haven't, Isobel, but the point is—"

"Well, you should, then you'd know. It tells how they love the earth and the sky and everything around them. And I had so much fun with Rebecca and her sisters today. Everybody else in this town is as boring as whey!"

"Isobel, their mother is divorced."

"Their mother is more fun than any mother I ever met! And what does that have to do with my being their friend?"

"It's the way she lets them run and do whatever they please. If you start running with them you'll pick up bad habits and get a bad reputation."

She looked stunned. "Why, Father, I'm amazed at you. They've only been in town two days and you're spreading rumors about them?"

"I'm not spreading rumors."

"Yes, you are. And Mother said, *Seek first, judge second,* isn't that what you always said?"

"Isobel, I'm only asking you to remember the manners you've always been taught, and the rules we've had in this house."

"I will, Father."

Twice she'd called him *Father,* which he took as a reprimand.

"May I go to their house tomorrow then?"

He had no logical reason to refuse. "If you change your dress first and act like a lady while you're there."

"I will."

"And you'll ride home to supper with me."

"I will."

As he rose and said good night, Isobel looked up at him and tried to remember if he'd ever hugged her the way Mrs. Jewett hugged her girls. She'd done it when they came home from school, and several times during the incredible evening. She did it for no reason at all, sometimes only when she'd pass them in the yard. Once when Lydia was reading, Mrs. Jewett reached over and rubbed her head, and Lydia had gone on as if she didn't even notice. *I'd notice if my dad ever rubbed my head,* Isobel thought. *Or if he ever hugged me good night or hugged me good-bye when I left for school.*

Suddenly, drawing up her covers, Isobel felt the sharp stab of loneliness she carefully hid from her father whenever it came. The image of her mother was fading. She used to be able to recall her face so clearly, but now she could only do so when she looked at the photograph Daddy kept on the bureau in his bedroom.

"Mother," she whispered in the dark, "Mother."

Sometimes she whispered it that way because she never got a chance to say it aloud the way other children did.

Six

There is no real spring in Maine. Roberta had heard it her whole life, and the following morning bore it out. The rare salubrious weather of the previous day had reverted to form and the skies had darkened to a thick woolly gray. The clouds, heavy with mist, skulked at sea level and dampened everything that moved through them.

Including Roberta.

As soon as the girls were off to school she set out for Boynton's Motor Car Company, buttoned to the throat in a short wool jacket and toting her umbrella. Opening her front door, she found no Gabriel Farley here yet. The plank was slippery and she skated down it, then passed the lumpy black smudge where last night's fire had been. Its sodden charcoal gave off an acrid smell, but the pleasant recollections of the previous evening put a bounce in her step. There were few things Roberta enjoyed more than lollygagging with her girls, and Isobel Farley had been a cheerful addition—a little shy, but an eager disciple.

By all indications, she would see a lot of Isobel around her house. If that meant running into Isobel's father occasionally, Roberta would simply have to grin and bear it.

She put him from her mind as she bobbed down Washington Street in shoes that grew damper with each step. At the north end of Main she stood under the sign she'd been unable to read the day she arrived. Beneath their names the Boyntons advertised SELLING AGENCY FOR HIGH-GRADE CARS. STORAGE & CARE OF CARS.

Inside, it smelled like rubber but was blessedly dry. The Boyntons had hooked up to electricity, so overhead lights dispelled the gloom. Roberta left her umbrella in the holder beside the door and stamped her feet on the horsehair mat.

"Good morning. May I help you?"

She looked up and encountered the bespectacled face of a heavyset man in his forties. He wore a moustache and a pin-striped suit.

"I hope so. I'd like to buy a motorcar."

Obviously, he hadn't been expecting this response. It took a beat before he replied, placing his palms flat together and rubbing them twice. "Certainly, madam. Hamlin Young at your service. And you are?"

"Roberta Jewett."

"Mrs. Jewett, right this way." He glanced at the door as he led her away. "Is your husband with you today?"

"I don't have a husband. The car is for me."

He paused beside a black Oldsmobile and puckered his brow. "Jewett . . . Jewett . . . you wouldn't be the sister-in-law of Elfred Spear, would you?"

"Yes, I would. Grace's sister."

"Ahh . . ." he crooned, tipping his chin up. "Someone told me you were moving to Camden."

Elfred, undoubtedly. He must have happened to mention Roberta was divorced, too, the way Hamlin

Young's eyes glinted with new speculation. She'd seen the reaction enough times to predict what would happen next: He'd take the liberty of touching her somewhere.

"I grew up here," she told him.

"Yes, of course. Now, whom did you marry again?"

"You didn't know him. The motorcar, Mr. Young," she reminded him.

"Yes, of course." There it was: He touched her elbow with the tips of his fingers. "Have you ridden in one yet?"

"Yes, a couple of times."

"Have you driven one?"

"Just once."

"You have! Well! That's amazing. I must admit, I haven't sold one to a woman yet. To the best of my knowledge, no woman in Camden has driven one."

"Then I'll be the first. I have some questions for you, Mr. Young, about the cost and the maintenance."

"We'll get to that later. First let me show you what we've got."

He touched her again while presenting the Oldsmobile Runabout, and again as he directed her to an Overland Touring Car. By the time they came to an ordinary Model T Ford she adroitly sidestepped and kept plenty of space between them.

"How much would this one cost?"

"Three hundred and sixty dollars, brand spanking new, including a planetary transmission system."

Only three hundred sixty. Elfred had said six hundred for a roadster.

"Would this one be started and operated like a C-Cab truck?"

"A C-Cab truck?" He peered at her more sharply. "Why . . . yes, it would. Have you driven a C-Cab truck, Mrs. Jewett?"

She realized her mistake immediately. "Why . . . yes . . . yes I have, and I managed quite well, I must say. If I buy this and it needs repair, will you do it here?"

"Yes, ma'am. We own the Camden Garage right next door, and in the back of it we operate our own machine shop with a staff of skilled mechanics. Upstairs on our second floor we've got supplies of all kinds and a nice waiting room for our customers. We've even got a telephone connection up there. You mind my asking whose C-Cab truck you drove?"

"Yes, I do, Mr. Young. What bearing has that on my purchasing this motorcar?"

"Well, I was just wondering if by any chance it might have been Gabe Farley's."

Exasperated, she replied, "Yes, it was!"

"Well, that's good, because Gabe bought it here. He'll vouch for what kind of work we do. Why, Gabe knows everybody in the place."

She was sure he did. She was also sure that everyone in the place would know she'd been out riding in his truck with him.

"Gabe is a good man. So he gave you a little driving lesson, did he?"

"A very little one, but enough for me to find out I *can* drive."

"Oh, I've no doubt. But I wouldn't be doing my job unless I warned you about some of the other things you'll have to know how to do if you drive for any length of time at all. Did Gabe mention patching tires?"

"Patching tires?"

"You'll have to carry a patch kit, which we sell right upstairs, but I'm not sure you'd want to do a dirty job like that."

"What else?"

"If the tire can't be patched, you'd have to replace it while the rim is right on the car, and truthfully, Mrs. Jewett, I don't think a woman could do that. It takes some muscle. I'm not lying, it's a heck of a job even for a man."

"How often do they go bad?"

"Depends on the roads you're driving. Some of them up here in the mountains get pretty bad. Rocks, wash-outs, what have you."

"But I could patch them?"

"You could. With a little lesson."

"Anything else?"

Roberta was sorry she asked. She was informed about the carburetor needing frequent adjustment, the transmission bands needing tightening and the fan belts replacing.

"But I thought you did repairs."

"These are all things that can happen out on the road."

"Oh," she said, showing her first hint of dismay.

"Don't get me wrong, Mrs. Jewett—I sell these things, and I shouldn't be running them down. They're good machines, and they're pretty reliable when they're new, but I wouldn't feel right about selling one to a woman without a husband, unless she knew what she was up against. In the long run you're probably going to wish you had a horse."

"I have no place to keep a horse."

"Well . . ." He lifted his hands lamely and let them drop. After a while he said, "You mind my asking what you need a car for?"

"I'm a public nurse, employed by the state of Maine. I'll be traveling a lot."

"Oh, I see." He could tell she was disappointed and touched her again, this time on the shoulder with an open hand that lingered a little longer. "I'll be glad to show you how to do some of these things if you decide to buy one."

His presumption snapped her out of her funk and made her jump free of his touch. "If a man can do it, I can do it. And if it's too heavy I'll get help. I'll be back, Mr. Young."

She went next to the Camden Bank. Mr. Tunstill, the vice president, raised his haughty eyebrows, gave her run-down shoes and threadbare jacket the once-over and informed her that his bank could not authorize one-hundred-and-fifty-dollar loans to women. Certainly not to women without men to support them. A public nurse? He was not impressed, nor could he help her. He suggested she find a man with an automobile and marry him if she wanted to drive.

"Good day, Mrs. Jewett."

She was back out in the drizzle in less than ten minutes, so angry she was unaware of the fact that inside her shoes, even her stockings were soaked.

Back at Boynton's, she asked Mr. Young what arrangements could be made if she didn't have enough cash. He was sorry, he said, but without a bank loan his hands were tied. Did he have any used motorcars? No, but he had some for rent. The rent, however, tallied up to a bad deal all the way around, so she ended up beneath her umbrella on the street once more. In an attempt to calm herself, she went to the post office and made arrangements for the delivery of her mail, then into Gold's Restaurant and splurged on a cup of coffee with two free refills. The waitress asked bluntly who she was, and when Roberta gave her name three women stared at her and whispered as if she had snakes growing where her hair should be. Two old geezers at the counter craned around and gawked over their bony shoulders.

By the time she left Gold's she was wishing she *had* a few snakes and could make them hiss and spit on her way out the door.

She had only one other possibility, and loathsome though he was, she decided to give him a try.

The town pecker, Elfred.

His real estate company was housed in the Masonic Temple block, in one of the new brick structures with the arched brickwork above the windows. Four people were working in the office when she walked in and asked for her brother-in-law. He spied her through his glass-walled office and nearly broke a knee leaping from his chair.

"Birdy!" He came at her with arms extended. "What an unexpected surprise! Georgie, meet my sister-in-law, Birdy Jewett." She was introduced to all and herded inside beneath Elfred's possessive arm while they were followed by inquisitive eyes. He stationed her on an oak chair beside his rolltop desk and swiveled his own to face her, rolling up so close their knees nearly touched. "What brings you down here, Birdy?" His eyes glinted wickedly. "You change your mind about what I suggested yesterday?"

"Stop it, Elfred!"

He grinned and leaned back comfortably, crossed his knees and extended a foot so it got lost inside the folds of her skirt. "I told Farley I'd leave the coast clear for him, but it looks like maybe I spoke too soon, 'cause here you are, and I'm mighty pleased to see you."

She boosted up and scraped her chair back six inches. He merely rolled his forward six and stuck his foot in the same place.

"Your employees are watching," she reminded him.

"All they can see is our heads and shoulders. What do you want?"

"A loan."

"Ooo, a loan," he singsonged, making suggestions with his eyebrows.

"For a hundred and fifty dollars."

"For that car you want?"

"That's right."

"What'll you put up?"

"Nothing. I'll sign a promissory note."

"Mmm, not good enough. You'll have to do better than that, Birdy." He began to run his black shoe up and down her shin. She rammed her heel into his knee-cap and thrust him backward, chair and all. He gasped and left his mouth open.

"No, *you'll* have to do better than that, Elfred, unless you want me to tell Grace you suggested diddling me within twenty-four hours of my moving into town."

He nursed his knee and said with remarkable amity, "Don't try to bamboozle me, Birdy, because I'm a bigger bamboozler than you are."

"You don't think I'd tell her?" She dropped her chin and stared him down, wishing again for a few snakes. "Try me."

Her threat began to sink in and Elfred lost his cockiness. "That's blackmail, Birdy, and you know it."

"Yes, and isn't it delicious. If you wish to prosecute me for it, go ahead. Of course, you'll have to weigh whether or not it's worth the risk of losing the respect of your wife and three children, because I *will* tell Grace, make no mistake about that. I'm not too happy with her anyway at this point. She must have been gossiping all over this town about my divorce, because women are looking at me squinch-eyed and men are posing like Greek statues as soon as they hear my name. And frankly, Elfred, you all disgust me. So don't put me to the test! I need a hundred and fifty dollars, and I can sign a promissory note, nice and politely, or I can put a serious crimp in your home life. Now, which will it be?"

Elfred's smug expression had curdled. "You've got a lot of nerve, Birdy, you know that?"

"Exactly. A hundred and fifty, please, Elfred, and make it quick before I decide to tell Grace anyway."

He scooted his chair to a black safe and started spinning its dial. She watched his shoulders, and when he turned, the wad of bills in his hands.

"I repeat, Birdy, this is blackmail." He handed her the bills.

She stuffed them into her jacket pocket while rising. "Have a note prepared and I'll sign it. All I can afford to pay you is five dollars a month, but it'll be on time, dear brother-in-law. Thank you very much."

She left him following her exit with a sour expression on his handsome face.

When she got back home there was a stack of lumber in her yard and Gabe Farley was hammering down a brand-new porch floor. His brother was with him. They were dressed in Wellingtons and slickers and neither of them saw or heard her coming until she was nearly upon them and paused in the yard beside the fragrant wood floor.

"Oh, Mrs. Jewett!" Gabe sat back on his heels. "Hello."

She offered no civility. So Elfred was leaving the coast clear for this one, was he? She wondered whose idea that had been, and couldn't find the grace to return his greeting.

"I didn't think you'd be working in the rain."

"Wait for a sunny day in Maine you'll never get any work done. This is my brother, Seth. This is Mrs. Jewett."

They exchanged hellos—hers cool, his curious—and she said to Gabriel, "My plank is gone."

"Sorry, you'll have to go around back."

She struck off in that direction but his voice stopped her. "Thank you for letting Isobel stay last night. She couldn't quit talking about it when she got home."

"You're welcome." She headed away again.

"She likes your girls," he called.

"They like her, too," she returned, without slowing or turning as she disappeared around a corner of the house.

Seth watched her go and said, "She doesn't like you much, does she?"

"No, not much."

"But Isobel stayed over here last night?"

"Just for supper. They boiled lobsters over the bonfire and read *Hiawatha*."

"Really." It was an observation, not a question. Seth watched Gabe stretch out a carpenter's rule, mark a plank and pick up a saw.

"I don't want her hanging around here too much though," Gabe said. "I get the feeling her girls run wild."

"Which you and I never did."

Gabe grinned at Seth over his poised handsaw.

They both got busy but talked in between the noise. "So what's going on between you and this woman?" Seth asked.

"Nothing."

"Then how come she races past so fast?"

"I interrupted a little scene between her and Elfred yesterday. I think she's embarrassed about it."

"What were they doing?"

"Not *they. Elfred.* He was doing what Elfred's always doing, only she wasn't having any of it. Matter of fact, she was squawking pretty loud when I put my nose into it."

Seth chuckled. Then he sobered. "How do you suppose his wife puts up with it?"

"Wives are usually the last to know."

After some cogitation, Seth remarked, "Jesus, trying it with his own sister-in-law. That Elfred's really a horse's ass, you know it?"

"Everybody knows it, but we've all laughed about it plenty, haven't we?"

"I guess we have."

"Yesterday I didn't think it was so funny though."

"So there *is* something between you and this woman."

"I told you, Seth—"

"Ya, ya, you *told* me. But something strange is going on around here. Undertones."

"Undertones? Boy, you're crazy. If I was looking for a woman, I wouldn't go for one who dresses like that and talks like that. She's about as far from Caroline as Pluto is from Earth."

"Oh, you've been comparing her to Caroline, have you?"

"No, I haven't been *comparing* her to *Caroline*. Look, just forget it, will you? Some days I wish I worked alone!"

When Gabe threw himself back into his work, he hammered like a piston.

At four o'clock the girls returned from school and Isobel was with them.

"Hi, Daddy! Hi, Uncle Seth!" The porch floor was done and the roof was in progress. All four girls yammered at once, "Wow! A new porch floor! Hi, Mr. Farley! Look at this! It can be our stage!" They got onto the fresh boards and clumped around, getting them wet and dirty, testing the sound of their heels, pretending they were skating or dancing. Rebecca spread her arms like a thunderbird and recited to the front yard.

" 'As unto the bow the cord is,
So unto the man is woman,
Though she bends him she obeys him,
Though she draws him, yet she follows,
Useless each without the other!'
Thus the youthful Hiawatha
Said within himself and pondered,'
Da-da-da-da, I forgot that, [this brought laughter]
'Dreaming still of Minnehaha.' "

The others applauded raucously and Rebecca took a deep, formal bow. Springing erect, she said, "Let's go get something to eat!" They all tramped inside and left the door wide open.

Gabe and Seth—one on the roof, one on a ladder—exchanged glances. Gabe shrugged. "See what I mean?"

Seth said, "That's the happiest I've seen Isobel in a long time."

Inside, the piano started clanging and the girls' voices could be heard as they charged through the house, into the kitchen, up the stairs. Sometimes there were shrieks, sometimes giggles, sometimes thumps. They could hear Roberta's voice calling, "Hey! Come down here and tell me about school!"

After a while they all piled outside, still in their school dresses, eating cold rice cakes. "Daddy, I'm taking the girls home to show them our house!" Isobel shouted.

He stopped hammering and peered over the edge of the roof. What could he say? His daughter had been a guest here yesterday. He could hardly admit he didn't want them tramping through his house. "Change your dress when you get there! And don't make a mess in the house!"

"We won't!"

Off they galloped through the mist.

On the roof, Gabe watched them. From the front door, with her hands on her waist, so did Roberta.

When the three Jewett girls saw Isobel's kitchen they came up short. "Golly, it's so clean," they said in awe.

"We keep it just the way Mother kept it. My father won't change anything, except he added electricity."

"How long has she been dead?"

"Seven years."

"How did she die?"

"Our horse kicked her."

"Oh, how awful."

"Then you know what my dad did?"

The Jewetts waited, rapt.

"He shot the horse. I saw him crying after he did it, and I was only seven years old but I remember it just as clear as a bell."

"Gosh," someone said, breathless.

"And ever since then he won't let anybody change anything in our house. He says he wants to keep it just the way she left it. I'll tell you a secret."

"What?"

"Her clothes are still in her bureau."

It was Lydia—an impressionable age ten—who asked in a whisper, "Could we see them?"

"Only if you promise not to touch them, because he'd

scold me if he found out. He's real funny about her things. Well, follow me, but remember—don't touch anything. You can only look, okay?"

While they tiptoed through the spotless parlor and up a set of narrow stairs, Susan whispered, "Who keeps your place so nice?"

"My dad and I do, and sometimes my grandma comes over and takes down the curtains and washes them—things like that. Here's their room."

Just inside the bedroom door, the girls stood respectfully silent and still. The bed was neatly made with a white coverlet. It had carved head- and footboards that matched the other pieces in the room. Isobel went to the bureau that had drawers along the right and a tall door on the left. She opened the door and said, "See? This was her nightgown, and these were her dresses."

"Golly, doesn't it give you the willies touching them like that?"

"Of course not, silly. She was my mother."

"Gosh, I wouldn't touch them if I could."

"I would," said Rebecca. "The amber one looks very pretty." Only an amber sleeve showed.

"That's the one she always wore to church on Sundays."

"We don't go to church," Lydia informed Isobel.

"Don't go to church! But everybody goes to church!"

"We don't. Mother doesn't like it."

"Well, are you heathens then?"

Lydia shrugged—a great big shrug—and turned her palms up. "I don't know."

Rebecca got piqued. "No, we're not heathens! Lydia, don't be so stupid!"

Isobel closed the door as if reluctant to have her mother's garments exposed to the godless.

Susan spotted the photograph in an oval frame. "Is that her?"

"Yes. Daddy has kept it here forever."

"Gee, she was beautiful." Susan picked it up and gazed.

"Don't touch, Susan, remember?"

"Oh . . . sorry." She replaced the picture in the spot where the linen dresser scarf was dented from the feet of the frame.

"I suppose we shouldn't stay in here too long, but I'll show you my room."

After the tour of her room Isobel obediently changed clothes, then offered them cinnamon jumble cookies, which were much preferable to the cold, rubbery rice cakes they'd eaten at the Jewett house. "My grandma keeps the cookie jar filled all the time, just like my mother did. She makes any kind I ask for." The four of them cleaned up the cinnamon jumbles and left an empty jar, taking two cookies each for later.

Roberta's girls, however, took home more than spare cookies. They returned bursting with the story of the dead woman whose clothing still hung in her husband's bureau.

"Mother, guess what."

"I couldn't guess. What?"

Rebecca did the honors. "Mr. Farley's wife was kicked by a horse and she died, then he shot the horse himself and killed it—"

"And it was his own horse!" put in Lydia.

"And Isobel saw him crying afterwards! Isn't that romantic?"

A shudder went through Roberta. She set aside her ironing and drifted toward the kitchen table where all the girls gathered, leaning far forward on their elbows. "That's not romantic. That's tragic."

"And listen to this! He keeps the house exactly as she left it and won't let anybody touch anything she touched—"

"Except for the electricity," Lydia inserted. "He had electricity put in."

"But everything else is just the way she left it and she's been dead *seven years* and her clothing is still hanging beside his in their bureau! We saw it!"

"And her picture is on his dresser—"

"And she's just beautiful. She had on this white dress with a tall collar and her hair was piled up in ringlets just like Lillian Russell's."

Roberta's gaze drifted toward the front porch where Farley had been working for two days. He was gone now and the place was quiet. She imagined him keeping a shrine to his beautiful dead wife, this carpenter who could irritate her so. When her attention returned to the girls, her expression had softened. "That's very pitiful."

"Isobel wouldn't let us touch anything 'cause she said he could tell if we did and she'd get a scolding. I don't think we've ever gotten scoldings, have we, Mother?"

"Of course you have. You just don't remember."

"You should see how clean their house is. And guess what, he and Isobel do most of it, but her grandma goes there every week and takes them cookies. Boy, I'm sure glad *we* don't have to clean every week!"

"She has a grandma then. Well, that's good." Roberta had never considered Farley in relation to a mother. Of course, it could be the dead wife's mother.

"She made the best cinnamon jumble cookies. We ate them all up," Lydia divulged.

"All?"

Lydia nodded, thrusting forward on her elbows nearly to the middle of the table.

"Well, he won't be too pleased about that. I don't think he wanted you over there in the first place."

"Why not?"

"You just told me why not. He's not used to having a tribe of wild hooligans traipsing through the place like I am. Now listen"—Roberta cheered up—"there's something I have to tell you. We're going to get our new motorcar tomorrow."

"We are?"

"That's right. A Model T Ford."

There were a lot of questions and rejoicing then, and the subject of the Farley household was dropped.

But in his house across town, when Gabe finished his supper and reached into the cookie jar, he found it empty and swore softly under his breath.

Seven

The girls had gone to school and Roberta was up and dressed the next morning when she heard the first hammer blows on the porch. What had happened to her animosity toward Gabriel Farley? Since the girls had come home with their story about his wife, her negative feelings seemed to have dissipated like yesterday's clouds from the sky. He kept popping into her thoughts, and whenever he did she always pictured him in a doorway, which is where he'd been yesterday when he'd so fortuitously interrupted Elfred. She had seen two sides of Farley: One considered divorced women fair game; the other rescued them from unwanted attention. One held that all marital troubles started with the woman; the other was a husband who had so worshiped his wife he'd kept a shrine to her for seven years.

What kind of man was this who was capable of such devotion?

Roberta admitted she was mystified by him.

His wife was beautiful, the girls had said, with hair piled high like Lillian Russell's. A quick glance in the umbrella stand mirror assured Roberta she was no Lillian Russell.

She spun from her own reflection. *Whatever are you thinking, Roberta Jewett! You finally got rid of one man and the last thing you want is another! Certainly not Gabriel Farley, who snickered the first time he met you!*

No, she didn't want Gabriel Farley. That glance in the mirror had been a mindless female reaction by which she set little store as she headed out her back door and around the house. She could hear the hammers in syncopation, ringing through the foggy day with an eerie bell-like tone that seemed to carry as if connected by slurs on sheet music. *Din-dinggg . . . dindinggg . . .* She snapped up her umbrella, rounded the front corner of the house and encountered Farley, constructing a new set of steps for her. Whereas yesterday she had all but snubbed him, today she paused.

"Good morning, Mr. Farley."

He straightened slowly, as if he'd stooped too many hours in his life. "Morning, Mrs. Jewett." Tilted over his left ear was the same plaid cap he'd worn the day she'd met him. It was covered with droplets of fog the size of frog's eggs.

At the far end of the porch his brother was putting up a railing. "Morning, Mr. Farley," she offered.

"Ma'am," he replied, remembering her snub of yesterday and continuing to work, leaving Roberta to face Gabriel with her anger displaced by the knowledge that he'd shot the horse that killed his wife seven years ago and had not disposed of her clothing since.

"Be glad to have your steps back, I suppose," he remarked.

"Yes, I will."

"Have 'em all done later today. Paint the porch as soon as there's a break in the weather. Don't want to leave raw wood to the elements up here in this soup pot."

"No, of course not. I hear my girls emptied your cookie jar last night."

He dropped his chin and drawled, "Waaal..." There's a way a man stands with a garden hoe. Farley often brought to mind such a pose, whether he had a hoe or not.

"I'm not very domestic," she admitted. "When they get around good food they sometimes lose their manners."

"My mother will load it up again."

Why would a man keep his wife's clothing? Did he take it out and touch it? The disconcerting picture of him rubbing a garment between his callused fingertips made him more human than Roberta wanted him to be. She shored up her wayward thoughts and said, "Well, I thought you'd like to know, I'm off to Boynton's to get myself a motorcar."

"You're buying one then."

"Yes, a Model T Ford."

"It's for sure you'll know how to drive it." He ventured a restrained grin.

"Yes, I will, won't I?"

"It's going to cause some talk, you being a single lady."

"Yes, I'm sure."

"Boynton's got a decent garage though. They'll take care of it for you."

"That's what Mr. Young said when I talked to him yesterday. Well, I'd best be off. See you later." She raised her voice to Seth. "See you later, Mr. Farley. Sorry about this weather."

When she was gone Seth remarked dryly, "Oh, she's talking to you today."

"Seems to be a moody woman," Gabe replied. Then he, too, went back to work.

She drove her spanking-new Model T Ford away from Boynton's carrying a myriad of accessories upon which Henry Ford had proudly emblazoned his company insignia: a spare fan belt, a tire-patching kit, a small tool kit, a canvas duster to protect her clothes and a pair of goggles for when she lowered the top. The only thing Mr. Ford seemed to omit his name from was the ten-pound can of carbide crystals that Hamlin Young gave her after filling her lamps . . . making sure he patted her hand plenty during the exchange.

"Now be sure to come back and let me show you how to adjust the carburetor!" he called after her.

In a pig's eye, she thought. *The carburetor you want to adjust is mine, and I'm not that big a fool!*

She motored down Main Street, bouncing on her new patent-leather seat, feeling sassy and free with the side curtains rolled up in spite of the drizzle. Her own motorcar, completely paid for! And nobody to tell her where she could go with it! She stopped at Coose's Hardware and carried her new gas can inside, had it filled and replaced the wooden plug herself with a jaunty slap. It was heavy, as Elfred had warned, but Mr. Coose wouldn't hear of her carrying it outside herself and did it for her. Away she went again, grinning at the astonished faces of the men she left behind. The mist continued, blurring visibility on the horizontally split windshield. But she peered through it at every driver she met, feeling superior to discover none were women.

Such elation demanded company, so she stopped at Grace's and gave several bleats on her Klaxon.

Grace stuck her head out the front door, slapped her own cheek and said, "Oh, merciful heavens, what will she do next!"

"Grace, come on out and take a ride with me!"

"Are you insane, Roberta!"

"Not at all! Come on, we'll go show Mother!"

"Mother will be furious!"

"Mother is always furious. Come with me anyway!"

From the opposite end of the walk she could tell Grace was waffling. "Without a man?"

"Oh, Grace, you don't need a man for *ev*erything!"

Grace's eyes veered down the street, then back to the car. "Oh, dear, Elfred will flip his wig! We aren't going far, are we?"

"No." Just for fun, Roberta added, "No farther than Portland!"

"Oh, Birdy." Grace flapped a hand, but this innocent collusion became more than she could resist. When they were girls it was always Birdy who got them in trouble, and as she popped inside to grab her coat Grace realized she was letting herself in for more of the same.

Their mother lived on Elm Street, one of the loveliest thoroughfares in town, in a sturdy two-story with a Colonial exterior and a Wedgwood-blue door and shutters. In the few short blocks it took to get there, the sisters reverted to giggles, driving along, ringing the brass bell beside the Klaxon, feeling smart and worldly in this man's contraption that drew open-mouthed stares from all the drivers they passed.

Grace went to the door. "Look, Mother, Birdy's gone and done it. She bought the motorcar!"

"Oh, that girl, she'll be the persecution of me yet!"

"She wants to take you for a ride in it."

"Not on your life! And you shouldn't be riding in it either! People will be calling you both loose women!"

"But, Mother, I don't see what harm can come of a little ride."

"Does Elfred know you're out running around alone?"

"No, but I'm not doing anything wrong." Grace's enthusiasm was fading fast.

"You get right back in that thing and tell your sister to take you straight back home before Elfred finds out!" She raised her voice and screeched at Roberta, "Elfred wouldn't like her out running around like some floozy! You might think it's just fine to go out and buy yourself a car, but this is a small town, and women don't do things like that! Now you take your sister home!"

She disappeared and slammed the door.

Grace returned to the car somewhat glum. "Mother's probably right. I knew it before I came with you."

By the time she had returned Grace to her house, Roberta's own spirits were dampened. She should have known better. Grace was not only under Elfred's thumb, she was under Mother's as well. She had been doing what the two of them demanded for so long that she had accepted oppression as her natural way of life.

When Roberta pulled up at home the reaction she

received was far different. Farley and his brother stopped pounding and moved toward the car like children toward a circus.

"Well, there she is!" Farley called. "And isn't she pretty!"

Forgetting her umbrella, Roberta had gotten out and met them at the bridal wreath hedge.

"Why is it that all you men call conveyances *she*?"

Both men stopped and casually admired the car. Gabe said, "Never stopped to think about it, just do." Seth started circling the Model T but Gabe stayed by Roberta. "Did you leave the spark lever up so you don't break an arm next time?"

"I did."

"And the throttle up, too?"

"The throttle, too."

"You learn quickly, Mrs. Jewett."

"It appears I'll have to. I've come home with a whole mess of repair tools that Hamlin Young assured me I *had* to have—a rubber patching kit for the tires and a spare belt for the fan and a bunch of screwdrivers and wrenches for the carburetor."

"And don't forget the transmission bands."

"Oh dear," she said, touching her lips melodramatically like a maiden in distress, putting them both in danger of laughing, for Roberta was as far from a maiden in distress as a black widow spider. The moment held a beat of disquiet while they stood in the rain enjoying each other completely, taken off guard by the realization that their acquaintance was taking a turn that neither of them had expected: They were slowly becoming friends.

Her voice held a teasing note as she spoke again. "What is this new nuisance, transmission bands?"

"Something that can be adjusted pretty simply with a screwdriver. You'll know when they need it because the pedals will go all the way to the floor."

"And then will I crash into the next fixed object?"

He did laugh this time, at her nonchalance in asking such a question. "It won't happen that suddenly. You'll feel it for a while. The car will start running jerky."

"I'll remember that—running jerky, tighten transmission bands." She watched him carefully for his reaction to her next remark. "I'm beginning to think a horse might have been much better after all."

He turned away and started circling the car so she couldn't see his face. "No, ma'am," he said quietly, "I don't think so."

Seth returned just then and said, "There's nothing like a Ford." While she stood talking to him she remained clearly aware of Gabriel's progress around the car, touching the braces that held up the leather top, reading the ceramic license plate, opening the far door, getting behind the driver's wheel and testing its fit in his hands (unobtrusively checking the lever positions, which brought her a secret smile), getting back out, stooping to check the level of the crystals in the carbide container, opening the brass headlamps and closing them again, eventually coming full circle, back to her.

Her amused smile was still showing when she asked, "Didn't you believe me?"

"I . . . um. . . ." He rubbed the underside of his nose with a knuckle.

"I told you I put them in the up position."

"I was just looking 'er over. These jitneys are pretty when they're brand spankin' new."

"Yes, they are." She decided to let him off the hook.

Seth said, "Well, I got a porch to finish," and went off to do so, leaving Gabe with Roberta, studying the Ford.

"You know," he said, "you told me you couldn't afford one. I'm just wondering . . . well, it's none of my business actually."

She grinned and told him, "I bribed Elfred." His surprised eyes flashed her way. "Over that incident in the kitchen."

"You didn't."

"Yes, I did. I told him I'd tell Grace if he didn't lend me one hundred and fifty dollars."

Amusement put crow's-feet at the corners of Gabe's eyes. "So old Elfred's finally come up against one woman he can't charm."

"That's right. And I would have done it, too, make no mistake about that!"

"I'm sure you would have."

"He's gotten by with his flirting for too long, and he's making such a fool of my sister. I suspect people are laughing at her behind her back."

She respected Gabe for not confirming her suspicion. Instead, his silence did so, bringing them through a muddled backlog of encounters that had shaped their acquaintanceship, starting with its unfortunate beginning when she had overheard his conversation with Elfred, to their standing in the drizzle beside the car he had taught her to drive.

"By the way, I never said thank you for rescuing me from Elfred," Roberta said quietly.

"Oh . . ." He crossed his arms and nudged at the gravel with the toe of his Wellington.

"I'm grateful you did."

He looked at her squarely and said, "This is a mighty uncomfortable subject, Mrs. Jewett, after the remarks I made about you. You know, I'm real sorry about that."

"Are you? Well, you've more than made up for it. You're forgiven, Mr. Farley."

He stood a moment, meeting her eyes, his face lighting with color. The spring mist put a gloss on his pink cheeks and painted the yard an Irish green. It put seed pearls on the nap of her worn wool jacket and a droop to the hair she'd twisted and gathered up earlier. It enriched the sound of Seth's renewed hammering, which startled some sparrows and sent them up scolding.

"Well, listen"—Gabe cleared his throat—"better get back to work, too. You let me know if there's anything I can teach you about the car."

"I will . . . thanks."

They walked toward the house separately, as if uncomfortable with the turn their friendship had taken, she to climb the fresh steps for the first time and he to help his brother with the railing.

It took some courage but that afternoon Roberta decided there was no sense in quailing: At five minutes to four she went out to crank the car so she could drive to school and surprise the girls.

Gabriel stopped working to watch her, and when the

engine fired and no bones were broken, he smiled and flagged his hand in approval.

The girls were boisterous and gay. "May Isobel and our cousins ride, too? They were going to come over and work on a play."

"I don't know if all of you will fit in here."

"Oh, we'll sit double . . . won't we, girls?"

So with seven energetic passengers Roberta drove away from school for the first time while the gawking children of everyone in town prepared to carry home the news to their parents. At her house they all tumbled out and scampered up the walk while Gabe witnessed once more what was becoming the normal routine at the Jewett home—a gaggle of girls creating bedlam at four o'clock every afternoon. The porch pleased them twice as much today with the railing all done and the roof shingled. Rebecca did another oration, this one from Shakespeare, then all the girls piled inside and back out again eating raw carrots, with a few slams on the piano keys en route.

At five o'clock, when Gabe and Seth packed up their tools to leave, Isobel begged, "Please, Daddy, may I stay just a little longer? We're having so much fun! And besides, I have to finish writing my part."

He had knocked on the front door and stood talking to her from outside. Behind her he glimpsed the girls all clustered around the piano writing and laughing, then growing curiously quiet as they wrote again.

"Well, all right," he agreed. "But I want you home by six, and you're eating supper with me."

"Oh, absolutely!" she said with wide-eyed innocence.

"And stay out of Mrs. Jewett's way."

"Oh, we're not in her way. She's helping us!"

"She is?"

"Aha."

He tried to peer past her again but couldn't see Roberta anywhere. "Well, just make sure you're home by six."

"I will. Thanks, Daddy."

When Gabe got home his mother was in the kitchen leaving some supper on the stove and filling his cookie jar. She was medium height and stocky, with fleshy arms whose undersides waggled when she moved. Her hair was the streaked gray of a mussel shell, parted on the side and rolled up around the rim in back with a rat. The way she moved, it was easy to see how she got carpenters for sons.

"Hi, Ma."

"Brought you some cookies," she said.

"Thanks."

"See the jar was empty."

"Ayup," he said as he hung up his cap and slicker.

"Who's that woman you're interested in?" she asked, point-blank.

"Nobody, Ma."

"I hear she's divorced."

"Ma! What did I just say?"

"I hear you had her out driving your truck."

Gabe rolled his eyes and went to the sink to wash his hands.

"She's been in town what—three days? Four?"

"Seth been blabbing?"

"Sure, Seth's been blabbing, and everybody else in

town. Is it true she bought her own car?"

"What's wrong with that?"

"I'm not exactly sure. Depends on what she's planning to do with it."

"She's a public nurse," he told her, drying his hands. "She needs it to do her job."

"Oh, you know that already, do you?"

"I'm working for her, Ma. Of course I'd know. So would Seth!"

"I hear she's got kids."

"Three of them."

"Isobel's been hanging around with 'em and they're wild as hooligans. That where she was after school today, running with them? I came with the cookies and she wasn't here. Where is she now?"

"They're putting on a play."

"A play! Where?"

"Well, a bunch of them are working on it . . . over at Mrs. Jewett's house."

"Ah, so that's her name now. I think I remember when she got married to some fellow she met when she moved away to Boston. Married him and never came back."

Gabe decided to button his lip.

"Well, I can see you're going to clam up and not tell me a thing, so I'm just going to say one thing. Caroline's been dead seven years and it's time you started thinking about another wife. But this one, Gabriel . . . be careful."

Gabe threw up his hands. "Ma, I'm fixing her porch for cripes's sake!"

"And teaching her how to drive and sending Isobel over there to eat lobsters."

"How did you find that out?"

"Gossip."

He snorted and dropped onto a kitchen chair.

"Well, don't get that look on you like the rest of the world's got a nose like an anteater. How do you think news gets around? There's new party lines in this town, in case you forgot, and I got one of 'em."

"Ma, look. I'm not marrying anybody. I'm not *interested* in anybody, and as far as Isobel goes, she and I are doing just fine. I appreciate your coming over like you do and baking us cookies and doing our laundry, but don't go telling people I'm interested in Roberta Jewett, 'cause it's just not true. I'm fixing her house and that's all."

Maude Farley seemed temporarily mollified. "Well, all right then . . . so long as it's true."

"It is. So . . ." He crossed his arms and relaxed. "What kind of cookies you bring?"

"Sour cream nut with maple frosting."

"Do I get one, or you going to poke 'em all in the cookie jar and hide 'em?"

"You should eat your supper first. I brought you some meatballs."

"Later. C'mon, c'mon . . ." He gestured impatiently for a cookie and she handed one over. He sat munching while she wiped up a few cookie crumbs and pushed a couple of things against the back of a tall free-standing cupboard with a built-in flour sifter.

Finally he asked, "Ma, what do you know about Hiawatha?"

"Hiawatha—who's he?"

"The Indian in the poem."

"Poem!" She peered at him from beneath beetled brows. "You taken to reading poems these days?"

"No, the girls are."

"The girls—you mean yours and Mrs. Jewett's?"

"Well . . . yes." He cleared his throat and sat up straighter.

"Well, I don't know anything about any Hiawatha. Listen, I changed your sheets, so I'm all done here."

"Okay . . ." He rolled up off the chair. "Give you a ride home then."

All the way there and back, then off and on for the rest of the evening, just like the evening before, he kept trying to remember those words Rebecca Jewett had spouted yesterday when she was standing on the porch with her arms thrown wide. Something about an Indian bow, and how it was like a man and a woman, and how neither one was much use without the other. What the hell was wrong with him lately? He wasn't useless without a woman—far from it. He and Isobel had done pretty darned well on their own. Thing was, he had women on the brain too much lately. Oh, well, it was spring, and like he'd told his brother, this was the time of year Caroline had died, besides being a time when restlessness was natural.

Still, whatever those words had been, they'd been pretty and they'd made him stop and think.

Roberta loved having the girls around the house. They were terribly noisy and rambunctious, but their spirit brought vivacity and humor into her life. With the addition of Isobel, and now her three nieces, the clan had grown until she hadn't enough chairs in the front room for them. They didn't care. They sat on the beds upstairs or on the living room floor, or clustered around the piano or the kitchen table.

They had decided to do a dramatization of *Hiawatha* instead of enacting the infamous sketch about Marcelyn's one-eared great-great-grandfather and were choosing stanzas and writing them out and talking about costumes. Roberta, called upon often to answer questions or provide ideas for sources of feathers and costumes, was easily lured away from whatever she was doing. If one of her daughters called, "Mother! Come in here!" she went gladly and listened to their ideas and answered questions like "May we push the piano over there so it'll be closer to the porch?" or "Listen to this! Does this sound like Indian music?" or "Do you think *Hiawatha* would work as an operetta?"

She learned a lot about the Farley household by listening to their chatter. Like all children getting to know one another, they asked questions, and Isobel answered, editing nothing. "There are a lot of old clothes at our house but my dad wouldn't let us cut them up because they were my mother's."

"My dad hates going to school for programs. He probably wouldn't come even if we did do it there."

"On Sundays we eat at my grandma's, but mostly I cook for my dad."

"In the evenings? Oh, I don't know. We do dishes and I study and if it's summer he goes out and fools with Mother's roses, and if it's winter he reads his newspaper. Sometimes I have to help him clean the house."

What Roberta pieced together was the picture of a very lonely young girl with a very boring existence who wasn't allowed to do much except household chores.

She began to notice Isobel's overt response to any sign of affection. Once when Roberta absently touched Isobel's hair while passing behind her, Isobel looked over her shoulder with an expression of such bald gratitude that Roberta hugged the girl farewell that night as she was leaving.

Isobel hugged her back very hard, and her eyes lit up as she exclaimed, "Oh, Mrs. Jewett, I just love it at your house! It's so much fun here."

"Well, you're welcome anytime, Isobel."

Roberta tried to remember if she'd ever seen Gabriel hug his daughter, but she didn't think so.

The following morning the weather had lifted and Roberta opened the front door early while the girls were still asleep. She stepped out onto the porch in her nightgown and stretched, feeling very much alive and optimistic. It was going to be a splendid day! And oh, what a sky! Clouds of deep rose fanned up like the fin of a sailfish, edged in gilt, carrying yesterday's gloom into the sunrise. The sea was tinted allover pink and through its surface the islands of Penobscot Bay seemed to be ascending as if they would lift completely free of the sea and become part of the pattern above. Below, in Camden Harbor, the rocky shoreline met the looking-glass water, and from it a snub-nosed little steamer headed out for somewhere, leaving behind a forest of reflected masts that lay as precise as real ones on the glassy surface. As she watched, those reflections were broken into shorter lengths by the slow-spreading wake from the steamer. Then from another mooring a fisherman pulled away in a double-ender, and as he cleared the other craft lying at anchor, Roberta made out his silhouette, standing in the boat as he pulled at the oars, like a Winslow Homer painting.

This then was Camden. This, her home and her children's home, perhaps for the rest of her days. And what would it bring? A happy place for the girls, it seemed already. Some strife with her family: This seemed sure. A new job, which she must see about, now that she had her motorcar. And Gabriel Farley . . . a friend or an annoyance?

The thought of Farley was too perplexing, so she turned inside to prepare for the day.

His brother didn't come with him that morning, but Farley was out on the porch with his paintbrush before the girls left for school. Of course, they wanted Roberta to give them a ride in the new Ford, but when she declined, they clattered off, streaming greetings that drifted inside and perked up Roberta's ears in the kitchen.

"Hi, Mr. Farley!"

"Mornin', Mr. Farley!"

"Hi, Mr. Farley—you painting today?"

She backed up a step and peered through the shotgun house out the front door, but wherever he was, he was not visible.

She heard the deep tone of his voice, but not the words as he returned their greetings. She could see the front end of his truck behind her car, but enough traffic passed on the street that she hadn't paid attention to the sound of his engine when he'd pulled up.

She decided to get to work and forgo good mornings.

The smell of his paint and turpentine, however, was a relentless reminder of his presence. Sometimes the faint thump of a ladder being moved would intrude upon her, and she questioned why she had not gone directly with a greeting as she would have to any other person.

At midmorning she went out with her pocketbook in hand, wearing her new cream-colored duster over her dress, with her driving goggles looped over her arm. Farley was on the south end of the porch, painting the wall.

"Well, good morning," he said, turning with the paintbrush in his hand.

"Good morning."

"Putting the top down this morning, are you?"

"Yes, I'm off to the administrator's office to get my assignments for next week."

"Time to go to work, eh?"

"Got to earn a living for my girls."

"Well, you've certainly got a beautiful morning for it."

"Yes, isn't it? And I thought all Mainers claimed they never have spring."

"Proves we're wrong. Saw a couple leaves sprouting on my wife's roses."

"She was a gardener, was she?"

"Yes, she was."

"I have a black thumb myself. The thing that grows best for me is weeds."

"She could make anything grow. Her gardens were her pride and joy."

"You still keep them?"

"No, only the roses. The rest is gone."

A lull fell, tinged by a degree of pensiveness that put the smallest damper on the fine spring morning. To dispel it Roberta summoned a more cheerful note. "Well!" She bent back to scan the decorative spandrel around the porch. "The paint is going to work wonders, isn't it?"

His gaze followed hers. "It'll look like a new place in no time."

"The girls will be glad to get you off their porch."

"*Their* porch," he repeated, chuckling soundlessly.

"They've staked their claim to it. The moment the paint dries their play goes into production. Seems we're all going to get invited to the premiere performance."

"All? Who's all?"

"All us parents. You, me, Elfred and Grace. I believe they've put Lydia in charge of ticket sales."

"You mean we're going to get charged?"

"That's right. You mustn't let on that I've told you though. I think it was supposed to be a surprise."

"I won't say anything."

They were back on comfortable footing and would have enjoyed chatting some more, but the paint was drying on his brush.

"Well, I'd better get going . . ." Roberta began buttoning her duster. ". . . let you get back to work."

"Good luck," he called as she headed down the steps. "Thanks."

He stood watching till she was halfway across the

lawn, then called, "You know how to put that top down?"

Walking backward, she answered, "I think I can figure it out."

"Be glad to give you a hand."

She swung about and continued toward the car. "Thank you, Mr. Farley, but I'll do just fine."

He dipped his brush and went back to work, but when her back was turned, he watched her open the car door and reach inside to loosen the bonnet spokes and collapse it like the hood of a baby carriage. Then she went up front, cranked the motor and brushed off her palms. She got in, put on the goggles and waved. "See you later! Happy painting!"—and off she went.

Watching her drive away, he mentally shook his head, but an undeniable seed of admiration had taken root in Gabe Farley. He wondered, as the Model T disappeared up the street, if Caroline would have managed as handily if he had been the one to die first.

Eight

The regional office of public nursing for the state of Maine was located in Rockland, seven miles south of Camden. There Roberta took her orders from a sweet-faced woman named Eleanor Balfour, who issued her white uniforms and caps, medical supplies, gave her assignments for the coming week and advised her she would need to get a telephone wire into her home for which the state would pay.

"A telephone wire?" Roberta's face lit with surprise.

"It'll simplify your getting assignments and ordering supplies. Occasionally emergencies arise, as well."

"And the state will pay?"

"Yes." At Roberta's continued amazement, Miss Balfour smiled indulgently. "It's one of these new contraptions that we're all getting used to. If you object to people all over town knowing about your private affairs, don't speak of them on the telephone."

"No, I won't."

"A reminder about our service," Miss Balfour continued. "It's as much teaching as it is nursing—in homes, in the schools, wherever you go, be prepared to preach cleanliness and hygiene. Keep your eye out for possible contaminated water supplies, any signs of communicable diseases, especially diphtheria, measles and scarlet

152

fever. Quarantine when necessary, and enlighten whenever possible." She pushed back her chair. "As you
know, Mrs. Jewett, a major portion of our fight is
against ignorance. And . . ." she added with a smile,
". . . muddy roads in the spring."

"Up in the mountains, I suppose they are," Roberta
commented as the two women rose.

"They don't call us nurses on horseback for nothing."

"I won't be on horseback, Miss Balfour. I own my
own motorcar."

"You do! Why, how excellent!"

"So far it is, and quite exciting."

"And you've mastered driving it?"

"If not mastered, at least minored."

Miss Balfour laughed. "Well, good luck, Mrs. Jewett."

She found herself excited and needing someone with
whom to share her exhilaration. Quite naturally, she
hurried home to Gabe, little realizing how much she
was looking forward to telling him her news.

"Hey, Mr. Farley, I got my first assignment!" Roberta
crowed as she barreled across the yard.

Gabe came down off his ladder and stood at the bottom, wiping his hands on a rag.

"Which is . . ."

"Inoculating schoolchildren against diphtheria. I'll
start right here in Camden, and get to as many as I can
before schools close for the summer."

"Jabbing children in the arm with those horse nee-
dles. They won't be too happy to see you comin'."

"Might save their lives though."

"Ayup."

"Have you ever been inoculated, Mr. Farley?"

"Nope."

"I'll do that for you, if you like."

"Oh, you'd relish the idea of jabbing me and making me howl, wouldn't you?"

Though Roberta was certainly not the coy type, she wasn't above a little teasing. "Do you howl, Mr. Farley?" she said with a glint of mischief.

He angled her a glance with some mischief of his own. "Been known to. Can't say I like pain much."

"Oh, come on. You've probably hit yourself with a hammer that hurt more than this little shot will."

Suddenly, down below, the mill whistle blasted. Situated as the house was, just above the stack, it was close enough that glasses tinkled together whenever the steam whistle sounded. Roberta covered her ears during the deafening bellow, and Farley winced. When it finally ended, their ears kept jangling.

"Phew, that thing is loud," she said.

"Can hear it for five minutes after it's done blowing."

"Well, it's noon," she remarked needlessly. "I'm hungry. Have you eaten your dinner yet?"

"Nope. Still in the truck."

"I'll make us some coffee if you want to come in and eat with me."

"Sounds like a good idea. I'm ready to take a break."

Ten minutes later they sat in her kitchen at a scarred wooden table. She was eating cold meat and cottage cheese while he worked on two hefty sandwiches. The room was far from neat, but he could see she had scrubbed it down and washed the windows. He could also see that her possessions were very meager.

"Guess what," she said. "The state of Maine is going to pay for a telephone wire for me."

"You don't say." He smiled, his cheek bulging with a bite of sandwich.

"So I can get my assignments and order supplies from Rockland."

"Well, congratulations."

"I think I'm pretty smart, getting a telephone."

He reached for his coffee cup. "Just watch what you say on it."

"Why?"

"Party lines."

"Oh, yes, that's right."

"My mother likes to listen in on them."

"Lots of gossip in this town, I take it."

"Ayup."

They ate awhile, then she asked, "So what does your mother hear about me on her party line?"

"Mostly that you're divorced."

"Mm . . ." She picked up two of his sandwich crumbs and ate them. ". . . that's pretty sordid, isn't it?"

It took some time for his grin to grow. Then he drawled, "Yes, ma'am, it is."

She sat back comfortably, enjoying him. "So tell me, what is your mother like?"

"My mother?" He thought awhile. "Oh, she's a nice woman. She does a lot for Isobel and me. She's a widow, has been for a long time, so washing our clothes and filling our cookie jar gives her something to do."

"Does she know my mother?"

"I believe she does, yes."

"But they're not friends?"

"Not exactly. Why?"

"Because my mother's not a nice woman like yours, I don't think."

He rested his elbows on the table and hooked a finger through his cup handle, remembering the one time he'd seen the mother and daughter together. "I could tell that day when she came over here that you two don't get along so well."

"We never did, actually. That's pretty much why I left Camden."

"How old were you then?"

"Eighteen. It was right after I graduated from high school. She wanted me to go to work in that infernal mill, and I absolutely refused. She thought I'd just settle down right here and wait on her, do everything she wanted, just like Grace. But my grandmother had died and left Grace and me each a small inheritance. Grace gave hers to Elfred to buy his first piece of property and start his business. I took mine and went away to college, which upset my mother a lot. She thought I should have done what Grace did, and of course she never stops reminding me how Grace stood behind her husband when he needed her to, and look what happened. . . ." Roberta mimicked her mother. "Elfred is one of the *wealth*iest men in town, and he's *so* good to Grace and the children. Why, look at that house he keeps them in!"

She dropped the theatrics and continued. "I, on the other hand, with my college education and my worldly ways, have disgraced myself by throwing off a husband and returning to Camden with little more than the clothes on my back and this rickety furniture, thereby becoming an embarrassment to my mother. She fails to see that if I hadn't pursued my nursing career, my children would have starved. Their father would have seen to *that*."

"He wasn't from Camden?"

"No. He was from Boston . . . from everywhere, really, wherever there was a roving card game, or a new get-rich-quick scheme, or a woman who'd come running when he'd crook his finger at her. He came home often enough to get me in a family way three times and to put the pinch on me for another stake . . . and another, and another, until I'd finally had enough. The last time he came I told him he was free to live with any woman he wanted. All he had to do was sign the divorce agreement. He refused, so I bribed him by offering him one last stake. Do you know how much it was?"

She met Gabriel's eyes while he sat quietly, attentive.

"Twenty-five dollars," she said sadly. "He got rid of a wife and three daughters for a measly twenty-five dollars."

He noted the hurt in her eyes, a pulling at the outer corners and a dying of animation. She looked away, staring off toward a window. The room grew very quiet. Roberta sipped her coffee but Gabe forgot his. All his attention was riveted on the woman whose face had suddenly lost its toughness. It lasted only seconds before her gaze returned to Gabe.

"And you know what?" In place of the hurt a touch of pride lit her eyes. "I've never been happier in my life. I don't have much, but I don't need much. And I certainly don't need a husband, nor do I want one. I'm rid of him, and my girls are thriving here. I may have a tarnished reputation, but I can say to hell with the rest of the world, because I know the truth. I survived with George, little more. What kept me going were my children, and they are what will continue to keep me going."

She got up and refilled their cups. His eyes followed her all the way to the stove and back. When she resumed her chair their eyes locked but neither of them said a word for a long stretch. Then, still without speaking, he pushed his stack of cookies toward her.

Silently she accepted one and for a while they sat eating, dipping the cookies in their coffee, thinking back over all she'd said, getting used to the idea of their becoming confidants, which they hadn't expected. This frank exchange was novel for them both, and they wondered if it was wise to push it further.

Finally, he asked, "Why did you marry him, then?"

"I don't know. He was pretty . . . and he was a charmer. Boy-oh-boy, was he a charmer. He talked a fancy game, and I fell for it, just like a dozen other women after me. Even my mother. I brought him here a couple of times right after we were married, and he kissed her hand and raved about her cooking and told her what a handsome woman she was. Well, she ate it up with a spoon"—a faraway look came into Roberta's eyes—"and blamed me for my marriage failing."

It was rare for Roberta to let her vulnerabilities show. Gabriel guessed as much and once again said nothing, only waited for her to go on. Soon she did, as if unable to staunch the flow now that it had begun.

"I stopped coming back when George's escapades began. I didn't want to answer questions about why he wasn't with me. But after I got divorced, I thought I owed it to my girls to give them a chance to know their grandmother. And Grace and Elfred and the girls, too . . ." She smiled wryly at Gabe. "Though now I include Elfred with some grave misgivings."

He returned her smile and she glanced away. Suddenly the spell seemed to have broken.

"Goodness, but I've bent your ear," she said.

"I don't mind."

"You're a very good listener."

"Am I? The truth is a man gets a little starved for adult conversation when he's living with a fourteen-year-old."

"I know what you mean. Though there's never a lack of commotion around here, a lot of it is exactly that—commotion. It is pleasant, talking this way."

"So, go on," he said, settling back, crossing his arms and stretching out his crossed ankles beneath the table.

"Oh no, now it's your turn. What about your wife?"

"My wife?"

"Or don't you talk about her?"

He assessed Roberta as if deciding whether or not to answer, then replied, "Not much, no."

"Why not?"

"Well . . ." He thought awhile.

"Keeping her memory sacred?"

His brow furrowed as he searched her for sarcasm. Finding none, he relented. "Maybe. Ayup . . . maybe."

She could see he would take some drawing out. He seemed to be a man who kept his own counsel.

"Your marriage was a lot different than mine," she prompted.

"Oh, yes . . ." He reached for a saltshaker and absently toyed with it. "As night and day." He sat ruminating for so long that she wished he had a crank, like her Model T, so she could get him started. When she'd all but given up hope of him speaking he pressed the bottom of the saltshaker against the table and said, "She was pretty 'bout perfect. I, ah . . ." He cleared his throat and sat up a little straighter, keeping his eyes on the shaker. "I knew I wanted to marry her from the time we were . . . oh, fourteen, fifteen, maybe. Seems like I always knew. She was kind, and gentle, and pretty as a rosebud. Me . . . I was . . ." He chuckled and shook his head. "Well, hell, you know . . . I was this big raw-boned thing with these big rough hands, and I thought no girl as pretty as Caroline would ever give me a tumble. And to top it off, I was a carpenter's son, and bound to be a carpenter myself. What could I give her? Why, when she said she'd marry me I was so . . . so . . ." He couldn't seem to come up with the word, but she waited, just as he had during her story. "I thought I was the luckiest man since the birth of time. And we had a mighty good life together. Bought that little house on Belmont Street, and she fixed it up like a dollhouse, and every day when I'd come home there she'd be with that smile, and supper hot on the stove and flowers around the house. Then Isobel came along, and Caroline wanted more babies, but . . . well, none came. Me, I was pretty grateful, because I didn't like what she had to go through to get Isobel. She had a pretty hard time of it. She was . . . well, she was a petite woman." He cleared his throat. "Anyway . . . Isobel came, and we had seven years after that before this one day—it was April, seven years ago next Tuesday, April eighteenth—she was getting into a buggy, going to ride out and enjoy the afternoon, she said, because it was one of those rare spring days when the sun was out and it was nice and warm, and she thought she'd take a picnic hamper up toward Hosmer Pond and see if the wake-robins were blooming yet. But she stopped downtown for something and just as she was getting back in the carriage the mill whistle blew and scared the horse." He paused, swallowed. "It reared . . . and . . ."

His story faded into silence as Roberta glanced at the telltale shine in his eyes and he stared out the window. Her throat had closed and her heart tumbled along like a stone in the rapids. Time passed in her dreary, cluttered kitchen, the sunlight doing its best to spread cheer from outside. He stared, and she waited.

When he finally spoke, his broken voice said as much as his words. "It's hard to lose somebody when you aren't done with them yet."

She didn't know what to say. This kind of devotion was beyond her.

Finally he realized he'd been sitting there with brimming eyes. "Well . . ." He pushed back his chair and got to his feet. "Been sitting here long enough. That porch isn't going to paint itself."

Turning his back, he tried to hide the fact that he was swiping at his eyes with the side of his hand. She tried to remember if she had ever seen a man this close to tears, but nothing came to mind. She and Farley had started out their dinner with such blithe spirits; she had not intended to wrench his heart so. She had merely sat quietly listening, just as he had when she'd been speaking. She could tell that he was chagrined at having shown her more than he intended.

"It's all right, Mr. Farley," she said kindly, rising too. "There's no need to feel ashamed of a few tears."

He nodded, hanging his head while she remained on the far side of the table, throat still plugged, studying the back of his hair as it lifted from his collar in sandy-brown spikes.

"Well, listen . . ." He half-glanced over his shoulder, making sure not to show all of his face. "Thanks for the coffee."

"Thanks for the cookies."

He walked out, giving her a view of nothing but his back.

Since he'd begun working at her house they'd run a gamut of emotions. Every day seemed to have its mood that bound the two of them, though she worked inside and he worked out. From blatant antipathy to moments of embarrassment, to a slow warming, beginning when he'd taught her to drive. But none had bound them as disquietingly as today's exchange of histories. From the stories they had told, each knew beyond a doubt that the other was suffering from a past that left no room for new love. She was done with men for good. He still loved his dead wife. But every clink and chink and shuffle and ding that they heard through the walls or through the open front door reminded them that they had created a bond between them this noon, and that nothing would ever change it. Forever they would know each other's vulnerabilities.

He heard a clatter once and stopped painting to listen. But he stood at an angle to the doorway and could not see in.

She heard the squeak of hinges once and waited a long moment before poking her head out and peeking across the living room to find he was starting to paint the exterior of the door. She just barely made him out through the square waist-high window, wielding the brush, looking up, unaware of her watching.

She pulled back, curved an index finger against her lips, shook her head and tried to put him from her mind.

By afternoon they both realized that putting each other from their thoughts was a pointless effort. They had said too much to do that. Besides, there was more to be said before the girls came home from school— ironically and in all probability *all* their girls.

She was pressing one of her uniforms when he called, "Mrs. Jewett?"

How odd. The sound of his voice suddenly put a flutter beneath her ribs. She set down the iron and went to the doorway between the kitchen and living room.

"Yes?"

He was standing just inside the threshold, empty-handed and smelling of turpentine.

"I finished up out here so I'm going to call it a day. Okay if I leave the paint cans and brushes under the porch over the weekend?"

"Of course."

"I work Saturdays down at my shop, so I won't see you till Monday. That is, I'll be back on Monday morning, but if you're gone before I get here, well, you have a good first day, will you?"

"Yes, thank you. I'll be working at the girls' school."

"Well, you take it easy on those kids, then."

She smiled guardedly.

"I'll have to be here inside your house next week, so I hope that's okay. When you're gone?"

"Of course. What will you do first?"

"That window upstairs. Then start on the walls."

"Fine. Just move anything that's in your way."

"Ayup. I will."

They stood for a moment, then he shifted his weight to the opposite foot. "About earlier," he said self-consciously. "I'm sorry. I shouldn't have told you all that."

"It's all right. I'm glad you did."

"No, I got a little carried away. I could see it made you . . . well, that wasn't . . ." He ran out of words and ended by clearing his throat. "Well, you know what I mean. Listen, I've got to go." Only now did he meet her eyes. "I imagine Isobel will be showing up here with your girls, so tell her to be home by six, will you?"

"Certainly. She'll be there."

He nodded once.

And stood there.

And so did she.

Each recognizing a faint reluctance to face two days without seeing the other.

"Better go," he said.

"Have a nice weekend."

"Ayup, you too."

Roberta had trouble keeping her word about getting Isobel home by six. The girls brought home another

new friend named Shelby DuMoss, as well as Grace's
girls, and all of them—eight, all together—decided to
head off up the mountain to look for birch bark. They
came back lugging a dead tree, from which they said
they were going to unroll the bark to make the shell of
a canoe for their play. From Gabe's lumber scraps they
took pieces to act as a frame, and were industriously
hammering and gluing when Roberta announced it was
time for the girls to go home.

"Oh, nooooo!" they all chorused. "Just a few
minutes longer? Please?"

"No, I promised Isobel's father."

Isobel went, but she was back the next day, and so
were all the others. Roberta took them on a hike up
Mount Battie, and they explored the budding haw-
thorns and dogwoods, the willows with their spring
skirts turned scarlet. They identified birds and came
upon a vernal pond in an old quarry where frogs sang.
They noted the locations of blueberry bushes for raiding
in late summer, and stood at the summit surveying the
vista of sea, islands and sky, the little blue loop of Camden Harbor shimmering in the sun, then dulling as a
thin cloud passed over it.

Later, they tramped downhill all the way to the shore
and came upon some boys on the rocks cleaning flounder, and got a bucketful in exchange for free admission
to their first performance of *Hiawatha*. It was easy to
see one of the boys had eyes for Becky and wanted to
please her.

Roberta fried the flounder and took them outside,
where she sat with the girls on the porch floor with their

legs hanging over the edge and their heels bumping the latticework.

It was there Gabriel found them, coming up on foot out of the pre-dark gloom to cross the front yard and stop at the base of the steps. He was dressed in dark clothing with his jacket buttoned against the evening chill, and once again he'd left his cap at home. Though they all saw him coming, none spoke as he approached, only thumped their heels and chewed their fish and licked their fingers.

"Evening," he said lazily.

"Evening," they all replied, and it came out in two such perfect, unison beats, like a cappella singing, that everybody got lighthearted.

"Figured I'd find you here, Isobel."

"I've had my supper, if that's what you're worried about."

"So I see."

"Mrs. Jewett fried us flounder."

He said nothing, but shifted his gaze to Roberta and let it stay.

"Evening, Mr. Farley," she said levelly. "Would you like some flounder?"

"No, thank you. I've had my supper."

"Oh, too bad." She swung her heels like the girls, and he could tell from the thumps that in the shadows they were making marks on his newly painted lattice-work. He counted the females. There were nine of them lined up like clothespins, each of them swinging her heels against his paint job.

"I like Isobel home by six," he told Roberta pleas-antly.

"It's Saturday. I didn't think you'd mind."

"She's got her hair to wash for tomorrow, and shoes to polish for church."

"Oh, that's right. Well then, Isobel . . . time to go, dear." Roberta leaned back to see Isobel down the line.

"Oh, I wish I didn't have to."

"Shh, Isobel," she whispered, "you'll hurt your father's feelings. Besides, it *is* late, and the others will have to be going, too."

Isobel got up and passed behind Roberta, who lifted one arm and looked at her upside down. Isobel leaned down and they gave each other unaimed kisses. " 'Night, dear," Roberta said softly.

" 'Night. And thank you."

Roberta watched carefully to see if Gabe would drape an arm around his daughter's shoulders as they turned and headed across the yard, but he didn't. He walked separately while Isobel's voice drifted back to the porch, telling about their trek up the mountain and how they'd acquired the fish. At the opening in the bridal wreath hedge the girl turned and called happily, "Good night, everybody." Then she and Gabe walked off into the growing dark.

On Sunday afternoon she showed up again, exasperated by having had to spend the hours since church at her grandmother's for dinner.

"My dad insisted. We spend *every* Sunday there till three o'clock. It's so *bor*ing!"

"But I promised your father you'd be home by six and you will, agreed?"

"Oh, all right," she said.

Shortly after she arrived, so did Grace, driven by Elfred in their black touring car. She barged right into the
house without knocking, as if it were her God-given
right to do so, braying, "Roberta, I've got to talk to
you! It's about these girls and the hours you've got them
keeping! Elizabeth DuMoss called me on the telephone
to ask just what kind of a place you're running over
here, keeping them here so late last night! She demands
to know just what was going on, and so do I!"

Elfred came in, too, and hung back just far enough
to give his nasty glances room to sail. He got out a cigar
and pursed it in his lips, twisting it back and forth and
wetting it, working it in and out like a plunger while
grinning suggestively.

Grace carped on. "My girls have been brought up
with manners! You had them eating fried fish with their
fingers, sitting on the edge of a porch! And you took
them tramping up that mountain and let them get their
dresses filthy!"

Roberta suddenly grew sick and tired of her sister,
who raised her girls like hothouse pansies. "Yes, I did,
Grace, and they loved every minute of it. As a matter
of fact, they didn't want to go home."

"Oh, Roberta," Grace gasped melodramatically,
"how you do wound me. I'd hoped when you moved
back here that we could get along better than we used
to, but I can see you're just as misguided and foolhardy
as you always were. And Elfred and I had come over
to let you know that we'd decided to give a small party
at our house to introduce you to some of our friends,
but now I don't know. You're attempting to undermine
me with my own children." Her voice broke as she

fished out a hanky and applied it. "And it does hurt, Birdy, it does."

Roberta opened her arms and folded her sister in a hug. "Oh, Grace, I'm sorry. I shouldn't have said that."

"But you've always done that, always! Made fun of my ways and my decisions. Whatever I do, it's not what *you'd* have done. Well, I haven't done so badly!" Grace pulled back defensively. "I've got my girls and my Elfred and we have a happy home and lots of friends, so who are you to belittle me?"

"I'm sorry, Grace," Roberta said, properly chastised, but keeping her eyes off Elfred, who had finally removed the cigar from his despicable mouth. If Grace wanted to convince herself that her marriage was made in heaven, who was Birdy to disabuse her of the notion? Let her live in her dreamworld. She took Grace's free hand. "If you can forgive me, I'd love it if you'd give a party for me. Truly, I would. And I'd love to meet your friends."

Grace sent a martyred glance at Elfred, making sure a few tears jiggled on her eyelids. "Well, if it's all right with Elfred . . ."

He came up close behind her and put a hand on her waist. "It's up to you, dear," he said sweetly, making Roberta want to puke.

Grace made a big show of deciding. "Well, I guess we could go forward with the plans. Saturday night, we thought. Maybe dinner and a little music afterwards."

"That would be just grand."

Then Grace spoiled it all. "We thought that if we were to come out publicly and show our support for you, let everybody see that we're still willing to have you in the house, then others in town will overlook your being divorced and will follow suit."

It took all Roberta's strained civility to keep from shoving Grace's fat face clear to the back of her fat neck. Willing to have her in the house! As if she were some pet hamster instead of a plain brown rat!

Jumping Judas, if it weren't so hypocritical, it might have been funny. Grace, with her philandering husband, willing to play the moral leader of the town while all of it was laughing at her behind her back. Elfred, working that cigar in his mouth like a butter churn, taking every opportunity to send salacious grins at his own wife's sister while men and women alike scorned him from a distance. They were truly two pathetic creatures.

After Elfred and Grace left, Roberta's anger remained. She played the piano some, but it failed to wipe out the hurt and disgust she felt. She was still agitated when she turned back her sheets and climbed into bed.

The house grew quiet. The girls settled down. Elfred, Grace. Grace, Elfred. *We're still willing to have you in the house and overlook your being divorced.*

It took well over an hour before Roberta grew drowsy. Her last thought before going to sleep was that she couldn't wait to rant about it to Gabriel Farley. He was the only one in this town who'd understand.

Nine

On Monday morning Gabe arrived before Roberta left for work. She was upstairs when the girls came bombarding her with good-byes, then clattered down the steps on the run, late as usual.

She went down seconds later in her starched white uniform and peaked white cap to find Gabe in the living room, wearing leather gloves and holding a pane of glass.

"Oh! I didn't know you were here!" she said, startled.

"Sorry. I thought the girls let you know."

"No!"

He stared as if he'd never seen her before. Her hair was coiled up much like his mother's, with the cap nestled into the crevice at the back. Her crisply starched uniform nearly reached her ankles and stood out like a bell, covered by a white apron with a bib that bent over her breasts like a piece of tin.

He'd never paid much notice to her shape before, but looking at her in that uniform was like looking at the Maine shoreline from the top of Mount Battie: The curves showed up, plain and plentiful. And she looked so tidy! When she was running around here with the girls, her hair looked like something the sea had thrown up on the rocks at high tide, but this neat roll was a real surprise. Why, even her run-over shoes were gone, in their place immaculate white oxfords.

He'd been gaping for some time before he realized it and got his mouth moving. "Gonna get that window replaced today."

"Yes, good."

Still he didn't move.

After a beat, Roberta jutted her head and said, puzzled, "Mr. Farley?"

He motioned as if wanting to point at her, pane of glass and all. "The uniform."

She looked down. "Is something wrong with it?"

"Um . . . no. It's . . . ah . . . no, it's . . ."

She waited, hiding her amusement.

"Nice," he finally finished, setting the pane of glass across his boots.

"The state issues them."

"Oh, so not only telephones, but uniforms, too."

"Yes. I'm lucky, hm?"

"Very lucky."

"Well, I've got to be going. Can't be late on my first day."

"Nope, 'course not." He curved his gloved hands around the glass and headed for the stairs.

"Oh, Mr. Farley?"

He stopped, set the glass across his boots once more.

"Will you be here all day long?"

" 'Spect so."

"This is a presumptuous thing to ask, I know, but the girls are going to beat me home. Would you mind keeping an eye on them till I get here? Try to keep them from eating me out of house and home?"

"Be happy to. 'Course, I'll be busy, you understand."

"Oh, yes, of course. I just thought, it's a pretty sure bet Isobel will be with my three, so maybe you wouldn't mind."

"Don't mind at all."

"Well, I'll see you then . . . sometime between five and six, I imagine."

"Ayup."

He watched her cross the living room and go outside. When she reached the porch steps, he called, "Oh, Mrs. Jewett?" She returned to the door and looked in. "You want I should crank that flivver so you don't get dirty?"

"No thank you, Mr. Farley, I can manage."

He remained in the shadows, far back from the door so she couldn't see him watching her. She made a sight cranking that car in her starched white uniform, checking everything he'd taught her to check, getting in and out while he cataloged each adjustment she made. When the engine fired, a big smile bloomed on her face and she brushed her palms together, glancing up at the house as if to win his approval.

He smiled too, and waited till she drove off, then carried the pane upstairs, thinking it would be a much lonelier day around here today.

The girls' bedroom was a mess. Neither of the beds was made, and dirty clothes were left where dropped. The two bedrooms shared one minuscule closet with doors left open in both directions. Books, fans, seashells, birds' nests, rocks, driftwood, shoes, dirty dishes, glasses of water, theater cards tacked to the walls—ye gods, you could barely see the floors.

Gabe wasn't nosy, but he took a peek into Roberta's

room and found it much the same. The most orderly thing in it appeared to be a stack of folded uniforms on top of her bureau. She had a beat-up chest and from one of its open drawers hung a petticoat with a soiled hem. She slept on the right side of the bed—he observed—on two stacked pillows, beneath a bedspread of yellow chenille. No curtains on the windows, only green shades with tattered bottoms, probably left over from crazy old Breckenridge.

Caroline would have set a match to the lot and called it a gain.

He looked for a picture of the husband but there was none. As he set to work glazing the new windowpane in place, he wondered what George Jewett had looked like.

The day went slowly without her. In only a week he'd grown used to the noises she made, clattering things, humming, playing the piano at ridiculous times, starting the car, coming out to talk to him, raising the smell of coffee brewing.

At noon he sat on the front porch steps and ate his sandwich alone, remembering how they'd sat together last Friday in her kitchen, talking. Time and again he thought, *But she's so different from Caroline,* little realizing the implication of his musing.

His mother found him there, eating the last of his cookies.

"Gabriel!" she called as she approached on foot across the front yard.

"Well, what are you doing here?" he asked, brushing the cookie crumbs off his palms.

"Came to see what you're doing to old Breckenridge's place."

"It needed lots of work."

"Porch looks good."

"Seth and I did that last week."

"Painted it too, I see."

"Ayup. Workin' inside this week."

"I want to take a look. I heard she's over at school giving shots, so I figured it was okay." She started up the steps around him.

"Hey, Ma, wait now! It's her place. I can't just let you walk in there!"

He was too late. She'd already gone in by the time he got to his feet.

"How's she going to find out? Lord, this all the furniture she's got? Piano's the best thing in the room, and it's seen some hard use."

"Ma, come on, I don't feel right letting you nose around in here."

"I'm not nosing around." Even making the claim she was standing in the doorway inspecting the kitchen. "I came to talk to you about Isobel."

"What about her?"

"Everybody says she's running with this woman's girls and I don't think Caroline would like it."

"Caroline is dead, Ma, and I've got to decide those things for myself. And aren't you the one who reminded me of it just a couple weeks ago?"

Maude turned. "Listen, son, you've been spending an awful lot of time up here yourself."

"Working for her."

"On Saturday night?"

"I wasn't here on Saturday night."

"I heard you were."

"Ma, you've been on that party line too much."

"All I'm saying is this here is a divorced woman, and you'd better mind your P's and Q's around her because the entire town knows it. And I don't want my granddaughter around these wild hooligans, getting a bad reputation."

"You know what, Ma?" He forced his voice to remain calm. "I'm getting a little mad here. Been a long time since I've been mad, but damn it, I'm a grown man and I don't have to explain my comings and goings to you. Nor do I have to explain them to a town full of gossips who don't know Roberta Jewett from Adam. This is the happiest Isobel's been since Caroline died. They hang around here, a whole gang of girls, singing and making up plays, and they take walks up the mountain and she fries them all fish, and if you want to know the truth, I've never seen a mother who spends so much time with her children, or one who enjoys them more. And they like her too. They laugh together, and she's in there playing the piano with them and having fun. Now what's wrong with that?"

"I'm just saying . . . you get your work done and get out of here, Gabriel."

He said it quietly, without rancor, but she knew he meant every word. "I think maybe the one who should get out of here right now is you, Ma."

He had a bad afternoon after that, worrying about what his mother was going to tell the other women on the party line, wondering why he hadn't just come right out and claimed there was nothing between him and

Roberta Jewett. It just burned him that people gossiped about her without ever having met her.

At midafternoon Seth showed up.

"Boy, is Ma steaming," he said.

"Ayup."

"What the hell did you say to her anyway?"

"Told her to mind her own business."

"That's about what I figured."

"She come down to the shop or what?"

"Damn right she did, and told me to get up here and see if I could loosen the rocks in your head."

"Town's too small for its own good. Everybody knows everybody else's business."

Seth looked mischievous. "Ma says she's all done filling your cookie jar."

Gabe angled his brother an amused glance. "Well, that'll sure fix me, won't it?" They both laughed and Seth thumped Gabe between the shoulder blades.

"So, you gettin' along pretty good with Mrs. Jewett or what?"

"No, nothing like that. We just talk a lot, that's all."

"Didn't think you ever talked a lot."

"About the people we were married to."

"Ohhh . . ." Seth said, tilting back his head sagely. ". . . about the people you were married to. Isn't *that* interesting?"

"Not you, too! Damn it, Seth, you're as bad as Ma!"

"No, I'm not. I'm just teasing, and I don't gossip either."

"Go on," Gabe said with an affectionate grin. "Get the hell out of here."

                    *   *   *

The girls—all four of them—came home after school, hungry, laughing, loquacious, and filled the house with life.

"Your mother said don't eat her out of house and home, and be sure you pick up after yourselves."

Gabe was surprised to find he enjoyed their banter and gaiety. They'd all had shots at school and compared arms and told about a younger girl who'd fainted. More than once he laughed, listening to them, continuing to patch plaster on the inside walls.

"We're going!" one of them called.

"Where?" he called back.

"Over to the Spears' to look at Aunt Grace's old dresses!"

"Change your clothes first! Isobel, you go home and change your . . ." He was ordering thin air. They were halfway across the yard and he was shaking his head, happy for their freedom, in spite of himself.

They were still gone at five when Roberta came home and found Gabe washing off his mortarboard and tools by the pump. She walked through the quiet house and followed the sounds toward the backyard, where he was down on one knee beside a bucket with his back to the house. He didn't hear her coming along the curled wooden boards that served as a walkway to the pump. She stopped five feet behind him and said, "I'm glad you're still here."

He whipped around a quarter turn, caught unawares. Then he settled back on one heel, with a wrist caught on the lip of his bucket, fingers dripping. "So how was your first day?"

"Not bad. Only three children fainted."

"Already heard about one of them."

"Where are the girls?" She reached up to remove a hatpin and her white cap. His eyes dropped to her breasts, then veered away to his tools, which he shook off and dropped into the pail.

"At your sister's. Went to look at her old dresses."

He rose, taking in details. Her apron was dotted with specks of blood here and there and her uniform was wrinkled. A wisp of hair had pulled loose when she removed her cap, and she tucked it behind her ear while asking, "You in a hurry to leave?"

"No. Got nothing at home but an empty house."

"May I talk to you about something?"

"Sure," he said, carrying his bucket, walking with her to the back step where she sat with her elbows on her knees. He sat beside her on the wooden step, leaving a discreet distance between them. She held her cap, monkeying with it while she spoke, pushing the pin repeatedly into the hard starched cotton.

"Would you be completely truthful with me?" she said.

"Depends on what you're going to ask."

She drew a deep breath. "Elfred and Grace came over yesterday and told me they were going to have a party for me, to introduce me into polite society, so to speak. She said that they wanted to show the good citizens of Camden that even though I'm a social outcast, they're willing to have me in their house anyway in the hopes that others will be equally as magnanimous."

Amazement broadened his expression and straightened his spine. "Your sister said *that*?"

"Well, no, not exactly in those words, but the essence was the same."

"She shouldn't have done that."

"Is it really that bad? Is everybody in this town talking about me just because I'm divorced?" She gave up fiddling with her cap and looked at him.

"What do you care what they say? People are thoughtless and ignorant sometimes."

"So they are."

He shifted his gaze to the pump. "I don't gossip much myself, so I wouldn't know."

"I asked you to be honest with me. Please, Gabriel."

He, too, had a family member with whom he was displeased. He wished he could unload his dissatisfactions with his mother, but to do so would wound Roberta even more, so he remained silent.

"Why is the woman blamed when the man is unfaithful?" she said.

"I don't know, Roberta."

"These people don't even know me."

"No, they don't. So you'll just have to face them down and show them you're a good person."

"You think I'm a good person?"

"Yes, I do. Now that I've come to know you, I certainly do. Makes me feel pretty sheepish, too, 'cause when you first came to town I was just like them, making jokes at your expense."

"Yes, I remember very well."

"Am I forgiven?"

"Do you want to be?"

He thought it best not to look at her while divulging, "My family thinks there's something going on between you and me, and they're giving me the raspberries."

"What exactly does that mean—the raspberries?"

"Nothing. Forget I said it."

"What? Are they teasing you? Warning you off? What?"

"Forget it." He got to his feet, picking up his bucket. "I shouldn't have said anything. I'd better go."

Her temper spiked because she wanted whole honesty and he pulled back, afraid of it. She was a woman accustomed to talking things out, not hiding things; facing issues, not suppressing them.

"All right. Be stubborn!" she snapped, rising too, and marching inside, letting the screen door slam between them.

He watched her go, quickly upset by her uncustomary show of temper. After standing awhile, trying to decide how to handle it, he followed her inside, into the smell of wet plaster and the dusting of graham cracker crumbs left behind on the kitchen table by the girls. She was wiping them up with brusque, angry motions, refusing to glance at him when he entered the room.

"I told them to clean up after themselves. Sorry they didn't."

She threw down the dishcloth and slammed a door that had been left gaping. He stood uncertainly for a bit longer, then went through to the front room where he'd piled some tools in preparation for leaving. He felt as if there were a brick in his belly, knowing he'd displeased her. Funny, how very heavy it felt. He got all his tools and his bucket in hand and stood for a minute, alone. Then set them all down again and went back to the kitchen doorway. She was standing at a window with her arms crossed, staring out. Her cap was on the table.

"Roberta," he said.

"What?" she snapped, without looking at him.

"It doesn't matter what they say."

She spun angrily and tapped her chest. "Not to you, but to me it does! My own sister! Your family! Everybody thinking the worst of me when none of it is true! None of it! Just because I'm divorced doesn't mean I don't have morals!"

"I know that," he said quietly.

She picked up her cap and brushed passed him, heading for the stairs. "Just get out of here," she ordered in disgust. "I don't need you. I don't know why I even thought I could talk to you! I have my girls, and they're better than the rest of this town put together!"

Up the stairs she went, and he after her, grabbing her by one arm when she was halfway up. There they stood, on two different levels, she looking down and he looking up, gripping her arm while, on some existential level, they were aware of his having invaded the private part of her house by following her toward her room.

"I shouldn't have said that about my family. I'm . . . I'm sorry."

Her expression remained flat and cold. "Maybe you should have your brother finish the work around here."

He felt a queer stab of loss. Seconds ticked by and he still held her in place. "That what you want?"

"Yes, I think it is." And after a pause, sarcastically, "Of course, just because he's married doesn't mean they won't think I'm entertaining him too, isn't that right? Would you please release my arm?"

He did, reluctantly. "You've got my brother all wrong. He's the only one who stands up for you."

"Oh, so you've been discussing me with him, too. That makes Elfred and your brother and how many others?"

Suddenly he grew impatient with her misconstruing everything he said. "Now stop it!" he shouted. "That's not true, and you know it. All right, maybe it was with Elfred, at first, but I apologized for that. And I don't go whispering about you behind your back anymore, not since I've gotten to know you better."

She forced a wry laugh, touched her brow as if clearing her head and went up the rest of the stairs. "What are we fighting about? I don't even know! You're nothing but my carpenter, for heaven's sake, and I'm standing here wasting my time with you?" She disappeared around the upstairs corner. "Tell your brother I want him to finish this job!" she shouted from her bedroom.

He shouted back, "I don't want him to!"

Her head reappeared. "Oh no? Well, I do!" She disappeared again.

"I started it, I'll finish it!" he yelled. Then even louder, "Roberta, get back here!"

She reappeared at the top of the steps, unbuttoning her apron behind her. "Stop yelling, Farley. Pack up your tools and go, because I don't know what's going on between us, but whatever it is, I don't need the aggravation in my life. I've got my girls, and my job, and my motorcar, and I'm happy as a lark. Now go, and send your brother tomorrow morning!"

Wham! Her bedroom door slammed.

When she disappeared for the final time he braced an

arm on the wall and hung his head, wondering why he was arguing with her . . . a bullheaded, know-it-all smarty who set about proving at every turn that she could get along without a man. After all, she had *told* him she didn't want anything to do with men. Why was he hanging around here?

In her room, Roberta slammed her door but it was warped and swung open again. She pressed her spine against it, letting her temper settle. Silence from him. A long silence while she wondered what he was doing down there. Then at last she heard his footsteps clunk away and the sound of his truck driving off.

She removed her uniform and put it in cold water to soak, then played the piano to calm herself.

While she was playing the girls arrived with some of Grace's old dresses, announcing that they were going to perform *The Song of Hiawatha* on Sunday afternoon on the front porch. Roberta made sure Isobel went home by six. She was back an hour and a half later though, and said, "Boy, is my dad a grouch tonight! All I did was ask him if he'd come to *Hiawatha,* and he nearly bit my head off! He said we always go to Grandma's on Sunday afternoon, and I got so mad I had to get out of there!"

Roberta thought smugly, *Good! He's upset me, let him be upset as well!*

He did not send Seth to finish the job for the remainder of that week. Instead, he made sure he got there after Roberta left in the morning and finished before she returned in the afternoon. She didn't know who was doing the work and told herself she didn't care. Each day she saw progress—the walls sanded, painted, the woodwork revarnished. A new doorknob on the back door. A shim put under one corner of the piano so it sat level. The heat register in the ceiling painted. Her bedroom door adjusted so it would close properly. And that's when she knew.

On Saturday she commandeered one of Grace's old dresses from the costume stack, took it in severely, polished up her run-over black shoes and drove over to the Spears' house for their party.

Who should be there but Gabriel Farley.

He was drinking from a silver punch cup when their eyes collided across the room. He raised his cup and she flashed him a dismissing smile, then avoided him while everybody else in the place was being introduced. Elfred was a respected businessman; his peers were all there: Jay Tunstill from the bank, Hamlin Young from Boynton's, plus many more, along with their wives. The women tended to offer sterile hellos and back off immediately after being introduced to Roberta. The men held her hand too long and ogled her when they thought she or their wives were not looking. Elfred touched her every chance he got, always on the waist or back, always under the guise of being the polite host, whether Grace was near or not.

By nine o'clock Roberta was ready to take a hatchet to his elbow. That's when the music started and Farley came up behind her in the conservatory beside an enormous potted palm.

"I'm not going to let you get by without speaking to me."

She glanced at him coolly. "Hello, Gabriel."

"You look very nice this evening."

"Thank you. So do you." He'd had a haircut and was wearing a black suit and white shirt and tie. His freshly shaved face was lightly burnished from outdoor work. Though his eyebrows would never lie neatly, their unruliness added to his appeal. He was, in fact, a sturdy, handsome man.

"Are you still mad at me?"

"Yes. Are you still doing the work in my house?"

"Yes."

"I thought so. Thank you for leveling the piano."

"You're welcome."

"And for fixing my bedroom door so it'll close."

"That's so it'll work the next time you want to slam it in my face."

"You deserved it. You made me very mad that day."

"Well, I'll be finishing up Monday, then I'll be out of your hair for good."

"Ah," she said, and took a sip of punch. "Well, be sure you leave the keys to my new back door."

"Of course."

She glanced over the crowd. "I thought maybe your mother would be here. I wanted to meet her."

"I told you, she and the Spears are not particular friends."

"Oh yes, that's right. I thought maybe she avoided coming because of her objections to me."

He refused to comment.

"I hear our girls are putting on *Hiawatha* on Sunday afternoon," she remarked.

"So Isobel tells me."

"I also hear you bit her head off and told her you always go to your mother's on Sunday afternoon."

"Damn that Isobel. Does she have to tell you everything?"

"I found it very amusing. But then I'm sure you hear things about me that I'd rather you didn't hear."

"I've heard a few. Roberta, I was wondering . . . could I walk you home?"

"No, you can't, Gabriel. I drove my car."

"Then, could I drive you home? Because I walked."

"Why on earth would you want to drive me home?"

He tried to hold his exasperation in check but could not. "Honest to God, Roberta, sometimes I really don't *know* why! Do you know what an exasperating woman you are?"

If she hadn't laughed, they might have been all right. But his honesty brought an unexpected outburst that could be heard above the pianist, who was playing a Strauss waltz. Several people turned around to look.

"Oh, all right then," Roberta conceded. "What the heck."

When the party ended she expected him to slip up to her car secretly after she was safely inside it. Instead, he fell in beside her in the vestibule and took her elbow as she was thanking Grace and Elfred.

"Maybe I should see that you get home safely, Birdy," Elfred offered.

"I'm seeing Roberta home, Elfred. No need for you to worry about her." At least a half dozen people overheard and saw Elfred's gaze drop to Gabe's hand as it commandeered Roberta's elbow.

On their way down the walk she said, "Hadn't you

better watch yourself? Your mother will hear about it on the party line."

"Roberta," he said pleasantly, "will you please shut up about my mother?"

She smiled and followed orders.

He cranked her car and drove it without any complaints from her. He'd expected the moment he made a move toward it she'd say, *I can do it myself, Gabriel!* It pleased him that she let him do something for her, for once.

When they reached her house he shut off the motor and walked her to the porch.

"I think we threw Elfred a curveball, leaving together," Gabe remarked.

"I wanted to throw him a lot more than a curveball all night long."

"He does like to let his hands linger on you, doesn't he?"

"Invites me to his house, then paws me in front of his wife. I could have clipped him."

"Why didn't you?"

"Next time, maybe. Thank you for rescuing me."

"You're welcome."

"So I take it you're not coming to see the play tomorrow."

"Oh, of course I'm coming. How could I not when they've been carrying on like some fancy Shakespearean repertoire company? Besides, if I didn't, I'd look like a degenerate next to you."

His irony put a smile on her face.

"Well, I'll see you then," she said as they reached the steps. He stopped and let her ascend them alone. Where he stood, moonlight shone; where she moved, shadows obscured. The screen door spring sang in the dark. "I like my new screen door," she said, letting it rest against her rump while looking back at him. "Thanks for getting it."

"You're welcome."

"And for bringing me home."

He should have turned and left. She should have gone directly inside. Instead he remained, washed by milky night light, looking up at her dim form above him with the white edge of the screen door slicing down her shoulder. A moment of motionlessness passed before she said, "Do we know what we're doing, Gabriel?"

Her near frankness took him by surprise, but he stood relaxed, in place. "I don't think so, Roberta," he replied.

There was no question they were thinking about kissing. The setting and situation were classic—a shadowed porch, moonlight white on the lawn, the smell of spring lilacs blossoming somewhere nearby, the streetlamps of the town circling the harbor below, a man and woman in party finery having made up after an argument. But the idea was folly. Too much had been said. Claims had been made that warned them any intimacy would be capricious at best, misguided at worst. If they gave in to their whim they would undoubtedly regret it later.

So they said good night and she closed the new screen door between them.

They were perhaps a little too proper with each other the next day when he came to her house to watch the play. Anyone who knew them could have sensed undercurrents. But the only ones who'd ever seen them together for any length of time were the girls, and they were too busy to notice. The closest Roberta and Gabriel came to each other was at either end of the piano when she asked if he'd help them move it across the front room to the open door so that it could be heard from the yard.

The production was poorly attended. Elfred and Grace found it beneath their dignity to sit on the grass of Roberta's front yard and watch their daughters cavort in Indian costumes. Sophie, their maid, came in their place. Myra had begged off with a headache, and Isobel's grandmother, while inquisitive enough to poke her nose into Roberta's house when Roberta was absent, withheld her presence on the off chance it might have been misconstrued as a nod of acceptance for the divorced woman.

But one set of parents came—the DuMosses, whom Roberta suspected wanted to check out the place where their daughter was spending a lot of time, and judge it for themselves. They were polite but reserved, and brought their own blanket to sit on.

Some of the kids from school came as well, including the boys who had given Roberta the fish. And—surprisingly—Rebecca's and Susan's English teachers, Mrs. Roberson and Miss Werm.

The girls had been truly inventive, having set some stanzas to music and constructed their version of a birch-bark canoe to act as a stage prop while Marcelyn recited, "Give me of your bark, O Birch-Tree!" They had made a shroud of black with a yellow beak for Trudy's head, and turned it around to reveal red on the

opposite side while she recited the part about how the
woodpecker's head got red. Each of them had chosen a
section of the legend to recite in costume: about what
makes the shadows on the moon, and why the rainbow
has colors, and why birds sing. Rebecca, wearing the
moccasins enchanted, whose stride measured a mile, recited the stanza about Hiawatha's wooing of Minnehaha. It began:

> "As unto the bow the cord is,
> So unto the man is woman;
> Though she bends him, she obeys him,
> Though she draws him, yet she follows;
> Useless each without the other!"

Roberta, sitting on the grass with her legs out-
stretched and crossed, leaned back on her hands and
moved her lips silently with the familiar words. She felt
Gabriel's regard like one feels sunlight, a concentrated
power focused in her direction, and when she turned
her head, he was studying her in somber reflection, as
if unable to help himself.

Bow and cord, man and woman.

It was a peculiar moment, endowed not with enchant-
ment but with the realization that resistance existed on
both their parts; further, that the *need* for resistance had
developed somewhere along the line, and it in itself was
a threat. How very ironic that they had stated their
stands—he still loving his wife, she soured on men by
the one she'd had—yet they felt their attraction for each
other working on them insidiously, complicated by so
many things: her divorced status, the town's view of

her, his mother's admonitions, their children's thriving friendship, their own friendship and vulnerability to gossip, the fact that two of their children's teachers could be watching them at this very moment.

Hoping their exchange of glances had not been observed, they returned their attention to the porch where the production continued.

> "Though she bends him she obeys him
> Though she draws him, yet she
> follows . . ."

Old Longfellow knew about men and women in this state.

> "Useless each without the other."

But I am not useless without Gabriel Farley, Roberta thought. I've proven that. I've made the difficult move here from Boston and I can raise my girls, provide for them, love them enough for two and be happy doing it. I have a house, a motorcar and a job that gives me security and dignity. Why would I want to jeopardize any of that by succumbing to any paltry attraction I might feel toward the man?

Neither did Gabe feel useless without Roberta. He too had a daughter he loved, a fine, clean, spotless house where everything ran smoothly (unlike hers), family who helped him out and cared for him, a thriving trade and the respect of the town. Why would he want to risk any of that by taking up with this divorced woman?

When the play ended, they remained polite but distant, applauding with the others, visiting with the teachers, gathering compliments on their daughters.

But while Roberta hugged hers unreservedly, Gabriel gave Isobel little more than an awkward pat on the back, and Roberta wondered if he was even capable of showing affection.

When her guests dispersed, Roberta bid him a goodbye kept intentionally impersonal, certainly far less enthusiastic than the one she bid Isobel. Isobel got the customary hug, smile and loving send-off that meant *Come back anytime.*

On Monday afternoon Gabriel was already finished and loaded up and cranking his engine when Roberta brought her car careening to a halt behind his truck.

"Gabriel! Wait!"

He let his hand fall from the crank and strolled forward to meet her.

"Something wrong?"

"No. I just promised I'd give you that inoculation, that's all. I knew this was your last day, so I finished up early and hurried home. Come on in the house and I'll take care of it for you."

"Oh, you didn't have to bother."

"It's no bother. Come on in."

He had little choice but to follow her or look like a fraidy-cat.

"This going to hurt?" he asked, growing tense inside.

"Mmm . . . a little. But it's so important. If we inoculate enough people we can lick diphtheria. Everyone counts. Next week I'll be driving over to Northport to start on the schools over there."

She led him straight to the kitchen and ordered, "Roll up your shirtsleeve."

She left him standing while she washed her hands and swabbed his arm with alcohol, then got out her equipment. "Look away if it bothers you." But he could not. What she was holding looked like a damned knitting needle, and the idea of having it jammed into his hide made Gabe blanch even before she gripped his arm to draw the skin tight. At the last moment she looked up and saw how pale he was. "Don't look," she said quietly. He turned away and closed his eyes. When the needle pierced his skin he flinched and whispered, "Sonofabitch."

"You all right?"

He sucked air through his clamped teeth and nodded.

"I've never heard you swear before."

"That hurts."

"It will for a while, and tomorrow you may run a little fe—" She looked up. His eyes were closed and he was weaving.

"Sit down, Gabriel," she ordered, guiding him backward to a chair.

"I'm sorry . . . I . . ." He couldn't finish. Everything was going white and distant.

"Spread your knees and put your head down." She put her hand on the back of his head and forced it down, her hand remaining on his thick sandy hair and the coarse-grained skin of his neck. It felt cool and clammy. She stroked it once, twice. "Better now?"

He nodded silently, his head still hanging.

She could see he wasn't.

"I'll get a cool cloth. Stay there."

He was still curled over like a vulture when she returned with the cloth. "Here . . . put this on your face. It'll help."

He took it in both palms and buried his face in it, bracing on his splayed knees.

"Take big, deep breaths," she said. "It'll pass."

While he followed orders she watched the rise and fall of his shoulder blades inside a tightly stretched red plaid shirt. She did what she would have done for any woozy child in school, put her hand there and lightly rubbed, making small, comforting circles on Gabriel Farley's muscular back.

Slowly Gabriel's light-headedness faded and he became aware of her rhythmic stroking. It had been a long, long time since any human being had comforted him in any way. Human affection had been snuffed out of his life with Caroline's death. His muzziness disappeared but he remained doubled forward, enjoying the feel of her gentle distraction, rocking slightly with each circle as her fingertips rode the valley between his shoulder blades. It was late afternoon, the sun streaming in the window and the call of gulls wafting in from outside. He'd spent some nice hours with her here inside her kitchen, where things were familiar. Outside somebody was mowing a lawn, the sound scissored through the house along with the green scent of clipped grass. And being touched, soothed was something he hadn't realized he'd missed.

"That feels good," he mumbled into the cloth.

So she rubbed him some more, watching him rock on the chair, so relaxed he'd given up all form of resistance.

After a while she bent forward at the waist to peer

at his right ear and jaw. "You're not falling asleep, are you, Gabriel?"

"Hmm."

"Feel better now?"

"Mm-hmm."

As her hand slid away from his shoulder he lifted his head. His face was damp from the cloth, hair pushed up and darker above his forehead where it, too, had gotten damp. His eyes were unguarded and steady on her. When he handed her the cloth his fingers closed over her hand and pulled.

"Gabriel, I don't think—"

"Don't say anything," he said, and toppled her onto his lap.

"Stop it, Gabriel."

"You mean that?"

"Yes. I'm not starting anything with you."

"I'm not starting anything with you either. I've just been thinking about kissing you, that's all. I got the idea you'd been thinking about it too."

"It's a stupid idea."

"You talk too much, you know that?"

When he kissed her she stopped resisting. His skin was cool, still damp, rough around his lips from the day's growth of whiskers. His tongue was warm and the slightest bit timid. She had fallen with one arm folded against his chest, the other free to roam. It did nothing of the sort but lay against his shirtfront inertly while at her back he still held the damp cloth. But he took his time, and grew surprisingly facile as the seconds stretched on. She opened her eyes once to see if his were closed. They were, and the glimpse of his eyelashes at close range brought an unbidden skitter along her limbs. It had been years since she'd kissed a man— the slobbering pleas of her husband had grown unpalatable years before their divorce—and she certainly wasn't going to let herself be unduly swayed by the first, thus becoming what all divorcées were rumored to be. So she let him do the work and remained merely amenable. By the time she sat up the wet cloth had wilted a circle of starch on the back of her white apron.

She rose from his lap in full control of her emotions and stood with her back to him. "This is a very bad idea," she said.

"I told myself the same thing."

"It was just that poem yesterday and all that claptrap about bows and cords."

"Maybe. Maybe not."

"Wouldn't that party line burn up if anybody in this town found out what we just did?"

"Well, I'm not going to tell them." He sat up straighter as if his head had finally cleared. "I've got more sense than that."

"No, of course not." She took several steps and found something to keep her hands busy: some greasy knives the girls had left leaning on the butter dish. "The girls will be home soon. Maybe you'd better go."

"Sure," he said, pushing up from the chair.

"Are you all right now? Is the dizziness gone?"

"Fine. Sorry I was such a baby."

"You weren't a baby. That just happens to some people."

"Well, thanks for the shot . . . I think."

At last she turned to face him. He would not have

guessed he'd just kissed her from the businesslike way she dealt with him. "Did you finish everything here? I mean, your work is all done?"

"All done. Like I said, I won't be bothering you anymore."

She didn't know whether to walk him to the door or stay where she was. In the end she stayed and he left without another word.

Ten

At his house evenings were lonelier for Gabe. Isobel spent every spare minute at the Jewetts'. He was of two minds regarding her desertion: On the one hand he didn't blame her for hanging around that place, with all its cheerful activity; on the other, he felt abandoned, for this was still her home, he was still her father, and she had responsibilities here. She cared about them less and less. The housework and any cooking was left to him. His mother—stubborn to a fault—had been as good as her word and refused to refill his cookie jar or come over to change the sheets. Naturally, she had stopped bringing leftovers, too.

One night during the week following his last encounter with Roberta, he had made a kettle of oyster stew for supper and was waiting for Isobel when the telephone rang. Two shorts and a long, that was his ring.

He went to the wooden box and lifted the earpiece from the prongs. "Hello?"

"Hello, Mr. Farley? This is Susan Jewett. We just got our new telephone!"

"You did? Well now, isn't that exciting."

"Mother said we could each make one call, and I said I wanted to call you because I was wondering if it would be okay if Isobel stays with us for supper."

He thought, *What are you having? Maybe I'll come, too.* He said, "Isobel's over there an awful lot."

"Oh, but we love having her! Don't we, Mother?" In the background he could hear the piano playing and pictured Roberta at the keyboard while the girls overran the house. Susan said, "Mother says of course we do, so *please*, Mr. Farley? Can she stay?"

"She probably has homework."

"But it's Friday night and school is almost over and the teachers are hardly giving us any. *Please*, Mr. Farley? We're trying to talk Mother into a clambake because pretty soon the tide will be going out and it would be so fun!"

"I've already made supper for Isobel and me."

"But can't she stay anyway? Mother, he won't let her . . ." Susan's voice got whiny and trailed away as if she'd turned from the phone. ". . . and I told him about the clambake and everything."

The piano ceased and a moment later Roberta's voice came on. "Gabriel?"

"Oh! Roberta . . . hello."

"We really do want Isobel to stay. Do you mind?"

It's lonely here, he wanted to say, but of course could not. "She's there so much."

"Because we enjoy her. The girls talked me into a shore picnic. They want to dig some clams."

"Well, in that case, I guess it'll be okay."

"Good . . . well . . . thanks, Gabriel."

He hurried on to keep her from hanging up so soon. "I just don't want her to wear out her welcome."

"No, she won't. And don't worry about her coming home after dark. I'll drive her this time."

"That's good of you, Roberta."

"No trouble at all, since we'll be in the motorcar anyway. Well . . ."

Her pause brought a fresh sense of imminent desertion, and he scrabbled about for something to keep her on the line. "So, how'd everything go up in Northport this week?"

"Fine. I finished there and went on to Lincolnville."

"Have any fainters on your hands?"

"Oh, Gabriel . . . you didn't faint. You just got a little light-headed."

"Well, I felt like a gol-dang fool."

"Why? You were right. It *is* a big needle."

A lull fell and he imagined her impatient to pack a hamper and get their outing under way. He knew he should release her, but only the silent house waited, and his pathetic oyster stew, and he wanted to keep her on the line for some deeper reason that he was unwilling to recognize. "Listen, Roberta." He cleared his throat and polished the edge of the oak telephone box with a thumb. "About what happened that day. I know you weren't too pleased with me and I just wanted to say I'm sorry. I shouldn't have pressed the issue."

"It's okay, Gabriel. It's all forgotten."

"No. No, I could tell afterwards that you were . . . well, you acted pretty distant and you couldn't wait to get rid of me. You didn't want to start anything in the first place and I should have let it go at that."

"Gabriel, the reason I didn't want to start anything is because of how this town has labeled me. I have to be more careful than most, and we both know that. So let's just forget it because it didn't amount to anything."

It didn't? Funny, but Gabe thought it had. Her remark left him feeling faintly emasculated.

"Well, I've been thinking about it all week, and I just wanted to clear that up."

"Gabriel? May I ask you something?"

" 'Course."

"Isobel says your mother has stopped filling your cookie jar and coming over to help out with housework. Is that because of me?"

"Isobel said that?"

"Yes, she did."

"There's not much housework around here with just the two of us and both of us gone all day long. And now Isobel seems to stay at your place most days after school."

"You haven't answered my question, Gabriel."

He cleared his throat. "No, it's not because of you."

The line went quiet for several seconds while Gabriel suspected she figured out he was lying. Then she surprised him by asking, "Well, in that case, would you be interested in continuing this conversation on the beach? If you're all alone you might as well come and dig clams with the girls and me."

He forgot about rubbing the phone box with his thumb.

"Well, that sounds mighty tempting, but you sure about this?"

"It's been years since I've done a clambake and I could use a little help with these four rambunctious daughters of ours."

"I'd like that, Roberta. Give me a couple of minutes to change and I'll be right over."

He showed up in fifteen minutes, dressed in tan duck trousers, canvas shoes and a roomy Norfolk jacket. Crossing Roberta's familiar front yard, his step was animated and he was whistling. He bounded up the porch steps in two giant leaps and called through the open front door, "Anybody here?"

The racket inside was laughable: clattering kitchenware, slamming doors, girls' giddy voices and Roberta shouting orders.

"I forgot, I don't have a spade. Isobel, call your father and see if he'll bring a spade! And a clam rake, too!"

He walked right in and stopped in her kitchen doorway. "I have a spade and a clam rake and some bushel baskets in the truck, plus a box of wood scraps to build a fire. Nobody's got to call me."

Roberta spun around and smiled brightly. "Oh, Gabriel, you're here!" She was back to the Roberta he first knew, the nurse's uniform gone, the hair falling from its tether, wearing her run-over black shoes and a sacklike dress of oversized blue-and-white squares with dollar-size white buttons down the front. The dress needed pressing, the shoes needed replacing and the hair needed tidying, but as he stood in the doorway observing the commotion he felt alive as he had not in days, being with her and the kids again.

"'Lo, Roberta," he said, low-key.

"That didn't take you long."

"Nope."

"Daddy, hi! I can't believe you're really going with us!"

Isobel bombarded him and hugged his waist. He dropped his hands to her shoulders but Roberta saw he was out of his element with spontaneous affection.

"Mrs. Jewett invited me," he told Isobel. "Hope that's okay."

"Oh, this is going to be so much fun! She says we can all dig clams."

"Thought you hated clams."

"Well, I do, but . . ." She released him and gave a sheepish one-shouldered shrug. "Gosh, I haven't had them since Mother was alive, and I've grown up a lot since then. I'll probably just love them!"

He glanced at Roberta, thinking this was going to be the best Friday night he'd had in years.

Roberta got busy again, putting a clam knife and salt and pepper shakers in the open hamper on the table. "Let's see . . . butter and lemon and salt and pepper. Too early in the year for corn on the cob, but we've got some sweet potatoes. Rebecca, get plates; Susan, get silverware; Isobel, some glasses, please; and Lydia, will you find a blanket, dear?"

Gabe watched as his daughter moved with the others to follow orders. She knew right where to find glasses.

He moved to Roberta's shoulder and said under his breath, "She certainly knows her way around your house."

"That's the kind of house I run, Gabe. Not much formality around here."

When the last items were packed into the hamper, she closed the lid and he took it from her hands. "Here, I'll carry that."

"We need a piece of canvas," she said.

"I brought that."

"And some fresh water?"

"Brought that, too."

"Hey," she teased, "you're a good man to have around. How'd you round up all that stuff in fifteen minutes?"

"That's the kind of house I run," he said with a grin. "Everything in its place so it's easy to find."

"And you found time to change clothes, too?"

"Ayup."

She returned his grin. "Talk about a couple of opposites; we're them, aren't we, Gabe?"

Opposites or not, they were both in glad moods as they herded the children outside like a regular family of six. Yes, it was a simulated family, but they felt seduced by the wholesomeness of tramping off on a simple adventure that would fill an evening with togetherness. The four girls got along extremely well, as if Isobel truly were a half sister. Roberta and Gabriel, now that the kiss was put behind them, found acceptable companionship in each other and, as before, enjoyed having another adult to talk with after years of having only the children.

The May sun was still twenty-five degrees off the horizon when they started out. Gabe cranked Roberta's car and she drove while all four girls stacked themselves in the backseat, singing, *We sail the ocean blue, And our saucy ship's a beauty.*

Roberta and Gabe could barely hear each other above "H.M.S. Pinafore."

"Where's the best place to dig?" she asked.

"Out at the Glen Cove flats."

"Oh yes, I remember. Down toward Rockport."

"You used to go there?"

"Sure, when I was in school. Did you?"

"In school and after I was married . . . with Caroline."

"But you haven't been back since she died?"

He studied her briefly, then shook his head. "Not since she died."

"So will it be difficult for you?"

"I don't know. I'll find out when we get there, won't I?"

In the backseat the girls were bellowing, "*. . . when at anchor we ride, on the Portsmouth tide . . .* "

She parked on the hill above the Glen Cove clam flats, and the girls tumbled out and went clambering over the rocks that had been nudged by a million tides to form a rugged rim around the upper scoop of the cove. Roberta and Gabriel stood beside the car and watched them bound away with bushel baskets and clam rakes while behind them the shadows of the mountains sloped down to the sea and stained the evening blue. Before them, the flats—mushroom brown and dull except where a powerless surf lazily licked the sand silver—collected the girls' footprints. Pebbles and driftwood pocked the washed surface, too. In places the retreating tide had left flotsam in ragged windrows that created a scalloped design along the shore. Among the rocks and over the sand, crabs scuttled, searching out their supper, dipping safely into their holes when the girls pounded past.

Gabriel studied the peaceful scene and said, "She wasn't particularly crazy about clams, but she loved to go clamming. Especially in the morning, when the sun was on the water and the islands looked ghostly out there in the sea-smoke. Sometimes she'd talk me into bringing her out early, even before sunrise, so she wouldn't miss the spectacle."

Roberta turned to study his profile against the back-drop of rocky shoreline. A faint puff of wind fluttered the hair against his forehead. Twilight painted shadows beside his straight nose and somber mouth.

"I envy you your happy memories. I wish I had more of them."

He dragged himself from his reverie to look at her. Motionless, he stood, while the girls' voices drifted up to them—"Oh, here's one! Dig! Dig!"—joined by the coarse chorus of some gulls whose mealtime had been interrupted, too. Roberta had the feeling Gabriel was seeing another woman, in another time, before he finally stirred himself and rejoined her in the present.

"I'll start digging the pit if you'll gather some sea-weed." He stepped out onto the rocks, sending the sand crabs scuttling again.

For the next quarter hour everybody kept busy. While Gabe built the fire and Roberta collected kelp, the three youngest girls searched the flats for tiny sand spouts, where they dug. Rebecca, barefoot, knotted her skirts across her thighs and methodically plied the shallow water, dragging the clam rake while keeping an eye out for telltale mud clouds on the bottom. As the girls turned up their bounty, Roberta washed it. The sun slipped behind the mountain and left the air cooler and bluer. The distant islands lost their gold tips and seemed to settle deeper into Penobscot Bay as if snuggling in for the night.

When the fire had subsided to coals, Roberta knelt

beside Gabriel and helped him layer the rocks, seaweed, foods and canvas, which they anchored at the corners with more rocks.

"There," Gabe said, sitting back on his heels. "In an hour we'll have a meal fit for a king."

"I'm starved," Lydia said.

"Yeah, me too," Isobel added.

"Why don't you all sing something?" Roberta suggested. "That'll make the time pass faster."

"I don't feel like singing," Susan put in. "Let's go see if we can outdig some sand crabs."

They moved off into the growing shadows, leaving their parents behind. Gabriel stretched to his feet. "I'll build us another fire so we've got something to poke at."

He did, and they sat on turtle-shaped rocks while the dusk and the dampness lowered upon the shore, cooling their backs while their faces grew as orange as paired sunsets in the glow of their small fire. The rocks were hard, but each of them had experienced clambakes before and would have disdained any more comfortable seat; after all, rock-sitting was part of the total experience. The fire pit seethed and sent out a soft, warm hiss that kept them company.

Roberta glanced up at the sky and recited,

> "Lo! comes the evening, purply soft
> To lift the glowing stars aloft."

Gabriel glanced over.

"Who wrote that?"

"I did."

He pondered a moment. "You Jewetts are really something when it comes to verses. You always manage to leave me in the dust."

"Leave you in the dust?"

"You know so much that I don't know, Roberta."

"Perhaps I do, but I cannot build a porch."

Sometimes she could really put him at ease, this woman in the wrinkled dress and tumbledown hair. He'd come to prize spending time with her, and he was beginning to admit it wasn't only because of the children. "I hadn't thought of that," he said. Now that he did, however, he felt less ignorant. "You write any more of that poem?"

"No, but I can if you want me to."

"Just like that?"

She shrugged as if the talent were common.

"You mean you could just spout lines that rhyme, without thinking for two hours and looking in books and crossing off mistakes?"

"I always liked poetry and music and drama. That's where my girls get it."

"So make up some more."

She squinted one eye at the rising moon. Her lips moved soundlessly for a while before she caught the line . . .

"Then just when dreams are turning fey
They slip and fall and turn to day."

He appreciated her silently for a while before speaking. "You're really something, Roberta, you know that?"

"And you think you're not?"

"Not like that, no. I've never been good with words. My brother just said the other day that I don't talk much."

"You do around me."

"Around you I seem to. Maybe because there's always so much talking in your house that a person feels like he's got to do some of it himself or get lost in the woodwork."

She laughed, then picked up a stick and poked the fire.

"Did you and your wife talk a lot?"

"Not a lot, no. We could be quiet together and still feel comfortable."

"That's nice. When my husband and I were quiet together it was because we had grown to such a state of disrespect that we had nothing to say anymore."

"The more you tell me about your marriage, the worse it sounds."

"And the more you tell me about yours, the better it sounds, which is quite an eye-opener for me, because I never knew anyone who had a happy marriage. I thought they were all lessons in tolerance."

"No, you're wrong there. Not all."

"All of them I ever witnessed. Take my parents, for instance. He was at the tavern more often than she wanted him to be, so she bellyached constantly; then when he was home she harped at him to fix this, mend that, but when he did, it was never good enough for her. She criticized everything he did, until I could understand why he liked it better at the tavern. I guess that's why I started escaping into my literature and music, so I could shut out their arguing."

He took time to mull over his own parents' relationship. "My parents got along pretty well. Sometimes her gossip aggravated him, but so did his pipe smoking. She said it clouded up her windows. He had a tendency to be lazy and she had a tendency to rush through everything, but, I don't know—they seemed to work things out."

Roberta said, "I think those who work things out are rarer than those who don't. I had a friend in Boston named Irene. She and her husband were really crazy about each other. But jealous! Heavenly days, they could get into fights about total strangers they passed on the street. If one of them returned a hello, the other one accused him of flirting, and the fight was on. If she went to the market for a loaf of bread, she had to account for every single minute she was away, and even then he accused her of ridiculous dalliances. So even though they loved each other, it never seemed enough. Why, it got to the point where they couldn't even be civil to their own friends, then after every fight Irene would come and cry on my shoulder. I used to do my best to comfort her until one day she accused *me* of making eyes at her husband. That ended our friendship, and I felt very bad about it.

"Then, of course, there are Elfred and Grace. That marriage is a farce if I ever saw one."

"I'd have to agree with you there."

They pondered the Spears for a while, Gabriel now poking the fire along with Roberta. Some sparks rose as he inquired, "Elfred been around bothering you anymore?"

"Not since the day you scared him off."

"Well, I'm glad about that. I have to admit, I got a little hot under the collar that day."

"Oh?"

"Elfred thinks he's God's gift to women, and until then I'd always laughed about it. But I didn't think it was funny that day."

Side by side, with their ankles crossed, they turned to study each other. They stopped poking the fire and let the tips of their sticks burn. The moon had risen and spread a gold-beaten path across the water. The buried kelp was beginning to give off an herbal aroma that contrasted with the rather musty one lifting from the warmed tarp. The soft slap of the waves lifted from the edge of the water, and in the unseen distance one of the girls shrieked, followed by a chorus of muffled laughter.

Finally Roberta asked quietly, "So how is it, being back here where you used to bring Caroline?"

"Not as bad as I thought it would be. Quite enjoyable, actually."

"Once before you mentioned a day you thought was going to be bad for you. April eighteenth."

"Oh, that."

"Am I treading on hallowed ground?"

"Surprisingly, no. A month ago you would have been, but—I don't know—maybe I'm healing at last."

"So what did you do on April eighteenth this year?"

"Fed her roses for her, same as I do every year. They climb on a pergola outside the kitchen door that I have to walk under every time I go into the house."

"Does Isobel do it with you?"

"No."

"Because she doesn't want to or because you never asked her to?"

"When I feed the roses is always my special time with Caroline. I . . . well, I talk to her then."

He was studying the fire. She was studying him. "Be careful, Gabriel."

He looked over. "Of what?"

"Shutting out your daughter too long."

He bristled. "I haven't shut out my daughter."

"She talks at our house. She tells us things."

"Like what? If she said I shut her out, it's not true."

Roberta could tell this was testy ground. "I'm not saying you do it consciously."

"If it wasn't for Isobel, I'd have lost my mind when Caroline died!"

"Have you ever told her that?"

"I don't have to tell her. She knows."

"Funny, she thinks she's in your way sometimes."

"In my way?"

Roberta tossed her stick into the fire, brushed off her hands and hugged her knees. "Affection is a curious commodity. It opens mouths almost as easily as it opens hearts."

"But why would she think she's in my way?"

"You never hug her, Gabriel. You never touch her. I've watched you and I can see that you don't know how. I imagine when Caroline was alive she did that for both of you. That's often how it is, the mother does the overt loving. But you're her only parent now, and she needs to know you love her."

Gabe said nothing. He stared into Roberta's firelit eyes for some moments, and she could see his jaw was clamped hard. "Showing it is hard for some people," she told him. "If you don't know how, watch me." He turned away so she could no longer read his face. "It's the little things that count, Gabriel. We say 'I love you' in a thousand ways; some have words and some don't— touches, smiles, maybe a little warning, like 'Keep warm.' 'Keep dry.' 'Watch your head!' 'Your dress is pretty.' 'Is that a new hair ribbon? It matches your eyes.' 'I'd love to come watch you put on *Hiawatha*.' 'Why don't we walk outside and pick some of Mother's roses together?' Have you ever done that with her?"

She was in too deep to withdraw now. There were things on her mind that she simply had to say, on Isobel's behalf.

"She's told me that she's not allowed to touch her mother's dresses, and that the couple times when she has, she's been severely scolded. Perhaps you should let her someday. What would you have felt like if you'd been told you could not touch any of Caroline's things after she died? You would have been so hurt, Gabriel."

He spoke at last, and she could hear his banked anger. "I didn't want her getting into them with her friends, and you know how destructive children can be."

"She's never had friends, Gabriel. She told us so. Not until my girls came along, because you always expected her to fill in for her mother on housekeeping duties, do her homework, meet responsibilities first and foremost. I've always thought quite the opposite. Teach children enough to get them by so they can fend for themselves when necessary, but give them their freedom. After all, they'll be adults just like *that!*"—Roberta snapped her fingers—"And then they'll have families of their own and all the responsibilities that go along with them. When they're children, let them be children. And that's what Isobel is at our house. That's why she likes it so much over there."

He faced her abruptly and argued with some ferocity, "But it was hard after Caroline died! You don't know how hard!"

"No, I don't. I can't know, because losing my husband was totally different than losing your wife. But I can imagine. And I can see you suffering still, and that tells me a lot. What I'm asking you to understand is that it was equally hard for Isobel, and you never shared that with her. You handled your grief separately from hers, and by doing so, you made her believe she was in your way. You're angry with me for being so blunt, I can tell."

"Y' damned right I am. You're accusing me of a lot of things here that I don't think I deserve."

"I'm not accusing you."

"The hell you're not!" He leaped to his feet. "You're telling me I haven't been a good father to Isobel, and just who appointed you judge!"

"I never said that."

"You've said plenty! Behind my back at your house— you just admitted it! What do you do, Roberta? Take a break from being my daughter's best friend to point out how her father suffers by comparison?"

"Oh, don't be ridiculous, Gabriel."

"Oh, now I'm ridiculous, am I? Well, maybe I have been, for letting her hang around there too much."

"Look what we found!" The girls were back, bearing a good-sized starfish. Isobel said, "We're going to boil it and keep it and maybe at Christmas if we painted it gold we could use it on the tree somehow."

"Not now, girls!" he snapped. "Roberta and I are talking about something important."

Roberta ignored him and reached out a hand. "A starfish . . . here, let me see." Then she examined the specimen and said, "Oh, it's a beauty."

Gabriel declared, "You're not bringing that thing into our house, Isobel! It'll start stinking before you ever get around to boiling it, and besides, we have a star for the top of the tree, so go throw it back."

Isobel looked nonplussed. "What's wrong, Daddy?"

What could he reply? He was being a boor and he knew it.

Roberta stepped in. "I think our food is done. Let's uncover it, girls."

"I'll uncover it!" he snapped.

Their outing was thoroughly ruined. Though jerky conversations were attempted while they ate, none were between Roberta and Gabriel. It was nearly ten o'clock when they repacked the hamper. He shoveled sand into the fire pit and Roberta sent the girls on to the car with the bushel baskets and clam rake. She watched him ramming the shovel into the sand and tossing some on the smaller fire with pent-up anger in every beat. Finally the coals disappeared and left them in moonlight. He threw two more shovelfuls and they listened to the lonely sound of the metal biting the sand.

Finally, she simply had to speak.

"You're really mad at me. I mean, *really*."

He leaned over to whisk something up off the sand, something unnecessary, she thought, to escape facing her. "Yes, I am, Roberta."

"Gabriel, listen to me. It's all right if you're mad at me. Just . . . just don't take it out on Isobel, okay?"

"Why should I take it out on Isobel! Jesus, Roberta, you think I'm some kind of a brute!"

"I do not. But sometimes when you're mad at me you get really grouchy with her. Just remember, this was me talking tonight, so if you want to take it out on somebody, do it on me because she doesn't deserve it."

Suddenly he turned on her and jabbed a finger northward. "You know, things ran pretty smoothly at my house before you came to town! I took care of my daughter and we got along fine! So don't think that you're the final word on how to raise children, because I was doing all right! And maybe you'd better take a look at that junk hole you live in and see if your own mothering could use a little improvement! While you're out running all over the county inoculating kids against diseases, your own are liable to catch ten others from the unsanitary conditions in your own damned house! And for God's sake, why don't you ever iron your dresses!"

By the time he finished he was shouting.

In the following silence they glared each other down and felt their blood race. Then he spun and strode across the flats, gripping the shovel handle like a javelin.

She planted her feet wide and yelled after him, "You damned bullheaded, closed-minded, jackassed plebeian dunce!" then kicked a spray of sand out of her path before heading after him.

When she reached him he was cranking the car as if he wanted to lift it and drag it home.

"I'll do it myself!" she insisted, knocking him aside. "Give me that!"

"Gladly," he shot back, and stormed around to the passenger side and got in, leaving her to struggle not only with the crank, but with the carbide headlights as well. After starting the drip, lighting the crystals and closing the lenses she finally climbed in behind the wheel.

It irritated him that he didn't have his own truck to drive and had to allow himself to be hauled around by *her*! She was too damned independent for her own good, and it was the last straw that tonight of all nights *she* was driving *him*! Furthermore, he didn't know what *plebeian* meant.

In the backseat the girls sat motionless, wary. No singing now, no chatter. Roberta put the car in gear and it jerked violently as she shifted. When it was rolling smoothly a timid voice from the rear asked, "What's wrong?"

They answered simultaneously.

Gabriel: "Nothing."

Roberta: "We had a fight."

"About what?" Rebecca asked.

Gabriel: "Nothing."

Roberta: "About what kind of parents we are."

He warned, "Roberta . . . "

"Oh, that's so typical!" she shouted. "Hide everything as if they have no right to know!"

"Roberta, I'll take this up with you privately, if at all!"

"If at all . . . Ha!" She threw back her head. "I doubt that you'll get a chance, Farley."

Rebecca had more courage than the others. "What does that mean," she asked, "what kind of parents you are? You're both good parents, aren't you?"

"It seems that Mr. Farley thinks—"

"Roberta, shut up!"

"I don't shut up around my kids, Farley!" she yelled. "That's why my family works! So don't tell me to shut up! You shut up! You're so good at it anyway, it should come naturally! Shut up all your feelings, and all your wife's old dresses, and the truth about what your mother and the respectable citizens of Camden think of Roberta Jewett and her girls! Well, we're just as good as anybody in this town, and you can go back and tell them that for me!"

Gabriel clammed up and glared outside at the roadside weeds flashing green in the carbide lights. A night creature with amber eyes disappeared into the ditch. Houses hunkered like sleeping elephants behind dark overgrown front-yard trees.

The backseat passengers rode silently.

Roberta took a curve too fast and brought Farley's back away from the seat.

"Slow down," he ordered.

Go to hell, she thought, and continued at the same breakneck pace. Into Camden they rumbled, over the streetcar tracks, past the mill and up the hill to Alden Street.

Nobody spoke as she stopped the car, catapulting them all forward in their seats. She set the various levers, got out and stopped the carbide drip. In grim silence they all started dividing property. He took the clamming equipment to his truck, but Isobel hovered behind, quite near tears.

"Thanks for the picnic," she told Roberta timidly,

then whispered, "Aren't you and my dad going to talk to each other anymore?"

Though Gabriel had the power to rouse her temper, Isobel's vulnerability did quite the opposite. She touched Isobel's jaw. "I don't think so, honey."

"But"—Isobel glanced at her father, who was lighting his headlamps—"can I still be your friend?"

Roberta dropped the hamper and took Isobel in her arms. "Oh, of course you can, sweetheart. We'll always be your friends." Isobel clung and tears stung Roberta's eyes. Against the top of the girl's head she said, "I'm sorry we made tonight end badly after it started out so fine."

From his truck Gabriel ordered sternly, "Isobel, come on, we've got to go."

Isobel drew back reluctantly. Rebecca, Susan and Lydia hovered nearby.

"Good night," Isobel said to them, then added with a note of pleading, "Can we do something tomorrow?"

"Sure . . ." Lydia and Susan responded lamely, uncertain of what the adults would have them say.

Gabriel's engine fired, and above its loud belching he shouted, "Isobel, come on!" His truck door slammed.

" 'Bye," she whispered, and Roberta heard tears in her voice.

Her own three said good-bye, and Roberta carried the hamper to the house while Farley chugged away, leaving the girls watching after him like a trio of birds just out of the nest but not yet ready to fly.

Eleven

*R*oberta and Gabriel had spent too much time together to shrug off their fight as if it didn't matter. It was an ending, and endings hurt. This kind did. Neither of them deluded themselves about how close they had come to a romantic connection. The truth was, they had grown to like each other, to enjoy each other's company, and the temptation to extend that friendship into some sort of light physical attachment had certainly been glimmering in their minds ever since the kiss. Roberta thought of it that way: as light physical attachment. Gabriel—he admitted after their falling-out—had occasionally imagined them as lovers, then cast aside the idea only to have it resurface with fair regularity.

The point was moot now. Their friendship had ended on a note of bitterness that carried through the days that followed. Whenever they recalled that night of the clambake, each of them thought how nice and workable their lives had been before they met. Then they grew agitated, remembering the unfair criticism they had suffered at the hands of the other.

Roberta thought, My house might be messy but it's cleaned as good as I have time for—and it's certainly not infested! Who is he to criticize the way we keep things when it suits all four of us? I'm a nurse who goes out and teaches others about hygiene, for heaven's sake! How dare he intimate that I don't give my children proper care? I won't have them living in some . . . some *museum* where nothing is touchable! They'll have fun in their home, and if it's a little bit messy, well, what will they remember most when they're older? The mess or the fun? And if he doesn't like the way I keep myself, to hell with him. Let him find some fluffy pink pea-brain who lives and breathes only to please him. She can *have* him!

Gabriel thought, She's got one hell of a big mouth for a woman who's never even seen my house, or how Isobel and I get along together, or how we handle being without Caroline. And for her to think I don't love my daughter—well, that's just rubbish! The thought of Isobel growing up and leaving me scares me half to death! Why, this place is like a jail cell without her, and when she leaves for good I don't know what I'll do. So maybe I don't fawn over my girl like Roberta does, but that's a woman's way. And maybe I make Isobel take her share of the responsibilities for keeping the place clean and neat, but that's what good parents do; they don't let their children run wild as squirrels! Roberta Jewett can raise her kids her way and I'll raise mine my way, and we'll see whose make a better impression on people around this town. And if I ever again have any dumb ideas about going over there and spooning with that woman, I hope somebody will knock my brains out for me!

One night about a week after the clambake Isobel was waiting when Gabriel came home from the shop.

"Daddy, guess what!" Her face was aglow with excitement. "We've been asked to put on *Hiawatha* for the whole school assembly!"

"That's wonderful, Isobel."

"By the principal herself!"

"Well, it's a good little production. She *should* have asked you."

"Mrs. Roberson and Miss Werm told her about it and said the student body should definitely have a chance to see it because it's an American classic. And after hearing about it, Miss Abernathy said it would be just perfect as a lyceum program during the last week of school. So we're going to do it, and I'm *so* excited! You'll come, won't you, Daddy?"

He began to say, But I've already seen it.

Roberta's admonition stopped him, flashing past like quicksilver. *We say 'I love you' in a thousand ways. If you don't know how, watch me.*

He found himself answering as she would.

"Of course I'll go. I wouldn't miss it."

His unexpected acquiescence widened Isobel's eyes. "You wouldn't?" Clearly she'd been prepared for excuses. "You mean it, Daddy? You really wouldn't?"

He chuckled self-consciously, caught by surprise himself. "I just said I wouldn't, didn't I? If I said I'll be there, I'll be there."

Overcome, Isobel flung her arms around him and hugged him hard. "Oh, Daddy, I'm so glad. I never thought you'd agree to see it twice. Thank you *so* much for saying yes!"

Suddenly it seemed as if Roberta was there, like some wide-winged guardian angel, standing over Isobel and looking out for her emotional well-being. When instinct told Gabe to draw back, the specter of Roberta ordered him: Don't miss this chance. He curled his arms around Isobel and touched his cheek to her hair. He sensed her surprise: a moment of stillness during which his own heart kicked up a flurry and he wondered why it had taken him so long. They remained close while he felt some sentimental cog slipping into place. Then she drew back and looked up at him with a smile of such wondrous amazement he found his reward on the spot.

The moment of closeness passed, bringing a rebound of shyness. Isobel colored and said, "Well . . . I have to go call Susan and Lydia and Rebecca. All right, Daddy?"

"All right," he said as his hands slid off her shoulders.

Watching her hurry away, he felt the afterglow lying deep within him making him into a more whole being than he'd been before. Such a simple thing—a hug, a kind word, a yes—but what complex reactions it evoked. Many years ago, when Isobel was an infant, he'd felt like this whenever he'd look down at her in her cradle, as if he were so full with life that one more drop of goodness would overflow him.

It astonished Gabe how often he thought about that hug he and Isobel had shared, how warmed it made him feel, and how it touched off remembrances of Caroline. Perhaps Roberta had been right: He'd left the emotional nurturing to his wife, and when she died he hadn't had the wherewithal to fill her shoes in that department. But had he actually *resented* Isobel's intrusion into his grief?

No . . . no, that was a preposterous accusation, one that still hurt. Why, he loved his daughter—wasn't this strong reaction the living proof?—and for Roberta to accuse him of resenting her was an emotional bruise that Gabe wouldn't soon forget.

The school performance of *Hiawatha* was held at two o'clock on a Thursday afternoon in the last week of May. Gabriel had worked all morning in the shop and went home at one o'clock to change clothes and freshen up, shave and comb his hair.

Roberta was working out on the other side of Bald Mountain, and when she headed in on Barnstown Road she had little time to think of clothes and combs.

He arrived with ten minutes to spare.

She arrived ten minutes late.

He sat in the rear, alone.

She sat in the third row next to her sister and mother.

He watched, still as a sleeping gull.

She moved her mouth along with the words.

The girls put on a splendid performance and, when it was over, were rousingly applauded. Miss Abernathy thanked and praised them, and after a smattering of final applause, the audience rose and shuffled out of the school auditorium.

Gabriel went straight outside.

Roberta headed straight for the stage steps where she met the cast coming down. The girls were talkative, excited, pleased with themselves, accepting many congratulations and being swarmed by the crowd, which moved toward the exit in a shifting mass.

Roberta managed to hug her own three, and Grace's girls, and finally, Isobel, who squeezed a little harder and longer than the others.

"Mrs. Jewett . . . gosh, it's good to see you again."

"I'm so proud of you girls! You all did a splendid job!"

"We really did, didn't we?"

"Everybody's saying so."

They drew apart, drank each other in and indulged in another hug that brought thickness to their throats.

"I've missed you around the house."

"I've missed coming over. But Daddy wants me to stay home more."

"Yes, I know he does. But you're always welcome, you know that, don't you?"

"Yes . . . I know."

Drawing apart, the girl and the woman saw affection in each other's eyes, and perhaps some withheld tears.

Gabriel was waiting outside in the sun when Roberta came out with one arm around Susan, the other around Isobel, surrounded by young people and trailed by her mother and sister. He stood out in the front school yard beside a thirty-ton hunk of stone called the Conway Boulder, which commemorated Camden's war dead. As she came down the schoolhouse steps, their gazes collided, bringing a mix of good memories and bad. If their hearts sent up faint flutters, neither of them revealed it. He stood as unmoving as the boulder itself, and she kept herself in the midst of her entourage. She might have turned aside and taken a different route to her motorcar, but the young people buffeted her along and she could see no graceful way to veer off. As the group moved toward Gabe, Isobel broke free and rushed forward to hug him.

"Daddy." She looked up into his face, radiant with

triumph. "Everyone is getting together at the Jewetts' for lemonade. May I go, please?"

Gabe looked up at Roberta, back down at Isobel. He simply couldn't find the heart to refuse her.

"All right. Home by supper though, huh?"

"I promise."

As she scampered off, he watched her rejoin the group.

Roberta observed the exchange with some surprise as Gabe heartily returned Isobel's embrace. When he raised his head their eyes met once more, but coolness emanated from them both. The gravity was there, un-deniable—a tug on the heart and the will—but pride made its demands, and now was not the time, not in the hubbub of early dismissal with excited first- and second-graders scuttling past, and her mother and sister watching. Their daughters knew how things stood be-tween them, too, and couldn't help but be curious.

So they exchanged no smiles, only a curt nod of his head and an answering one from her before she turned away aloofly and moved on.

Grace clasped Roberta's elbow and hissed in her ear, "That's the first time I've seen Gabe Farley at one of these things."

Myra, sour-faced, said, "You aren't seeing him any-more, are you, Roberta?"

She repressed a caustic reply and answered dutifully, "No, Mother."

As the group moved away, Gabe found his eyes fol-lowing the X of apron straps on Roberta's back. Her white nurse's cap caught the sun like snow on a moun-taintop. Her mahogany hair was rolled up in a coil that had been neat this morning but was tattered now. A stab of loneliness caught him along with a mental image of her house. He wished he could follow her home, sit on her front porch and listen to the young people talk and laugh, visit with Roberta and sip a cool drink.

They reached her car and all the kids piled in— must've been close to a dozen of them, but Roberta didn't care. She bussed her sister and mother on their cheeks, and just as she was about to crank the engine Elfred appeared and offered to do it for her. Gabe wasn't sure where Elfred had been: not in the auditorium, he was sure. Apparently he'd come by to collect his wife and mother-in-law and give them a ride home. At any rate, he detoured long enough to offer his usefulness to Roberta, who declined (with pointed distaste) and cranked the car herself. Against his will, Gabriel smiled at her spunkiness. As she walked around and opened the driver's door, he thought she paused a second to glance over at him. But someone walked between them and cut off his line of vision, and when it cleared, the car was rolling away.

Two things happened during the lemonade session that afternoon that remained on Roberta's mind later. Isobel told her, "My dad says he's going to hire a woman to do our laundry and take care of the house . . . at last." And Rebecca—fresh from neatening her hair and applying a faint tinge of lip rouge—came out to the porch and sat apart from the other girls, talking and laughing with the boy who gave them the fish he'd been cleaning that day on the rocks. His name was Ethan Ogier and she asked permission to leave the gath-

ering and walk with him uptown to have an ice-cream
soda at the drugstore.

The school year ended on Memorial Day, and summer was officially launched with a grand parade and
picnic at which Roberta once again fended off advances
from Elfred when Grace and Myra were not looking.
He cornered her at her car where she'd gone to get a
blanket. His attack was more audacious this time, and
she ended up slapping him hard enough to leave a red
welt on his cheek before he finally backed off and returned to Grace, flinging a threat over his shoulder. "I'll
get you yet, you little slut. Don't think I won't. You're
giving plenty of it to Farley—you can spare a little for
me!" He never returned to the picnic after that, and
though Roberta wondered how he'd explain the bruise,
she never asked, nor did Grace mention it. It would be
fifty below zero in July before Grace would admit she
was married to the most notorious philanderer in Knox
County. Grace was easily the most deluded person Roberta had ever known.

June arrived, bringing hot days to the little seaside
town of Camden, spilling thick green down the moun-
tainside, and silvering Penobscot Bay. Wild daisies
tripped in a slanting path down the foothills to the scalloped shore. Bracken ferns paid homage at the feet of
white birches. All the berries—blue, straw and choke—
bloomed in sheltered patches, while columbine waved,
wild and sweet, in the soft summer breeze.

Summer changed the harbor and the busy quay
around it. Racks of salt codfish appeared near the

wharfs, redolent as they dried in the sun. The fishing boats went out earlier and returned later. The summer people came, filling the cove with sails and occupying the cottages out along Dillingham's Point and down by Hosmer Pond. At Laite's Public Beach swimmers donned their woolen bathing outfits and took to the water by the dozens. The gang from Roberta Jewett's front porch swam there, too, and spent time rowing and fishing off Negro Island, and taking picnics up on Mount Battie where the cooler breezes gave relief from the mugginess at water level.

Isobel was often with them, for Gabe had hired a thirty-six-year-old widow named Elise Plowman to do his housekeeping, laundry and some light cooking. His mother remained estranged and his daughter seemed happier than she'd ever been as she once again took up porch sitting and mountaintop exploring with the Jewett crowd. Though Roberta's house became the official summer hangout for an even larger number of both boys and girls, Rebecca did less with her sisters and more with Ethan Ogier.

As summer advanced, Roberta grew to love her work more and more. It took her from county line to county line, and kept her out some days till nearly dark. The newly formed field of public nursing, legitimized by the presence of the Red Cross in the continuing war in Europe, gave its nurses the "freedom to initiate" and the "mandate to educate," so she did. As she crisscrossed the countryside, she began searching out homes that had diapers on the line and stopping at these to check on the welfare of both the babies and their mothers. She gave lessons on infant care, and learned through the county grapevine who was expecting, then called at those homes to give prenatal advice and assign midwives. She initiated a program aimed at the prevention of typhoid fever and other communicable diseases arising from bad sanitation and ignorance. She began an anti-tuberculosis crusade with the help of printed materials supplied by the state and implemented by examination and supervision of the susceptible cases. She gave eye and ear examinations and visited the sick who were newly released from the hospital, and the blind who did not know help existed for them.

She learned more about running a Model T motorcar than she cared to: how to lift the floorboards, remove the cover of the transmission box and adjust the transmission bands with a screwdriver; how to put rubber patching compound on a cut tire, wrap it with a towel and bind it with wire to go an extra fifty miles; how to back up the steepest hills when the gas level was low, so the gravity feed wouldn't stall the engine. She even learned how to start the car with the key instead of the crank—tuning her ear to that particular buzz in the ignition coils that said there was gas in the cylinder and the pistons happened to be in the right position, though she never knew (if the key start managed to work) whether the Tin Lizzie would take off forward or backward.

On the last day of June she had been sent out to do a checkup on a six-week-old infant and its mother, and had climbed some of the worst roads Knox County had to offer. It was a hot, hazy day. From up on Howe Hill, Penobscot Bay appeared to be simmering. Pearly haze hung over it, dulling the water surface along with a layer of filmy clouds that hung with desultory shiftlessness around a murky sun. The wooden steering wheel felt greasy beneath Roberta's hands as she hurtled down the washed-out roadbed. She hit a rock and bounced high and hard . . . and when she landed, the engine stopped running. She was nosing along a sharp downgrade and kept coasting till she approached the intersection of Hope Road, where she bumped to a halt with the car pitched over sharply in the weeds and rocks of the right-hand verge.

"Blasted machine!" She thumped the steering wheel and struggled to open the door. With gravity working against her, it took a hard shove before it budged and she was standing on the gravel road with her hands on her hips, disgusted. She looked around: a *T* in the road, dust settling behind her, brown-eyed Susans and skunk cabbage bobbing in the ditch, grasshoppers jumping and munching among the the quack grass and dandelions around the car, wild mustard blooming tiredly in the dry-wash ditch and the incessant note of the katydids hidden in the weeds and grasses.

The clouds shifted away from the sun and the heat pelted down, baking the top of her head while she wondered what to check first. Fan belt? Not likely, since the radiator wasn't hissing. But she folded back the hood anyway and peered inside. The heat from the engine was horrendous, but the fan belt was in place and things looked the way she remembered. She jiggled the spark plug wires, checked the magneto terminal. They looked okay. So it could be the transmission bands, but even if they needed adjustment, it shouldn't have stopped the engine this way. As she was removing the front seat to check them she thought about checking the gas. She hauled the seat out and leaned it against the running board, then removed the gas cap from the hole between the floorboards. Using the wooden dipstick, she found her problem—bone dry. Hauling the green-and-white Valvoline gas can out of the backseat, she heard an oncoming engine; she straightened and waited. A black touring car appeared at the crest of the hill from the east and slowed as it rolled down a slight decline and approached her. Even before he pulled to a stop she recognized Elfred.

He was hatless, smoking a cigar and smirking as he turned off his engine and got out—all the while keeping an eye on her.

"Well, what have we here . . . a damsel in distress?"

She tucked a strand of hair behind her ear and answered, "Not at all. I'm just refilling my gas tank."

"Well, allow me, Mrs. Jewett," he said, handing her his cigar. "Here, hold that, will you?"

He'd left his suit jacket behind and was dressed in a white shirt with a high, round collar, gray pin-striped trousers and wide black suspenders. Even in the heat of late day his collar and tie were cinched tight. Though the starch beneath his suspenders had wilted, it was apparent his shirt had been fresh that morning. Elfred had a penchant for neatness. Neat on the outside, sleazy on the inside, she thought, studying his white shirt-back as he picked up the gas can.

"That's kind of you, Elfred, but I really could have done it myself."

"Nonsense. What kind of cad would pass a stranded woman so far from town without offering a hand?" He

removed the wooden plug from the Valvoline can and
jockeyed himself into position to pour while she stood
waving his cigar smoke away. The air was so motionless
she could find little breeze to help, and no matter which
way she turned, the smoke seemed to follow. As Elfred
poured, she studied the seam down the rear of his trousers. She looked away, prompted by a wave of dislike.
The stillness, the remoteness seemed magnified by the
unchanging song of the katydids and the oppressive
heat.

Finally she asked, "What are you doing clear out
here?"

"Looking at the Mullens' place. She's decided to sell
rather than run it by herself. What are you doing?"

"I had a case up there. . . ." She motioned. "A new
mother with a six-week-old baby. Checked her over and
gave her some instruction on infant care. There's a lot
of ignorance everywhere. It kills a lot of children needlessly, especially newborns."

He half-glanced over his shoulder, then back down
at the gurgling gasoline.

"I haven't seen you since the Memorial Day picnic."

"I've been busy, running all over the county."

He quit pouring and backed out of the front seat with
the can. "You know, I didn't like how you treated me
that day." He put the wooden plug in the can and
tamped it once with a cupped palm. "You put a mark
on my face that I had trouble explaining to Grace."

Roberta scrabbled through her mind for something
to say while he stored the can in the backseat, then
sauntered toward her, wiping his hands on a white linen
hanky. Shuffling to a stop before her, he stored the

hanky in a rear pocket, then reached her way. She took one quick step backward.

"You're a little jumpy, Birdy," he said, reclaiming his cigar with an insidious grin. "Aren't you?"

"I'd better get going. The girls are expecting me at five."

"Not so fast there." His hand lashed out and grabbed her arm. "Don't I get any thanks for helping you out?"

She pulled back, but he hung on. "Thank you, Elfred. Now may I go?"

"That's not much of a thanks, Roberta. I was thinking of something a little more personal."

Elfred could put more lecherousness into a grin than anyone she'd ever known.

"Let me go, Elfred." She tried to pry at his fingers, but he threw his other arm around her and spread his legs, hauling her up hard against him, his moustache an inch from her lips.

"Let you go? And what if I don't?" He grinned wolfishly, his face so close she could smell the cigar on his breath, the gasoline on his hands. "What if I find out for myself just what's so precious under those skirts that you save it all for Farley? What if I do that, huh, Birdy?"

She wedged an arm between them and pushed. "Let me go."

"Not this time, Birdy. This time nobody's here to stop me." He lowered his face but she whipped hers aside.

"Elfred, please . . . don't!"

"Show me, Birdy . . . come on."

"Elfred, I said don't!" Her rising panic seemed to add to his fire.

"Come on, Roberta, don't be so stingy." The struggle intensified. So did her fear.

"Stop it, Elfred!" He hauled one way, she strained the other, and their combat stirred up dust on the road.

"All that hot stuff you been holdin' at arm's length . . ." She tried to knee him, but her skirts hampered her attempt, and he was cagey with his moves, keeping to one side or too close. "Don't tell me you don't like this. . . . I heard about divorced women. . . . They like it any way they can get it, isn't that right, Birdy?"

"Let me go!"

He grabbed her hair, yanked her head back and kissed her, thrusting his tongue against her locked lips. Her white cap fell to the road. Her skull felt as if it were being ripped from her temples. The smell of cigar smoke filled her nostrils while continuing to rise from behind her as he grappled for control. She kept pushing at his chest while his mouth bruised her lips—pushing! pushing!—until he finally lost purchase and his hand slipped along her back. When he shifted for a new grip, her chance came. One hard shove, and she tripped him, spinning, breaking free, running.

She took five steps before he brought her down on one hip, screaming, against the running board of the car. The loose seat fell, and her shoulder struck metal. She slid to an angle, half on the gravel, half on the seat. Pain ripped through her hip and her right shoulder.

"Ow!" she cried. "My arm! Elfred . . . my arm!"

It was wrenched beneath her as he flung her over with surprisingly little difficulty.

"Turn over here, damn it!" He straddled her thighs while she fought him as best she could.

"Elfred, please ... don't ... please ... Elfred, my arm ..."

Her left arm was free. She struck him with her fist, so hard he yelped, rocked to one side, and she got free. Up she scuttled, but her dusty uniform and apron were tangled in his trouser legs and he grabbed a fistful of her skirt. She towed him two feet along the gravel before he hauled her backward and sent her sprawling.

Over on her back.

Right where she'd been.

Pinned by the neck by one of his strong hands while he loomed above her, enraged now, and bruised.

"Goddamnit, Birdy! I'm gettin' mighty tired of this! You're gonna put out, and you're gonna do it now!" The coal of his cigar came up close beneath her chin. She screamed and pedaled wildly, but the gravel scraped away beneath her heels. He held her by the throat, his teeth clenched, his hair fallen on his forehead, his face vicious. A scarlet bulge was blossoming near his eye.

"You're gonna stop fighting, Roberta. Got that?"

Her terrified eyes answered.

"Now I don't wanna burn you, Birdy, but I will!"

Her nails dug uselessly at his hand, scratching her own throat instead.

I can't breathe, she tried to say, but could not.

His face grew scarlet and trembled as his wrath built. He tightened his grip and shook her some, rapping her head against the gravel. "I'll teach you to treat me like shit! You think you're too goddamn good for me, don't you, Birdy? Well, I got women all over this county can't wait to pull their pants down for me. So why not you, huh? What's so goddamn exclusive about Birdy Jewett?"

She lay moon-eyed, gripping his wrist, the gravel grinding into her neck and head.

I can't breathe, she mouthed.

Finally he released her throat just enough to give her breath, and moved the cigar away. His expression turned feral and he spoke through crimped lips. "Now you're gonna do it, Birdy." He glanced at his lap. "Go ahead."

"You'll have to kill me first," she whispered raspily.

"No, I won't." His cigar returned . . . closer this time. So did his face, wreathed by the fetid smoke.

"Don't make me burn you, Birdy. I didn't intend to do that, but you got to learn to do what a man says, then he'll let you off easy. Now do it. Unbutton me."

She strained to lift her chin free of the heat. Unable. Eyes wild with fear.

"Don't underestimate me, Roberta. That's been your trouble—you've always underestimated me. Now, you're gonna do it, Birdy. Go ahead."

"Please, Elfred . . ." Tears leaked down her temples and made wet patches on the dusty gravel.

"Do it." He touched her with the cigar and she screamed.

And unbuttoned his trousers.

"Now yours." Her eyes were shut in humiliation, but she felt him raise up and shrug off his suspenders, transferring the cigar to the other hand. The rest was easy, even though she refused to aid him further. A knee to her stomach, a flip of her skirts, a yank at her waist-

band, a tug on his own drawers . . . and at last he flung
the cigar into the weeds. She bucked then, and tried to
throw him off and scratch his face, but it was useless.
He pinned her wrists above her head, grinding gravel
into them as he got between her knees and forced them
wide with his own.

She felt the hot tears seep from between her quivering
eyelids as her brother-in-law defiled her. She endured it
by placing herself beyond what was happening . . . beyond his bestiality and grunting . . . and the smell of his
cigar smoke . . . and of gasoline . . . and of sweat on his
skin . . . beyond the pain of the rocks grinding into her
from below . . . and the ignominy of being entered
against her will, of being treated like a disposable non-
entity, less than human. She withdrew into the singing
of the katydids, and the promise of cool water, and the
chirping of birds and the sounds of her children's voices
on the front porch in the evening twilight, marveling at
fireflies and reading James Russell Lowell's "The Vision
of Sir Launfal."

And what is so rare as a day in June?
Then, if ever, come perfect days . . .

When it was over and Elfred withdrew, sitting back
on her legs, she flung an arm over her eyes and remained motionless.

He fumbled with a handkerchief and his shirttails,
then his weight shifted. Bracing a hand on her belly, he
boosted himself up, forcing her breath to escape in a
grunt.

"That damn gravel is hard on the knees," he said as it crunched beneath his shoes.

With her eyes still covered, she threw down her skirt and willed herself to remain inert until he was gone. How easy it would be to kill him right where he stood. Had she a gun she would quite willfully point it at his head and pull the trigger, feeling no remorse whatsoever.

Reptiles like Elfred deserved to be slaughtered.

"Come on, Birdy, you better get up."

She felt his hand on her arm.

"Don't touch me," she said, jerking free of his detestable touch, her eyes still covered. She spoke in a dead calm. "You touch me again and I swear I'll murder you, Elfred. Not now, but soon. I'll find some weapon, some knife, or one of my syringes with the right kind of drugs in it, or some rat poison, or maybe the foot feed on my car will conveniently stick when you're crossing the same street I'm driving on, or whatever it takes, but I'll murder you, Elfred, if you ever in your life again lay one finger on me."

She didn't need to shout or dramatize. The certainty in her voice made Elfred move slower, halfway through raising his suspenders.

"Look, Birdy, it wouldn't have had to be so rough if you'd have given in weeks ago. I tried it nice and persuasive with you, but you just wouldn't listen."

"Is that how you rationalize the crime you've just committed?" She refused to move her arm and look at him. "If I get pregnant out of this, you can forget about me jeopardizing my own life by getting it cut out by some midwife. But your bastard will show up in a basket on your doorstep, Elfred, with a note telling Grace and the girls why it's there. Now get away from me. Get your despicable, perspiring, bloated body away from this place before I get in my motorcar and run you down where you stand."

When he left, she was still lying in the road where he'd raped her, her arm still across her eyes.

Twelve

Only when he'd driven off did she roll to her side, coil tightly and hug her belly. More tears came, and a fierce trembling over her entire body, but she resisted succumbing to total dysfunction. *I can't, I can't*, she thought, keeping some narrow corridor of her mind open to reason, drawing upon an inner strength that deemed control necessary for survival. The delayed shock rattled her body, riveting her head against the sharks'-teeth gravel, but she wept quietly, letting the tears roll onto the stones, which darkened like tea stains beneath her temple.

Get up. Go for help. She heard the inner voice but, rising, she would have buckled, so instead she lay waiting out the shakes. It felt as if she were watching someone else rattling away here in the middle of this remote track, looking on from the edge of the ditch while the victim of the afternoon's violence curled on her side with her arms lashed hard around her belly and tears leaking from her eyes. Meanwhile, the katydids went on caroling, and a covey of goldfinches fluttered into a patch of purple thistle, chattering companionably. She was aware of them subliminally, and of the stems of some puny chickory weeds poking up against the horizon, and of the horizon itself—brilliant green meeting brilliant blue, while uncaring nature forged on with its summer schedule and left a ravaged woman to gather her forces in the road.

Time passed . . . five minutes or ten . . . she knew not which, before the voice got through.

Get up. Go for help.

She hauled herself upright and sat braced with one hand, appalled at her body's inability to be controlled by will. It continued to tremble as if enfeebled, and no amount of reasoning would restore her calm. She stared numbly at her dusty skirts, at her left shoe where the roadbed had scraped away the shiny white toe and left bare leather. Some crows flapped over, calling loudly. Her head hurt.

I need a bath . . . please . . . somebody, help me get his slime off my body.

She pushed to her feet and rose unsteadily, the gravel embedded in her palms like gems in a mounting of flesh. Pieces of it fell as she lifted her skirts and pulled up her underclothes, holding the buttonless waistband of her pantaloons in place. She shuffled to the car, leaving behind her white cap and one mother-of-pearl button among the heel scrapes in the road. The front seat was lying where it had fallen, beside the running board. She wrestled it into the Ford, then set the levers, cranked the machine and drove down off Howe Hill onto Hope Road, along the Megunticook River beside Washington Street and eventually through town to Belmont Street.

The voice in her head told her where she must go. She didn't want her children to see her in this condition, nor her mother—and going to Grace's was out of the question—but why inflict her troubles on Gabriel Farley, a man who didn't want to be bothered? Sheer self-preservation drove her to his door, her thoughts scarcely thoughts, but mindless instinct to seek refuge.

Lifting her knuckles to his screen door, she heard the voice chanting again: *Let him be home . . . let him be home . . .* Somewhere in her distant perceptions she detected the smell of meat roasting and coffee brewing, but suppertime and its humdrum routine were unrelated to this day.

She knocked and he came, holding a dishtowel he'd been using as a pot holder, appearing in the doorway above her like Saint Michael the archangel disguised in blue chambray and khaki.

"Roberta?"

"Gabriel . . . I . . ."

"Roberta, what's wrong?"

"I didn't know where else to come."

"What happened?" He moved swiftly around the screen door, his eyebrows beetling in concern, as he cast aside the dishtowel.

"The girls are home . . . and . . . and . . . the girls are home . . . and . . . I don't want them . . . the girls . . . oh, Gabriel . . ."

"What happened?" He gripped her arms and felt her shuddering deep within.

"I'm sorry to be such a nuisance." She acted peculiar, foggy, like a sleepwalker.

"You're not a nuisance, Roberta. Now tell me what happened."

She stared at his throat for some time, as if unable to make sense of her presence here, then turned her head with mechanical smoothness and studied the white siding beside his back door.

Almost dispassionately, she told him, "Elfred raped me."

"Oh, Jesus," he whispered as her knees gave, and he plucked her up into his arms and carried her inside.

His kitchen walls whizzed past as she objected, "Is Isobel here? Isobel can't see me. Gabe, stop."

He hurried through his house, up the stairs, around the corner into a bedroom and laid her on a soft bed.

"That sonofabitch," he said, filling her range of vision as he braced his hands beside her shoulders. "He *raped you?*"

"I tried to stop him, but it was no use. He was so strong, Gabe, and I . . . I . . ." A sob interrupted.

"Where did it happen?"

"Out on Howe H-Hill." She swallowed and controlled her sobs. "My car ran out of gas and he stopped to h-help me fill it, and then he . . . he . . ." She tried not to cry, but the memory jumped up and replayed in her mind, and with it came the shakes again. She flung an arm over her eyes and felt Gabriel touch her dirty sleeve.

He saw flagrant evidence—the gravel ground into her wrist, her dirty clothes, the purple bruises on her throat.

"Did he do this?"

From behind her arm she said, "I didn't do anything to encourage him, Gabriel . . . honest . . . you've got to believe me."

"I believe you, Roberta." Touching a bruise on her throat, he repeated, "Did he do this?"

"I fought and I screamed, but he was stronger than I

thought and there was nothing I could do. First he held me down, and when I wouldn't stop fighting he b-burned me with his c-cigar."

"Oh God . . ." He drew her up and gathered her close while she wept, while pity and rage created a maelstrom of emotions within him. He clasped her to his breast, her forehead at his throat, his eyes closed, terrified to ask where she'd been burned. His heart was racing as he pictured the worst. But he forced himself to ask, "Where?"

She pulled back some and ran the edges of her dirty hands across her eyes. "Under my chin."

Under her chin. Sweet Jesus. He'd kill that goddamned sonofabitch. He took her shoulders and urged, "Lie down, Roberta. Let me see."

When he saw the red-rimmed blister his rage trebled. But he forced himself to think of her first and vengeance second.

"I've got to put something on that."

He moved to rise but she clutched his sleeve. "No, Gabe, please. Isobel will be coming home for supper and she can't find me here looking this way. I don't want my girls to find out."

He covered her hand with his own, squeezing hard. "Isobel's at your house. I'll call there and tell her to stay awhile. You rest and I'll be right back." He rose from the bed, extending his hands to prolong his touch as he moved away. "I'll only be a minute, Roberta."

His hand slid away and she heard him hammer downstairs as if someone were after him with an axe. She closed her eyes and listened to the call bell ring as he summoned the operator, then his voice, indistinct, as he gave the number. Of the conversation with Isobel, she heard only snatches. "Mrs. Jewett and I are talking . . . would you . . . yes . . . our house . . . you later . . ." Then nothing more.

She rested, with her hands at her sides, fanning them over the soothing nap of the bedspread that had probably been selected and washed and tucked beneath the pillows countless times by his wife. Odd, but the thought of that dead woman whom she had never known brought courage and strength to Roberta.

She sat up unsteadily and balanced herself with both hands, looking down blearily at the spread. It was patchwork. The walls were papered in gray, spattered with yellow roses.

He found her that way, sitting up looking somewhat stronger.

"I brought some boric acid and pineoline, but you should see a doctor."

"No," she said with surprising vehemence. "No doctor! It'll be all over town and my girls will hear about it. If I wanted that, I would have gone straight home."

"But you're hurt, Roberta, scraped up and burned."

"The burn is nothing." She took the tin from his hands and tried to open it, but her shaky hands couldn't manage. "It'll heal up in a week, and the real hurt is much deeper than any doctor can cure."

He retrieved the tin, opened it and said, "Lie back. I'll do it."

She did as ordered, lifting her chin while he dusted the burn with boric acid, then dabbed it with pineoline jelly. She winced, and he did too, hating that he had to hurt her after all she'd already been hurt. "I'm sorry," he said, but she set her jaw and tolerated his ministrations with remarkable stoicism.

When she heard the cap go back on the pineoline her eyes opened and met his. He rose from the side of the bed and she sat up, too, swinging her legs over the edge and raising one dirty hand to her hair. He stood before her, out of his element, uncertain, but realizing she was still in no condition to get to her feet and walk out of here.

"You're sure about the doctor?"

She nodded, her eyes downcast.

"Then what do you want me to do?"

"A bath," she said quietly to her knees. "I'd like a bath."

Her answer jolted him with unwanted images and a keener realization of the sordidness remaining, even after the act was over.

"Of course," he said, turning to the dresser.

She studied the blue chambray on his back as he moved away and opened a drawer.

"I'm so much trouble to you," she said.

"Yes, you are. But not in the way you think. Not today." He selected something then moved on to a highboy, followed by her eyes. Momentarily he returned to the bed and laid some clothing beside Roberta. "These are some things of Caroline's. She was a lot thinner than you, but that's a dress she wore while she carried Isobel, so it should do. I'll bring up some water."

He went off, leaving her with his wife's precious, untouchable clothing. She picked up the garments, overcome by his generosity and how far he'd come during this eventful summer, from where he'd been when they first met. She held the dress by the shoulders and it cascaded over her knees, an umbrella of violet-sprigged muslin with two small permanent stains on the front yoke. The stains—evidence of a real life, in the real world—released Roberta's tears once more. She put her face into Caroline Farley's maternity dress and silently told her, I love your husband. I don't want to, but I do, and he doesn't want to love me either, but I believe he does. You see, I'm nothing like you, and it scares him, and he fights his feelings for me because he thinks he's being disloyal to you. I know perfectly well that if he ever breaks down and tells me, it'll never be like it was with you. But he's a good man, and you were lucky. Thank you for letting me borrow your clothes.

Gabe stopped in the doorway, holding a dishpan of hot water, with a towel slung over his shoulder. Roberta raised her face from Caroline's dress, which she held bunched up in both hands. There was a prayerfulness to her pose that caught at his heart.

"Water was still warm in the reservoir." He entered and set the dishpan in the center of a hooked rug. "Brought you some soap and a washcloth and towel, too." He laid them on a nearby chair, then turned to find her watching him, her hands fallen to her lap in the folds of the sprigged muslin.

"Thank you, Gabriel," she said.

"When you're dressed, call me and I'll carry the dishpan out."

"I will. You're very thoughtful."

After an awkward pause, he moved once again, then stopped abruptly.

"You sure you can stand up okay?"

She did, to show him. "You see? I'll be fine."

"Okay then, take your time." He gestured with lifted palms. "There's no hurry."

She sent him a weak smile and he headed for the door.

"Gabriel, there's one more thing I need to ask you to do for me."

He spun in place. "Anything."

"It's an indelicate matter, but I don't see any other way than to ask. You see . . . I don't want his baby. If there should accidentally be one, I don't want it. Do you understand what I mean?"

He colored and shifted his weight, dropping his eyes to the rug. "Guess I do."

"Could you mix up some of that boric acid in a quart of warm water and bring me my bag from the motorcar? There's something in there I can use."

He cleared his throat, still unable to meet her eyes. "Of course. Be right back."

The bedroom door was closed when he returned with the things she had requested. "I'll leave it out here, Roberta," he called, tipping his head toward the door.

"Thank you, Gabriel," she said from inside his room.

"Listen, I've got to leave for a while. Will you be all right for a little bit?"

"I'll be fine."

He shifted his weight to his other hip, roughed up the hair behind his right ear and decided that—indelicate subject or not—he could be just as brave as she.

"Commode's under the bed, Roberta. Feel free to use it."

Beyond his bedroom door, all was silence. He pictured her standing on the other side and wondered what she'd use, then felt like a damned pervert for giving in to curiosity at a time like this. But hell, he'd been married to Caroline for eight years, had lived with her through a wedding night, a pregnancy and a birthing without running up against anything this earthy. He felt as hot-faced as the time he'd seen the fat lady at the carnival who couldn't close her legs. But this was no time for dissembling. Roberta had been raped, and reality needed facing. Remarkable, how she faced whatever life handed out to her and turned the stronger for it.

He put a palm on the door frame and told her, "You wait here for me. Don't walk home, understand?"

"I won't. But Gabriel? Where are you going?"

"To my shop," he lied. "Quick stop, then I'll be right back."

"Wait! Gabriel, could I ask you one more favor, since you're going out anyway?"

"Anything."

"My nurse's cap . . . I must have left it up there on the road where it happened. I don't want anyone to find it, and I need it for tomorrow morning. Would you mind driving up and getting it for me?"

"Just tell me where."

"At the bottom of Howe Hill where it meets Hope Road. There's a *T* in the road."

"I know where it is. Take me about twenty minutes. You be okay?"

"I'll be just fine . . . and thanks a lot, Gabriel."

"All right, then . . . I'll be back."

He made plenty of noise clomping down the stairs so

she'd know he was gone and had total privacy.

Outside, he didn't think twice about taking her car. It was parked out front, and when he cranked it he was concentrating on Elfred with so much rage he nearly lifted the front tires off the ground. He motored straight to Elfred's house, gripping the wheel and scowling, feeling his pulse elevate with each passing block until his adrenaline was pumping sweet vengeance through his bloodstream. *An eye for an eye isn't good enough*, he decided. *In Elfred's case we'll go maybe twenty to one.*

The Spears' front door was open and voices came from the rear of the home. It was post-suppertime for most families, and Elfred's was probably just finishing up the meal.

Gabe pounded on the screen with the edge of a fist and shouted, "Elfred, get out here! I want to talk to you!"

In the depths of the house, the voices silenced.

Gabe beat the screen door again. "Elfred, get your ass out here right now or I'll come in there and drag it out!"

More silence, followed by whispering.

"Elfred, you know what this is about, so I can settle it in there in front of your family or out here in the front yard! The choice is yours, but you better make it soon or I'm comin' in!"

Down the center hall Elfred's head appeared around the dining room archway. Somewhere behind him, Grace murmured, "Elfred, what is it? Is that Gabriel Farley?"

Elfred said, "Farley, are you crazy?"

Gabe opened the screen door and ordered, "Get your

ass out here, you chicken-shit bastard! I came to give you what no woman can give you, and my blood is pumpin' mighty fast, Elfred, so don't make me come in there and get you, 'cause you'll only make it worse on yourself!"

Elfred, visibly frightened, wiped his mouth with a linen napkin, then hid behind it for a moment.

Gabe stepped inside and let the door slam loudly.

Elfred pointed a finger and said, "You get out of here, Farley, or I'll have the police on you."

Gabe marched down the hall. "I'll get out of here when I've finished my business with you, you bastard." He collared the surprised diner and hauled him straight down the hall in a headlock, opening the screen with the top of Elfred's head while his feet pedaled to keep up. The Spear family spilled through the archway and some of them screamed as they watched the man of the house unceremoniously used as a ramrod.

"Elfred! Oh, dear God!" Grace cried, following.

Gabe hauled Elfred down four steps, still in a head-lock, choking him with his necktie. Every word Gabe spoke came out in a clear baritone bellow. "Now, just so there won't be any question, this is for the woman you raped, Elfred, 'cause she can't do it herself. 'Course you knew that when you raped her, didn't you?"

He landed the first blows while Elfred's head was still couched at his hip. Four of them—*crunch, crunch, crunch, crunch*—that broke Elfred's pretty little nose and put a matching strawberry on the eye Roberta had missed. He released him by thrusting a knee up and flipping him backward against his own front steps. When he landed, a rib cracked and Elfred screamed. His children and wife were standing in the doorway blubbering and crying, but Gabe worked on Elfred for another minute or so, hauling him to his feet time and again before Elfred's rubbery legs would finally no longer support him. Then Gabe dropped him like a used saddle, Elfred's limbs folding under him like stirrup straps while Gabe bent above him and rifled his vest pockets. He withdrew a cigar, nipped the end, spat, struck a match with his thumbnail and puffed four stinking clouds of smoke into the lavender evening air before grabbing his prey by the hair and yanking his listless head back.

"One last thing, Elfred. An eye for an eye, a burn for a burn . . . only let's not hide it. Let's put it where everyone will ask about it."

Elfred still had enough fear left to scream as the cigar coal approached the center of his moustache. In the end, Gabe's common sense reared up and stopped him when he'd only singed Elfred's moustache enough to ruin it.

"Ehh, you shit-sucking maggot," Gabriel said in disgust, flinging him aside and letting him fall as before, limbs crumpled in assorted directions, as Roberta's had been when Elfred took her down. Gabe stood over him, his adrenaline still pumping, his powerful carpenter's muscles scarcely taxed by the minute and a half of pulverizing the man who had preyed on women for years. "You had this coming for a long time, Elfred, and I'm happy to be the one to do it. Anybody wants to know where to find me, I'll be at home, waiting to testify as to why I ground you into chicken mash. You hear me, Elfred? The law asks, you send 'em my way." He touched the brim of his floppy cap, which hadn't so much as shifted on his head, and bid, "Evenin', Elfred," before turning to Roberta's car, whose engine was still running.

In his bedroom, after Gabe left, Roberta bathed herself inside and out, shuddering at times with recollection. She scrubbed her flesh until it hurt, unable to scour away the filthy feeling of Elfred's hands and male parts abusing her. Sometimes tears interrupted but she swiped at them angrily, unwilling to be bested by anyone as low and bestial as Elfred Spear.

Don't let me be pregnant, don't let me be pregnant, she begged in silence. Sometimes she mumbled the words, then catching herself at it, refused to be reduced to a demented heap of blubbering, and clamped her lips shut stubbornly.

Once she said aloud, clearly, "Elfred, you'll pay! Mark my words, you'll pay!" little realizing Elfred already had.

When she had toweled dry, she donned Caroline Farley's maternity dress. It was tight across the bodice but it covered her and smelled of lavender from Caroline's bureau drawers. The shift Farley had given her was too short-bodied, so she left it folded on the bed, eschewing her own soiled underclothes, which she rolled in a ball and tied with the legs of her pantaloons. On the dresser top a comb and hand mirror lay, just as Caroline had left them. She removed what pins were left in her hair and combed it with stern strokes, sending bits of gravel ticking onto the floor at her heels. While she combed, she studied Caroline's picture. A dainty rose of a woman, with every delicate feature a man could desire, while in the mirror Roberta's own reflection showed broad cheekbones and bold features with little to recommend them, save strength, which most men disdained. Of that she had plenty. The comb moved through her hair almost defiantly, and when she'd finished, she laid it back on the crocheted dresser scarf and said, "Thank you, Caroline. I'll do something nice for your daughter. How will that be?"

Then she sat on the chair to wait for Caroline's husband, who seemed to be taking terribly long. She had been there less than a minute when a fuzzy brown cat appeared from beneath the bed, said, "Mrr . . ." and jumped onto her lap.

She knew it by name, though they'd never met.

"Hello, Caramel," she said as it paused in a crouch, sniffing her chin, then circled and found a place next to her wad of clothing.

"Well . . . so you're Caramel," she said, and lifted a hand to scratch the creature's neck. "What do you think is taking your master so long?"

When Gabe finally knocked, Roberta was dozing with her chin on her chest.

"Roberta?" he called quietly, and her head bobbed up.

"Whmm?" she replied, disoriented.

"May I come in?"

"Oh, Gabriel . . . yes . . . yes, come in."

He opened the door partway and peered around it. The sun had set but Roberta had turned on no lamp. In the shadowed room she was only faintly sidelit from the one north window whose pane had turned violet. Her hair hung straight down her back. She'd stuck her bare feet into her white shoes, and held a roll of clothing on her lap, which was shared by Caramel, whose eyes squinted closed after identifying her master. Caroline's dress looked misplaced on Roberta's much broader shoulders, but he found himself ready to accept it there.

"I'm sorry," she said, sitting up straighter. "I fell asleep."

He pushed the door against the wall and moved into the room where the smell of Ivory soap still lingered. "That's all right. That's good, actually. I worried that you might still be crying . . . or scared . . . something."

He paused at her knee and she looked up. "I've pretty much decided that tears and fright are worthless. What's done is done, and I'm not going to let myself be ruined by it."

"I hated leaving you alone, but I had to."

"You've been very kind to me tonight, Gabriel. Kinder than you would have had to be, especially considering how badly it ended the last time we were together."

He stood near her chair, looking down on her upturned face, wondering what was to become of the two of them.

"Here's your cap," he said.

When she reached for it, her hand paused. "Turn on the light, Gabriel."

"Why?"

"Turn on the light."

He hid the hand behind his back, hat and all. "Why?"

"Your hand . . . what have you done?"

"You know what I did. I beat the living daylights out of Elfred Spear."

"Oh, Gabriel." And after all the drying up she'd managed, her eyes filled again. She dropped her head and put a hand to her face, trying to hide the evidence of her feelings for him, because once again this was not the time or the place to reveal them.

He settled into a squat at her knees and put the cap on the floor beside the chair. Rather than touch her, he touched the cat, rubbing its throat with one callused finger. "I'm sorry, Roberta, but I couldn't let it pass. Everybody's going to know now—your kids, Elfred's wife, his kids. But a bastard like that has got to be stopped sometime, and if I didn't do it, who would?"

She nodded behind her hand and said, "I know. It's just so unexpected . . . your fighting for me. Nobody's ever fought for me. I've always had to fight for myself."

He reached out and put a big, bluff hand on her hair. He felt her silent weeping and went onto his knees, putting his other hand on her hair, too, drawing her forward till her forehead bumped his collarbone and his mouth rested on her mahogany hair.

They remained that way a long while. Until the window grew darker and Caramel woke up and found herself surrounded by too many people. Silently she leaped to the floor and padded off into the darkened house.

Then Gabriel whispered thickly, "I went out there to get your cap, and I found a button, too. And I saw the scuff marks in the gravel where he took you down, and so help me God, I wanted to go back to Elfred's house and finish him off. In all my life I've never wanted to harm anyone, but tonight I want to kill Elfred. I believe if you'd ask me to, I would."

Roberta pulled up her head and made out only the

dim outline of Gabe's features. "How badly did you beat him?"

"Bad. I broke some bones."

"Oh, Gabe. Do you think they will arrest you for it?"

"I don't know. It's a possibility. Either way, the whole town is gonna know."

She sighed and fell against the chair back, closing her eyes.

He sat back on his heels, close, but not touching her. "You thinking about your girls?" he asked.

"And yours . . . and you. Because you know what everyone's going to say about me, don't you? I'm divorced. I must have asked for it."

"But I know the truth. I saw the evidence!"

"And you know what they'll say next, don't you? That I came to your house first. What business did I have coming to the home of a single man in a state like that? Why didn't I go to my mother? But do you want to know why I didn't go to her? Because she'll say the same thing as all the rest. That it was my fault."

"No, Roberta . . . she wouldn't."

"Yes, she would. It's how she thinks. It's always the woman's fault."

He thought for a while, then said, "Roberta, I'm sorry if I made it worse by beating him up."

She took pity on him and touched his collar. "It's all right, Gabriel. And if you stop to think about it, there is some rather exquisite sense of justice in knowing that Elfred's true character has come to light at last. After all, how can Grace ignore it now that it's right before her eyes?"

"But his girls know, too, and they don't deserve that.

I shouldn't have done it in front of them."

"No, Gabriel, you shouldn't have. But you did, and they, like all the rest of us, will just have to live with what they know about their father. Perhaps that will be the greatest penalty Elfred will pay—the loss of their respect and love."

"So you don't intend to let the law know what he did to you?"

She dropped her hand from his collar and slowly shook her head. "Absolutely not."

"I didn't think so." He sighed and rose from his squat, towering above her again. "But it's so unfair. He should have to pay like any other criminal."

"Gabriel, let's not talk about it anymore." It was full dark now and he saw only the faintest edge of her face as it lifted. "I'm very tired and I want to go home."

"I'm going to take you."

"No, please . . . the girls . . ."

"The girls know what's up between us. We're not fooling them."

"What's up between us, Gabe? I don't seem to know myself."

"You're tired, you said, and you've been through a lot. This isn't the time to get into that, so hang on, Mrs. Jewett. I'm going to do something I've only done once before in my life, on my wedding night."

A second later she was in his arms like a child on her way to bed.

"Gabriel, put me down. I'm not Caroline."

"I know you're not Caroline. I've known that for quite some time," he declared, heading for the stairs. "Turn on that light. The switch is down by your hip."

A moment later the switch snapped and the brightness made both of them squint as he carried her down the stairs.

"You don't listen very well," she said, circling his neck with both arms, for any other way the ride was awkward. "I said to put me down."

"Heard you."

He took her through the kitchen and opened the screen door with her feet and went out into the starlight through the strong scent of roses.

"You just carried me under Caroline's rose arbor."

"Ayup," he said.

"And if you drive my motorcar you'll have to walk back home."

"Ayup," he said. "Done it before."

"And if anyone happens to be letting his cat in for the night and sees us we'll both have to leave town."

"Piss on 'em."

She couldn't help but smile; he was not his usual mild-mannered self tonight. He dropped her feet when they reached her car, and opened the passenger door for her, then slammed her inside. It took a minute for him to set the levers, light the headlamps and do the cranking. When he got in, he sat for a moment before putting the automobile in motion.

"Listen, Roberta. When you're feeling up to it, you and I should have a talk."

"About what?"

"About some of the things we said to each other the night of that clambake."

"Oh, that."

They rumbled away from the boulevard down the

dark street, their lamp beams bouncing with every pile of horse dung and pothole they crossed.

"Don't you think we should?"

"Yes, I suppose so."

"All right then, you let me know and I'll come over whenever you say and we'll get that straightened out."

"You think we can?"

"Don't know, but we got to try, don't we?"

"Yes, I suppose we do."

"All right," he said as they approached her house. "Now, what are you going to tell the girls about tonight?"

"The truth. What else can I do when I'm wearing Caroline's dress? Besides, I had a lot of time to think while you were gone, and I decided that I've never hidden the truth from my girls before, and we've always fared just fine. I'll figure out a way to tell them that won't traumatize them."

He braked, shut off the engine, set the levers and said, "All right, Roberta, we'll do this your way. Nothing but the truth."

"What about Isobel?"

He considered a moment, then answered, "She's the same age as Susan."

"But she's led a much more sheltered life. Besides, it really isn't her problem, is it? I'm not her mother."

He offered no response because he didn't know what to say.

Roberta lay her hand on the seat near his thigh. "I'll tell you something. I really don't know what I'm going to say when I walk in there. All four of those girls are innocents. They don't deserve to learn that the world has cruelty like Elfred's, and when I think about them finding out it makes me detest him all the more. He's their uncle, Gabe . . . their uncle! Just think about that."

They did, for some time, in silence.

Finally Gabe sighed. "Well, let's just go in there and see what they say. I'll take my cue from you."

"Thank you, Gabriel," she said.

They got out of the car and she waited while he stopped the carbide drip to the headlamps. Then they walked to her house to face their children, together.

Thirteen

The house smelled strongly of chocolate. The front room was dark, but through the lighted kitchen doorway Roberta glimpsed all four girls gathered around the table, leaning on their elbows, eating something from a flat pan. They were talking loudly and Lydia must have been entertaining, for she suddenly rocketed off her chair, whizzed in a circle and flailed her arms as if she were a dervish.

The others were laughing as Roberta and Gabriel entered the room.

"Hello, girls. We're here," she announced.

They all glanced at the doorway, and their faces lit at the sight of Roberta and Gabriel together again.

"You're *both* here!" Rebecca exclaimed.

"We're both here."

"Does that mean you've made up?" Lydia asked.

"I guess it does. What's in the pan?"

"Fudge. Becky made it for supper."

"Fudge? For *supper*?"

"Well, you weren't here, so we didn't know what else to have. And besides, we were in the mood for it."

Susan had been eyeing her mother curiously. "What's that you're wearing?"

Isobel answered, "It's my mother's dress."

264

"Why are you wearing her mother's dress?"

Roberta looked down at the worn garment. "Because I had an emergency and needed something quick, and Gabriel offered to lend me this."

"He did?" Isobel turned her wide eyes on her dad. "You *told* her she could wear Mother's clothes?"

"That's right," he said, feigning nonchalance, helping himself to a piece of fudge.

"But that's a maternity dress!"

Roberta explained, "I'm bigger than your mother. This was the only thing that fit."

Rebecca had been holding back, more suspicious than the rest. "What happened to *your* dress?" she asked, her attitude suggesting she wasn't buying these surface explanations.

"It got soiled."

Gabe bit into his piece of fudge and Isobel asked, "What happened to your hand?"

"Fistfight."

All four girls spoke at once.

"What!"

"A fistfight!"

"Over Mother?"

Everybody grew animated, and the babble sounded like a flock of pelicans. Rebecca's demand rang out at the end. "What's going on here?"

Roberta's eyes sought Gabe's. "I think we'd better tell them and get it over with."

"All right, whatever you say." He set down his fudge and said, "Susan, get your mother a chair. She's been through a lot tonight."

Susan went into the living room and returned with

the piano stool. When Roberta sat, Gabriel surprised everyone by taking up a stance behind her with his hands over her shoulders.

"What I have to say goes no farther than this room. Is that understood?" Roberta's eyes scanned the circle of solemn faces. Two of the girls nodded. "You neither confirm nor deny it, no matter what you might hear around town, no matter what your friends or any others might say to you."

Rebecca spoke for all. "You have our promise, Mother."

Roberta scrabbled through her mind for the proper place to begin. She extended her hands to the two girls nearest and said, "I think I'll need some hands to hold. This is going to be difficult." Holding Lydia's and Susan's hands, she told her story, avoiding overtly graphic descriptions and searching for veiled language.

"The reason Gabriel's hands are bruised is because he beat up your uncle Elfred for attacking me. I was out in the country and my car ran out of gas. Elfred came along and offered to help me fill my tank, and then he thought I should kiss him to thank him. When I refused, he got very rough with me and tried to force me to kiss him. He hurt me very badly and my clothes got dirty and I was very, very scared."

It was apparent that only Rebecca understood the full import of what Roberta was telling them. Her face showed it. Though she sat at the table with the rest, she had advanced to a plane of adult speculation that immediately distanced her from the three younger girls. She asked no questions, but Roberta knew they were rampaging through her head.

"Your uncle Elfred is not a nice man. He's a . . . well . . . how shall I say it?"

"Womanizer," Gabriel offered, still bolstering her as before.

"Yes, I guess that's as good a word as any. Do you all know what that means?"

The younger girls looked at each other and shrugged sheepishly, their hands clasped between their knees under the table.

"He likes to flirt with other ladies besides Aunt Grace. Only sometimes it goes further than flirting, and he gets demanding. That's what happened to me."

Lydia asked innocently, "Did he hit you, Mommy?" She had given up calling Roberta *Mommy* long ago, but it crept back into her vernacular now that her mother's well-being was threatened.

"Well . . . no." Roberta thought for a beat, then said more energetically, "But I hit him. Pretty hard, too."

"You did?" Lydia's eyes brightened. "Golly!"

Before any of the youngsters could ask for details of the attack, Roberta steered the conversation on another tack. "Now listen to me, because this is important. Your cousins were there when Gabriel beat up their father, and so was Aunt Grace. So I'm not sure they'll want to come over here and do things with you anymore."

"Can't we ask them to?" Susan inquired.

"Not for a while. Let things settle down a little bit. And as for going over to their house, I'm afraid that's going to be against the rules from now on."

Lydia looked dismayed, and Roberta could see a jag of whining coming on. Sure enough, Lydia whined,

"But Sophie makes the best praline cookies. We all love her praline cookies, Mother."

"Nevertheless, I don't want you over there."

Rebecca was staring at Gabe's hands on Roberta's shoulders. Her concerns far outstripped an end to Sophie's pralines.

Roberta took a deep breath and sat up straighter. "Gabriel and I thought you should know what happened, but I'm all right now, so you don't have to worry. I went to his house and he took good care of me, so now all we have to worry about is you four who ate nothing but fudge for supper, isn't that right?"

Though Roberta tried to end the discourse on a cheerier note, one of the group was noticeably more glum than the others when the evening broke up. Rebecca, already becoming estranged from her siblings by her infatuation with Ethan Ogier, withdrew to her bedroom, leaving the others to bid Isobel and Gabriel good night. They all wandered out to the porch where Isobel gave Roberta a good-bye hug and said, "I'm sorry Mr. Spear was so mean to you."

"Thank you, Isobel. But don't worry about me. Good night, sweetie." Fireflies were glimmering in the shrubs as the three girls went ahead. The neighborhood lay quiet beneath a moon-washed sky and the air had the dewy coolness that would leave the painted porch floor misted with moisture in the morning. Gabriel lingered on the porch with Roberta, feeling protective and loath to leave her. There, in the shadows, he put his hands on her shoulders, inquiring, "Will you be all right?"

It had taken a lot to bring out that touch of affection,

she thought, but he still had a long way to go. "I'll be fine. I just need some rest."

A mosquito came buzzing, and he fanned it away from his ear. "You think you'll stay home tomorrow?"

"I need every cent I can earn. I'll be working."

"In the country?"

"In Rockport in the morning. In the afternoon I don't know where until I get my orders."

"I'll worry about you, being out and about in your car from now on."

"No sense worrying." She, too, waved off a mosquito. "Nobody but Elfred would present any kind of threat to me, and you've taken care of him."

"Nevertheless, I'll worry."

"I'm not the kind who'll tuck my tail and hide, Gabriel. I simply have to do what I have to do, and if I have to drive through these mountains to support my girls, so be it. I'm not saying there won't be times when my heart won't jump into my throat if I see a man approaching me, but I'll just have to learn to live with it, won't I?"

He took one of her hands and covered it with his own. Their surroundings gave enough light for her to see the outline of his nose and chin, and pinpricks of reflected light from his eyes as he said quietly, "You're quite a woman, Roberta, you know that?"

"Actually, I think I'm pretty ordinary, but it's nice to hear you say that anyway. Thank you, Gabe. And thank you for beating up Elfred. I surely hope it doesn't get you into a bunch of trouble."

He used their joined hands to knock a mosquito off his temple. "I don't think it will, because underneath it all, Elfred's a coward, and if he accuses me publicly, he'll also have to explain why, publicly, and I don't think he's got the guts to do that."

Just then Isobel called, "Dad, come on! The mosquitoes are biting me!"

"Me, too," he said to Roberta, and dropped her hand. "Well, good night. I'll try to stop by tomorrow night and see how you are."

"I'll be here," she said, and moved to the top of the steps as he descended them. He passed her girls bounding back to the house, hounded by mosquitoes, too.

"Night, Mr. Farley!" they chorused.

"Good night, girls. Take good care of your mother now."

The girls mounted the steps in two leaps and Susan shrieked, "Come on, let's get inside before they eat us alive!"

In her bedroom ten minutes later, Roberta hung Caroline Farley's worn, stained lavender muslin maternity dress on a hook behind the door. Strewn around the room were her own discarded clothes from as long ago as a week. But the care she disdained for her own possessions she lavished on the dead woman's garment as dutifully as if Caroline herself were watching: She centered it carefully on a hanger, and touched the stains gently before her hand trailed away and fell to her side.

Oh, Gabe, she thought, *what are we going to do?*

Removing the dress left Roberta naked. She put a hand to her lower belly and closed her eyes, hating Elfred Spear. Glancing down at her stripped limbs, she felt a wave of despair and the repressed urge to shed

tears for herself. She had never been vain, not even re-
motely. Indeed, bodies, to Roberta, were merely the ves-
sels housing the soul and mind and spirit. They needed
fuel to power those souls and minds and spirits, as well
as occasional maintenance, but beyond this, Roberta
thought little of the human body's physicality. Looking
down at herself she saw very clearly her mediocrity—
size, texture, shape. All showed the history of a woman
who had borne three children and spent a lifetime of
hard work with little time for self-care. But her flesh—
plump, unfirm though it was—was her own, no one
else's to use as he wished.

She had no full-length mirror in the room, only a
small rectangular one with a chipped plaster frame,
hanging above a bureau. Passing it, she caught a faint
glimpse of her breasts, and hurried to cover them with
nightclothes, as if Elfred might still be lurking.

Even when she had donned her faded summer nightgown and tried to think of tomorrow instead of today,
the thick-throated urge to cry persisted. Two opposing
wills urged her. One said, *Cry*. The other said, *Don't
cry*. She was struggling between the two, straightening
out her unmade bed when Rebecca knocked and said,
"Mother, may I come in?"

Roberta grabbed the sheets and rubbed both her eyes
before calling, "Sure, Becky. Come ahead."

Becky slipped in and hovered near the door, showing
an uncharacteristic reserve. Backed up against it, she
stared at her mother and attempted a flicker of a smile
that failed dismally.

Roberta sat on the edge of her bed, trying to appear
unemotional. "Still up?"

"I've been waiting."

Oh, Becky, I'd hoped you wouldn't understand. I wanted to spare you that. Roberta's features dissolved into an admission of sadness. Too quietly she admitted, "I guess I knew that."

A stretch of silence brought the night closer and sharpened the need for truth. Where to go from here—one woman of thirty-six who knew too much about the world in which men and women met and clashed; one of sixteen who only suspected. One who wanted to protect, one who wanted to know.

Rebecca found the courage to speak first. "You didn't tell everything, did you?"

The terrible lump formed in Roberta's throat again and brought with it an overwhelming sorrowfulness. Her lips shaped the word *no*, but it failed to emerge as she wagged her head sorrowfully from side to side.

Rebecca slipped across the room and sat on the opposite side of the bed at a diagonal from her mother. She was barefoot and dressed in a white nightgown. Her hair had been braided in a coronet that day—she'd been experimenting with hair since Ethan Ogier had been paying court—and it formed a shock of loose squiggles, like unfurled rope fanning her shoulders. When she sat, she unconsciously pressed back against the footrail as she had against the door, but her mother understood: Tonight her daughter would grow up in a way neither of them wanted.

It took a while before Becky could say, "You don't think I know about it, but I do. About what Uncle Elfred did to you." Her eyes were big with the certainty of it. "He did, didn't he?"

Forever after, Rebecca would never be the innocent girl she had been, but Roberta would not lie to her daughter. She nodded slowly, twice.

"I know what it's called, too. I've heard the boys say it." Becky's voice held tinges of both defiance and fear.

"It's a terrible word."

"I knew it had to be because the boys were whispering when they said it, and when they caught us girls listening they got mad and told us to get out of there." Tears appeared in her eyes and she looked down at her nightgown and the outline of her knee beneath it. A sudden outrage replaced the horrified wonder in her voice and she made a fist on the bedspread. "How could Uncle Elfred do that to you? It's so horrible."

"Yes, it is. It was. But I couldn't let the younger girls know."

Rebecca nodded sadly.

"Elfred's been making innuendos to me ever since I got here. He's a sly, insidious lecher, the absolute worst kind. Always does it when Grace's back is turned. Poor Grace, married to a hypocrite like that."

"Does she know what he did to you?"

"Gabriel says so. He didn't try to keep it a secret why he was beating Elfred to a bloody pulp right in his own front yard. And Grace was right there watching. She heard what Gabe accused him of."

"Will she divorce him like you did our dad?"

"I don't know, Becky. My suspicion is that she'll think I lured her poor beleaguered husband on, that it was all my fault, just because I'm divorced. She and Grandma are in cahoots on that."

"But how could she think that?" Rebecca grew indignant. "She knows you'd never do that! You're a good person, and you've always taught us to be good, too."

"Ah, Becky . . ." Roberta slumped back, partially on her pillows, partially against the headrail of the bed. "If only the rest of the world were as fair-minded as you." She closed her eyes for a moment. "It's not though." They opened again and she appeared relaxed, idly plucking at the chenille as if to pick it from its backing. "And that's the reason I told the girls they can't defend me, because there are going to be people in this town who take Elfred's side. He's a man, after all, and men somehow get excused from perpetrating vicious acts like this. Women get blamed—that's just how it is. Especially divorced women." She rolled her head to face Rebecca. "But you and I know the truth, and Gabriel knows, and that's all that really matters to me. Anything others might say means little or nothing to me. I'm only sorry if it hurts you girls, especially if it makes your sisters realize exactly what happened." She hauled herself upright again. "That's one of the aftereffects of this that I hate Elfred all the more for. For robbing my babies of their innocence. Look"—her hand lifted and fell—"here you are, having this discussion, when you should be totally unaware of any such thing, living your young life without this blight on your memory. Oh, Becky . . . I wish I could undo it for you."

At her mother's sudden surge of emotionalism Becky got up and hurried around the bed. "Oh, Mother, I wish *I* could undo it for *you*." Seated at Roberta's side, Rebecca embraced her as if she were the mother and Roberta the daughter.

Roberta allowed herself some tears . . . but few. She and Rebecca had always been close, but even closer since her divorce. As the oldest, Becky had uncomplainingly assumed the responsibilities that fell her way, often playing surrogate mother in Roberta's absence. Tonight, her sweet concern brought peace and healing; the tender pat of her hand on Roberta's shoulder made both of them feel much better.

Against Roberta's hair, her daughter said, "Isobel's dad was awfully good to you though, wasn't he, Mother?"

Roberta drew back and held both of Becky's slim hands.

"I was so glad to have him there. He's really a very kind man."

"I felt bad when you two fought."

"So did I."

"And I'm glad you're back together again."

"So am I."

"So is Isobel!"

They found enough levity for smiles, then Rebecca divulged, "Isobel told me that she wishes her dad would marry you."

"Did she?" Roberta smiled softly, picturing Isobel, whom she, too, loved. "I'm afraid that won't happen though. We're just too different."

"What kind of different?"

"Oh, you know. He's fastidious, I'm messy. He lives by a schedule, I hate clocks. He thinks you have to sit at a table with a fork and knife, and I think tables were made for resting your heels on. Also, his family objects to me because I'm divorced."

"Oh." A beat passed before Rebecca asked, "But would you marry him anyway if he asked you to?"

"I don't know. Would you want me to?"

"Well . . . not for us—I mean, we get along just fine without him, and we have lots of fun together, just the four of us. But you seem happier when you're with him."

"I didn't realize that." After some thought Roberta added, "Well, maybe I did realize it, because when I saw him at school that day and he didn't speak to me, I felt just terrible. And after that I couldn't stop thinking about him. I don't know, Becky . . . once you've been married and it hasn't worked, you get sort of scared of trying again. And like you said, we four Jewetts get along pretty darned well on our own, don't we?"

Becky reached out and closed two buttons at Roberta's throat. "But he beat up Uncle Elfred for you, and let you wear his wife's dress, and he let Isobel start coming here again whenever she wants to. I think he loves you, Mother. I think he loves you very much and he just doesn't know it yet."

With that, Rebecca sedately rose and kissed her mother on the top of the head. "Don't you worry about anything. I'm going to take extra good care of you from now on, and whether he marries you or not, I think Mr. Farley will, too."

Mr. Farley, at that moment, was contemplating the same thing: taking care of Roberta Jewett. He was standing in his bedroom in his summer underwear, discovering some gravel on the coverlet where her head had been. *Goddamned Elfred Spear, he ought to have his balls cut off!* Gabe reached down and rubbed a couple of grains between his fingers, then dropped heavily to the edge of the bed, sitting there a long while, picturing what that bastard had done to Roberta. And she, so full of pluck and life, never hurting a flea. Truth was, she was one of the most loving people he'd ever met. Good to her kids. Good to his kid. Good to him. Probably really good to the sick people she took care of all over the county as well. It was just no damned fair that a woman like that should fall prey to slime like Elfred. Ask anybody who knew him and they'd say that Elfred was sure a fine businessman, and owned a big beautiful house, and had himself a real nice family. And couldn't that man make money, hand over fist! Apart from how "good" Elfred did, they might chuckle about his never-ending peccadilloes. But did they stop him? Did anybody ever try to stop men like Elfred?

No. Instead, they gossiped about women like Roberta because she had a little white piece of paper that said she didn't have to be married anymore to a no-good sponger who had never taken care of her or his kids to begin with! Had her husband ever loved her? Hard to believe a man like that had much love in him. If he did he would have been home more and kept her happy instead of taking up with other women and leaving her to support those kids alone.

Poor Roberta, she'd had a hell of a life, always scrabbling for a living, never complaining about it. But now . . . what if she had one more? What if that sonofabitch Elfred had left her pregnant? Wouldn't that give the good matrons of Camden grist for the next twenty years' gossip? And those three nice girls of hers would pay a price, too. Lord, Lord, it just wasn't fair.

Gabe was no expert, but he'd done some figuring about how long it had taken from the time Elfred raped her until the time he left her alone to bathe, and it seemed to Gabe that no matter what she'd done after he closed the door, nature had had plenty of time to take its course.

He supposed she must be lying in her bed worrying about the same thing. What if? What if?

He sighed and rose like an old man, straightening muscle by muscle, then flipping down the coverlet off his pillow. He turned off the light, stretched out for the night and folded his hands beneath his head.

But all he could think about was Roberta, Roberta, Roberta beside him where she'd be safe from men like Elfred for the rest of her life.

She was still asleep the following morning when the telephone rang downstairs, blending into some weird dream she'd been having. Bolting up, she felt her pulse hammering as she sat in her rumpled bed, trying to sort out why the school bell was ringing at home, and where the girls were on Saturday. Oh! It was Friday, and judging from the angle of the sun, she should be on her way to work.

The phone rang again.

"Oh my," she mumbled, scrambling out of bed, noting the alarm clock said seven-thirty. She took the stairs with her hands on both walls, breaking her downward plunge, and grabbed the receiver off the prongs as the bell jangled for the fifth time.

"Hello?"

"Morning, Roberta."

"Oh . . . Gabe." She rumpled her hair and squinted at the bright kitchen window. "What are you doing calling at this hour?"

"Wondering how you're doing today."

"I just woke up and I'm going to be late for work, but other than that I'm doing all right, Gabe. Really I am."

"Well, good. Something I want to talk to you about, but not with Central listening in. You suppose you could meet me at noon someplace?"

"At noon?"

"Or whenever would be best. I thought you might be able to get away for a bit after you check in at your Rockport office. I'm doing a job down that way myself, and we could maybe meet, say, oh I don't know . . . out by the south end of Lily Pond off Chestnut Street?"

"Sure, I guess I could."

He gave her some specific directions and they agreed on eleven-thirty.

"See you then," she said.

"Ayup," he said, "see you there," and hung up. She stood for a few seconds with her hand on the receiver after she'd hung up, wondering what he wanted. She remembered his concern yesterday, his protectiveness, but that was what anyone would do in such a situation, it wasn't the normal Gabriel. Well, she'd know soon enough, and in the meantime she was later than ever.

When she arrived at their meeting place his truck was pulled off the road into the shade beside a clearing that led down to the pond. Around the edge of it water lilies spread the surface with plate-sized leaves, dotted with big yellow blooms. Across the water houses were visible, but on the near side the residences were secluded in the woods, and only a rock pile broke the stretch of open land between two sections of thick, green forest. Someone had scythed the wild grasses and left them to dry in the sun. The heady scent of shorn clover made ambrosia of the air. To Roberta's left, a split-rail fence divided the woods from the field, and on its far side a small herd of black and white cattle were chewing their cuds and twitching their tails. Two of them watched Roberta as she got out of her car, shaded her eyes and waved to Gabe.

He was propped against a waist-high boulder forty feet away, wearing a straw hat and chewing a piece of grass. When she waved, he boosted himself up and walked back toward her. She enjoyed watching his lanky movements, the relaxed stride of his legs in his blue denim pants and the slight riffle of breeze against the rolled-up sleeves of his white shirt. They met in the middle of the clearing, where grasshoppers caromed off the hem of her uniform and landed on the toes of his worn leather boots.

"Smells good out here," she said when they were still ten paces apart.

"Clover," he said.

"Peaceful, too."

They came abreast of each other and stopped. "So peaceful I realized too late that you might not be very anxious to meet another man out in the middle of nowhere with nobody else around."

"Oh, Gabe, I'm not scared of you."

"Well, I hope not."

The bright midday sun reflected off her white clothes

and made her squint, even with the sun at her back.

"Pretty hot out here in the sun," he said. "Come on, let's go sit in the shade by the truck."

"All right."

She turned and walked beside him through the stubble of clover and meadow-grass, lifting the fallen bits of green with the toes of her white nurse's shoes, as he did with the toes of his boots, stirring its perfume, which grew heady beneath the hot, hot sun. In the distance, one of the cows mooed as if asking where they were going. The woods formed a rippling green wall as they moved toward it.

"I been watching the frogs . . ." he said.

"Mm . . ."

". . . eating flies."

"Mm . . ." She smiled at their feet as they ambled along, she stretching her strides, he shortening his, so they'd match.

"A few turtles in the pond, too."

"We'll have to tell the girls. They'll be right out here to get one."

"When I was a boy we used to eat turtle. My mother made soup out of it."

They reached the cool, welcome shade beside his truck and she turned to face him.

"That what you brought me out here to talk about, Gabriel? The frogs and the turtles?"

From beneath the brim of his straw hat he studied her, unsmiling. His white shirt collar was open, soiled inside from his morning's work, and bits of sawdust clung to his shoulders. His throat was the reddish brown of a man who rarely closes his collar button. His eyes were the gray-blue of new smoke, and serious.

"No, it's not. Did you eat dinner in town?"

"No, I didn't."

"Oh, of course not. It's not noon yet. 'Course, I know you don't set much store by noon, but I went ahead and brought us a couple of sandwiches, and I thought we could just sit here on the running board and eat them if you were hungry."

Gabriel, who never wasted words, was jabbering. She wondered why.

"What kind of sandwich? Turtle?"

"Nope. Beef." He opened his truck door to get them. "Matter of fact, you aren't going to believe this, but I went over and asked my mother to make them this morning."

"Your mother—well, she must not have known you were going to share them with me."

"Ayup, she did. I told her." From the tool caddy in the back of the truck he found a steel brush and swept off the running board.

"Sit down, Roberta."

She sat, and he sat, putting a sandwich tin between them. He took out a fruit jar full of iced tea and un-capped it, and set it in the weeds between their out-stretched feet. Opening the tin, he offered it to her.

"Thank you."

They began eating, companionably quiet for a spell before Gabriel said his piece, looking off sort of easterly across the meadow at the green rim of woods. "What happened to you yesterday—that bothers me something terrible. I couldn't sleep last night for thinking about it and worrying about you."

"But I'm not your worry, Gabriel."

"May not be, but I worry just the same. What if . . . well, what if what you did afterwards didn't do the trick? I figured it out, Roberta, and close as I can guess, it was almost an hour from the time Elfred pulled his dirty work and when you took that basin of water into my bedroom. Let's just say that the timing turned out to be just right and what you did in there you did too late, and you still were pregnant. If that happened, I'd marry you, Roberta. That's what I came here to tell you."

Her cheekful of sandwich nearly dropped out of her mouth. She closed her lips and swallowed, staring at Gabriel's profile while he continued studying the sunny field of mowed clover.

"You would?"

Turning his face to her, he nodded.

"If I were pregnant."

"That's right."

"To protect me from gossip."

"Something like that." He took another bite of beef sandwich.

"What about the things you said we needed to talk about? I thought that's why you were meeting me out here."

"In a case like this—I mean, supposing—we'd just have to overlook our differences."

"Overlook my messiness and your fear of showing your emotions, is that what you mean?"

She watched him carefully, and sure enough, he finally found the wherewithal to blush. He finished his sandwich and took a long drink of iced tea from the fruit jar, studying the opposite woods again. He set the jar down and wiped his mouth with the edge of a hand.

"I figured it was a way out of a fix for you."

She was quiet for so long he finally looked over and found her packing away the uneaten portion of her sandwich in the tin.

"What's the matter?"

"You really think I'd make a second disastrous marriage after the first one ended that way?"

"Disastrous?"

She put her feet flat on the ground and covered her knees as if they were baseballs she'd just caught. "A marriage of convenience isn't exactly my style, Gabriel. I should think you'd know that by now. I may not be dainty and perfect and feminine like Caroline, but I have feelings, the same as she did. And if a man wanted me, I'd expect him to show it by doing some serious courting—unless the way you've been acting is what you consider serious courting. But by my standards it's not. The thing is, Gabriel, I think you're scared. I think you love me and you're scared to death to say so, so instead you use this trumped-up excuse for suggesting we should get married, only I'm not about to fall for it and live with another man who doesn't have the faintest notion of how to be a husband. I'd rather give birth to a bastard and raise it myself than tie myself up to a man who's still in love with his first wife. So, I appreciate the thought, and underneath, it's probably very selfless of you to offer, but no thank you, Gabriel. Not unless you love me." She pushed off her knees and rose, adding without a touch of rancor, "Thank you for the sandwich. Sorry I didn't feel like finishing it, but maybe next time." She strode toward her car while he leaped to his feet.

"Roberta, wait!"

"I've got to drive clear up to Bangor this afternoon. Sorry."

"That's a fine way to fling a man's offer back in his face!" he shouted at her back.

"I thanked you, Gabe, didn't I?" She tossed a half-glance over her shoulder, and he grew angrier, watching her proceed to her car and get set to start it. He stomped across twenty feet of mixed weeds and caught up with her, forcing the crank handle from her hand.

He, angry, and she, stone calm, faced each other in the dappled shade of noon with a herd of cows looking on.

"What do you want me to do?" he said, exasperated as only this woman could make him.

"I've already told you."

"Roberta, we're middle-aged people, for cryin' out loud!"

"Which precludes courtship? Emotion? Spooning? Gabriel, if that's what you think, then you're worse off than I thought you were."

"I thought I was doing you a favor by offering you a way out."

"Yes, I know that's what you thought. I'm sorry I can't accept, and I thank you again for your largess. But on those terms . . ." She shook her head, letting the thought trail. "I've spent enough loveless years with a man. I'm the kind of woman who needs the real thing, in all its"—she gestured wide—"its flamboyant outrageousness, and I don't think you're ready for that yet.

I really do think you're not over Caroline yet. Don't get me wrong, Gabriel. I'd never ask you to give up your memories of her. But you'd have to love me as much as you did her, otherwise it would never work. I would forever be walking in her shadow, and the shade would be too cool for me to tolerate."

She wrested the crank from his hand and applied it. Momentarily they stood surrounded by the noise of the sputtering engine.

"Roberta!" he yelled above it. "All of our children want us to marry, can't you see that?"

She yelled back, "Of course I can! Examine your motives, Gabriel, and when they're the right ones, ask me again!"

As she headed for the car door, he wanted to haul her back and manhandle her into submission. But that's what Elfred had done yesterday, and gentlemen didn't do such things.

So he let her get in, and shift what needed shifting, and back away and turn around and leave him standing in the shade wondering what he'd done wrong.

Fourteen

*M*yra Halburton belonged to an organization called the Greater Camden Ladies' Tea, Quilting and Benevolent Society. One of its members was Tabitha Ogier, the grandmother of Ethan Ogier. Another was Maude Boynton, whose husband owned the motorcar company. And Jocelyn Duerr, a neighbor of Gabriel's, and Ellen Barloski, who was a great-aunt of the Spears' housekeeper, Sophie. Hannah Mary Gold was a first cousin to Seth Farley's wife, and Niella Wince lived kitty-corner across the street from the Spears. Sandra Yance's daughter was a nurse for young Dr. Fortier III. . . .

And the roster twined on and on.

Two days after Elfred Spear's beating, the Benevolent Society gathered for its biggest event of the year, a garden luncheon beneath the elms in the backyard of its president, Wanda Libardi. Wanda also belonged to a musical trio called the Sweethearts of Song, who opened the luncheon by singing "Beautiful Dreamer" while standing beneath the rose arbor against a backdrop of seven-foot hollyhocks in Wanda's bountiful garden.

The real entertainment began, however, once Wanda and her cohorts ceased warbling and the group at large got down to some of its *benevolence.*

Maude Boynton brought up what everybody there was wondering about. "Myra, is it true what we've all been hearing about Elfred?"

"I don't know, Maude. What have you been hearing?"

"That he was beaten within an inch of his life by Gabriel Farley."

"I guess there's no sense in trying to hide it. But Gabriel Farley will pay for what he's done! Mark my words!"

Sandra Yance said, "My Susan saw Elfred when he came into Dr. Fortier's office. She said he looked like somebody used him for an anvil."

Ellen Barloski looked bereaved. "Oh . . . that handsome face of his, all bashed up . . . what a shame. Poor Grace must be mortified."

Jocelyn Duerr asked, "Your divorced daughter has been seeing a lot of Gabriel, hasn't she?"

Myra prickled up. "I don't actually keep tabs on what Roberta does. Running all over the country in that motorcar of hers—how could a mother possibly keep track of a daughter like that?"

While Myra fended off the leading question, the other women exchanged pointed glances that said, *Later.*

The group spent a pleasant two hours milling around the yard, admiring the gardens, filling their plates at a buffet table and eating petite tarts and crustless sandwiches. Whenever Myra was out of earshot, covert whispers filled her wake, as insistent as the smell of coffee wafting out of the house. Sensing that the undercurrent was caused by the turmoil in her family, Myra made her excuses and left early.

To a woman, the other members of the Camden Benevolent Society stayed under the elms until they had
seen Myra's skirts rustle off through the garden gate.
The hostess opened the gossip herself.

"Well, now that she's gone I must say . . . I'm surprised she didn't say more. She's always got so much to
brag about—Elfred and his money, Grace and her fine
things. But now that the gossip's going the other direction, she's certainly clammed up, hasn't she?"

"Whatever Myra Halburton says, that younger
daughter of hers is behind this rivalry between Gabriel
and Elfred. Why else would two grown men who've
been friends for years get into a fistfight that way?"

"And right out on the front yard where everyone
could see it!"

Tabitha Ogier said, "My grandson has been spending
quite a bit of time at that Jewett house this summer.
Seems he's got an eye for the oldest girl. Some of the
things he's heard over there . . . well, let me tell you, it
would make your hair curl."

"I saw that Jewett woman over at Gabriel Farley's
house the night they say he beat up Elfred. Parked her
car there just as bold as brass, and I happen to know
his daughter wasn't home at the time."

"Well, I haven't spoken up till now—out of respect
for Myra—but I actually *saw* the fight." Niella Wince's
lips were pursed up with self-importance.

"You didn't!"

"Most of it. Out my bedroom window. Goodness
gracious, a person couldn't help but look with all that
yelling going on. What Gabe was yelling a lady
wouldn't repeat, but let me tell you, it didn't leave any

question that that divorced woman thinks every man is fair game, whether he's married or not."

They all chewed on that for a while, then someone said, "Poor Grace."

"Oh my, yes, poor Grace."

"And poor Caroline. What would she think if she were still alive?"

"And those children. For heaven's sake, imagine what they've been exposed to with a mother like that."

"Myra Halburton wouldn't hear it from my lips, but I said it years ago when Roberta left Camden because it wasn't *good* enough for her—I said, 'Mark my words, that girl's going to fall into no good, moving off to the city that way.' And sure enough, doesn't she come back eighteen years later divorced and footloose, thinking she can carry on her indiscretions on our doorsteps as if we were blind and stupid."

"Gabriel Farley's been at her place plenty, let me tell you. They say it started the first day she got into town. He and Elfred both went running up there to her house like a pair of regular tomcats. And they've been there plenty since."

"What about those Jewett children? Shouldn't somebody look into it and see that they're removed from their home if it's being run like a bordello?"

"Who?"

"Well, I don't know, but somebody should do it."

"Well, it's not going to be me."

"But aren't we the Benevolent Society? Doesn't that make it our duty?"

"Now, just a minute. I don't know that being the

Benevolent Society gives us the right to intrude on someone's personal affairs."

"Oh, doesn't it? Then who should look after the welfare of those children? After all, they're the grandchildren of one of our members."

"Then let Myra Halburton look after their welfare."

"Can't you see that poor Myra is too mortified by
these activities of her younger daughter to admit what's
going on? And you've got to feel sorry for her, too.
After all, what mother would want to face her own
child with an accusation of being an unfit parent?"

"I may have said she's been seen at Gabriel Farley's
house, but that doesn't make her an unfit parent."

"Then what does? She's a hussy, through and
through. Married, divorced, twitching her tail before
the nicest single man this town has to offer, spoiling
him in the process, then trying to break up the marriage
of her very own sister. I'd say that's a hussy. Furthermore, she leaves her children untended at all hours of
the day and night, and they say her house looks like a
pigsty. I say we speak to someone in authority and have
them go over there and see what's what. Those children
might be better off living somewhere else."

"But who's going to do it?"

"You're the president, Wanda. I think you should do
it."

One single Benevolent member had remained silent
throughout all this holier-than-thou exchange. Elizabeth
DuMoss, normally genteel, spoke up with a ferocity
that startled her peers.

"Now just a minute, all of you! I've been sitting here
listening while you planned your little war against a

woman who is not here to defend herself, so I'm going to do it for her. First of all, let me say I'm ashamed of every single one of you for your unbridled gossip the minute Myra's back is turned. You call yourselves a benevolent society, but I'm afraid today you've made mockery of the very word, and I can't sit silent any longer and let you continue this charade.

"I'm a fourth-generation member of this group, and I'm sure my great-grandmother would be appalled if she knew how its once-charitable intention has turned to such high-handed matters as deciding people's fates. I know I'm just one voice against many, but I couldn't live with myself if I didn't say something, and what I have to say is primarily about Elfred Spear, not Roberta Jewett.

"Every woman in this yard has conveniently over-looked the fact that Elfred Spear is a shameless de-baucher who has pinched bottoms and ogled breasts and fondled women he has no right to touch whenever the opportunity arose. He's embarrassed us at public and private gatherings by touching many of us, though few of you will admit it. He mocks his wife while her back is turned, and makes a joke of his marriage with his countless adulteries. He hasn't enough respect for his own children to hold his lechery at bay when they are present, but conducts it right under their noses as if it is his God-given right to insult any female in the universe. We all know he does it—sidles up to women any-where he pleases and makes sly innuendoes about what's under their skirts. And any of you who'll deny it are outright liars.

"So I ask you, why have you all placed blame on

Roberta Jewett when the real villain here is probably Elfred Spear? I've sat quiet while you crucified her simply because she's a woman and divorced, and not one word about Elfred's fornicating has been mentioned. Well, I'm mentioning it because he's gotten away with it long enough. This is our chance to stop Elfred Spear. All we have to do is stand behind Mrs. Jewett, and stop the rumors rather than spread them. Is that so difficult to do? To give the woman the benefit of the doubt? And what is her greatest crime? Is it that she's divorced, or that she's living her life the way many of us wish we could live ours—living where she pleases, driving her own motorcar, supporting her three children as she sees fit, carrying out a job that brings her the satisfaction of earning a salary she can use as she wants without having to ask a man for pocket money?

"I ask every woman here—are you disdainful of Roberta Jewett or jealous of her?"

As Elizabeth DuMoss stopped speaking the women beneath the elms held so still the buzz of the bees in the hollyhocks could have been cataloged into individual notes. Some faces were red with embarrassment, others white with rage, but none were impassive. Some women stared beratingly at Elizabeth, others gazed sheepishly at their laps. Some hid behind their coffee cups, others hid behind their silent self-righteousness.

Elizabeth gathered up her gloves and parasol. "I leave you with a gesture which to some of you may seem excessive, but which I see as essential to my self-respect. At this time I formally resign my position as treasurer of the Greater Camden Ladies' Tea, Quilting and Benevolent Society and submit my resignation from the club. I find I cannot be affiliated with an institution that would put its time and efforts—and probably some of its treasury funds as well—into bringing undeserved emotional duress upon a woman like Mrs. Jewett. In doing this, I follow the dictates not only of my own heart, but of my foremothers as well, one of whom was a founder and charter member of this society. On her behalf, and my own, I bid you good-bye."

Elizabeth DuMoss, having said her piece—and said it with magnificent mastery—snapped up her parasol and left the gathering. Before she reached the garden gate, she heard the furor burst forth behind her.

She went straight to the shop of Gabriel Farley on Bayview Street. Finding him out on a job, she repaired to his home where, receiving no response to her knock on his screen door, she opened it and dropped a note onto his rag rug.

Mr. Farley, it said, *I must speak to you immediately. The Benevolent Society is going to try to undermine the reputation of Roberta Jewett and get her children taken away from her. We cannot let that happen. Please call me at 84 or come by my house this evening as soon as you possibly can. Elizabeth DuMoss.*

Elizabeth DuMoss was a pretty woman with soft brown eyes, gentle manners and an exceedingly rich husband who owned one of the largest houses in Camden, on Pearl Street, as well as the limestone quarries in Rockport. Elizabeth was one year younger than Gabriel Farley and had been infatuated with him from the time she was in fourth grade. She loved her husband in countless ways and had established a faithful, workable marriage. But he was thick through the middle and tight-fisted with his money, and though she wouldn't have traded her life with anyone's, there were several levels on which she nevertheless envied Roberta Jewett.

Her unrequited first love was one of them.

When he rang her bell at six-fifteen that evening she rose from the dinner table and told the maid, "I'll get it, Rosetta. Please, go on serving dinner." She trod through her home with the grace of a hostess accustomed to handling callers, and approached the front door with the assurance of one who understands her unassailable place at the head of a small-town society.

"Hello, Gabriel," she said, opening the screen door and admitting him into her richly papered foyer.

"Hello, Elizabeth." He extended his hand and she gave hers. "How are you?"

"Oh, I'm fine. At least I was until the Benevolent Society meeting this afternoon."

Their handclasp held, and their mutual knowledge of her longtime regard for him lent the moment an intimacy that was present whenever they met. But along with it came a mutual respect for her married state and the fact that she was the mother of four children.

He dropped her hand and said, "I got your note."

She held up a finger and said, "One moment, Gabriel." He watched her move down the hall to the dining room archway and speak to her family. "Excuse me, Aloysius, Gabriel is here now. Children, continue with your supper. We won't be long."

A chair scraped back and Aloysius DuMoss brought his considerable girth and walrus moustache into the hall. He was extending a hand as he approached Gabriel and said, "Let's step into the morning room where we can talk in private."

What was said among the three of them in the DuMoss's morning room drove Gabriel Farley straight to Roberta's front door within five minutes of his meeting with them.

The girls were on the front porch when he arrived, slung into hammocks and canvas chairs, reading and whisking away mosquitoes with wilted lilac branches. Ethan Ogier was there, too, sitting with his back against a railing spindle, playing catch with himself by throwing a hard rubber ball against the wall beneath the living room window where it left a smudge in Gabriel's white paint job, which no longer looked as immaculate as it had last April.

They all said, "Hi, Mr. Farley," too steeped in laziness to pay him much mind.

"Your mother home?" he asked as he mounted the stairs in two giant steps.

"She's in the kitchen."

"Okay if I go right in?"

"Mom!" Susan yelled over her shoulder. "Mr. Farley's coming in!"

He opened the screen door as she returned to her reading.

Roberta met him in the kitchen doorway, wiping her hands on a dishtowel that looked as gray as the shop rags Gabe used on his tools.

"Well . . . back so soon?" she said. "You come a-courtin'?"

He turned her by an arm and whisked her into the

kitchen where they could not be seen through the doorway.

"If it's courting you demand, you're going to get it, Roberta, because I want to marry you."

"Goodness, that's quite a change from this afternoon when you indicated you really didn't *want* to marry me, but would if you had to, to save me from disgrace. Now, which one is it, Gabriel?"

"I swear to God, I never saw such a saucy woman in my life. Would you shut up and listen to me?"

"Shut up . . . oh, now that's really poetic. Whoo!" She fanned her face with the dishtowel. "Makes a woman's heart race about forty miles an hour to hear sweet talk like that. Who taught you to—"

Gabe shut her up with a kiss.

He plastered his very impatient mouth over her very impertinent one and flattened her up against the pantry door. When he had her effectively silenced, he put his arms to use as well. Those long muscular carpenter's arms slid around her and scooped her away from the door against him, and as their bodies aligned, all of her sassiness and all of his exhorting melted into oblivion. She went up on tiptoe and he adjusted his head, and they meshed together splendidly, like some perfect mortise and tenon he might have fashioned to last two hundred years. With an arm at her waist and an open hand in her tumbledown hair, he kept her there where both of them had often imagined her being, kissing the bejesus out of her.

It was fiery and insistent and tinged with the awareness that a porchful of young people could come slamming into the house at any moment.

And deuced if they didn't.

Right in the middle of that important first willing resignation, when Roberta was bent back over Gabe's arm
and his dusty carpenter's trousers were nestled into the
gathers of her wrinkled white nurse's apron, two girls
showed up in the doorway. There they were, going at
it like long-lost lovers when they heard Susan whisper,
"My mom is kissing your dad," then two giggles that
brought Gabe's head swinging around as he ordered
over his shoulder, "Out, you two!" and belatedly,
"Hello, Isobel."

Roberta peeked around Gabe and seconded the order. "Yes, out. And don't come back till we tell you
to."

Gabe resumed his stance and said, "Kids . . . sheesh,"
before Roberta brazenly pulled his head down for more.

Their kisses got better then—the children knew, and
would stay away, and the hurdle was jumped at last.
They took each other . . . and plenty of time . . . and explored some while a mosquito came buzzing and was
ignored. She sampled his mouth and he sampled hers,
and they used their hands on what was allowable.
When primal urges became adamant, he pulled his midsection back, flattened his forearms against the door
and stood that way, breathing hard against the bridge
of her nose. His eyes were closed. So were hers. Their
heartbeats were still doing a quickstep and there was a
mosquito bite on Roberta's cheek.

"He got me," she said, smiling.

"Who?"

"The mosquito."

"Where? I'll kiss it."

"Right here." She tapped her cheek and he kissed it, bending to reach, leaving his forearms on the wall.

"Thank you," she murmured.

"Any more?" he queried. "Here?" He grazed her eyebrow. "Here?" And her nose. "Here?" And her lips.

"Mmm . . . yes, there."

While he kissed her mouth as if it were a slice of watermelon, she scratched the bite on her cheek. Still preoccupied with his amorous attentions, he pulled her hand away.

"Here, don't do that. It only makes it worse."

"Quit talking when you're kissing me. I've been without kissing for too long to put up with that."

"Boy, you're bossy," he said, and followed orders.

Some time later they came up for air, and she looped her arms loosely over his shoulders. "Oh, Gabriel," she said, gazing into his eyes, "what took you so long?"

"What do you mean, what took me so long? Do you remember the first time I kissed you? You didn't even kiss me back, just sat there like a lump of dough. It takes a man a while to get up his courage after getting treated like that."

"I did not sit there like a lump of dough."

"Yes, you did, Mrs. Jewett, as if you were analyzing it. And then you excused me from your house as if to say, 'Duty done, good-bye.'"

"I don't remember it that way at all. I just thought it was a bad idea."

He grinned. "Obviously you don't anymore."

"No, Mr. Farley, I don't anymore."

"Good, because you've got to listen to me. You've got to marry me because the—"

She pushed his arm aside as if it were a turnstile.

"No. Listen . . ." He caught her and kept her between him and the wall. "You've got to because the Ladies' Benevolent Society is talking about raising issues with the law over your mothering, and they're making noises about trying to force your kids away from you somehow. And it's my fault, don't you see? Because I bashed in Elfred's face, and they figured we were fighting over you so you were probably carrying on with both of us, and somebody saw your car at my house afterwards, and if they go to the authorities you'll have to tell them what Elfred did to you, and I don't think you want to do that."

She stared at him with her hands pressed to the wall behind her.

"Who told you all this?"

"Elizabeth DuMoss."

"Shelby's mother?"

"Yes. She belongs to that society. Belonged—actually, she quit today when they started raising these preposterous issues. Gave 'em a piece of her mind, too. Then she came to see me and warned me what they were planning to do."

She stared at him again and said, "My mother is a member of the Benevolent Society."

He closed his eyes and breathed, "Oh, God." She pushed on his arm and he let his hands slip from the wall, releasing her. "I'm sorry, Roberta."

She walked toward the dry sink, turning her back on him. "Why would Elizabeth DuMoss stand up for me?"

"Because she knows what kind of a snake Elfred is."

She snapped him a look. "You told her what he did to me?"

It took him a beat to answer. "No, not exactly."

"Then what? . . . Exactly."

"I didn't tell her. I think she just guessed from what she heard about me beating him up. Roberta, look"— he moved up close behind her and tried to make her turn around—"this is all my fault. If I'd have used my head and cornered Elfred out in the country someplace where nobody would have known I was the one to beat him up, this wouldn't have happened. I'm sorry. It was stupid and selfish of me, because all I was thinking about was myself and how angry I was. I never stopped to think about how it would implicate you. Please, Roberta . . ." She had been resisting his effort to turn her around so he slipped an arm across her collarbone and pulled her back against him. "Please don't get that way with me again. Don't throw me out and get all independent and uppity. Let us fight this thing together."

"Why would you want to, Gabriel?" she asked, gripping his arm with both her hands. "Why? I've got to know. If it's true, go ahead and say it so we can both know where we stand."

The right side of his mouth was pressed against her hair. His heart was pounding against her back. But he took the plunge and whispered, "Because I love you, Roberta."

The grip of her hands on his arm tightened, as if she were afraid he might slip away and change his mind.

"I love you too, Gabriel, I hope you'll believe that. But if I don't run off and marry you in a week or two or three, you mustn't be discouraged. I've only kissed you for the second time today, and half the time I've known you we haven't been on amicable terms. Besides that, you know me. You know that I have to fight my own battles and win my own way, whether it's getting rid of an unfaithful husband or keeping my beloved daughters. So I have to fight this my way."

"And marrying me wouldn't be your way."

"No."

He turned her to face him and held her by her upper arms. "Roberta, please . . ."

"No, because if I did that, anything they'd say about me would go unchallenged, and I'm a good mother. A good one! I won't let anybody say different!"

"But if you'd marry me they wouldn't challenge you at all, so why put yourself through that?"

"We don't know that I'll have to. So far it's just a rumor."

He could see he wasn't going to convince her tonight, so he pulled her loosely into his arms and they stood in an easy embrace.

"Gabriel?" she said quietly after a while.

"What, love?"

"Thank you for asking me, and for telling me you love me, and for being here to bolster me. You've been doing that ever since I moved to Camden, and I've never told you how much I appreciate it."

"You're welcome. You bolstered me too."

"I riled you up."

"That, too. But somehow I always came back for more, so I must have enjoyed it."

She rested against his sturdy bulk and it felt good to be there. In Roberta's life there had been too few times when she'd rested against a man's sturdy bulk.

"Do you know what you just called me?" she said after a while.

"What did I just call you?"

"Love. You said, 'What, love?' "

"Did I?"

She smiled against his neck and said, "There might be hope for us yet. Also, because you're a very good kisser."

He smiled. " 'Course I am. And you're not so bad yourself, once you decide to get started."

She let herself stay in his arms a bit before getting back to a sterner reality.

"I've made a decision," she said.

"Which is?"

"To talk to my mother and see what she knows about this Benevolent Society." Roberta drew back and looked into Gabriel's eyes. "Because if she's a party to this . . . if she's one of the women who wants my children taken away from me, I can't remain in this town, Gabe. Surely you must understand that."

It hadn't entered his mind.

He gripped her arms again. "Don't scare me that way. Now that I've finally overcome my fear of loving you, don't scare me, Roberta."

"It's how I am, Gabriel. I see things very clearly— which path I should take, which one I should avoid. Then I chart my course and follow it. Is that the kind of woman you'd want to marry?"

"Here . . . yes. Not in Boston or Philadelphia or some other town I've never been to. Camden is my home. This is where I want to stay."

She pulled back slowly until she was standing free. "Then we'd better wait and see, hadn't we, Gabe?"

He sighed and felt heavy with foreboding. Though he was reluctant to agree, he knew at that moment she was thinking much more clearly than he.

"Yes, I suppose," he finally agreed. "We'd better wait and see."

And on that forlorn note they went out to face the glowing eyes of their children for whom they had no answers yet.

Fifteen

Going home should have been more inviting, Roberta thought as she approached Myra's house. Stepping into a mother's kitchen should feel like a welcome respite, a lush sinking into loving security that ought to have outlasted growing up and becoming independent oneself, and moving away and having babies of one's own.

Instead, approaching Myra's back door brought only dread.

Roberta knocked, which brought a regret of its own: She'd never felt comfortable simply opening the door and walking in like Isobel did at her house.

Instead of *Roberta dear, come in, are you all right, let's talk,* she heard, "Oh, it's you."

She entered uninvited.

Myra's kitchen was painted a dull moss green and smelled of drying chamomile and tansy, for the teas she brewed all winter. The same painted wooden table dominated the center of the room, and the same wooden bowls and crockery canisters lined the open shelves. The same displeasure corrugated Myra's face.

"Hello, Mother," Roberta said resignedly. "May I sit down?"

"Have you been to Grace's?"

"No, Mother. Why would I have been to Grace's?"

"Well, I don't know. To set things right, I hoped."

Roberta studied her mother a long time, silent, oppressed, thinking, *I will never treat my children this way. Never. No matter what they've done.* Finally she sat, taking the chair she had not been invited to take while Myra remained standing with the table between them.

"No, Mother, I came here hoping to do that."

"Well, *I'm* not the one you hurt! You should see your sister. She's been crying for three days!"

"Over what?"

"Over what!" Myra's eyes bulged as she seated herself erect as an eagle on the farthest chair from Roberta. "How dare you come here and say a thing like that. May God forgive you for what you've done to your sister."

"What have I done to my sister?"

"Made a fool of her before this whole town, that's what!"

"Would you like to hear my side of it, Mother? Just this once? Because I think you should. I think you should hear my side of what that bunch of wizened old biddies is gossiping about at the Benevolent Society!" As she spoke her voice grew stronger and her head jutted forward. "I think we should finally air what we both have known about Grace and Elfred, and their *miserable* marriage"—she rapped the tabletop—"and Elfred's philandering . . . and how you've refused to acknowledge it for what? Ten years? Twelve? As long as they've been married?" Her knuckles kept hitting the tabletop as she made each point. "And I think we should talk about why. Today. Here. Now. Get it all out in the open because I can't live this way anymore, wondering why you dislike me so much!"

Myra's mouth snapped shut. Her eyes receded.

"Don't be foolish. I don't dislike you."

"No? Well, you could have fooled me!"

"I'm your mother, for heaven's sake," Myra said, as if that explained everything.

"Mothers stand behind their children. You never did, not for as long as I can remember. It was always Grace, Grace, Grace! I couldn't please you if I had married the King of Siam! So why not?"

"Roberta, you're overwrought." Myra popped to her feet.

"Y' damned right I am! Sit down, Mother! You're not running away from this."

Myra sat. Roberta composed herself and lowered her voice to a more reasonable level.

"When I was in seventh grade I won a poetry award, and they were giving me a certificate at school, but you didn't come to watch me get it. Do you remember why?" Myra sat wide-eyed and silent, as if watching a cobra. "Because Gracie got sick, that's why. Poor little Gracie had one of her ten colds a year, or an earache, or something else equally as unimportant. You could have left her with Daddy, but you didn't. You stayed home and took care of Gracie and let me receive my award without either of my parents in the audience. When I got home I ran in to give you my certificate and do you know what you did with it?" Myra didn't, of course. "I asked you where it was a day or two later, and you said, 'Oh, it must have gotten burned up with some newspapers.' And I went to my room and bawled my eyes out.

"But I learned something from that experience. I learned not to depend on my mother loving me or supporting me, because you never did. Whatever I achieved, or wanted to do, you denigrated in one way or another, did you know that? When I graduated with honors you thought I should have stayed and worked in the mill. When I said I was going to move to Boston you said, 'You'll be sorry.' When I said I was getting married you said, 'Is he rich?' When Grace said she was getting married you bragged to the whole town about how handsome Elfred was, and how successful he was going to be someday. I wrote and asked you to come when I had my babies—well, the first two, anyway. After that I learned not to ask because you weren't going to come anyway. Of course you never came. As my children grew up and I wrote to tell you about their accomplishments you never failed to write back praising whatever Grace's kids were doing at the moment. When George began his affairs and I needed someone so badly, what did you offer then? Nothing. Not to come to me or comfort me in any way. That was probably when Grace had her shingles and you had to go over there and cook for them. And when I finally couldn't put up with any more of George's women, or with his fleecing me for every penny he could get, I got rid of him the only way I knew how, but—what else would you do, Mother?—you blamed me for the divorce. You actually *blamed* me!

"And now!" Roberta rose and bent over the table as her ire elevated. "Now that gang of know-it-all old hypocrites you have tea with has decided I'm not a fit mother and they're talking about going to the authorities to try to get my children taken away from me. And if you're a part of it, Mother, you'd better hear the whole story first!"

Myra gasped. "How could you believe—"

"I could believe it because you've never once in your life spoken up for me. They say I've been having an affair with Gabriel. I'm not. They say I'm having another one with Elfred. I'm not. But let me tell you about your precious Elfred. From the time I set foot in this town, he's been trying. After all, I'm just a loose divorced woman, right? I must be easy prey for a slick, handsome devil like him, right? After all, he's seduced woman after woman while his wife was right in the room—the whole town jokes about it, but Grace pretends it isn't happening. That's why she gets the shingles, Mother! Because her husband has promiscuous affairs with anyone he can, only this woman"—Roberta tapped her chest—"wouldn't fall for it. This woman"—Roberta's voice began losing its fight and she sank back onto her chair—"this woman said no, and slapped him, and forbid him in her house . . . until . . ." With her forearms flat, Roberta gripped the sides of the table. "Until three days ago when my car ran out of gas out in the country on Hope Road, and Elfred came along and found me." Very softly, she asked, "And what do you suppose he did, Mother?"

Myra had drawn back hard against the rungs of her chair and covered her mouth with four fingers.

A beat of intense silence passed before Roberta said, "He raped me."

Behind her hand Myra whispered, "Oh no."

"That's why Gabriel beat him up, and that's why
Grace has been hiding, and that's why my car was seen
at Gabriel's house late that night—he was doing what
my mother should have done, taking care of me, holding me while I cried, letting me take a bath at his place
and calming my fears. But I couldn't come to you—isn't
that sad, Mother? I couldn't come to you because you'd
have blamed me, just as you always have. You'd have
said surely I must have done something to tempt Elfred.
You're probably thinking it now, aren't you?"

Behind her hand, Myra quivered.

"Well, I didn't. And because I didn't, he gave me
this." Roberta tipped back her head. "It's a cigar burn.
It's how he made me stop fighting."

Tears had actually formed in Myra's eyes as Roberta
leveled her chin and sat back tiredly in her chair. Her
emotional weariness equaled that of the night she was
raped, combining as it did a fresh recollection of the
assault with the confrontation she'd undertaken here today. Myra, however, kept her reactions under tight rein,
sealing herself off in a peculiar trancelike fashion, showing little more than the glitter of tears in her eyes.

Studying her, letting her own weariness show, Roberta said quietly, "Now I have to know, Mother. Are
you one of the Benevolent Society who wants to see my
children taken away from me?"

It took Myra a long time to gather her equilibrium
and whisper, "No. I didn't know a thing about it till
now."

Roberta breathed a hidden sigh. "Well, that's one
good thing anyway." She waited for her mother to ex-

press anguish or concern about her condition, the way Gabe had, but Myra was too steeped in her selfishness to go that far. She sat instead, gazing through her tears at a spot to the left of Roberta's shoulder, perhaps mourning the end of her delusions about Elfred and Grace.

"Maybe I did favor Grace," she said to the window frame. "Yes, I . . . I suppose I did. But there was a reason." She paused, still without meeting Roberta's eyes.

"Well, tell me," Roberta said impatiently. "I'm waiting."

Myra collected herself dramatically, heaving an over-burdened sigh and letting her jowls and shoulders sag while dropping her eyes to her joined hands. "I was raised in a very strict household—church every Sunday, reciting the Commandments every night at bedtime on our knees. There was no swearing there, no laughter, very little fun. Fun was godlessness, work would get you closer to heaven, they preached, and I believed them. It was a somber upbringing, but I loved them, my mother and father. They had come over from Denmark and used to tell us about the land there, and about our grandparents.

"At any rate, they arranged a marriage for me to a rather somber young man named Carl Halburton. There wasn't much to our courtship, no . . . well, you know . . . none of the silliness and mooning you'd associate with it today. But we married and he was a good man. Never very outgoing or warm, but a hard worker and a good provider. When Grace was born he was very proud.

"But I had never . . . Carl and I . . . we . . . it

wasn't . . ." Myra looked down at her fingers, which worked a tabletop doily as if crumbling dough. She cleared her throat and began again. "Well, let me tell it this way. . . . A train spur came through town, and a crew came to lay it. They ran those tracks right behind our backyard, and this one particular young fellow used to see me out there hanging clothes, and he'd wave to me, and once he came over and asked if he could get a drink from the pump in our yard. And then he started coming to visit with me even after the crew moved up the line. He was a very handsome, smiling fellow, always full of mischief and jokes, very different from Carl. He made me laugh . . . and he told me I was pretty."

The room had grown still. Not even Myra's fingers worked the doily any longer.

Roberta knew, even before the story continued.

"What was his name, Mother?"

Dreamily, Myra answered, "His name was Robert Coyle."

"He was my father, wasn't he?"

"Yes."

It was a peculiar moment in which to feel close to her mother, that moment in which Roberta was told she'd been lied to her whole life long. Yet she had never seen softness in Myra before. It smoothed her wrinkled brow and relaxed her aging eyes, making Roberta wonder what her mother would have been like if Robert Coyle had stayed.

"He left, of course, with the railroad crew. And Carl knew right away that the baby wasn't his. He and I didn't . . . well, you know. Not often. And then, after

Robert left, not at all. Not ever again. Carl treated me politely, like a guest in his house. And when you were born, he announced that your name was to be Roberta, as a constant reminder of the sin I'd committed with another man. It didn't take me long to realize what a good man I had in Carl Halburton—steady, dependable, somebody I loved . . . but by then it was too late. He went on shunning me till his dying day.

"Grace was his. You weren't. He never let me forget it, so I suppose I wanted to pass down some of my regret to you."

Though Roberta waited, no apologies accompanied Myra's soul baring.

"But, Mother . . . I was still yours."

Myra shifted in her chair, pressed the wrinkled doily to the tabletop and said, "Yes . . . well . . . it was hard."

There was little dignity in begging for crumbs at this point, and Myra might have mellowed enough to tell the story, but it seemed she was not going to confess any love for her daughter or apologize for withholding it. What was done was done.

Roberta sat back and glanced around the room as if coming awake from a séance. "Well, you taught me one thing, Mother."

"What's that?"

"Never to cheat my own children on love."

Myra turned pink at the cheek and her mouth got stubborn. "I tried very hard with you, Roberta, but you were always so headstrong . . . and different. Whatever I told you to do, you did the opposite. That's not easy on a mother, you know."

Some people can never admit they're wrong, Roberta

realized, and her mother was one of them. She continued to be so concerned with herself that she was blind to her faults.

"Does Grace know all this?"

"No. I never told her."

"You wouldn't have told me either if I hadn't insisted."

"No . . . I suppose not."

"So what about this Benevolent Society taking my children—you say you don't know anything about it?"

"No! Nothing!"

"Who's the head of it?"

"Oh, Roberta, you aren't going to go kicking up a fuss over there, are you?"

"Mother, listen to yourself! These are my children I'm fighting for. If you won't tell me, I'll find out somewhere else."

"Oh, very well, it's Wanda Libardi, but she's a friend of mine, so don't go accusing her of instigating anything that isn't true."

It was typical of Myra that she would be more concerned about her friends' hurt feelings than the welfare of her own grandchildren and daughter, but by now Roberta had become inured to her callousness. Why, she hadn't offered a single word of commiseration about the rape or the burn, no expression of horror, no word of blame for Elfred. It was as if after those few meager tears she had blocked it out of her mind. Was she actually going to pretend she'd never been told?

"Mother, you do believe me about the rape, don't you?"

"Oh, please, Roberta."

"Why would I make up such a story? And where do you think I got the burn if I was lying?"

"You and Grace are both my daughters . . . what do you expect me to do?"

Open your arms and close them around me.

In reality, such a response would have been so out of character it would have been difficult to accept. Never having been shown physical affection by her mother, Roberta realized she really didn't want it now. She'd had Gabriel when she needed comfort most. And the children, especially Rebecca. They would continue to be her emotional mainstay.

"Nothing," Roberta finally answered, accepting within herself that she truly meant it. She expected nothing from her mother and she got nothing. But she meant what she'd said earlier, that she had learned a valuable lesson from Myra's coldness, and it had stood her in good stead through sixteen years of being a mother herself. Her children would never want for affection, attention and approval, not so long as she drew breath.

Surprisingly, now that Roberta had expunged her anger, she felt more amicable toward Myra.

"I really mean that, Mother. I don't expect anything from you. I just needed to get my feelings out. I guess if you continue being good to Grace, she needs it more than I do anyway. I got rid of my unfaithful husband, and I'm secure within myself. She still has both of those problems to work out yet. Well, listen . . ." Roberta pushed back from the table and rose. "I'd better get going. I took time off work to come up here and talk to you, and I'll have to make it up. I'm the only public nurse working this area."

Myra looked relieved that the visit was over. She rose, too, keeping to the far side of the table. "Are you mad at me for telling you about your father?"

"No. It doesn't change what I felt for Carl. He'll always be the Daddy I remember, and if he wasn't an affectionate father, he made sure we had what we needed. That was enough."

"Well, that's"—Myra gestured vaguely—"that's good then."

An awkward silence fell. Roberta couldn't wait to get away and end it. At thirty-six years old she had done a lot of growing up today, and it felt good to have it behind her.

She could not take the time to go up and accost Wanda Libardi about whatever the Benevolent Society had in its craw. She had work to do and ground to cover, miles to drive and cases to visit.

And so much to think about.

Her girls. Gabriel. Gabriel's recalcitrant family. The frightening possibility of pregnancy. What the town was saying about her. What Grace was saying to Elfred. How Elfred was explaining his battered face. Elfred's girls and what they might have heard about their father. Whether or not to marry Gabriel. Whose house they'd live in. How they'd get along, being such opposites. The Benevolent Society. Elizabeth DuMoss tipping them off. Gabe and Isobel coming over for supper tonight. The instructions she had given Susan and Lydia about when to put the meat loaf to cook. Rebecca and the Ogier

boy who'd gone out sailing this afternoon. How wonderful Gabriel's kisses had felt. How ironic it was that
she and Rebecca were embarking on new relationships
at almost the same time. The fact that she'd better have
a talk with Rebecca about that.

She was late getting home, and the others were already there when she arrived. Gabe's truck was parked
on the boulevard, and a new swing hung on the front
porch; Susan, Lydia and Isobel were crowded on it. Rebecca and Ethan Ogier were petting a strange cat that
had wandered into the yard, and Gabriel was sitting on
the front step reading a newspaper.

He put it down and got up as she slammed the door
of her Ford, and he walked across the yard to meet her.
A fine and unexpected leap lifted her heart at his approach. He was freshly bathed and combed, dressed in
ordinary khaki pants and a white shirt that his new
laundress must have starched and ironed. It had fold
lines and a place for a collar, but none was buttoned
on. The evening was warm and his sleeves were rolled
to the elbow, exposing his tanned forearms. As he
moved toward her he wore a relaxed smile, and she
thought how odd it must look to her neighbors to see
the man waiting while the woman came home from
work. But waiting he was, with all their children lounging on the porch beside him, continuing their preoccu-
pations with an acceptance that granted her absolute
freedom to walk toward him with a smile of anticipation on her tired face.

"Hello," she said, amazingly happy to have him waiting.

"Hello."

"Where did the swing come from?"

"Made it for you."

"Rebecca and Ethan will be glad."

"So will I, after dark."

Her gaze dropped to his lips, and she let a beat pass before replying, "So will I. Thank you. It's very nice."

They had stopped in the break of the bridal wreath bushes where the long shadows from the neighbors' trees laid strips of gold and green across the yard. From the end of the block the sound of a horse's hooves passed, and up on the porch the swing chain was creaking. Gabriel stood with his back to the house, Roberta with her back to the street.

"Know what I wish?" he said.

"No. What?"

"That I could kiss you."

"I wish you could too. I found myself thinking about kissing you a lot today."

"That's a good sign. Does that mean you'll marry me?"

"Not necessarily. But I thought about that, too, especially after I talked to my mother."

"Oh?"

"She said she didn't know anything about the Benevolent Society taking my kids away from me."

He nodded three times, very slowly, as if his mind was on something else. A half-smile narrowed his eyes, which roved over her hair and face. "I've never told you before, but I really like you in your uniform."

"Do you? Why's that?"

"The way you roll up your hair over the edge of your

cap, neat and tidy. The way your apron straps cross in the back. Your clean white shoes."

"You'd like me all neat and tidy all the time, wouldn't you?"

"I guess so."

"What if I'm not? What if our house is not? What if my children are not and you were married to me, then would we fight about it?"

"I don't know."

She took a turn assessing him and liked what she saw.

"If we were married, where would we live?"

"I don't know that either."

"Where would you want to live?"

"Your house is too small."

"And your house is too Caroline's."

"Are you going to be jealous of her?"

"I doubt it. I actually spoke to her picture when I was alone in your room."

"What did you say?"

From up at the house Susan yelled, "Hey, are you two going to stand there and talk all night? We're starving!"

Gabriel glanced over his shoulder and called, "Be right there," then turned back to Roberta and calmly repeated his question. "What did you say?"

She liked his unflappability along with his blue eyes and sharp-edged lips, his thick eyebrows and his overall generous size.

"I told her that I love you."

"You did not."

"Yes, I did. I said, 'I love your husband, Caroline Farley.' And I do, Gabriel."

She saw very clearly how she had stunned him anew with her declaration. He got slightly breathless and his lips dropped open as if he wanted to lower his head, close his eyes and delight them both right there on the front path.

"Roberta, I don't understand you. You love me, yet you won't say you'll marry me."

"Come on, you two!" Isobel yelled. "It's almost seven-thirty and the meat loaf is done!"

This time it was Roberta's turn to glance at the porch, leaning to see around Gabe, then straightening without answering Isobel.

"Let's take this up on the new swing at eleven o'clock or so," she suggested.

"That's a long time from now."

"Well, maybe I can get the girls to go to bed by ten. I'll do my best. Now let's go see if Isobel set the table all neat and tidy, or if my girls just planned to pull the meat loaf apart with their hands."

He let her lead the way to the house, and when she'd passed him by he said from behind her, "*I* set the table all neat and tidy."

"Oh." She smiled to herself. "Well, who knows? We might work out some kind of connubial compromise after all."

That supper seemed to take forever. Another kingdom come seemed to pass before the girls had cleaned up the dishes. Then they decided to try folding some origami designs, and by the time Roberta convinced them to start picking up paper scraps, it was well after ten. Following that, Gabriel felt obliged to drive Isobel home. And at quarter to eleven at night he didn't want everyone up and down Alden Street to hear his truck returning to Roberta's house, so by the time he walked back up the hill it was after eleven.

She had washed up quickly, rubbed on almond cream, changed into a calf-length dress and a sweater and was waiting inside the living room screen door in the dark when he came up the porch steps.

"Hi," she whispered, opening the door stealthily and stepping outside.

"Hi," he whispered back.

"I didn't think they'd ever go to bed."

"Me either."

"Does Isobel know you came back?"

"No. She doesn't have to know everything."

"Neither do my girls. I can't believe I'm sneaking around meeting a boyfriend at my age."

"Me either, but it's kind of fun."

"All except for the mosquitoes."

"They weren't so bad when I was walking back. Maybe they'll leave us alone. Come on."

He took her hand and they tiptoed to the swing and sat, his arm slung loosely around her shoulders. They spoke only in whispers.

"You took your hair down."

"To keep the mosquitoes off my neck."

He reached over and put his hand on it . . . then in it . . . finding her skull with his fingertips. "Now what were we talking about when the girls called us in for supper?"

This was what they'd been waiting for all day, this moment of reaching, touching, tasting once again with his head bowed over hers. It was immediate, that first kiss, and earned by a long day's wait. They were eager and ardent from the instant they touched, roused by their hours of anticipation and the inky intimacy of the shadows beneath the porch roof. However inhibited Gabriel Farley was in the light of day, he shed his inhibitions on the privacy of that porch swing. The kisses Roberta had missed during the waning years of her marriage she received over and over in a roundelay of sweet repetition. A mosquito came and bit her ankle right through her cotton stocking and she tucked her legs up, covering her feet with her skirt, relinquishing none of the sweet suckling hold she had on Gabe's mouth. It was open above hers, his breath beating against her cheek, and his hand on her back stretching everything—her sweater, her dress, her skin—making flat circles that substituted for more intimate caresses.

There were questions rapping at her harried heart and she tore her mouth free to ask them.

"How long since you've done this?"

"Since Caroline."

"How many years?"

"Seven."

"George stopped kissing me years ago, unless he wanted money. It got so I hated it with him . . . but I missed it . . . oh, I missed it."

They kissed again, making up for lost time, curling against each other with an impatient embrace. Then two mosquitoes bit him at once—one on his neck, another on his wrist. He shook off one and slapped the other and said against her lips, "Let's go in, Roberta."

"No, I can't."

"We'll be quiet. Nobody will know."

"I'll know. You'll know. And I won't give this town the satisfaction."

He drew back his head and said, "But that's silly. All we're going to do is stand behind the living room screen door where the mosquitoes can't get at us. I promise. That's all we're going to do."

"I can't, Gabriel. If I weren't divorced it would be different, but that's just what the town expects me to do—take men into my house at night when my girls are sleeping."

Another stinger sank into his jaw. He hit and missed it and said, "Then go get a blanket."

"Oh, Gabriel, you can't be serious." He could hear the makings of a chuckle in her tone. But just then she killed a mosquito on her face.

"Roberta, this is just damned ridiculous. Go get one."

Dropping her feet off the swing she said, "All right, I will."

He sat there slapping mosquitoes while she tiptoed across the porch, opened the door without making a peep, disappeared and returned as noiselessly as she'd gone.

"Here," she whispered, flinging the blanket as she resumed her place beside him.

"Where did you have to go to get it?" he asked, flipping and settling it until he got it just right.

"Clear upstairs in my bedroom."

"Think they heard you?"

"I don't care if they did. I have a right to sit here on my own front porch swing, don't I?"

He chuckled and got them situated to his liking with the blanket shrouding all but their heads.

"Hey . . . I like this," he murmured, slipping a hand beneath her arm, narrowly missing her breast. "Come here."

There are ways to combat modesty and yet maintain it . . . and he found them, leaning back into a corner of the swing and dragging her with him until their limbs were stretched and aligned like the folds of the blanket that covered them. One six-minute kiss later, when their mouths were getting tender, and the mosquitoes had found their bare faces, and his empty hand could be denied no longer, he flipped the blanket over their heads, and there in a tent of total darkness where the scent of his bay rum consorted with that of her almond cream, she scolded, "Gabriel!" And giggled.

"Shh . . ." he whispered, and cupped her breast. And stopped her breath for that singular moment, then started it again . . . faster.

Five minutes later their mouths were swollen and so were some other strategic parts, when a voice outside their blanket said, "Mother? Is that you under there?"

Gabe and Roberta turned to a couple of pillars of clay. Only these pillars looked like they were half-carved and the sculptor had gone to lunch. There they sat—well, lay, actually—two bumps beneath a dark blanket, like half-finished works of art. From the outside it appeared to Rebecca that her mother was trying to push herself up and pretend she hadn't been lying against Mr. Farley's open legs, because one of hers was hanging in midair as she struggled against gravity.

"Mr. Farley? Is that you, too?"

There was some whispering under the blanket, and the four legs managed to untangle. The two bodies managed to square themselves side by side, and finally Roberta lifted the blanket far enough to peep out. Rebecca had turned on the living room light and its distant rays picked out two very messy heads of hair and four eyes that peered out sheepishly, like a pair of raccoons caught in the headlights.

"Yes, Rebecca?" her thirty-six-year-old mother said, striving for dignity where there was none.

"Mother? What in the world are you doing under there!"

"Talking."

Some embarrassing seconds ticked by before Gabriel jumped into the gap.

"Ah . . . the mosquitoes," he explained lamely, folding back the blanket.

"Well, why don't you come in the house?" Rebecca said sensibly. "There are no mosquitoes in there."

"Good idea," Farley said, and peeled Roberta's skirt off his left pantleg. "Let's go in the house, Roberta."

He had no idea she was on the verge of breaking up until her laughter escaped her pinched lips and sent up a "Ppppppt!" like a draft horse breaking wind. When she started laughing, he couldn't help himself and started, too.

Rebecca grew indignant and planted her fists on her hips. "Mother, for heaven's sake, get in the house right this minute before the neighbors see you out here with that ridiculous blanket over your heads! Good Lord, a person would think the two of you were twelve years old!"

She slammed in the house, cranked off the light and left the two on the porch laughing with two fistfuls of blanket pressed to their mouths. Roberta was so breathless she could scarcely get the words out.

"Oh, Gabe . . . oh my word . . . if we get married . . . we'll have to tell this story to our grandchildren. Oh, Gabe . . . you should have s-seen yours-self coming out from under that blanket."

He rubbed his hair with one big paw, leaving it worse than before. "Oh, well, what the hell. They know anyway."

She laughed some more, then sat beside him until her breathing leveled off. She hooked both hands over the edge of the swing seat and glanced at Gabe on her right. "Let's say good night. We're too old for this anyway."

"Too old for what?" he said suggestively.

She whispered, "Not for that. Just for this." She rose, taking a tail end of the blanket along. It was pinned under his butt, and he hauled away until it towed her back to him. She dropped one knee onto the swing seat and fell against him, their momentum sending them and the swing backward. His wide hands caught her high around the ribs, his thumbs just beneath her breasts.

"Marry me, Roberta," he said seriously, lifting his face as she looked down on him.

He had made a true effort to please her, and she liked the change, the way he had come a-courtin', as she'd said she wanted—on a porch swing under a blanket, no less. And he'd loosened up a great deal where Isobel was concerned, and certainly the girls were in favor of their courtship. But courtship was one thing and every-day life was another—with mothers, and brothers-in-law, and ladies' societies.

"Maybe," she replied, and kissed him good night.

Sixteen

Toward dawn the next morning, Roberta had a nightmare about the rape. She awakened herself with a scream and gained consciousness to find that she was cowering against the headboard, sweating and weeping, her heart driving like a ramrod in her chest.

Rebecca came tearing around the corner from her bedroom, wearing a wrinkled nightdress, terrified out of a sound sleep.

"Mother, what's wrong!"

"Oh, Becky . . . oh . . . oh . . ."

Rebecca flew to the bed and held Roberta fast. "Were you dreaming?"

"It was terrible." Roberta's voice shook as she clutched her daughter. "It was Elfred again, doing that awful thing to me, only just before he did it he . . . he lifted his head and it was Gabriel, not Elfred, and I was so heartbroken that he had deceived me and that he wasn't the kind of man I thought he was, and I kept trying to fight him off, and I was pushing at him and telling him he was a liar, only I couldn't get the words out. Oh, Becky, it was just terrible."

Becky petted Roberta's hair and kept her close. Her own heart was banging as if she'd had the nightmare herself.

"It was just a dream, Mother. Look, it's almost dawn and the girls are still asleep, and everything's just wonderful. Don't be afraid."

Roberta began to calm, and her grip slackened.

"Why would I dream such a thing about Gabriel?"

Becky sat back, capturing her mother's hands, rubbing her thumbs across Roberta's knuckles.

"I don't know, but last night you were sitting on the swing with him and it didn't look to me like you were trying to fight him off at all."

"Oh goodness . . ." Roberta glanced at the window. Pale lavender dawn was flowing over the scarred sill, and the lacework of leaves lay motionless on the branches of a maple tree outside. As she remembered the previous night, her terror subsided and her heartbeat slowed. "You were very displeased with us."

"Not really. You woke me up, creeping upstairs to get that blanket, I suppose. Then I lay there wondering why you were up so late and if you were okay. I just couldn't believe it when I looked out on the porch and saw you two with that blanket over your heads. But I'm not displeased with you, not really. I'm happy you've got Mr. Farley."

"Really?"

"Why wouldn't I be when you're so happy yourself?"

"I am, aren't I?"

"He's given you a wonderful summer, given us all a wonderful summer, actually—our first Camden summer, filled with so many good memories. I think you should marry him, Mother."

"He asked me again last night."

"Are you going to do it?"

"I suppose I am, eventually."

"I keep thinking about how safe you'll be with him, then men like Uncle Elfred can't hurt you, and the gossips of this town will have to find somebody else to whisper about. And I've been thinking a lot about how pretty soon Susan and Lydia and I will be all grown-up, and when we find husbands and move away from home you'll be so lonely. I'd love knowing that you were with Mr. Farley. And at holidays we'd all come home—we three and Isobel, too—and imagine what a good time we'll have. Coming back to Camden for another seaside summer, probably with a whole mess of babies. Oh, Mother, you've got to marry him, you've just got to."

Roberta took her daughter in a loose embrace. She was totally calm now, her heart welling with appreciation for this remarkable young woman whose loving and caring attributes made her truly special.

"Have I told you lately how much I love you, Becky?"

"Of course you have."

"Well, let me tell you again." She kissed Becky's cheek, hard. "I love you, Becky, light of my life. I don't know what I'd have done without you these last two years. The older you get, the dearer you get."

Becky looked squarely into her mother's eyes and said very simply, "Marry Mr. Farley, Mother. I think you love him more than you know, and sometimes you can be too independent for your own good."

"Can I now?" Roberta chided good-naturedly, tipping her head.

"Yes, you can . . . so think about it." Becky got up

and padded barefoot toward the doorway. Reaching it, she paused and said over her shoulder, "Besides, if you marry him you two won't have to kiss under a blanket on the porch swing anymore. You can come in the house where you belong."

Less than one hour later, Roberta called Gabe on the telephone.

"Good morning, Gabriel," she greeted.

"Wh . . ." His surprise was evident even before he said so. "Why, this is a surprise."

"I didn't wake you up, did I?"

"No, I was up having my coffee, getting set to go to work."

"Did you sleep well?"

He cleared his throat. "Actually, no, I didn't, Roberta."

"Oh?" she said, dropping an undertone of flirtatiousness into the single syllable. "Why's that?"

He chuckled deep in his throat and the sound prompted pleasant shivers up her trunk.

She laughed with him, and for a while the operator had only silence to listen in on.

"I've been thinking," Roberta went on, "there's a Boston troupe at the Opera House tonight. They're doing an Oscar Wilde play and I promised the girls I'd take them. Would you and Isobel want to come along?"

"Oscar Wilde?" Gabe said.

"The Importance of Being Earnest."

"Oh."

She could tell he knew nothing about Oscar Wilde or his plays.

"Have you ever been before?"

"To a play? Ah . . . no, no I haven't."

She smiled and imagined him feeling out of his element. "It's all right, Gabriel. I haven't built any porches or grown any rosebushes, but that's not saying we both can't learn."

In his silence she recognized a return of the concupiscence between them and wished—amazing herself suddenly—that he were there, that she could see him even if only briefly, be kissed by him and feel the vibrancy of his presence, be cleansed by it and lose the shadings that remained from her nightmare. Tonight seemed such a long time to wait.

"Gabriel? What do you say?"

"I'm willing to give it a try."

She smiled and felt young. And energized. And impatient!

"Gabriel?" she said, realizing that romantic longing is not reserved for only the very young.

"What, Roberta?"

"Tonight seems a very long time away."

She had a hectic schedule at work that day, with plenty of medical tasks to occupy her mind. But Gabriel occupied it, too, in spite of the diversity of her chores.

She took a bean out of the nose of a five-year-old boy whose mother had made it worse by trying to extract it with a buttonhook. She sent to the doctor a man with a toe that had swollen his foot to twice its size after he'd chopped through his shoe with an axe and split the toe joint. She retaped the fractured ribs of a teamster who had been flattened up against a fish shed wall when his lead horse spooked at the sound of a steam whistle down on the docks. She verified an outbreak of measles at a farm southwest of town, and treated not only the family's three children, but also their pet pig, who had erupted with the pustules at the same time as the toddlers.

Between all these jobs, she drove, covering a total of sixty-five miles. And while she bounced and bumped and rocked over dry gravel roads with her hair jarring loose and her uniform getting cloudy, she thought of Gabriel and planned how, at the end of the afternoon, she'd indulge in a full-blown bath, and would wash her hair and pin it up the way he liked: It wouldn't hurt her to indulge him this one time on the night she intended to accept his proposal of marriage. She would put on her single good linen dress with the bell sleeves and the fagoting across the bodice, and she would say to him, "Gabriel, I accept your proposal. I'd be very proud to be your wife."

But when she got home in the late afternoon a strange woman was sitting on her new porch swing, dressed in a hat that looked as if bees should be carrying nectar into it. Beneath it her straight summer suit and brown lace-up oxfords looked severe. So did her prim white gloves.

She wasn't swinging, just sitting properly with her ankles crossed and her purse handle caught over her wrist. When Roberta drove up, she rose and waited at the top of the porch steps.

"Mrs. Jewett?" she said, at Roberta's approach.

"Yes?"

"My name is Alda Quimby. I'm a member of the

Camden school board, and I've been asked to come and speak to you by our chairman, Mr. Boynton."

"About what?"

"Is there somewhere we can speak privately?"

"No, there's not. The front porch will have to do. Sit down where you were and I'll stand. Just a minute though, I've got to say hello to my girls first." She went inside, shouting, "Girls! I'm home!"

There happened to be five of them there that day, plus two boys—Ethan Ogier and his younger brother, Elmer. They were all in the backyard, some sorting through a collection of seashells and some lounging on the back steps, while Elmer Ogier hung upside down by his knees from the clothesline pole, trying to impress the younger girls.

Roberta went through the kitchen and called out the back door, "Hi, everyone, I'm home!"

Susan came to the opposite side of the screen and whispered, "Who's that woman, Mother?"

"I don't know. I'll tell you later. Pump me some bathwater, will you, Susan? Thanks."

Back on the front porch Alda Quimby remained standing as Roberta came out in her dusty uniform.

"Now, Mrs. Quimby . . . what can I do for you?"

"I'm here on official business, Mrs. Jewett, and I may as well warn you, it isn't pleasant."

Roberta knew exactly what it was, and exhibited no patience.

"Well, spit it out then. That bunch of dried-up hussies known as the Benevolent Society thinks I'm not a fit mother, isn't that right?"

Mrs. Quimby's mouth dropped open, then snapped

shut tight as a mussel shell. Her hat was ringed with cabbage roses the color of her own nipples—*if she has any,* thought Roberta. The flowers fairly trembled on her self-righteous head.

"Mr. Boynton's wife is a member of that society and she brought some things to her husband's attention—"

"That he was too lily-livered to come here and talk to me about himself, probably because he thinks I won't buy my next motorcar from him, and he's right. I won't!"

"It's come to our attention that your children are left to fend for themselves five days a week, and that in your absence a number of the other town children have taken to gathering here at your house without any sort of adult supervision. Is that correct?"

"I work to support my children—*that's* correct!" Roberta snapped.

"Some of them are in your backyard right now."

"That's right."

Mrs. Quimby's mouth puckered as if she were getting ready to sip hot tea. "You're divorced, I believe."

"Yes, thank God. And I'm a licensed nurse, and the owner of this house, and the owner of that motorcar, and quite capable of raising my children on my own."

"Mrs. Jewett, I'll save us both some time and make this as plain as possible. Complaints have been waged about your causing a fistfight between two men in this town, one of whom is married—and is, to add to the shamefulness of the incident—your own brother-in-law. The fracas, I'm told, was witnessed by his own wife and children, who—rumor has it—heard the vilest language that night, and heard things about you that no child should ever hear, and which, I might add, raised eyebrows from one end of this town to another. One of Camden's most *respected* businessmen has subsequently been walking around deplorably defaced, and your motorcar has been seen late at night parked in front of the other man's house. He's been seen on your front porch so much that concern has been expressed for his daughter's welfare as well. Your children have been heard to say that they had to eat fudge for supper because their mother didn't come home until after dark, but left them to fend for themselves at mealtime. And *today* there's a rumor that you and Mr. Farley were seen spooning on this very swing at midnight last night!

"Mrs. Jewett, I'm sure you'll understand that the members of the school board must concern themselves with the welfare of any child whose well-being is threatened by a lack of normal daily parental care, and whose home is being run like a bordello."

Roberta scarcely trusted herself to remain on the porch lest she send Alda Quimby bouncing backward down its steps on her know-it-all, highfalutin' ass.

"You erudite jackasses don't know the first thing about what makes a good parent!" she shouted. "If you did, you'd be at Elfred Spear's door right now. I'll ask you to leave, Mrs. Quimby, and if you want to question my morals or the care I give my children, you'd better be prepared to do so through legal channels, because I shall fight you until I'm dead before I'll let you take my girls away. Now get off my porch and don't ever set foot on it again!"

"The school board asked me to—"

"Get off, I said!"

"Mrs. Jewett, at the next school board meeting—"

"Off!" Roberta gave Mrs. Quimby a little help. "And tell that pantywaist Boynton to do his own dirty work next time instead of sending a *woman* to do it for him!"

She didn't have to push Mrs. Quimby again. One step in her direction and the woman scuttled off with her cabbage roses trembling.

When Gabriel arrived that evening he found Roberta in a state of extreme agitation, still in her soiled uniform with her bath untaken. She filled him in on what had happened, then raved, "How dare they!" pacing up and down her living room. "Gabriel, I'm so mad I could kill somebody! I swear, if I owned a gun, I would! They send that prissy know-it-all over here with her Virgin Mary white gloves and her hatful of cabbage roses to tell *me* I don't know how to raise my kids!"

The girls were all hovering around, as incensed as their mother.

Rebecca said, "I'll go tell that school board a thing or two!"

"Yeah, our mother is the best one in the world!" added Susan.

Isobel said, "I'll tell them too, the idiots!"

"Could they really take us away from her?" Lydia asked, at ten still young enough to be more fearful than angry.

"I don't think so," Gabe said. "Roberta, I'm so sorry."

Then something most wonderful happened: Gabriel took Roberta in his arms right there in the middle of her living room with all four of their girls looking on.

And nobody thought a thing of it. She put her face against his neck and folded her arms up his back, and for that moment, while she took strength from him, the six of them felt a supreme rightness about being together.

"Oh, Gabe," she told him, loud enough for the girls to hear, "I'm so glad I've got you right now."

"Don't you worry, Roberta, I won't let anybody take *anything* away from you—ever."

Her eyes were closed and tears had darkened her lashes. "I've never been much of a crybaby, but I must admit, I've been close to it since that woman left."

"Well, that's perfectly understandable. Now listen, I'm not the only one behind you . . . the girls are too . . . aren't you, girls?"

He opened the circle of two and it became a circle of six as their daughters came and closed in around the two of them. If there was ever a moment when the two families bonded, this was it. There in the house that had brought Roberta and Gabriel together, where they had overcome their first aversion for each other, and had fought and forgiven and shared their first kiss, and where their children had become fast friends, they formed a ring of connectedness on this occasion when it was so badly needed.

"Now, listen," Gabe said, "we're not going to let this keep us from going to the theater, are we?"

Roberta despaired. "Oh, Gabe, I haven't even changed clothes, and I was going to take a bath and fix my hair."

Gabe checked his watch. "Do something quick. We'll wait, won't we, girls? Besides, it's not fair to keep the girls from having fun just because Alda Quimby and her bunch have got hair balls in their craws. What do you say?"

Alda Quimby had annihilated Roberta's wonderful day and changed it from one of exhilaration to one of vexation; now here was Gabriel, trying valiantly to rescue the mood: a true reversal of roles for him and Roberta.

"Oh, all right," she conceded, "but I might need some help. Becky, can you come upstairs with me and bring a basin of water?"

While the others went out on the porch to wait, Roberta hurried upstairs to get ready.

Around seven-thirty that evening Maude Farley was doing some hoeing in her vegetable garden when her son Seth came walking around the side of the house and made his way to the end of the row of green beans. The gnats always bothered Maude when she got sweaty, and they got awfully pesky at this time of evening, so she'd tied a dishtowel on her head to keep them out of her hair.

"Hi, Ma," he said.

Maude flung a piece of quack grass into a bushel basket and turned. Her face was shiny and pink beneath the big white knot. "Well, Seth, what're you doing here?"

"Came to talk to you about something."

"You mind if I keep working while you do it?"

"Aurelia sent over a dish of apple betty for you, left over from supper. Why don't you wash your hands and dig into it, and we'll sit down on the step over here and talk?"

Maude had bent down and pulled another weed. It hung from her dirty fingers as she straightened to study her son. "Well, all right," she said, tossing the weed in with the others, then leaning her hoe against the bushel basket.

She had a backyard pump. Seth worked the handle while she washed her hands, then leaned over to wipe the excess water on the grass. Walking toward the back step, she said, "Apple betty, huh?"

"She knows how you like anything with apples in it."

"Aurelia's a good woman. You're lucky to have her. You mind going in and getting me a spoon?"

They sat on the back step and she ate the apple betty while they both looked over her vegetable and flower gardens, which covered much of her backyard. The late-day sun laid elongated shadows beside the tomato bushes and the cucumber vines. She didn't need to plant so many vegetables anymore, but she was one for giving food away to her kids. A family of wrens was raising its second batch of babies in a little white house that hung on a low branch of a box elder tree. The male flew in with a worm, poked it into the hole, then perched outside and started serenading.

"Ma, I came to talk to you about Gabe and Roberta Jewett."

She stopped eating for a couple of seconds. "He been seein' a lot of her?"

"A lot."

"Mm." She started eating again.

"I know you don't like her, but you'd better prepare

yourself, 'cause he's asked her to marry him, and if you ask me, you're being just plain stubborn about that woman. Hell, Ma, you haven't even met her."

"How could I? He doesn't bring her around here to introduce her, does he?"

"Why would he, as outspoken as you've been?"

" 'Pears you two have been doing plenty of talking."

"He tells me a lot. Matter of fact, the longer he's known her, the more talkative he gets."

"He know you're over here lecturing me?"

"Nope. Did that on my own. Thought you needed it."

"Everybody in town's talkin' about how the Benevolent Society and the school board are up in arms over how she raises them kids of hers, and my granddaughter's practically living at her place. So is he."

"Oh, he is not. He's courtin' her—wouldn't you expect a courtin' man to go sit on a woman's front porch now and then?"

Maude finished her apple betty and set the bowl aside. She pinched the corners of her lips clean and said, "How come you're takin' sides on this?"

" 'Cause Gabe's so happy. Haven't seen him this happy since Caroline died, and if you were around him more you'd see it for yourself."

She gazed off into the distance. Finally Maude sighed and pushed her dishtowel off her head. Unknotting it, with her elbows on her knees and her skirt drooping, she said, "Guess you're right. I have been stubborn. Didn't like the idea of my boy getting tangled up with a divorced woman."

"Well, I'll tell you what—you keep it up and you

won't see much of him, 'cause if she marries him his loyalties will be to her, and that would be just silly for the two of you not to be on friendly terms just 'cause she was married once before."

"So she hasn't said yes yet?"

"Not as far as I know. But the way their kids get along together, and just from things he says, I think she will."

She stared at the dishtowel in her hands. "Aw, you're probably right. Being stubborn is lonely business. I miss takin' him cookies, and what am I going to do with all those cucumbers and tomatoes in the garden? You and Aurelia can't keep up with 'em."

He put his hand between her shoulder blades and kissed her temple.

"Guess where she's got him tonight," he said.

"Where?"

"At the Opera House."

She pulled a face, leaning away but panning him. "Oh, go on," she said.

"No! That's right. At the Opera House."

She snorted a little bit as she laughed. "Well, isn't that a wonder—at the Opera House."

"He's changed, our Gabe."

"But what about all those rumors that he beat up Elfred and she was seeing both of them?"

"Aw, Ma, come on, what do you know about Elfred Spear? Put that all together with some new divorced woman coming to town and figure out what Elfred would try."

"With his own sister-in-law?"

"That wouldn't stop Elfred."

She thought for a minute. "So Gabriel was defending her."

"Same as I'd have done for Aurelia if it had been her. And I'll tell you something—it better not ever be her or I won't leave Elfred alive. I'll finish him off for good, the randy bastard."

They sat for a while, judging Elfred and Roberta Jewett. Finally Maude pushed up and said, "Well, I might go over there tomorrow and put some ginger creams in Gabriel's cookie jar, see if that housekeeper wants a few slicers for his supper."

Seth studied her back as she braced it and tried to get the kinks out. "Guess it got too late for weeding," she said. "Gnats might not bother anymore, but the mosquitoes will."

The Jewett-Farley clan attracted plenty of gawkers at the Opera House that night. During intermission Gabriel bought them all lemonade, and they stood beneath the lobby chandeliers sipping, watching people's glances carom away as if everyone in the place weren't whispering about them.

One couple came to greet them: Elizabeth and Aloysius DuMoss. They crossed the lobby and Elizabeth made a show of extending her hand to both Gabriel and Roberta.

"Good evening, Mrs. Jewett . . . Gabriel . . . I see you have both of your families out tonight. Hello, girls."

They all chorused a hello, and she said, "Mrs. Jewett, may I have a quick word with you?"

She led Roberta aside and got straight to the point. "Forgive me for intruding on your evening, but I thought you should know . . . there's a movement afoot to bring up this unpleasantness about you at the school board meeting Monday night. I hear you threw Alda Quimby off your front porch this afternoon, so the battle lines are drawn."

"That was fast. I only tossed her off about three hours ago."

"The new party line."

"Oh . . . that."

Elizabeth reached out and gripped Roberta's forearm imploringly with her gloved hand. "Listen to me. Don't let them cow you, and don't be scared. They've got no power to do this. It's all been caused by a bunch of gossiping women leaning on their husbands and putting bugs in their ears. They've got no right! No right at all!"

Roberta was stunned by Mrs. DuMoss's ferocity.

"Perhaps not, but they're doing it anyway, and no matter what I might have threatened, I don't have the money to hire a lawyer to advise me of my rights."

"You don't need money. If it should come to that, I have money, and I would be the first one to come to your aid."

"You? Why, Mrs. DuMoss!"

"Please . . . Elizabeth."

"Elizabeth. Why, I'm speechless. Why ever would you make an offer like that? And what would your husband say?"

"He would be the first to say, 'Go ahead, Elizabeth.' "

"But why? You scarcely even know me."

Elizabeth squeezed Roberta's arm somewhat harder,

then released it. "I know enough. And we won't let them get away with it."

The last act of the play was lost on Roberta. She kept remembering Elizabeth DuMoss's words and wondering what in the world had prompted them. She wondered about the school board meeting and if she would be summoned to it, or if they simply would go ahead gossiping about her while she wasn't even there. In her view, all they were doing was gossiping, if what Elizabeth said was true and they had no authority to threaten having her children taken away.

When the play was over they all rode home in Roberta's motorcar, and the girls were starving, as usual, so Roberta made popcorn and said, avoiding the front porch swing, "We'll be in the backyard. Come on, Gabriel."

Outside the grass was heavy with dew and the lights from the kitchen windows slanted across the lawn. They could hear the girls' voices from around the kitchen table, and smell the marigolds that were blooming near the pump as they passed it and headed for the deep shadows beneath the elms.

Gabe tugged on Roberta's hand and turned her around. "Now tell me what Elizabeth said."

"She said I shouldn't be scared, and that she'd fight the school board with me, and that they have no right to do what they're doing, and that if it means hiring a lawyer, she'll pay for it herself to stop them. But she didn't tell me why. Gabe, she hardly knows me."

"Elizabeth is a fine woman. Her word carries a lot of weight in this town."

"But why would she do such a thing?"

"I don't know."

He drew on her hand and she fell against him, flinging her arms around his shoulders. "Oh, Gabe, this has been the most mixed-up day. All day long at work I was planning how I was going to come home and get all cleaned up the way you like me, then I was going to tell you I'd marry you, only when I got home that Quimby woman was on my porch, and then I never got my bath taken and I never got my hair washed, and now all of this talk about the school board has just robbed this whole night of all its magic."

"Hold it a minute. Back up to the part about you marrying me." He settled her against him with his arms locked low across her spine. "Did you mean that?"

"Oh, Gabe, how could I not marry you? We're practically married already, the way the girls spend time together, and the way we're always back and forth at each other's houses. Besides that, Rebecca told me this morning that I'm much more in love with you than I realize, and that I'm too independent for my own good."

"So are you going to marry me or not?"

"Yes, I am."

"Well . . ." He let out a gust of breath. "That took you long enough."

"But I don't want that damned school board to know it. If anything comes of this inquiry, I want to fight it on my own merit as a mother, not by crawling to them and asking their mercy because I'm going to be married, with a man to take care of me from now on."

"Rebecca's right. You *are* too independent for your own good."

"First I beat the school board, then we let the news out, okay?"

"Roberta," Gabe said, frustrated, "what does it matter?"

"It matters, Gabe. By now you should know me well enough to realize that it does matter to me."

"But why do you have to be so stubborn?"

"I promise I won't be about everything. Just about this. Please, Gabriel."

He sighed and said, "All right, Roberta, we'll do it your way." His hands dropped from her waist and she felt cheated out of the romantic spirit that should have accompanied the last few minutes.

"Gabriel," she said, capturing his hand as he pulled away. "I'm sorry I ruined the moment when I accepted your proposal. I had it planned much differently."

He acted a little sulky, so she carried his hand to her mouth and kissed it. "Gabriel," she whispered, "come on . . . don't be mad. Aren't you even going to kiss me?"

"Well, hell, we wouldn't want the school board to find out," he said.

In the dark she grinned at his childishness and took it as a challenge.

She drew on his hand and crooned, "Gabriel?"

He let himself be dragged back to her, but still didn't take her in his arms. With his back to the house he said, "How many faces are looking out the kitchen windows?"

"None. But if you won't kiss me, I'll kiss you. It's all right . . . just stand there passively and I'll show you. That one goes there . . ." She put his right hand on her waist. "And that one goes there . . ." And his left arm around her back. "And these go there." Putting her lips on his, she hove against him and hugged him melodramatically.

He freed his mouth to say, "Roberta, I swear—"

"Swear it later," she said against his mouth. "Right now I want to give that school board something to talk about."

Seventeen

$\mathcal{R}$oberta received no summons to the school board meeting, but if she was going to be talked about, she was going to be there. A frailer spirit might have cowered, but cowering would have been greater cause for shame than being scrutinized in public for one's mothering, for which Roberta had no reason to apologize.

At seven-thirty P.M., when the school board convened in the central auditorium of the high school for its last meeting before the fall school term, Roberta was present. So were Gabriel and his brother, Seth and Seth's wife, Aurelia, as well as most of the members of the Greater Camden Ladies' Tea, Quilting and Benevolent Society, a number of teachers, and Elizabeth and Aloysius DuMoss, whose charitable contributions to the school board had, in 1904, helped build the very building they were meeting in. Other nosy townspeople who'd gotten wind of the contretemps between the board and Roberta Jewett came also, hoping to spice up their lives with additional fodder for gossip.

For some reason Roberta failed to fathom, Alda Quimby acted as spokesperson for the board. After Mr. Boynton had called the meeting to order and the board had discussed some mundane school business, the chairman quietly deferred to Mrs. Quimby, who clamped her hands together on the tabletop and glanced past Roberta's shoulder without ever meeting her eyes.

"Mrs. Jewett . . . now, if we might ask you a few questions regarding the issues brought to our attention by certain members of the Benevolent Society . . ." Alda cleared her throat and Gabriel squeezed Roberta's hand.

"Ask anything you want," Roberta replied from the second row. "Do you want me to come up there and face the gallery as if I were testifying in court?"

There was a visible amount of sheepish shifting on the chairs up front.

"That won't be necessary. You can stay where you are."

In the back of the hall a group of young people who had been expressly forbidden by their parents to attend the meeting quietly opened the door and slipped inside to stand along the rear wall. Roberta's children were there, and Isobel, of course; Shelby DuMoss and the Ogier boys, plus a cross section of others ranging in age from nine to sixteen who had, at various times, lounged around the Jewetts' front porch or gone on nature hikes up on Mount Battie, eaten boiled lobsters in the front yard or put on plays or gone clam digging or gathered around the piano to sing while Roberta or one of the girls pounded the keys. The last three to enter—later than the others—were Marcelyn, Trudy and Corinda Spear.

Alda Quimby noted their arrival and stalled for a moment, glancing at her fellow board members, who conveniently kept their eyes averted.

Alda pursed her lips and began again. "Mrs. Jewett,

you moved here, I believe, this past spring."

"That's right," Roberta said, loud and clear, so everyone in the hall could hear.

"And you came from Boston, where you had recently gotten a divorce."

"That's right. Is that a crime in the state of Maine?"

Mrs. Quimby glanced at her constituents, but none of them offered any help. They were all studying the tabletop.

"No, it's not. So when you moved here you bought the old Breckenridge house and fixed it up with the help of Mr. Farley."

"Yes."

"And you secured work as a traveling nurse, employed by the state."

"That's right. I'm a graduate of the preparatory nursing course at Simmons College in Boston."

"So you travel around the countryside in an automobile which—"

"Which I purchased from Mr. Boynton here. Hello, Mr. Boynton, it's nice to see you."

Boynton turned as red as a boiled lobster and looked as if his collar was going to pop off.

"So your job as public nurse takes you away from home from early morning until sometimes late at night."

"Some days."

"During which time your children fend for themselves."

"My children are sixteen, fourteen and ten and have been taught to be self-reliant. Yes, they fend for themselves when necessary."

"Your house, Mrs. Jewett, has become rather a gathering spot for other young people of Camden, has it not?"

"I guess you could say that."

"Where they are allowed to stay past suppertime and into the late hours of the night, whether there is any supervision there or not."

From the back of the hall a young voice called, "Why don't you ask us those questions?"

Other young voices added, "Yeah, why don't you ask us what we do there?"

"And what Mrs. Jewett does with us."

"And how much fun we've had on her front porch this summer doing stuff that nobody else in this town ever thought of teaching us."

Roberta's head had snapped around, as had Gabe's and every other one in the room.

"I told them they were not to come here," Roberta whispered.

"It's their lives, too, Roberta," Gabe replied, low.

"But what if the subject of Elfred comes up?"

"I don't know. We'll just have to wait and see."

The children were marching boldly down the center aisle between the rows of wooden folding chairs, led by Rebecca. "We've got some things we want to say before this goes any farther. If you adults can speak up, so can we."

"Children are not allowed at school board meetings!" Mrs. Quimby shouted above the clatter of footsteps as the children headed straight for the front of the hall.

"At our house we're allowed to speak. Why shouldn't we here, when it's my mother you're accusing?" Becky fearlessly led her legion to battle, speaking in an orator's voice that had gained a sense of drama from all the plays she'd been putting on since childhood. "Everyone in this room should be lucky enough to have a mother like mine, then we might have more open minds and less bigotry right here at this very moment. Don't think we don't know what kind of things you whisper behind her back just because she's divorced. Well, the best part of our lives began when she got rid of our father."

Lydia chimed in. "All he ever did was go away for weeks at a time and never even come home at night."

Susan added, "He only came home when he ran out of money. Then he'd take it from her and leave again."

"So we were all really happy when my mother got divorced," Becky said, "and she has a job that we're all very proud of, too."

"She's a nurse, and she helps people," Lydia told everyone.

"And she owns her own motorcar and she runs it herself, which most women would be afraid to do." That was Susan.

"But our mother's not afraid of anything."

"Not even of you. She wouldn't have *had* to come here tonight to answer your questions, and neither would we . . ." Rebecca's glance took in her cohorts. "But we thought you should know what we do at our house."

Isobel stepped forward. "Before Mrs. Jewett came here, I was a really lonely girl who didn't have many friends or pastimes I was interested in. You all know my mother is dead, so I didn't have anyone at home after school and during the summer days either. Then I met Susan and Becky and Lydia and their mother . . . and everything changed. I guess the first thing we did together was put on *Hiawatha*. She let us use her front porch and roll the piano right next to the front door—"

"And make any costumes we wanted . . ." Shelby DuMoss led a roundelay of remarks that fell from any child who wished to speak. Even the three Spear girls chimed in.

"And props . . . gee, my mother wouldn't let us make a mess like that on our front porch!"

"Then she let us put on the play for our parents."

"Only not many came."

"But we put it on at school, didn't we, Mrs. Roberson?" Becky turned to find her teacher in the crowd.

In row four, Mrs. Roberson stood up. "They certainly did, at my and Miss Werm's invitation, for the entire student body. And it was very well done indeed. If any of you thought the performance was originated and rehearsed at school, you stand corrected. It was all a product of the children's own ingenuity. Miss Werm and I attended the performance on Mrs. Jewett's front porch and saw immediately how the children were encouraged to take part in some very healthy activities there. Of course, we heard about them in school, too."

Miss Werm stood up. "Not only drama, but music as well. And I believe I heard something about nature walks that she conducted."

"Oh, yeah! She took us up Mount Battie and we identified trees and collected insects and she'd recite poetry."

"At school we never liked poetry before, but when

Mrs. Jewett taught us, it was about stuff we could understand."

"It's always fun at her house because everybody laughs there."

"And nobody tells us to be seen and not heard."

"And there's always something to do." These remarks were made by the Spear girls.

"She taught me how to tell a tern from a gull."

"Sometimes we'd be real hungry and she'd let us boil lobsters ourselves, right out in the yard over an open fire."

"And I'm reading a book by Robert Louis Stevenson. . . ."

"And we're probably going to make it our next play."

"If Mrs. Jewett will let us."

Silence fell across the hall, a vast, memorable silence in which the gilding of Roberta Jewett's reputation began. In the midst of that silence, Gabriel dropped Roberta's hand and rose calmly to his feet. Holding his floppy cap in his hand he looked straight at Alda Quimby and spoke in a deep, sure voice.

"And I have watched my daughter blossom into a vibrant young girl during this summer. What she told you earlier is true. She was lonely and bored until the Jewetts moved to town. Then Mrs. Jewett opened her heart and her home and took Isobel in as if she were one of her own"—he looked down at Roberta—"and for that I am eternally grateful."

Without histrionics, Gabriel resumed his seat.

At the table up front, Alda Quimby was still trying to keep from looking like a jackass.

"Mr. Farley," she pursued, "there is another issue we haven't taken up, and it's a rather . . . well, shall we say a delicate matter of which it appears you are a major factor. But in light of the presence of these children . . ."

On the right side of the hall Elizabeth DuMoss stood up, dressed to the nines and radiating social grace.

"I believe I know what that issue is, and if it pleases the board, I think I can shed some light on it. You all know me, and my husband, Aloysius." He nodded. "And this is our lawyer from Bangor, Mr. Harvey. If the children have finished speaking their piece, a short private session might be in order at this time. Mr. Chairman, Mrs. Quimby, would you mind repairing to another room with us so that we can get this over with as quickly as possible?"

"Of course, Mrs. DuMoss."

"I believe Mrs. Jewett and Mr. Farley should be present, too."

"Certainly, Mrs. DuMoss."

"Aloysius . . ." she invited, and as he stood, she took his arm. "Mr. Harvey." Harvey rose and followed.

When they had gathered in a classroom down the hall, and the door was closed behind them, Aloysius DuMoss introduced Mr. Daniel Harvey. Harvey, a tall, courtly fellow with an affable mien, suggested that everyone seat themselves in the school desks. They did so, with the board members choosing the second and third rows while Roberta and her supporters folded down the front row, which consisted of seats only, with no writing surfaces.

Mr. Harvey stood in front of them like a teacher. He let his eyes graze over every person in the room before addressing them in a voice calculated to soothe rather than arouse.

"Members of the school board, Mrs. Jewett, Mr. Farley . . . Mr. and Mrs. DuMoss have asked me to be present tonight to represent them and you, Mrs. Jewett—should the need arise—in what they hope shall be the immediate silencing of these allegations. We are speaking now of the allegations regarding licentious conduct on the part of Mrs. Jewett in which Mr. Farley has been implicated, are we not?"

The members of the school board, intimidated by the unexpected presence of a Bangor attorney, bounced gazes among themselves, then Mr. Boynton harrumphed and replied, "Yes, we are."

"Thank you, Mr. Boynton. Mrs. DuMoss has some information she wishes to impart on the subject. First though, the DuMosses have asked that the members of the board read and sign this confidentiality agreement to ascertain that whatever is spoken in this room shall remain confidential *ad finem*." Mr. Harvey produced a typewritten paper and passed it to the chairman of the board.

Mr. Boynton complained, "Mr. Harvey, this is highly irregular. This is nothing but an informal inquiry."

"On what appear to be some highly sensitive moral issues which could damage the reputation of anyone so accused if they were to be aired in public. Mrs. DuMoss informs me that the children of a certain Mr. Spear were present in the meeting hall tonight. Since what she has to say involves him, she feels they should be protected from hearing it at all costs, either firsthand or secondhand. To that end, she has requested that each member of the board sign the confidentiality agreement which I shall notarize and which Mr. DuMoss will keep under lock and key."

"But"—Mr. Boynton glanced at the paper—"you're asking us to sign a paper disallowing us to defend ourselves regarding our decision in this matter."

"Exactly. But the decision will be the board's nonetheless, and once you've heard what Mrs. DuMoss has to say you'll understand her reasoning."

The board had never come up against such a bizarre request before. However, given Aloysius DuMoss's largess to the school district in the past, and the future funding they'd stand to lose if they displeased him at this juncture, Mr. Boynton had little choice.

"Oh, all right. We'll sign and get on with it."

Mr. Harvey produced a silver pen and ink vial, dipped the nib and handed it to Mr. Boynton first. The room remained so silent that the scratching of six signatures sounded like dogs at a door.

"Thank you." With the signatures completed, Mr. Harvey capped his ink vial and slipped his pen into a leather sheath. "I shall let Mrs. DuMoss proceed."

Elizabeth rose and, followed by her husband, ascended the podium and pulled out the chair. Mr. Harvey sat in one of the desks they'd vacated, while Aloysius DuMoss stood at his wife's shoulder as she seated herself and gathered her thoughts. Linking her fingers on the desktop, she spoke in a reserved, cultured voice.

"What I have to tell you tonight I've held inside a long time. It has been cause for great distress to me for years and years. You all know me . . . you've known me all my life and realize that I have no reason to lie. What I tell you will be the truth, and my husband will vouch for it, because he's known about it for years as well.

"Since the telephone wire has come to Camden we all hear things on our party line that we wish we hadn't. There are people who spread the news they hear as if it were their God-given right to do so. I don't abide by it, but it's inevitable that gossips will talk, and I hear rumors like anybody else.

"I recently heard a rumor about a fistfight between Gabe Farley and Elfred Spear. Everyone in this room knows it's true that the fight took place, because we've all seen Elfred walking around looking like a bowl of Harvard beets. The night of that fight Gabe yelled something in Elfred's front yard that nobody in this room has had the courage to say, and that I believe must be said. The word was 'rape,' and I know about it because it happened to me."

Aloysius gripped his wife's shoulder as she struggled to overcome a wave of emotion. Her throat worked and the knuckles on her linked hands turned white.

"When I was seventeen years old Elfred Spear raped me." Tears suddenly glittered in Elizabeth's eyes and she lost her ability to speak. Her husband dipped his head near hers and fortified her with a whispered word and the continued presence of his hand upon her shoulder. "It's all right, dear," she whispered, touching his hand. "I can do it."

She cleared her throat and continued. "The particulars aren't important, only the fact that I was an innocent virgin on my way home from an evening with my friends when I accepted a ride from a young man I thought I knew. One I trusted. The ramifications of that night have affected me the rest of my life. My marriage to Aloysius began in fear. Only his patient love has seen me through the nightmares that took years to go away. Since the Benevolent Society's attack on Mrs. Jewett, my nightmares have returned."

Elizabeth's eyes sought and found Roberta's, and their kindred pasts brought the glisten of tears to both their eyes.

To the room at large, Elizabeth stated in the most ladylike tone, "I damn Elfred Spear all over again for what he did to me. I did not deserve it. I did nothing to encourage him—nothing! I was female, and for Elfred, that was enough. We all know that for Elfred that's always been enough. Yet how many of you—especially you men—laugh away his antics as if they were no more than childish pranks while the women he preys upon are sentenced to eternal silence because if they were to speak up, they would be accused, just as you've accused Mrs. Jewett. And don't say you haven't, because I was at that Benevolent Society meeting when that despicable gossip got blown up into this farce you have perpetrated on a woman whose only crime was returning to her hometown as a divorcée.

"For that you have labeled her, and *that's* what this inquiry is about, isn't it?" Elizabeth let a beat of silence drill her accusation home before continuing.

"It's much easier to point a finger at a divorced woman than at a pillar of our town society, isn't it? Especially one you all do business with each day. Well, you do business with my husband, too, and I bless his loving heart for standing behind me in my wish to confront you tonight with a plea to stop persecuting Roberta Jewett. If you don't, you should know that our estimable fortune will be behind Mr. Harvey in defending Mrs. Jewett in whatever way is necessary. There will be newspaper reporters here, too, challenging your motives—to say nothing of your right—to bring her before this board for questioning. And in the process, Elfred Spear's wife and children will be dragged through the trail of evildoing he's left behind. I'm a mother of four. I simply don't believe children should suffer something like that. Therefore, the confidentiality agreement I've asked you to sign. Gentlemen . . . and lady . . . I leave you to decide where to go from here." Elizabeth added, "Just one more thing. I have resigned my post as treasurer of the Benevolent Society because I cannot, in all good conscience, be affiliated with a group that makes a mockery of their very name. Thank you."

Elizabeth sat back and relaxed her hands. Her husband patted her shoulder as she looked up at him. To Elizabeth's credit, she had never threatened a withdrawal of future school funding from the DuMoss coffers, nor had she stated unequivocally that Roberta Jewett had been raped. But it was evident by the mood in the room that the school board had no intention of grilling her further.

Mr. Boynton said, "If we could have a few minutes to talk this over . . ."

Five people left the room: The DuMosses and their lawyer, Roberta and Gabe. Out in the hall, when the schoolroom door closed behind them, the two women stood before each other in a moment of poignant silence before pitching together and hugging hard enough to wrinkle their bodices.

"How can I ever thank you, Elizabeth?"

"Perhaps you already have. I've let it out at last, and after all these years, it feels so good. I wouldn't have done that but for your own misfortune." Elizabeth pulled back and said, "I was afraid I was divulging things about you that weren't entirely my right, but I thought that by making them sign the agreement . . ."

"Say no more. You were utterly tactful, and I wanted them to know about Elfred, too, so you spoke for both of us."

"I'll tell you one thing," Elizabeth said, putting on a more cheerful face. "Alda Quimby will pay the price for spearheading this inquiry. It'll drive her crazy that she can't tell this to every woman in that Benevolent Society."

The schoolroom door opened and Mr. Boynton stood before his pack of board members, who avoided eye contact with everyone in the hall.

"The inquiry is dropped," he said simply. "Sorry, Mrs. Jewett."

The six school board members silently filed away, leaving behind five people with ample cause for smiles.

Gabriel hugged Roberta. Then Elizabeth. At her ear he said, "Thank you, Elizabeth, from both of us."

"You're welcome, Gabriel," she said, accepting the first hug he had ever given her before taking her place beside the husband who had loved her enough to stand by her through this ordeal and many others.

Daniel Harvey extended his hand to Roberta. "Mrs. Jewett, it's nice to meet you at last. I must say, I admire you already after listening to those children. I'd been brought on to defend you, but they were doing such a splendid job I wouldn't have dreamed of stepping in. Also, there's a little thing on the law books called *defamation of character,* and I thought if I let that school board go for a little while, they might do us a favor if we ever had to challenge them in court. Which I'm glad is not the case."

"Thank you, Mr. Harvey."

She thanked Mr. DuMoss also, then Elizabeth suggested, "Why don't we all gather at our house for a glass of sherry to celebrate? Roberta, I'd like to get to know you better. Gabriel, what do you say?"

He deferred to Roberta.

"That sounds wonderful," she decided. "But do I dare leave my girls alone?"

They were all laughing even before Elizabeth replied, "The school board will probably find out and call an inquiry."

Outside on the schoolhouse steps they encountered their children, who'd been inside when the meeting was abruptly called to an end.

Roberta opened her arms to all three . . . plus Isobel. "Here they are, our obedient children who stayed home just the way we ordered them to."

They all spoke at once.

"We did it!"

"We saved you!"

"Mother, I was so proud."

"Oh, Mrs. Jewett, you won! You won!"

Amid the celebrating there was a moment more somber when Roberta looked up and saw her three nieces hovering nearby. She went to them and hugged them, too. "Marcy, Trudy, Corinda, thank you for what you said tonight." She wondered exactly what they knew about their father and hoped they were ignorant of his gravest faults, for their innocence was of far more importance than his guilt. "How is your mother?" Roberta asked.

"Just fine."

"Will you tell her hello and give her my love?"

"Sure."

"And tell her that I'm getting married soon."

Corinda's eyes widened in excitement. "You are, Aunt Birdy?"

"To Mr. Farley. But, shh! Don't spread it around here tonight. Wait till tomorrow, all right? We haven't told the girls yet."

Corinda giggled as they parted company with Roberta's hand slipping from her niece's shoulders with a lingering melancholy. Gabriel came up behind her and sensed her sadness over the irreparable rift between her and her sister. He touched her waist and said, "It's hard not getting along with your family. I know because my mother's been standoffish all summer, and I've really missed her. But guess what." She looked back over her shoulder at his cajoling smile. "She came over yesterday and filled my cookie jar while I was at work."

"Oh, Gabriel, did she really?"

"Ayup."

"I'm so happy for you."

"So'm I, actually. Think this means she's ready to meet you. Speaking of which, there's someone else here I want you to meet."

It was his sister-in-law, Aurelia, who, along with her husband, Seth, was invited to join the group heading over to the DuMosses' for libations. From Aurelia and Seth Roberta felt only open friendliness, as she did from the DuMosses. *How fitting,* she thought, *on this night when my life takes a significant turn, that I get to know at least some of Gabriel's family.*

The children strayed away in a group to walk to their various homes, leaving the adults to make their way to the DuMoss home in automobiles.

It was there, in the DuMoss parlor, after their first toast to Roberta's victorious evening, that Gabriel proposed a second toast.

"To my future wife," he said, chiming the rim of his cut-glass goblet upon Roberta's. "Three days ago Roberta consented to marry me."

Felicitations poured forth, accompanied by hugs and one seemingly sensible question from Seth. "Then why didn't you announce it earlier and save yourself all this unnecessary hell tonight?"

"She wouldn't let me," Gabriel replied.

"It's my nature to be stubborn," Roberta informed them all.

Gabe spoke into his sherry glass. "You can say that again." When the laughter had subsided he looked into Roberta's eyes while speaking to the others. "You see, she wanted to win out over the school board on her own merit, not because she would have a man to take care of her and her children in the future. But she's going to have one, just the same."

"I can take care of myself, Gabriel Farley," she declared very clearly.

"I know you can. I've watched you doing it all summer. But two can do it better."

She grinned and said, "I'll concede to that," then touched his glass again while the others in the room looked on and felt as if they were privy to the inside workings of the relationship between Gabriel Farley and Roberta Jewett. The pair had a camaraderie that surpassed the usual fluttering hearts and damp palms of most courtships. And as for the stringent housewife-provider setup that prevailed in most marriages . . . anyone in the room could see their marriage wouldn't be run that way.

She would crisscross the countryside in that sassy motorcar of hers, dressed in a white uniform. And he would probably be left to fend for himself in a house that didn't get cleaned as often as it should, and would eat late suppers inexpertly prepared, or learn to cook himself.

Elizabeth lifted her glass in an official toast. "To the future Mr. and Mrs. Gabriel Farley!"

And as many glasses touched, Roberta realized she would have her first true Camden friend in Elizabeth DuMoss.

Eighteen

*W*hen Roberta and Gabe got back to her house that night, it was eleven-thirty, the kitchen light was on and all four girls were eating divinity with spoons.

"We tried to get it thick but our arms got tired beating it," Isobel explained. "But it's really yummy. Want some?"

"What are you still doing here?" Gabe asked. These days when he questioned Isobel this way he did it almost breezily.

"I live here, didn't you know?" she replied cheekily, licking a spoon.

Gabe slung an arm loosely around Roberta's neck and said to his daughter, "Know something? You're going to. Tell 'em, Roberta."

She took a relaxed grip on his wrist and let her arm dangle from it. "Your father and I are going to get married."

"Heck, we knew that," Isobel replied, still sucking.

"Sure, we knew that," Becky seconded.

"We just didn't know when," Susan added.

"When, Mother?" Lydia asked.

Roberta deferred to Gabe. "When, Gabe?"

"When do you want to?"

"When should we?"

Isobel answered, "Sooner the better so we can all live together."

Roberta turned to Gabe again. "Where we going to live?"

"Here," he replied, as if he'd known all along. "Gonna knock a hole in that wall over there and add on a bedroom for us, and the girls can share the two rooms upstairs."

"I get Isobel in my room!" declared Susan.

"Mother, does she?" Lydia whined. "I want her in mine."

Rebecca dipped two spoons, which she handed to the adults. "Here, try some. Better get used to it, Mr. Farley, 'cause sometimes that's all you get for supper around here."

"Oh, Becky, honestly," scolded Roberta, amused. "Don't tell him stuff like that. He'll believe you."

"And don't call me Mr. Farley anymore. How about Gabe?"

"All right, Gabe. How's the divinity?"

"Mmm . . . not bad."

"Who's going to stand up for you, Mother?"

"Who wants to?"

Three hands went up. "I do, I do, I do!"

Susan immediately disparaged her younger sister. "Don't be silly, Lydia, you're too little to be a bridesmaid."

"No, she's not," Becky defended. "Why couldn't she be the bridesmaid just as well as you?"

"I know. We'll draw straws," Roberta decided.

"I've got a better idea," Rebecca said. "Let's draw spoons. Everybody lick your spoon off, and only one of us dips ours in the candy. Then we put them all in the clean kettle and you hold it above your head, Gabe, and the one with the divinity gets to be mother's attendant or bridesmaid or whatever you call it."

Gabe said to Roberta, "Is this what life is going to be like all the time, living with you four? Making a game out of everything?"

"Ever a game," she told him. "Always going for the fun in life so that when you take the deep six you do it with lots of memories." To the girls she said, "Somebody dip that spoon."

Lydia dipped. Gabe raised. And everybody drew.

Rebecca got the candied spoon, and Roberta felt a secret spark of pleasure: It was right that Becky stand up for her; after all, she'd been predicting and encouraging this union for some time. Everybody got a hug, though, along with an invitation to plan something special for the wedding ceremony, and to talk about where it should be held. It seemed natural to say yes when the girls asked if Isobel could stay overnight so they could begin the planning.

Minutes later, Gabe and Roberta were back out on the front porch in the dark, saying good night.

"You really are going to let the girls plan your wedding?"

"Well, sure . . . some of it, anyway. We do everything together."

He took hold of her arms and pulled her toward him. "Roberta, you're something," he said, bending his head.

It was different, kissing as an engaged couple. Betrothal removed certain restrictions. His hands moved over her as if she were a fine piece of wood he had sanded and polished and was checking for smoothness. He stood between her and the yard, in the deepest shadows at the opposite end of the porch from the swing, getting more and more reckless as the seconds stretched into minutes with his open mouth plying hers and his hips riveting her against the wall.

Her arms were raised, her hands on his neck and hair until their breathing became labored and he began making inroads into her clothing. He had never done that before.

With her mouth and hands she pushed him away and whispered, "Stop, Gabe."

He freed her abruptly, sensing her rising fear. He could barely make out her face in the blue-black shadows.

"I'm not Elfred, Roberta. I won't hurt you."

"I know . . ." she whispered, then as if to convince herself, "I know."

"But he's scared you, hasn't he?"

"Some. Maybe."

He thought awhile, damning Elfred and fearing for the blight he might have left on his own and Roberta's future.

"Okay, well, listen . . ." He stepped back, catching her hands, holding them. "You're right. Best thing to do is wait with everything, prove the Benevolent Society wrong, eh?"

She kissed him on the corner of the mouth and said, "Thank you, Gabe, for understanding."

Though they tried to pretend a small wedge had not been driven between them, it had. Though they tried to pretend it would not be driven deeper on their wedding night, they knew it was a distinct possibility. Necking on the porch swing or in the shadows of the backyard with all their buttons closed was one thing; facing a marriage bed was another. He wondered if she'd delay their wedding interminably to avoid facing her own fears.

"So when can we get married?" he asked.

"Oh"—she let out a puff of breath—"I don't know. How long will it take you to get an addition on the house?"

"Is it all right if I do that? We haven't even talked about it."

"Of course it's all right. I'd love to stay here, and your plan makes perfect sense. After all, Isobel has spent so much time here, and so have you, that it practically seems as if it's been our home already."

He thought about his work schedule. "Seth and I have got some jobs we've already agreed to do, so I can't start here for a couple of weeks."

"Well"—she thought for a moment—"what about mid-November? We could set the wedding date for then."

It seemed light years away, but Gabe hid his disappointment and said, "Guess that's all right."

"That's it then. Mid-November."

"Roberta, I'd like to give you something—an engagement ring or a brooch. Should have had it for you tonight, but I thought you might like to pick it out yourself."

They both realized how different this second time was from their firsts, when breathless anticipation held no clouds, and proposals were delivered with the proper trappings. They wondered what had happened to the carefree couple who had entered the house to announce their intentions so jauntily less than a half hour before.

That couple reappeared on Friday when they went to pick the engagement ring—a modest diamond surrounded by four smaller diamond chips—and got back to Roberta's house to find it empty, for once. He took her to the living room settee and started kissing her, and hauled her across his lap, and bent her back into a corner against a loose pillow.

This time she stopped him immediately, dragging his hand away from her breasts the moment he made a move toward them, gripping him in a tight hug that forced his arms around her back, while willing her desire away.

Hugging so, like two in peril, they counted the weeks till their wedding, wondering if by then she would have overcome her aversion to being touched.

Afterward, and at other times between then and their wedding, he went away to wonder what ultimate damage Elfred had done, for she would go only so far before overt temptation became intrinsic fear. It ran through her sometimes when he least expected it, and he realized that as a groom, he had been given a more delicate second bride than first. Roberta would need an inordinate amount of patience and understanding on their wedding night, and perhaps for many nights to follow.

The girls had something to say about waiting until mid-November. They wanted the wedding to be held on the front porch, and there was a good chance that by mid-November it could be covered with snow.

So they moved the date up to October fourteenth, and Gabriel got busy with the addition. The bedroom wing was weatherproof but still shy of being finished when their wedding day arrived.

Roberta awakened early, rolling her face to the window where a perfect roseate dawn was ascending into a sky of flawless, unbroken blue.

We must live right, she thought. *It's going to be a perfect day for a wedding.* Nevertheless, she curled deeper into her rumpled double bed, staring at the color outside, realizing that tonight she'd be sharing a bed with Gabe. She suppressed a shudder at the thought, then pressed a hand to her trembling stomach.

Roberta Jewett, you love Gabe, and he is not Elfred, and you're being silly, so just get these ridiculous fears out of your mind and act like an eager bride.

How could a person want something and fear it, too?

Sometimes the day seemed to crawl, sometimes fly toward four o'clock. When she was dressing, with the girls traipsing in and out of her bedroom, asking for last-minute items, exclaiming over her dress and her hair, seeking approval of their own, her nerves were as on edge as if she were seventeen and a virgin.

The girls all had new dresses, and though they all looked adorable, Rebecca, in a very adult ankle-length dress of apricot satin, looked quite breathtaking. And so grown-up! Roberta thought.

Shortly before four Lydia called, "Gabe and Isobel are here!" and she heard them knock below. She'd never have believed she'd have butterflies in her stomach from meeting a man at the door, but on her wedding day, she did.

When she saw him standing on the porch, spit-shined and wearing a spiffy new black wool suit, the toes of his new boots gleaming like onyx, she thought, *Why, I love him more than I loved George. Certainly I know him better. I would never in a million years have anything to fear from him.*

She could tell immediately that he was far from calm. His freshly shaved cheeks were as rosy as the dawn had been, and he didn't seem to know where to hang his hands.

He said, "Hello, Roberta."

And she said, "Hello, Gabriel," very formally. Then they both laughed nervously as she pushed open the screen door.

Isobel said, "Gosh, Roberta, you look so pretty!"

Belatedly, he said, "Yes . . . yes, you certainly do."

She was decked out in ivory, an Austrian-draped dress that fell in layers from beneath her breast and showed her high-top shoes. Her hair was swept up in back around a white silk rose, much as she wore it with her nurse's cap.

"And you look very elegant. You bought a new suit."

He cleared his throat and glanced down briefly, his chin catching on his high white collar and thick, black, knotted tie. "Ah . . . yes."

Not even when they'd first met had they been so formal and stiff with each other. Yet, ridiculous as it seemed, neither of them could stem their nervousness, which made the children whisper among themselves.

"I thought we'd wait outside on the porch," Roberta said.

"Oh, certainly!" Gabe replied, as if he'd done something wrong by stepping into the living room.

Some guests began arriving: Seth, who would stand up for Gabe; Aurelia and their children; Gabe's mother, Maude, whom Roberta had met on two occasions and with whom she'd forged an uneasy peace; the Du-Mosses and their children; Mrs. Roberson and Miss Werm; Eleanor Balfour from the regional nursing office and Terrence Hall, who clerked for the Farley boys.

And, of course, Myra.

Grace was conspicuously absent, though Roberta really hadn't expected her to attend: Grace was living in her insular sphere, pretending as she always had that the rest of the world was misguided and her marriage was made in heaven.

Elfred wasn't at the wedding either, of course. Word around town had it that his business wasn't doing particularly well. He had been overheard saying he was going to be forced to take out a second mortgage on his house.

The minister from the Congregational church suggested they get started.

Because it was to be a very informal wedding, there was no wedding march, only a shuffling and placing of the wedding party up on the porch, with the children trailing down the steps.

While the mothers of the bride and groom were watching the wedding party assemble, Maude remarked, "Your daughter looks quite lovely today."

Myra's mouth formed a doughnut of disapproval. "I told Roberta not to wear white, but she's never listened to me. Grace told me that's *just* what Roberta would

do, and sure enough, look at her! A woman never wears
white on her second wedding!"

"I'd call that ivory."

"Well, it's white enough to be disgraceful!"

Maude shot a surprised glance at this woman who
was about to become her son's mother-in-law, and decided he'd need all the kind, thoughtful mothering he
could get from his own mother if he was to be saddled
with Myra Halburton on his wife's side.

The ceremony was ordinary by any standards, except
for the fact that the bride accompanied her daughters
on a piano rolled up to the living room door while the
trio sang "Oh Promise Me" in three-part harmony; and
Rebecca recited an Indian verse.

When she turned at the porch rail, she discovered that
her Spear cousins, who had been ordered to stay home
by their mother, had appeared across the street and
were watching the proceedings from there. Rebecca
stood proud and tall and let her resonant alto carry
clear out to where they stood.

> "As unto the bow the cord is,
>   So unto the man is woman,
>   Though she bends him she obeys him,
>   Though she draws him, yet she follows,
>   Useless each without the other!"

Ethan Ogier, who had ridden up on his bicycle, stood
beside the Spear girls and whispered reverently, "Wow,
doesn't Becky look pretty today?" And in his sixteen-
year-old heart he vowed, *I'm going to marry her someday.*

On the porch, Reverend Davis asked the groom, "Do you take this woman?" and when Gabe answered "I do," four girls mouthed the words along with him. They did the same when Roberta gave her response. And when Gabriel kissed his bride the three youngest girls flashed smiles back and forth at one another while Becky sent a prolonged gaze across the street to Ethan.

The kiss was brief and self-conscious on Gabriel's part. He had come some distance toward being comfortable with demonstrations of affection, but kissing before an audience definitely rattled him. When he lifted his head, Roberta saw that his face was ripe as a peach, and she thought how peculiar that they should have survived the first stages of courting with relative ease, only to become uneasy with each other on their wedding day.

All the girls swarmed around and gave him kisses on his cheek, too, which added several degrees of heat to his cheeks. And the guests came forward, too, with hugs and congratulations, and separated the bride and groom for a while.

The wedding feast was all finger food, passed around by the four new stepsisters, who had helped their mother make it. Among the cold sandwiches were fudge and snow-white divinity (no spoons required this time) and Gabe's favorite sour cream cookies, which his mother had volunteered to make.

Roberta found Becky midway through the soiree and suggested, "Why don't you take a tray of sweets and offer them to your friends across the street. That way they don't have to break any rules."

Becky looked up at her mom and got misty-eyed.

"Know what, Mrs. Farley?" she said. "I've got absolutely the best mother in the world."

As Roberta kissed Becky's cheek Gabe strolled over and stopped beside them. When Becky headed away with the tray he asked quietly, "What are all the tears about?"

Roberta watched Becky go and said, "Oh, Gabe, I'm so happy. We're going to make such a wonderful family."

He dropped an arm over her shoulders and they stood side by side as Becky reached the group across the street. Marcelyn glanced over and saw them watching . . . and waved.

Gabe and Roberta waved back.

"Poor Grace," Roberta said. "She will stick with that man till death do them part, and never know what kind of happiness she missed."

Gabe could think of only one reply: He gently kissed his wife's temple.

Roberta smiled up at him. "Well, look at you," she said, pleased by his very prim kiss, "the man who was so afraid to show affection."

"I wish it were evening," he replied. "I'd show you a lot more."

She quickly glanced away, and he wondered how many times she had said no to him since they'd been engaged. She'd even insisted on no honeymoon, her excuse being that she'd had her job for only six months and didn't want to ask for any time off. Also, she argued, the girls shouldn't be left alone, though he didn't see why either Maude or Myra couldn't stay with them for a week.

"No," Roberta had said again.

So he'd left the business to Seth and tried his best to get the addition finished by tonight.

And this was it . . . it was shortly after 6 P.M. and their guests were leaving . . . and the girls were going off to sleep at Gabe's house with Grandma Maude . . . and the new bedroom wasn't quite finished but it had a new bed, and the bathroom had a claw-foot tub and a real water heater run by electricity . . . and Gabe had no idea how to approach the next couple of hours.

The yard emptied.

Gabe and Roberta stood on the front porch steps listening to the autumn silence. Beyond the rooftops the sea looked like a plate of sky-blue enamel broken by the distant, jutting islands that burned up out of the water like small fires. Vibrant orange and blue—the entire vista—with occasional spires of evergreens poking through, and white boats coming home at day's end.

Nearer, the ferns around Sebastian Breckenridge's anchor had turned rusty and curled back toward earth, in the direction from which they'd come. The iris leaves had long since yellowed, and the bridal wreath bordering the yard had been touched by frost and hung like an orange waterfall. A line of meditative gulls trimmed the ridgepole of a rooftop below, and as Roberta and Gabe watched, one of the birds broke rank and took wing, followed by others, who flocked over their own front yard to cock their heads and deliver their tuneless squawk to the man and woman standing on the steps.

"I remember when you built this porch," Roberta said.

"Six months ago."

"Is that all?"

"Whoa, did you hate me."

Roberta chuckled. "I did, didn't I?"

"Remember the day you first saw the house? You came in the bedroom and found me making off-color jokes about you being a divorced woman. Lord, was I wrong."

He had been watching her, waiting for her head to turn so he could read her eyes. She turned, and if there was anxiety within her, she hid it well.

They stood there on the edge of evening, Gabe wondering how she felt about making love before dark, Roberta afraid that at the last minute she'd ruin their wedding night over something that was none of his doing.

"Are you tired?" he asked.

"Yes . . . I am."

"Want to go in?"

In answer she turned and her footsteps slurred across the hollow porch floor. The screen door opened lazily, then closed them inside, followed by the inner door with its scarred dentil trim below the curtained window.

They crossed the living room without haste and stood in the kitchen doorway—Gabe's right shoulder curving behind her left one—inspecting the room, which the girls had left cleaner than it had ever been. On the table sat a plate of candy and Caroline's philodendron plant.

Watching Roberta's eyes pause on it, Gabe asked, "Do you mind?"

"No, of course not. Isobel asked me if she could bring it over. Actually, it dresses up the room . . . and you know I'm not very good at doing that myself. There are things Isobel can teach me."

He had never met another human being like Roberta, so unsusceptible to jealousy, so open to change, to discovery. She had accepted not only Gabe and Isobel, but a third person as well, for Caroline was an integral part of their past, and she understood this. Jealousy was foreign to Roberta, for she was so comfortable with herself that there was no need for it in her life. She saw her shortcomings as clearly as she saw her strengths, and neither denigrated herself for the one nor lauded herself for the other. She simply lived life day to day by her own code of *happiness first*.

"Roberta?" he said.

She turned from the philodendron to him. "Hm?"

"I love you. I've been standing here realizing just how much."

"Why, Gabe," she said as he curled her into his embrace.

She would have said *I love you too*, but he kissed her with a tenderness so exquisite that it made her heart hurt. Kissed her and kept his hands only on her back. When the kiss ended he embraced her full length, so hard it hurt her ribs, and kept her flush against his body without moving, her chin caught on his shoulder and her breasts firmly cushioned against his chest.

With his lips closed he pulled in a deep breath, then exhaled unsteadily, and she knew the next step was up to her.

She leaned back, hands coming to rest on his chest, and said, "If you don't mind, I think I'll use the new bathtub."

"I don't mind," he said, releasing her.

While she went inside and closed the bathroom door, he removed his shoes, his tie, his collar and jacket.

The water ran. And stopped. And *blipped* as if a foot went in. And *blupped* in a lower tone as if a body went in.

He sat on a chair in their new bedroom, staring at the new wooden finish work he hadn't had time to varnish yet, at the bed she'd made up with all new bedding, everything white.

Some soft splashing sounded, the burble of a cloth being wrung out.

He rose and turned the chenille spread and the blankets down and thought about getting in, then changed his mind and returned to the chair, leaving the bedding downturned and waiting.

The water began draining . . . then silence.

He waited where he was.

Finally the door opened, emitting a billow of moist air and the flowery scent of powder. She stood in the doorway closing two buttons on the yoke of a blue cotton nightgown, neither prim nor promiscuous. Her hair was brushed and her feet were bare. And her eyes came straight to his.

"I've never had a bathtub before. Thank you, Gabriel."

"You're welcome," he said.

She glanced at his bare feet, his unbuttoned shirt: It was obvious he'd been sitting there waiting.

"Did I take too long?"

"No! No, not at all."

"Do you want to . . ." She motioned behind her, leaving the invitation unfinished.

"Oh . . . sure." He went in and deliberately left the door ajar, brushed his teeth, washed his face and came back out with a towel in his hands and his suspenders hanging.

She was sitting on the edge of the bed facing him. He went around to the other side and, with his back to her, removed all but his short-legged union suit and got in.

When he lay down, she lay down, covered to their waists.

It was still shy of seven o'clock and even on the east side of the house, far from dark.

He crooked his right arm beneath his head and looked over at her. She was looking at him.

"Gabriel," she said matter-of-factly, "I was not a virgin on my first wedding night, so this is very awkward. I feel like I am one tonight."

He rolled to face her, keeping plenty of distance between them, and the elbow still crooked beneath his ear.

"I would've thought you would be," he said.

"No, I wasn't. Were you?"

"Yes, I was."

"Somehow that doesn't surprise me. So you've been through this before."

He cleared his throat, then nodded instead of speaking.

"All of this is unlike me," she said. "I am no cowering wallflower. I never have been."

He took her hand and held it on the clean sheet between them, watching his thumb as it played over hers.

"Roberta," he said, and lifted his eyes to hers. "Tell me what scares you most."

"The memories come back. I can only go so far and then they all come back and it's as if I'm on my back again on that gravel road, and I know perfectly well it's you I'm with and not him, but it happens—I get scared and I can't help it. It's not like me, Gabe, honest, it's not! But I don't know what to do . . . how to get over it."

He continued rubbing her hand with his thumb, letting her get used to seeing him on the other half of her bed. His eyes kept steady on hers as he wondered how to proceed.

Finally he tugged on her hand and whispered, "Come here . . . " and rolled to his back, dragging her halfway across his chest, then releasing her hands. "We've both done this before," he said. "Do what you want."

She lay above him looking down while he flung his wrists back and let them lie pulse-up on the pillow. She studied his eyes for a long moment while neither of them moved so much as an eyelash. Her right hand lay on his chest right where he'd released it, over his heart, which she could feel beating as fast as her own.

A tress of her hair fell from behind her ear across his chin. He did not move, only met her gaze with his steady one, waiting.

She threaded the stray hair behind her ear and slowly leaned down to kiss him. What he denied his hands, he allowed his mouth, opening it beneath hers and moving it persuasively as his head angled on the pillow. Her hair fell again, and in pushing it back she touched his hot face, then spread her hand on his cheek with her fingertips at the corner of his eye.

She ended the kiss and they opened their eyes, so close they could feel the radiant warmth of each other's skin, and the fanfare of fast breathing that fell from between their parted lips.

She whispered, "Gabriel . . ." and got to her knees beside him, lining his cheeks with both palms.

He whispered, "Your hands are hot."

"So is your face. And your heart is racing. I can feel it beneath my arm."

"Is yours?"

"Yes," she whispered, kissing him again, tipping forward off her heels until her breasts hung pendulous within her nightgown. Midway through the kiss she found his upturned wrists and circled them with her hands, squeezing as if to pinion him in place and keep him from lunging up when he was only lying as before, posing no threat at all. His pulse beat up against her palms and her freed breasts felt heavy as she knelt over him. Desire came as a gift, an onslaught free of fear or memory.

She slung a leg across his hollow belly and straddled him, watching his eyes darken and his nostrils dilate, still holding his wrists against the pillow. Then she carried them, blue veined and strong, to her breasts, and let her eyes close as his palms filled with her flesh. She sat upon him thus, head tipped back, her hands over his, their joined hands flexing together until hers fell and his remained, rocking her backward and forward to some primal rhythm they heard in their heads.

Minutes later she fell forward and stretched her limbs

along his, murmuring a behest into his open mouth, carrying his hand once again, expelling her breath at the return of goodness when he complied.

There was bedding between them. They wrestled it down and lay on their sides, legs opening, knees lifting, coming together first in wishes, creating their own welcome torture of waiting. They drew back with luminous gazes and shed their garments—hers first, his second— and lay in the gloaming that shaded their skins with the falling evening, venturing first glimpses of each other.

They spoke the universal language of lovers, with throaty sounds of wordless praise, and touched freely.

Then they were coupled, still on their sides, face-to-face on a single pillow, eyes open . . . then closed. Grips loose . . . then tense. Breath flowing . . . then held.

She opened her eyes at the final moment and saw him with his lips drawn back in the near grimace of ecstasy, and marveled that she could bring him to such straits.

She smiled, and let her eyes close once more, and claimed her victory over Elfred Spear.

She would see Elfred intermittently in the years that followed, crossing a street or passing in his motorcar. But they never spoke, nor did she and her sister, Grace. Once, when Roberta was entering the bank, Grace was coming out and they nearly collided. "Oh! Birdy!" Grace said, without thinking.

Roberta smiled, her heart racing, and said, "Hello, Grace, how are you?"

But Grace gathered her dignity about her like an ermine cape and moved on without further word. Roberta watched her go with a heart full of pity.

"Poor Grace," she whispered, touching her own heart.

The Spear girls, though forbidden, found ways to come to Roberta's house and take part in plays and musicales with their cousins.

Myra came too, when invited, but never stayed long and always left in a huff over some disagreement with her younger daughter, whom she'd never been able to bend to her wishes as she could her older. Roberta would watch her go. And sigh. And whisper to herself an echo of what she'd said the day she ran into Grace.

"Poor Mother."

Then her husband would come up quietly behind her, and slip an arm around her waist and kiss her temple. And soon the girls would be there too, watching their grandmother huff away as if the world had done her a grave injustice . . . again.

"What makes Grandma so ornery?" they'd ask.

And Roberta would reply, "Who knows?"

And then one day they asked and Gabriel replied, "Jealousy."

Roberta snapped her head around to gape at him. "What?"

"She's jealous of you. Don't you know that? So is Grace. Because you've always been so happy and you've made your happiness yourself."

"Really?"

He just put a half-smile on his mouth and left it there.

She considered his opinion for some time, then kissed him on the jaw—they kissed quite regularly in front of the girls now—and said, "Why, thank you, Gabriel. I never would have figured that out for myself."

"That's because you don't have an ounce of jealousy in you so you can't see it in others."

"Hm," she said thoughtfully.

He closed the door and walked, with her hard up against his side, to the kitchen where the supper dishes were waiting to be washed. Stopping in the doorway with his arm still around Roberta, he called back over his shoulder, "Whose turn is it tonight?"

Someone called back, "Not ours!"

Someone else called back, "Not ours!"

It was nice having teams ... when they did their work. But there were always so many more inventive things to do!

Gabe looked down at Roberta, who made the equivalent of a facial shrug.

"Oh, hell," he said, "should we do 'em?"

"Naw, let's leave 'em."

"They'll be all dried up tomorrow."

"But tomorrow it'll be somebody else's turn."

He laughed, then cocked on eyebrow suggestively, "So what else should we do instead?"

She went up on tiptoe and whispered something in his ear.

He faked a gasp and said, "Mis-sus Farley! At this hour of the day!"

Then they snagged jackets from the hooks by the door and headed toward the front of the house, calling up the stairs as they passed, "Hey, girls! Be right back. Gotta take a run over to the shop real quick!"

And ran out into the twilight, giggling.